Closing Costs

Also by Seth Margolis

Closing Costs

SETH MARGOLIS

St. Martin's Press
New York

This is a work of fiction. All of the characters, organizations, and events portrayed in this novel are either products of the author's imagination or are used fictitiously.

www.stmartins.com

Library of Congress Cataloging-in-Publication Data

Margolis, Seth Jacob.
    Closing costs / Seth Margolis.— 1st ed.
        p. cm.
    ISBN-13: 978-0-312-35368-1
    ISBN-10: 0-312-35368-5
    1. Women real-estate agents—Fiction.   2. Real-estate business—New York (State)—New York—Fiction.   3. Rich people—New York (State)—New York—Fiction.   4. Socialites—New York (State)—New York—Fiction.   5. New York (N.Y.)—Fiction.   I. Title.

PS3563.A652C56 2006
813'.54—dc22   2006040843

First Edition: August 2006

10 9 8 7 6 5 4 3 2 1

For Maggie and Jack

Closing Costs

Prologue

Lucinda Wells stepped onto the roof garden atop the Metropolitan Museum and headed directly for the railing at the south end, navigating through a wriggling crowd and an obstacle course of ghastly sculptures too large, apparently, even for the cavernous rooms of the museum below. The benefit, for a children's hospital or animal shelter, was in full swing, having been moved outdoors at the last minute due to the spring heat wave. She nodded at several familiar faces and smiled toothily at the *Times*'s omnipresent party photographer, who walked by without snapping. At the railing she took in the view, the best in Manhattan, she always thought, and she'd seen them all—from terraces on Fifth Avenue, from penthouses in the newer condos farther east, from high-floor spreads on Central Park West. Nothing beat the view from the roof of the Met. Just a few stories above the tree line, it was like the prow of a vast ship cutting across an undulating ocean of greenery. Nice image, that. She should probably jot it down somewhere and use it in a memoir or perhaps a novel—if only she had time to write! To gaze at the amazing skyline from a high floor was to feel small and humbled, no matter what or how much you'd achieved in life to be able to afford such a view. From the Met's roof you felt as if you might actually control not only your own destiny but that of a large swath of this otherwise incorrigible city. She looked left to Fifth Avenue and absently noted the addresses where she'd sold apartments: 550, 660, 750, and so on up to Ninety-sixth Street, above which she never ventured professionally. She looked sternward to the West Side and guessed that she'd sold apartments in most of the better buildings along CPW. Straight ahead to the south she checked off another dozen. A voice intruded on her mental inventory—a curt "Hello, Lucinda"—and then a quick retreat lest conversation ignite. Well, she was just a real-estate broker after all, and these partygoers were much more than that: financiers, entrepreneurs, inheritors. But she wasn't offended, because she knew with absolute certainty that her station on the lofty New York food chain was quite near the top. Shelter was what it was all about, and for a certain strata of New York, which included just about everyone on the roof of the Met at that moment save the gorgeous cater-waiters circulating micro-appetizers on doilied trays, she controlled access to the finest shelter in the city. You are what you eat, it was said—well, that might have been true at one time, when only the rich could afford leg of mutton or suckling pig or lobster thermidor or whatever it was the rich used to eat. But nowadays anyone could pop into Zabar's and pony up a few shekels for Scotch salmon or foie gras. Clothes make the man? Not when knockoffs, perfectly good knockoffs at that, were hawked on half the street corners in Midtown. No, today you are where you live. Shelter makes the man. With the right outfit, genuine or not, you could look like a million bucks anywhere in public, and you could eat like a millionaire at least once in a while with a decent credit line on your gold card. But you couldn't fake it in your home. A home was your skin, your true face to the outside world. Surveying it all from the roof of the Met, Lucinda didn't care who chose to talk to her. Because she knew she held the keys to the kingdom.

One

"It's time to sell," Peggy Gimmel announced to her husband, Monroe, at the kitchen table on the second Tuesday morning in May.

"Not in this market," he said without looking up from the stock tables in the *Times*. "We're about to hit bottom. This is a *buying* opportunity."

"The *apartment*, Monroe," she said with slow emphasis. "It's time . . . to sell . . . the apartment."

He grunted and slowly moved the magnifying glass down the column of stock prices. Luckily their kitchen faced the sunless courtyard or he'd start a fire.

Monroe was obsessed with the stock market. All the financial experts on cable talked about needing a long-term outlook to make money in the market. But what kind of long-term outlook could a man of eighty-two have? *Listen, at my age I don't buy green bananas.* How many times a week did she hear that line at the bridge table or supermarket? Now Monroe was buying stocks in companies with unpronounceable names stuffed with *x*'s and *z*'s. Companies that could use a few more vowels, in Peggy's opinion. Who knew what these outfits did for a living, other than take investors' hard-earned money? True, for a few years there he was actually making money—on paper, of course; God forbid he should sell anything. There was no talking to him, really, he was so full of himself and his fancy investing skills.

"I made more this week from Z-linq than I made in a year selling blouses," he'd say. *What the hell was Z-linq*, she wanted to ask, *and what's with that* q, *anyway?* Then the markets turned sour and so did Monroe. He rarely spoke anymore, and when he did he sounded angry and resentful. All day he watched the stock prices march across the bottom of the TV screen as if it were an EKG reading. *His* EKG.

"Sonia at the bridge club thinks we could get nine-fifty."

He didn't react—what was a million dollars to a Wall Street *macher* like Monroe? But $950,000 was exactly $925,000 more than they'd paid thirty-six years earlier, when the apartment went co-op. Back then everyone told them they were crazy to buy an apartment in Manhattan. A piece of paper, that's what you'll own, they told her. Co-op, schmo-op, get yourself a real house with some ground if you want to throw your money away on real estate. But it was buy or move out—an eviction plan, they called it; the term nearly gave her a coronary, even back then when she was young (well, younger)—so they borrowed from Peggy's brother and took the plunge. Oh, how she wished she could tell those people what the place was worth now. Monroe's parents. The Fishmans, who had rented next door but moved to Bayside rather than throw their money away on a piece of paper. Her friend Frieda Brand, who thought the whole world was out to swindle her and every other Jew on the planet. Even her brother, who lent her the money after hocking her to China about what a mistake they were making. But they were all gone, them and half the people she knew. It was like crossing the finish line of some long, exhausting race, then turning around, ready for the applause, only to find that all the contestants and all the spectators had already left the field. Old age isn't for wimps—who was the genius who said that?

"Lily recommended the broker she used to buy her place," she told Monroe.

Still no reaction.

Their daughter's apartment on Park Avenue was roughly three times the size of their place, but Lily said the broker she'd used wouldn't mind. Her actual words, "wouldn't mind." Some world, when people wouldn't mind collecting the commission on a million dollars. Then again, Lily's husband, Barnett, probably earned that much in one day on Wall Street.

"Who needs three bedrooms, anyway? When was the last time we had overnight visitors?" The grandchildren never spent the night, probably thought you needed a passport to come to the West Side. Or shots. "We'll buy a smaller place, or we'll rent." Monroe had put down the magnifying glass and picked up a pen. He circled something, his hand trembling as it always did. He'd probably circle the wrong stock, she thought, and maybe *then* they'd make some money.

"We'll invest the difference," she said to get his attention.

"Invest?" He glanced at her. His blue eyes had faded in the fifty-two years they'd been married, but they were still the youngest thing about him, like the sequins on that Anne Klein II cocktail dress she'd paid a fortune for that still glittered like diamonds every time she opened her closet even though the dress itself was faded and limp. His eyes still glittered like diamonds, at least for her.

"In Treasury bonds, Monroe. Think of the income."

He frowned and turned back to his portfolio. She'd call the real-estate broker at nine-thirty; she certainly didn't need Monroe's permission for something as unimportant as selling their home! Peggy smiled and got up for a second cup of decaf. Sometimes she wanted to tell Lily not to worry so much about what Barnett did or said. She was a strong, intelligent woman who danced around him like a geisha. Maybe she was grateful for the big apartment and the trainer and the drapes in the living room that cost $750 a yard. *Just don't overdo the gratitude,* she wanted to say, *just wait until you're both old like us. Then you'll see that the women always get the upper hand in the end.* And it's worth the wait getting last licks in life. They get terrified you'll die before them, these husbands, that's why when the wife goes first, they either remarry in a hurry or drop dead in six months. But her women friends, when their husbands went they threw a nice funeral at Riverside Chapel, settled the estate lickety-split, and then hit the road. Package tours to Europe first, to get their feet wet, then Asia and Africa and even the Galapagos, for God's sake, with bridge games and theater subscriptions and concerts at Lincoln Center to keep them occupied between cab rides to JFK.

Relax, she wished she could tell Lily, *relax and wait.* But the last thing her daughter wanted from her was advice. She sat down with her coffee, took the phone from its cradle, and dialed her daughter's number.

. . .

Lily Grantham heard the phone ring from the bathroom, where she was toweling off after her morning shower. Barnett had long since left for his office downtown.

"Let it ring!" she shouted. But her voice died somewhere in the long hallway that connected the master bedroom suite to the nine other rooms in the apartment. After two rings someone picked up.

"I'm not here!" she shouted, again futilely. Only one person ever called her before nine o'clock.

Awaiting the inevitable summons to the phone, she tossed the wet towel in a corner and began her daily appraisal before the mirror. Face: almost wrinkle free, thanks to a bit of work around the eyes (her high forehead had always been smooth). Breasts: she wouldn't pass the pencil test, but they hadn't hit her navel yet, and in the right bra they still looked great. Tummy: flat, as well it should be, thanks to the tightly regulated diet prescribed by her nutritionist, Lori LaChant, and the eight million sit-ups a day with D'Arcy, her trainer, who'd lately added a dash of sadism to her regimen by hurling a medicine ball at her abdomen mid–sit-up. Legs: long as ever, incipient saddlebags taken care of by Dr. Nabaladan last year. The battle won another day, she thought with the usual surge of anxious relief.

"Mrs. Grantham, it's your mother." Nanny's nasally British voice had no trouble finding its way through the bedroom and into her bathroom.

"Tell her I'll be right there."

"I'll finish up the children's breakfast," Nanny said unnecessarily. She never missed an opportunity to remind Lily that she handled most of the child-related chores on the ninth floor at 913 Park Avenue.

She slipped on a white, floor-length terry-robe and went to the phone on her side of the bed.

"Hello, Mother."

"Did I wake you up?" Peggy Gimmel asked, as she always did when calling before noon. Lily sighed. That made two people with censure in their voices, and it wasn't even nine o'clock.

"I'm just getting out of the shower."

"Listen, sweetie, you said you knew a real-estate broker."

"Lucinda Wells."

"Good, give me her number."

"Are you sure about this? You've lived there so long, and it's not as if you have a mortgage to pay."

"It's just too big. The other day I found dust on the radiator in the guest room. Dust!"

Her mother had always looked on dust as something animate, an Anschluss of tiny living creatures who invaded her home the moment her back was turned.

"You could get a cleaning lady."

"Or I could move."

"I just think you should give it some more thought. Lucinda's very aggressive. Once you get her involved, you'll find it hard to turn back."

She couldn't explain it even to herself, but the thought of her parents moving made Lily very uneasy.

"I know it's hard to think of us selling the home you grew up in."

"That's not it," she said quickly, but she felt a shiver of vulnerability. They lived in two different worlds now, but Peggy could still read her mind. The truth was, she found her childhood home depressing, from the half-century of accumulated cooking odors that greeted her on the elevator landing to the thirty-year-old rust-colored shag carpet on the living-room floor—she always half expected to see John Travolta disco into the room in a white suit. And yet the idea of someone else living in 6D brought on something that felt close to panic.

"Listen, you don't have to pretend with me."

"Mother, I don't—"

"What's her phone number?"

Lily tossed the phone onto the unmade bed and went to get her address book.

Rosemary Pierce opened the door to her apartment and let in a tornado. Lucinda Wells blew past her into the tiny foyer, its floor all but obliterated by the twins' baby paraphernalia: double stroller, car seats, diaper bag, toys. Rosemary had meant to clean up. She was always meaning to clean up. She peeled off the "Knock lightly, no doorbell—babies sleeping" note she'd taped to the front door and closed it.

"This is faaaaabulous," Lucinda said. She turned around slowly but pointlessly, as the entire, patently unfabulous apartment was all too visible from a single angle: cramped living room, alcove kitchen, two small, dark bedrooms, one darker bathroom. "I love what you've done with it."

What they'd *done* with it was allow an invasion of *stuff* since the twins, Patrick and Edward, were born four months earlier. The focal point of the living room was two battery-operated swings in which the boys had been sleeping for five minutes. If Rosemary played her cards right, twice a day she could get both babies asleep simultaneously and have some time to herself. Yesterday she'd pulled off a full nine minutes of serenity.

"It's a bit of a mess, really."

"You'll move a few things out for the open house," Lucinda said. "I'll get someone in to help you."

Lucinda Wells had been recommended by a friend whose friend had used her to find an apartment. She looked about thirty-five, tall and leggy with a long, lean face to which she'd expertly applied a diverse palette of makeup, particularly around her jutting cheekbones and large, deep-set eyes. Her dark-brown, blond-highlighted hair fell to her shoulders. She wore a lavender cotton sweater that showcased small but shapely breasts, along with khaki linen pants and a pair of aggressively pointy high-heeled pumps.

"Just a few things have to go for the open house. We'll leave one of the swings here—buyers like to know that an apartment can handle an infant, even if they don't already have one. But two might be off-putting."

Two children or two swings? Rosemary was just five pounds above her prepregnancy weight but felt enormous and logy next to the coiled spring of Lucinda Wells.

"How big a place are you looking for?" she asked as she headed through the living room into the master bedroom. "I forgot how small the bedrooms are in this line. That's a king-size bed, am I right?"

"Yes."

"How big?"

"Oh, well, we'd like at least two bedrooms and two bathrooms. Anything bigger would be great, though we understand in this market—"

"How far north are you willing to go?" Lucinda sat on the unmade king-size bed and took a Palm Pilot from a leather satchel.

How far north—was she looking for a geographical or financial response?

Rosemary was a graduate of Wellesley and had a Ph.D. in art history from Columbia. She'd been a specialist in twentieth-century decorative arts at Atherton's, the auction house, but had to take a medical leave in her eighth month when pregnancy-related high blood pressure had been diagnosed. Five months out of the workforce—the *paid* workforce, she reminded herself—and she already felt hopelessly out of touch. *So five minutes ago,* to use an expression she had employed to deride clients who just didn't get it. Now she feared she was the one not getting it. Even *so five minutes ago* seemed so five minutes ago.

"If you mean how far uptown, we'd like to stay below Ninety-sixth Street if possible, on the West Side. My husband's office is near Union Square."

"Internet?"

"Actually, e-business infrastructure." Rosemary heard an edge of defensiveness in her voice. People were still mourning the death of dot-com stocks. "Positano Software . . . the stock's held up quite well."

"Went public when, about four months ago?"

She easily guessed what Lucinda was after. Six months was the lock-up period for most new offerings. After six months insiders could start to cash out; until then, their wealth was all on paper. If the company had been public only four months, executives wouldn't have any liquidity—meaning less borrowing power and less appeal to co-op boards.

"That's right. Guy is the founder," she added, the defensive edge sharper now.

The day Positano went public—the company was named for the town in Italy where they'd spent their honeymoon—Guy's stock was worth forty-seven million dollars. She'd found the amount unreal, obscene, even terrifying. Her parents were high-school teachers in a small town near Pittsburgh where the owner of the local Jiffy Lube franchise was at the top of the economic heap. They were middle class and proud of it and had bequeathed to her a deep-rooted suspicion of wealth. She felt strongly that forty-seven million dollars, even on paper, was a dangerous sum of money. You could never work hard enough to justify such an amount. It had taken Guy months of pleading before she agreed to call a real-estate broker, by which time Positano's stock had slid forty percent. They were reliving the Internet boom-and-bust all over again, but this time if felt more personal, just the two of them.

"Six rooms minimum, south of Ninety-sixth. . . ." Lucinda tap-tapped the data into her Palm. "Can you go as high as one-point-three?"

"We *could* go that high—assuming, of course, we could get a good price for this place."

Lucinda arched her pruned eyebrows. "I could get you seven-ten, seven-twenty," she said with a shrug, as if tossing off the price of a quart of milk. "Unless you want to sell quickly, in which case seven-even. I'll have a queen-size brought in for the open house." She looked hopelessly around the small, cluttered bedroom.

"The closets are actually quite large," Rosemary said, opening Guy's closet to make her point. His golf bag tumbled out.

"I sold 6A and 9A," Lucinda said. "Trust me, I know the closets in this line."

Rosemary shoved the golf bag back into the closet, displacing a row of suits Guy never wore anymore. His long bathrobe, which hung on a hook behind the door, prevented the door from closing securely and the golf bag fell out again.

Lucinda got up from the bed and stepped daintily over the bag, as if avoiding a corpse. "I'll have to call you later about the open house. And I'll see what I have in inventory to show you."

Imagining a gigantic warehouse containing an *inventory* of dark apartments, Rosemary followed her into the living room, where Lucinda glanced at the swinging twins.

"Is that cute?" she said. "And I love the window treatment."

"I can't wait for more space," Rosemary said.

"New Yorkers dream in floor plans," Lucinda said. "No, really, it's their most recurring dream, more common than that one about studying for the wrong test. Freud said that walking in and out of rooms in a dream is really about sex—penetration, I suppose. Did I mention I was a psych major at BU? Helps in this business, trust me. But with Manhattan apartments going for two thousand a square foot in top buildings, dreaming of walking in and out of rooms has nothing to do with fucking, it's just the desire for more space, case closed. The people I deal with would trade a year of sex for a walk-in closet with custom shelving. Make that five years! Trust me, Freud never saw a real-estate market like this one."

She handed Rosemary a business card at the door. "I'm going to love working with you," she said, as if that mattered most. She reached in her pants pocket and took out a small cell phone. "Last year I sold seventy million in co-ops, but this year I'm already ahead of that by twenty percent, and with this stock market."

Rosemary closed the door and heard the nasal beeping of a dialing cell phone from the other side. She went to the living room and sat on the sagging sleeper sofa, where she watched her boys' syncopated rocking. Back and forth, back and forth. Patrick, Edward, Patrick, Edward. She had a bad feeling about this move. They needed more space, that much was irrefutable. But with the stock market going nowhere, was this really the time to buy? Guy's salary was just over a hundred thousand a year: Positano was losing buckets of money—*truckloads*—on just a few million dollars in revenue, so anything larger would be unacceptable to investors. She felt herself frowning and imagined that she looked much like her mother at that moment, an anxious and disapproving Republican.

Patrick, Edward, Patrick, Edward, Patrick, Edward. She almost wished they'd wake up—they always regained consciousness with a united howl—so she'd have the distraction of changing their diapers, feeding them, burping them, then changing them again, then feeding them . . .

No, she'd let Lucinda Wells find them their dream home. Guy was a risk taker, and she could learn something from him about trust and optimism. Hadn't she tried to talk him out of leaving his job at the brokerage to start Positano? He'd ignored her and was now worth . . . what was the stock price that morning? Twelve and a half or twelve and three-quarters? Well, somewhere around twenty-five million dollars.

Oh, God. Just thinking about that number, reduced as it was, made her face flush and her stomach tighten. A number like that had to change things, and not always for the better, she felt certain. The apartment was just the start.

Two

"The tile!" shrieked Lucinda Wells in the foyer of the Gimmels' apartment at 218 West End Avenue. She glanced down, her lavishly made-up face contorted by unfathomable emotion. Peggy Gimmel observed her carefully. Was she impressed by the gleaming marble-look linoleum or terrified that a gaping hole would open up and send her sprawling down to the fifth floor?

"We had it put in when we bought the place," Peggy said. Next to the real-estate broker her voice sounded meek and hesitant. She cleared her throat. "We've never replaced a single tile."

"Why would you?" Lucinda Wells glanced sharply at her. Did she expect an answer? Peggy shrugged. She'd called the agent only that morning and had been surprised at her offer to come over that day.

"I didn't have time to straighten up," she said. This was accurate but hardly relevant, since the apartment was always immaculate.

"I sold 12D, did your daughter tell you that?" Lucinda said as she led Peggy into her own living room. "I love it, I really do. The . . . the carpet." She swept her right foot over the rust-colored shag as if scraping off dog poop.

Peggy wondered if Lucinda Wells had sold an apartment in every building in New York. She certainly had the energy for it, the metabolism of a nuclear reactor. Her eyes blinked continually like tiny cameras, recording everything. Click. Click. Click. Peggy half expected little flashes to go off.

"The crown moldings!" she cried. Click click click. "These old porcelain light switches, I haven't seen these in *years*." Click click click. "Oh my God, frosted sconces!" Click click click.

She turned abruptly and marched back through the foyer and into the dining room. Peggy checked discreetly to see if her sharp heels had left impressions in the marble-look tile.

"Incredible," Lucinda said. "I love what you've done with the space."

We did *it thirty-five years ago,* Peggy almost said, but she felt a rush of gratitude nonetheless. She'd heard Lily, on the phone with a friend, refer to the apartment as Neanderthal, and that was twenty years ago.

"You haven't changed anything, even these old radiator covers." Lucinda gave the metal cover a sharp rap.

"Is that good?" Peggy managed to ask

"Is that *good*? Are you *kidding*?"

Was that an answer? Was she expected to reply?

Lucinda charged into the kitchen. "I grew up in a kitchen just like this." She turned slowly at the center of the room.

"It gets quite a bit of afternoon sun," Peggy pointed out.

"Tell me about it! I'm dying to see what you've done with the maid's."

There was hardly room for the two of them in the tiny room behind the kitchen, so Peggy waited in the back hallway for Lucinda to make her inspection.

"I see you don't have live-in help," she said as she squeezed past Peggy and headed back into the kitchen.

"Lily's been gone for twenty years, and even when she was home we never had anyone—"

"Joking!" Lucinda said, and beat her to the den by several seconds.

"Oh, hello! Am I disturbing you?" she said to Monroe, who was sitting on the sofa staring at FNN.

Monroe turned slowly from the television and looked blankly at the intruder. He probably saw stock prices marching across her face.

"This is Lucinda Wells, a real-estate broker. This is my husband, Monroe."

"A pleasure," Lucinda said. "Do you mind?" But she had already charged into the room. "Buyers like to see an extra bedroom turned into a den," she observed. "Shows the possibilities. How about this market, anyway?" She tapped the TV screen with a red-lacquered fingernail. "*Quelle* nightmare."

Monroe stared at her, mouth agape.

"The venetian blinds!" Click click click. "That same shag carpet . . . how coordinated!" Click click click. "A console TV—when did you last see one of *those!*"

Monroe's eyes fixed on the broker's long, impossibly narrow calves as she headed for the door. His mouth formed a slack, lascivious grin. Peggy swatted his shoulder as she followed but, truthfully, felt relieved that something, even the stilts of an anorectic real-estate broker, could distract him from the tumbling price of Cisco.

"We never did much with it," Peggy said in Lily's old room. Indeed, the room was a shrine to Lily's teenage years in the seventies.

"So this is where it all began," Lucinda said with a trace of awe. She might have been describing the nursery of Amelia Earhart or Madame What's-her-name, the French scientist. All Lily was was the wife of a rich banker who attended a lot of parties that got written up in the papers. Peggy frowned. It wasn't as if the apartment was some sort of Third World hovel from which Lily had clawed her way to Park Avenue.

"She went to P.S. 87, just a block away," she felt obliged to point out.

"How extraordinary." Lucinda peered closely at the room's details, like a tourist at a presidential birthplace.

"Crinoline bedspreads," she said. Click click click. "Bamboo wallpaper. You must have cornered the market in rust shag, LOL."

Up to that point, the broker's inspection had made Peggy uncomfortable, but the tour of the master bedroom felt as invasive as a gynecological exam.

"Love how the spreads on the twin beds match the floor-to-ceiling drapes." Click click click. "And the color of the drapes . . . how did you ever find the perfect rust?"

She nearly swooned in the master bathroom as Peggy waited outside.

"These fixtures . . . you could advise the Met on preservation." Click click click. "Why do people insist on ripping out these old flushometer toilets? *Why?* And I love the medicine cabinet, the silvering is such an authentic touch."

She emerged, slowly shaking her head. "Perfect," she cooed, stretching her arms as if she'd just stood up from a massage. Then the arms fell to her sides. "Where can we talk?"

Before Peggy could reply, Lucinda headed straight for the living room and plunked herself down on the sofa. The plump goose-down pillows nearly swallowed her.

"Did you have a price in mind?" she asked when Peggy caught up.

"My friend Sonia said she thought we could ask eight—"

"Two-point-three," Lucinda said with a pursing of glossed lips.

Million? Peggy almost asked but thank God didn't. She sat in an armchair next to the sofa as blood rushed up into her face.

"Maybe you were expecting more, but my policy is, be realistic. Manage expectations. Two-point-three is a lock. How do you feel about that?"

Dizzy came to mind, but Peggy cleared her throat and managed to say, "Fine."

"I'd like an exclusive for six weeks, though I'll sell this place sooner than that. Classic sevens don't come on the market every day. I'd like to schedule an open house for next week."

"Next week?"

"What kind of place are you planning on moving to?"

"We hadn't really—"

"Two bedrooms? One and a half baths? I assume you'll want to stay in the neighborhood." Lucinda sat forward and narrowed her eyes. "You're not thinking of moving to Florida, are you?"

"Of course not," Peggy said quickly, and decided to wrest control of the conversation. "We'd like something smaller, obviously. Two bedrooms, two *full* baths." She couldn't imagine why they'd need the second tub, but it seemed important to contradict Lucinda on at least one point.

"Doorman, sunlight, move-in condition. I can find you something for one-point-two, one-point-three."

Leaving a million in the bank, Peggy thought. Her face warmed again as she considered how she was going to keep Monroe's speculative hands off a million dollars.

"A condo, of course. You don't want to face a board interview."

"No?"

"You'll have to reveal everything. Your investments, liquid assets, the details of your sex life."

"Our—"

"Joking! Most of the newer buildings in your price range are condos. No board approval. You own your own apartment outright. In co-ops like this one you own shares in a corporation, and a board evaluates your fitness to buy. It's a very intrusive business, worse than a gyno exam, LOL."

"Ell-oh—"

"So we'll stick to a condo and spare you the stirrups, okay?" Her wink revealed a huge, blue-painted lid.

"This is all happening so quickly," Peggy said, glancing quickly around the room as if for the last time.

"Listen, you can't drag this sort of thing out. You'll make yourself crazy." Lucinda sprang to her feet and stood directly in front of Peggy. From down below her face looked especially long and narrow, and her bony shoulders arched forward, ospreylike. "Okay to leave the contract for the exclusive with the doorman?"

Peggy had learned that Lucinda's questions didn't require answers. She followed her to the front door and unlocked it.

"You have a beautiful apartment, Mrs. Gimmel. Exceptional. It'll go like *that*."

Peggy shut the door and leaned heavily against the wall. Her home for thirty-five years, reduced to a sharp snap of Lucinda Wells's fingers. She closed her eyes and tried to imagine herself and Monroe in another apartment. Something new and white, without moldings to dust, and perhaps there'd be a view. She could picture the apartment easily enough, sunny and clean, heat and air-conditioning whispering through those nice little ducts you didn't have to clean or have serviced, but she couldn't quite place her and Monroe inside it. They were like the drapes in the living room, built specially for these windows. Where else would they fit?

She shook her head to clear it and opened her eyes. It was time to go, absolutely. Only this morning she'd dropped a spoon on the kitchen floor and, when she bent over to retrieve it, noticed a streak of schmutz under the toe kick, an entire civilization of crumbs and hair and dust that would never, in the past, have escaped her efforts.

And the money. She didn't dare *think* of the sum that broker had mentioned. When had prices gotten that high? Why hadn't she noticed? Never mind that, who the hell could afford to buy their place? Lily and Barnett, obviously, but they'd sooner move to the Congo than West End Avenue. Then who? It struck her as perfectly logical, in an absurd way, that anyone who could afford to buy the apartment wouldn't want to.

She'd lie down for a few minutes and try to forget the whole thing. She walked by the den and cast a weary glance at Monroe, his face shimmering with reflected stock prices, untroubled by the momentous decisions awaiting them. In the master bedroom she lay down on her bed with a sigh and closed her eyes. An afternoon nap—already things were going downhill. It was the money, of course. Money was always the issue, too much or too little, either way. So much money—surely a sum like . . . a sum like that woman mentioned would have consequences.

Rosemary Pierce ran from the living room to the kitchen to the bedroom, a twin in each arm, searching for the cordless phone. Like the TV remote, it was never where she needed it to be. If Heisenberg were alive he'd invent another, and far more useful, Uncertainty Theory to explain why the very act of searching for a small household appliance guaranteed that it would be somewhere you didn't even think to look. She gave up looking when the answering machine picked up after four rings. Patrick was wailing for a feeding and Edward was taking quick gasps through his puckered mouth, always the prelude to a full-throttled crying jag.

"Please leave a message for Rosemary, Guy, Patrick, or Edward after the beep," she heard herself say. "One of us, most likely Rosemary or Guy, will call you back." A cute idea at the time, but she imagined most of their friends were already tired of it. She'd make a new message as soon as she had time, perhaps when the twins left for college.

"It's Lucinda. Are you there? Rosemary?"

"Believe it or not, I *do* get out," she shouted at the answering machine. "Just not today," she added more quietly. "Or yesterday, actually."

"Okay, I'll make this quick. I found your apartment. I knew the minute I walked in. I'm standing in front of the building right now, it's just around the corner from you, three bedrooms, three baths, full-service building, eighty percent financing . . . needs work, of course, I mean the place is a total dump, a wreck, I haven't seen that much shag carpeting since I lost my virginity to Matthew Bronstein on the floor of my parents' den, and we all know how long ago *that* was, LOL. Anyway, it's got incredible bones. The apartment, not Matthew Bronstein."

Lucinda released a high-pitched laugh that sounded very much like the answering machine beep and triggered a complete meltdown from Edward.

". . . the bathroom fixtures and the window treatments . . . yuck. Some of my clients wouldn't see the possibilities, but I know you can, with your art background. Rip out the whole fucking thing and start fresh. God, doesn't that sound heavenly? Oops, I'm getting another call. Listen, this one won't last. You can have it for just north of two mil if you make a preemptive bid right away. Call me."

Rosemary walked back to the living room and lowered herself and her boys onto the sofa. She put them on the sofa, one on each side, pulled off her T-shirt, scooped them back up, and applied one to each breast. In seconds they were slurping contentedly.

Positano Software was down another twenty-five cents that morning—she'd taken to logging on to Yahoo Finance to check up on it whenever the twins were sleeping. That still left more than enough to buy the apartment—more than enough *on paper*, that is, and the operative word was *finance* the apartment, since buying implied an actual exchange of money and they wouldn't be parting with a cent.

The whole idea of buying/financing a new place in this climate made her incredibly uneasy, but she was eager nonetheless to see the apartment Lucinda had found. She looked down at her boys, milking her dry. Soon they'd need high chairs and big-boy toys—where would all that go? They were growing so quickly. She imagined them inflated like balloons in the Macy's Thanksgiving Parade, engorged on her milk until they no longer fit in the small apartment, their plump arms and thighs forced out the windows like icing through a pastry bag. Yuck, as Lucinda would say. She spotted the phone in the seat of one of the baby swings and decided she'd call Lucinda as soon as the boys fell into their postprandial nap.

Three

Guy Pierce loved the moment when people first entered his corner office at Positano Software. Like the woman from Goldman Sachs—what was her name? He checked the card she'd just handed him. *Kristin Liu, Vice President, Private Client Investment Services.* She'd probably walked into his smallish office on the third floor of a nondescript East Twenties building thinking, Nothing special. Thinking, I should have insisted that he come downtown to us, maybe offered lunch. And then she saw the tank.

"Wow," said Kristin Liu. "Amazing. Incredible."

They always reacted like that to the huge aquarium that formed most of the wall between his office and the main conference room. Nine hundred gallons of salt water, state-of-the-art filtration system, fifteen different breeds of fish, nine types of coral. Practically an entire saltwater reef, right in the center of Manhattan. Positano's architect had been against the idea, and the CFO, a twitchy bean counter named Henry Delano, had been appalled by the cost (the floor had to be specially reinforced, the tank custom-built, and he'd been particularly enraged by the Indonesian Fighting Fish—*Christ, even Le Bernardin doesn't get a hundred bucks a fish*). He'd almost resigned when he learned of the $25,000 owed to the aquarist who'd designed, installed, and stocked the tank. *The fucking aquarist is more profitable than we are!* But the tank impressed the hell out of potential customers, and it gave employees a lift, just knowing that a company that hadn't existed five years ago could have the coolest office accessory in town. Hell, even a Prada-clad banker from Goldman Sachs couldn't take her eyes off it.

"How long have you had this?" she asked.

"Since we moved in four months ago."

"Just after the IPO—I guess that's one use of proceeds that didn't find its way into the prospectus."

He forced a chuckle. Was she being censorious about the extravagance of the tank or just making a little joke?

"Clients love it," he said.

"I'm sure they do." Kristin Liu looked elegantly slender in a sleek black pantsuit. She had shoulder-length, bluntly cut, glossy black hair and wore rectangular glasses with thick black rims. Banker-cool. Chinese, he guessed. Half the bankers on the IPO were either Chinese or Indian. In the new Positano corporate brochure, a fifty-two-page four-color, embossed, debossed, and die-cut extravaganza (another use of proceeds), many of the photographs showed Asian people in front of monitors, at airports, in meetings. Asians signaled intelligence, globality, and tech-savviness, the brochure's designer had told him. The new Jews.

Kristin Liu sat on the gray faux-suede sofa across from his desk and he took an armchair facing her.

"I thought I'd begin with an overview of what we do in Private Client Investment Services," she said. "PCIS," she added with a prim smile.

He nodded for her to begin, though he already knew what PCIS was all about: making rich folks richer. Goldman hadn't been one of Positano's IPO underwriters—Positano wasn't quite up to snuff for the tier-one bankers like Goldman and Morgan Stanley, especially after the Internet bubble had burst. But now that the company was public, bankers with the whitest of shoes were all over him. He had three million shares of a public company—snuff enough even for Goldman.

She took a large, comb-bound pitch book from a sleek leather briefcase and began turning the laminated pages as she launched into a canned presentation. He didn't pay much attention. Instead, he considered, with some pleasure, how his situation had changed in five short years. Back then he was a lowly systems manager at a brokerage firm, toiling anonymously in the Secaucus processing center. Secaucus! Talk about back office: hundreds of pallid techies tending networked computers in row after row of small, airless cubicles. The veal farm, they'd called it. The likes of Kristin Liu, wining and dining clients, investing billions of their capital, barely knew the place existed. Client statements were produced, mailed, archived—who even stopped to consider how it all got done? Not Kristin Liu with her thousand-dollar pantsuits and killer eyewear.

His assistant, Dinitia Siting, poked her head in. "Guy, Rosemary's on the phone."

He apologized to Kristin Liu and picked up the phone next to the sofa.

"Hey, what's up?"

"I found an apartment," she said. He could hear the twins wailing in the background and felt a guilty sense of relief that he wasn't there. "It needs some work . . ."

She sounded more wary than enthusiastic. Rosemary simply had no faith in the future of Positano's stock. Yes, it had taken a nauseating dive in recent months, but fluctuations went with the territory. The company was on track to achieve profitability in two years, revenues were doubling every six months . . . true, there would be no secondary offering anytime soon (the market just wasn't ready), but he had Goldman Sachs sitting right there next to the saltwater reef, ready to make virtually any amount of money available to them.

"Great, when can I see it?"

"Lucinda, the broker, thinks we need to make an offer quickly—if we're going to make an offer. Otherwise she's going to schedule an open house next week."

"I'll look at it tonight, then. Why don't you set it up. I'm in a meeting now . . ."

"You haven't asked how much."

I've got Goldman Fucking Sachs here, honey. Who cares how much?

Trying to sound interested, he asked, "How much?"

"Two million three hundred thousand dollars." She dragged out each syllable, as if she were writing the figure on a check.

"Okay, that's in our range." He smiled indulgently at Kristin Liu. Perhaps sensing Rosemary's anxiety, the twins' wailing escalated.

"Try to set it up for tonight, then," he said. "I have to go. Love you!"

He hung up and looked at his visitor. "My wife thinks she's found our dream home. But she's nervous about the price."

"It's a strong real-estate market," Kristin Liu said. "Real-estate values trail equities by a year or more, in our experience."

Our experience. She was probably twelve when the last bear market hit.

"But we have strategies that could make her more comfortable with your situation. I was just getting to the zero-cost collar—are you familiar with that?"

A banker from Morgan had already trudged through it with him. Basically, you locked in, or collared, a floor price for your stock in return for giving up most of the upside potential. It cost you nothing, the ultimate hedge for executives with all their wealth tied up in their company's stock.

"When Rosemary and I met, I was writing code for an investment firm," he said. "I don't think our new . . . situation has completely sunk in with her."

Kristin Liu took off her glasses and leaned forward. "Would it help if I walked her through this presentation?" she asked with the soothing, slightly impatient tone of an oncologist addressing the spouse of a mortally ill patient. Guy almost laughed. Just the mention of a zero-cost collar would send Rosemary into fits of insecurity. In Rosemary's world, nothing came without a cost, certainly not collars.

"I don't think that would help. I think it's more . . ."

Without her glasses Kristin Liu looked suddenly, unexpectedly hot. She was intimidating in that Asian, smartest-kid-in-the-class way, but the absence of eyewear humanized her somewhat. Her skin was flawless, and her tiny, nearly round mouth seemed perpetually on the verge of a chaste but promising kiss. He checked her left hand: no wedding ring. Five years ago such a woman would have had nothing to do with him. He was acceptably handsome, he supposed, but a haze of disappointment had trailed him like body odor as he trudged out to the Secaucus veal farm by subway and PATH train, dressed in ill-fitting polo shirts and khakis back when dressing like a slob wasn't yet a New Economy status symbol. Now he was CEO of a high-flying technology firm with three million publicly traded shares and New York's largest tropical fish tank in his office, and though his wardrobe hadn't changed much (Who had time to shop? Who cared?), he'd noticed that women reacted differently to him, a sexual energy seemed to animate conversations with women these days, an energy he'd never noticed before—because it hadn't been there! Kristin Liu, for example, was gazing so intently at him just then, so seductively, he thought, that he had to cross and then uncross his legs just to disguise his growing interest.

"I used to feel a million miles from the real business of the firm," he said, sensing that she was eager to hear his tale of rags to riches—or back office to front office. "I was out in New Jersey making sure monthly statements and year-end tax forms went out on time, while you . . . I mean, the bankers, were making million-dollar decisions before breakfast and taking wealthy investors to Lutèce and the Four Seasons."

She nodded and squinted sympathetically. He recalled reading that Lutèce wasn't considered wonderful anymore—was it even open?—and felt a twinge of the old insecurity.

"I graduated near the top of my class at Columbia, a math major. I never thought I'd end up in a code-writing factory in New Jersey. I felt like I'd never get out of there. Then I got a call, five and a half years ago, from a managing director. Apparently a few customers—excuse me, *clients*—were starting to send e-mails to their brokers. Some of these clients had never even met their brokers face-to-face, they'd inherited them along with the fifty mil in Daddy's estate. Daddy never owned a computer, but his kids did, and they wanted to move their relationship with their brokers online. So the brokers suddenly had these annoying messages waiting for them in the morning, full of annoying questions about earnings per share and dividend yields, and they couldn't keep up. So they asked me to design a program that would automatically send back an e-mail saying, you know, the basic bullshit: 'Thank you for your important and keenly insightful inquiry. We're working on getting the information you need and will respond as soon as we can, so please don't send us any other fucking messages, okay?'"

Kristin began to squirm. Too bad for her. He loved telling the story of Positano's beginning the same way Rosemary liked relating the twins' births: that first, twin-revealing sonogram, the rush to Mount Sinai six weeks ahead of schedule, the last-minute C-section. Positano's birth was no less dramatic.

"It took me about five months to design that program. A real beauty, though kind of basic compared to what came after. E-mail messages were automatically sent, the brokers returned to . . . to their four-star restaurants, and I settled back into my cube in New Jersey without so much as a thank you from anyone on Park Avenue. And then, one night, I couldn't sleep."

He loved this part, his Eureka moment, and didn't care whether Kristin Goldman Sachs was interested or not.

"I was tossing and turning when it hit me. What if I sold the program I'd designed to other companies? Everyone and his grandmother was selling shit online. My little program could handle incoming e-mail without human intervention. Complaints, order inquiries, you name it. A week later I gave notice, hocked myself and Rosemary up to our eyeballs to buy the hardware I needed, and basically re-created the e-mail program I'd developed for the brokerage house in our living room. My first customer was AutoTrade.com. Once I had their endorsement, things really took off and the venture funding started to flow."

"Fascinating," Kristin Liu said in the same unfathomable tone she'd used to praise the tank. She turned a page in her pitch book, but he wasn't done.

"I keep reading that the Internet has unleashed this creative force in the world, that's its changing the entire economy, but when I go to trade shows and technology investor conferences, you know what I think?"

She cocked her head and moved the pitch book a few inches closer to her, as if preparing to defend it.

"I think the Internet has been the salvation of guys like me. It's moved us from the back office to the front office, right to the top of the food chain. Math majors, code jockeys, computer nerds—we're cool now, *I'm* cool now."

She didn't respond. Well, he could hardly expect her to offer an endorsement.

"Some people think the Internet's peaked," he said. "That's bullshit, of course, it's just the stock market talking. We haven't even seen what the Net can do. We're working on the third release of our Sorrento product, which automatically scans incoming e-mails for designated key words, maps them along predetermined quadrants, and develops a customized response . . . within seconds! I've got customers lined up out the door waiting for it."

She glanced doorward, then back at him.

"If I had to go back to the veal farm, if this was all some kind of *Brigadoon* thing, I think I'd die a slow death, like a plant without light."

"But you won't have to," she said, reseizing the conversational thread. "We have strategies for locking in the value of your assets now. Forever." She thrust the pitch book toward him.

"I don't want to hedge my bets. Positano is a great company, it's got a great future. Why would I give up the upside just to play it safe?"

"You don't have to hedge your entire investment in Positano. We can arrange a strategy that—"

"I'm not hedging a single share."

She considered this a beat, then flipped over several pages of the pitch book. She was Goldman Sachs and probably had an MBA from Harvard, but he had three million shares of a publicly traded company.

"Let's talk real-estate loans," she said.

The red-eyed vireo alit on a maple branch so fragile it seemed a miracle it didn't snap. But the branch dipped gracefully, then swung back to its original position.

Lily Grantham wondered what it felt like to execute a graceful plié on so slender a branch. She adjusted her binoculars and tried to read the vireo's expression. It looked wary and rather satisfied but hardly thrilled. Birds were hard to read, which is what she admired about them. She'd never liked dogs or cats, with their transparent tail-wagging and purring, so cheesily gratifying to people who required that kind of thing. Birds were elusive and inscrutable, they lived among us, but they remained apart, resourceful and independent.

This was the first red-eyed vireo she'd seen all year. She was in the Rambles, the remotest and wildest section of Central Park, which she visited several times a week with her top-of-the-line 12X36 image stabilizing binoculars and a sandwich. She was aware of other bird-watchers, many of whom seemed to be there every day, huddling in small groups to share their latest sitings. She eschewed this camaraderie, which seemed antithetical to the whole idea of bird watching. Socializing, in Lily's opinion, was very unbirdlike.

The red-eyed vireo remained obligingly still as she admired its subtle coloring, that patch of mauve under its throat that signaled its maleness, the dusky brown of its tail feathers. A few weeks earlier, she'd seen the first grosbeaks of the year, the finches. The pair of red-tailed hawks over at 960

Fifth, where the Zelwins had their duplex, would be fortifying their nest on the ninth-floor balcony in preparation for the spring breeding season. Such seasonal inevitability depressed her in most contexts, but with birds she found it reassuring. Why they returned to Manhattan, which struck her as inhospitable to all living creatures except the very rich, she couldn't imagine.

A voice intruded on her solitary contemplation, trilling the words "red-eyed vireo." She lowered her binoculars and saw two middle-aged women several yards away, just a few feet from the maple tree, their binoculars trained upward. She felt robbed, violated, and found herself wondering, irritably, what kind of life the two women had that they could spend what her mother would call *a perfectly good afternoon* watching birds. That this was precisely what she was doing with her ample free time only fanned the fire of her irritation. Soon an elderly man joined them and quickly aimed his binoculars on the red-eyed vireo, *her* red-eyed vireo, in response to the breathless exhortations of the women. She heard him say, "Welcome back, my little friend!" to the delight of the two women.

She felt like clocking him with her binoculars. *It's just a bird,* she wanted to call out as she stood up. In fact, she didn't particularly like birds, anxious, jumpy creatures drawn, like delusional actors, to the bright lights of Manhattan as they made their grimly regular commute up and down the Atlantic coast, hundreds of them each year colliding into the tallest buildings and plunging to the Midtown sidewalks. But for reasons she really couldn't explain, even to herself, she liked to be among them, spying anonymously on their private, unfathomable world. She sorely wanted to take a final look at the vireo, reclaim it. But pinned in the gaze of three other pairs of lens-enhanced eyes, the vireo wasn't the same bird she'd discovered on her own a few minutes ago. She headed home.

"Lily?"

The sound of her name sent a buzz of alarm down her back. No one knew about her bird watching in the Rambles. It was one of the few completely private aspects of her life. She looked to her left and saw a man, jogging in place, panting. Early forties, she guessed, *her age*, with shaggy brown hair, a loose, sweaty, Hershey-logoed T-shirt tucked into those skintight Lycra running shorts that turned even an average endowment into a mortifying codpiece. She had no idea who he was, which was a relief.

"Lily Gimmel?" How long had it been since anyone had called her that? *There is no such person,* she almost said. "Larry Adler," he said.

Suddenly she was so nonplussed—the loss of her red-eyed vireo, being recognized, hearing her name, her old name, then *his* name—she could only nod dumbly.

"How have you been?"

He stopped jogging in place and placed his hands on his hips, as if presenting the codpiece for her consideration.

How had she been? A throwaway line from anyone else, but from Lawrence Adler, the question seemed huge, impossible.

"I've been . . . and you?"

He winced. The last time they'd been together, almost twenty-five years ago, they'd made love three times on the floor of the maid's room of her parents' apartment at 218 West End Avenue while Peggy and Monroe slept obliviously down the hall. Three times in one night . . . the memory gripped her in a dizzy sadness.

"I'm great," he said. "Put on a few pounds, but I'm running again." He patted his stomach like an old dog. She used to love watching him run around the track when he'd been the star athlete on the Bronx Science track team. Competing so earnestly had been terribly uncool back in the seventies, and there hadn't been many people on the bleachers with her. As Larry passed her he'd shoot her a quick glance, his face all nervous concentration and focus. Like a bird's, she thought now.

"I read about you in the paper sometimes," he said.

She felt another shiver of vulnerability; after all, she knew nothing of him. Then again, what did he know of her, except the name of her husband, the parties she attended, the dresses she wore? (What else is there to know? a voice asked her. A little birdie, she thought with a panicked glance at the maple branch.)

"What have you been doing?" she asked.

"Same old same old. I've been running the store since my dad died six years ago."

"The Broadway Nut Shoppe," she said softly. The words felt like a sigh as they left her lips "I didn't realize it was still there."

"Remember how you used to visit me when I was working behind the counter? I offered you whatever you wanted and all you'd take was one non-pareil. Never more than one."

"The Broadway Nut Shoppe," she repeated, recalling the comfy smell of roasting nuts in the back, the taste of the nonpareil as it slowly melted on top of her tongue until only the tiny dots remained.

"I even moved into my parents' old apartment on West Eighty-second Street. My father had just died and I needed a place to live. I think my dad would have died a second time if I'd let a rent-controlled apartment leave the family."

"My parents are still in their place," she said. And then she remembered that Peggy was determined to sell the apartment and felt an inexplicable jolt of insecurity.

"I guess this apple never fell far from the tree," he said without a trace of embarrassment. "But you've really gone places. I mean, look at you."

She actually glanced down, feeling suddenly absurd next to his Lycra'd casualness. Khaki trousers, pale blue Turnbull & Asser oxford shirt, Ferragamo boots—all she needed to complete the picture was a riding crop.

"I have to get back," she said.

"I wouldn't have pegged you for a bird-watcher."

"Oh, this." She raised the binoculars. "It's just something I do. It's . . . I mean, it's nothing."

"You look fantastic," he said.

So do you, she almost said, but instead she gave a little wave with her free hand and turned eastward.

"We never talked about what happened," he said. "I must have called about sixty times. Your mother said you weren't home, or you were home but you were sleeping, or sometimes you were in the shower."

She turned back to him. "I didn't know what to say."

He looked pensive for a few moments, during which she dreaded his re-crimination, which she deserved. She'd sent him a Dear John letter from Mount Holyoke and then avoided him over Christmas vacation until he stopped calling. But he finally smiled.

"You look great," he said again, and she wished to God she didn't, though she knew she did, albeit in a horsey. *Town & Country* way. He jogged off to the west, and she began walking home to the east.

Four

Prying Monroe from the apartment on a Tuesday night was like luring a gopher from its hole.

"It's just for a few hours," Peggy assured him. "Our new broker has a hot prospect who needs to see our apartment." She'd picked a restaurant on the East Side, to justify the interim stop she had planned, which set off a new round of grumbling.

"It's the East Side of *Manhattan*, Monroe, not Tokyo. You'll be back in time for the ten o'clock news." He returned to the money channel, or whatever it was called, with a surly growl.

At seven that evening they took the Seventy-ninth Street crosstown bus to the East Side. When they got to Fifth Avenue, Peggy stood up.

"You said the restaurant's near Second."

"We have a stop to make," she said. "Come on or we'll miss it."

They debussed from the front. She took Monroe's hand and led him up Fifth. Ahead, in front of the Metropolitan Museum, a swarm of vehicles, many of them black Town Cars, jammed the avenue. Flashbulbs flickered like fireflies in the night air.

"We're not going to the museum, are we?" Monroe said. "Looks mobbed."

"It's an opening, Monroe. And the only way we're getting in there tonight is if we pay a thousand bucks apiece."

"That include dinner?"

Mister Big Shot, she thought, with his shrinking portfolio.

Most of the action was on the museum side of Fifth, so they had the facing sidewalk to themselves. As they slowly moved uptown, the noise from the other side of the street grew louder. Car after car pulled up and deposited guests, then sped off downtown to God knows where to wait out the night. Photographers with big, old-fashioned cameras stood to the side of a long red carpet that ran from the sidewalk up the staircase and into the museum. A banner over the doorway read DUTCH ART FROM THE AGE OF EXPLORATION, whatever that meant. Peggy supposed she'd see the exhibit eventually. Ruth Firestein would sooner skip a grandson's Bar Mitzvah than miss a big museum show, and Peggy didn't mind accompanying her, though she could live without the highbrow commentary that Ruth had picked up from an art-appreciation course she took a hundred years ago at the New School.

"What a hullabaloo," Monroe said. "Where are we going?"

"To dinner, eventually. Let's wait here a minute."

They stopped directly across from the museum staircase.

"I need to sit down."

"You sit all day. Look!"

She stepped behind a narrow tree and pulled Monroe after her. She'd rather die than be spotted by Lily and Barnett—and vice versa, she didn't doubt.

Lily wore a long, backless gown of some sort of shimmering fabric; it glistened like chain mail whenever a flash went off. Her hair was swept up onto her head, with a few wisps on either side hanging down helter-skelter; she'd probably paid someone a lot of money to decide just which strands to leave alone. A flash went off and Peggy thought she spotted diamonds twinkling on Lily's ears. Barnett had on a tuxedo, of course. They stopped just before ascending the stairs, turned to their left, and posed for a few shots. Barnett put his arm around her waist—he could probably circle it with both hands—and they just stood there, smiling. At one point he reached over and adjusted her hair, repositioning one of those free-standing wisps. A second later he did it again.

"What a nerve," Peggy said. "She should tell him to suck in that gut of his."

"That's Lily!" Monroe said, just getting it. "Let's catch her before she goes in." He started for the street but Peggy grabbed his elbow.

"Are you off your rocker, Monroe?"

"But it's Lily and—"

"I know who they are. And I also know that they wouldn't appreciate us intruding on their evening."

They were slowly climbing the grand staircase as the photographers turned their attention to the next arriving couple.

"Is that why you brought me here, to spy on them?"

Lily and Barnett disappeared into the museum and Peggy felt a huge weight descend on her. What a stupid, humiliating thing she'd done.

"I just wanted to see what she was wearing," she said quietly.

"You could ask her next time."

She looked at him and frowned. "Or I could shoot myself. Let's get a taxi, Monroe. And promise me one thing, you won't ever tell her we were here, okay?"

"We'll take this down for sure," Guy Pearson said, rapping on the wall that separated the Gimmels' living room from their guest bedroom.

"Loftlike," Lucinda Wells purred.

"We'll open up the kitchen to the foyer, definitely."

"A California kitchen."

"You think there's room for a Jacuzzi?" he asked in the master bathroom.

"You'll have to incorporate a closet," she replied, "but you could add a whole wall of closets to compensate. It's doable. Everything's doable."

Everything's doable—that could be her motto, Guy thought. And his. He almost told her about the fish tank but decided he'd let her discover it for herself—he'd insist they hold the closing in his office. She thought she'd seen everything, but he'd bet the price of the co-op they were looking at she'd never seen a nine-hundred-gallon aquarium in place of a wall. He wanted the apartment. It was way bigger than the house he'd grown up in in Flatbush, Brooklyn—the *entire* house, not just the first floor his family had rented. It was easily five times bigger than the closet they lived in now. Just imagining the four of them ensconced in such an abundance of square footage made him light-headed.

"What kind of financing are you considering?" Lucinda asked him when they returned to the living room. She sat on the big sofa and motioned with a proprietary sweep of an arm for him to sit next to her.

"All cash," he said with a touch of bravado. "Goldman Sachs is lending me the money."

"Against your shares in Positano?"

She was good. He watched her cross her long, thin legs, her right kneecap forming a perfect circle under sheer stockings. She was sexy in a harsh, aggressive way that might once have intimidated the hell out of him. Now he had three million publicly traded shares and Goldman Sachs throwing money at him and he almost wished he were single again, just for one night—an hour would do—to show Lucinda Wells just how manfully unintimidated Guy Pearson was.

"They'll lend me whatever I need to buy this place," he said. "Obviously I won't have to put up all of my holdings as collateral."

They shared knowing smiles.

"Co-op boards are leery of collateralized loans," she said when the smiles had subsided. "If the price of the shares drops, and the loan is called . . ."

"That's ridiculous. I'll be pledging less than ten percent of my holdings. And Positano's not dropping. Our revenues this year are running at twenty-four million, we're on a path for breakeven in Q4 of next year. And this is West End Avenue, for Christ's sake, not Park or Fifth."

"Excellent point. I'm just raising the kinds of issues the board will be raising. The issue of running revenues, for example."

"What?"

"You mentioned that your revenues were *running* at twenty-four million. But you haven't actually *achieved* that level of revenue as of yet."

She was very, very good and he hated her. "Run rate refers to annualized revenue based on the most recent quarter. In our most recent quarter we had six million in sales, so we're running at—"

"Twenty-four million. I get it. And so will the co-op board, if we present the issue in the right context."

Guy looked around, irritated. The apartment hadn't been touched in thirty years at least, the owners had probably bought as insiders for a pittance and couldn't afford to buy it today if they scraped together every cent they had, and now *his* worthiness was in doubt?

"The Gimmels—they're the owners—want two-point-three. I tried to get them to ask less, but they had this price in mind even before I entered the picture. They're very shrewd, so if you're serious—"

"I'm serious."

"Then I suggest we offer something close, say two-point-one-five. We'll work our way up to two-point-two. That'll settle it."

Guy imagined the wall facing him succumbing to a sledgehammer, big chunks of plaster plunging messily onto the rust-colored shag carpet, plaster dust settling on the workmen like powered sugar as they hacked away at this deplorable impediment to his manifest destiny of wide-open square footage.

"Make an offer," he said, barely moving his jaw, which had the desired effect of forcing his voice down an octave.

"Two million one-five?"

Her use of the *m* for the first time that night gave him pause, but he managed to toss off a dismissive "Whatever."

Across town at the Met, dinner was served. Normally, Lily Grantham loved fund-raisers at the museum, the heady impertinence of relegating priceless artworks to an unnoticed backdrop for a crowd of begowned and bejeweled society folk raising money for some charity no one knew or cared anything about. Surrounded by dozens of round tables set with good china and elaborate arrangements of spring flowers, the Temple of Dendur, squat, unnoticed, and completely out of context, glowed preternaturally, like a meteor just fallen to earth. But tonight she felt restless and bored. Her thoughts turned with maddening regularity to her parents selling the apartment, to Larry in the park, to the theft of her red-eyed vireo.

"Darling." Barnett kneed her under the table. "Alan and Kate have invited us to Connecticut next weekend."

"That would be lovely," she said without any notion of what she'd just agreed to. Alan was Alan Flutterman, of Flutterman, Petrovsky & Wald. Kate was Kate Grier Flutterman, wife of Alan Flutterman of Flutterman, Petrovsky & Wald.

"It's sooo beautiful right now," Kate Flutterman was saying. "We had ten thousand daffodil bulbs planted last fall, all the same color, yellow with white centers."

"White with yellow centers," her husband corrected.

Why are they telling me this? Lily wondered. Nothing was making sense. She glanced at the Temple of Dendur, which looked small and embarrassed. Whose idea was it to drag that homely pile halfway around the world, only to have it end up as a party decoration? Everything and everyone seemed out of context.

"The children love riding," she heard Barnett say. "What's the name of the stables where they take lessons?"

"Claremont Riding Academy," she said, surprising herself. Kate and Alan Flutterman nodded. Barnett brushed a strand of hair from her forehead. A young waiter with the blandly handsome face of a soap opera actor put a plate of food in front of her. Salmon and sweet peas and potato croquettes.

Conversations lurched forward all around her as she ate. Normally she was the galvanizing center of a table, the focus. She could talk to anyone about anything. True, some nights, as she took off her makeup and gown in her dressing room, she wondered if she'd gone too far in making everyone feel included, important. She wondered if other women in other dressing rooms on Fifth and Park were complaining to their husbands that Lily Grantham had monopolized attention with her encouraging questions and too-ready laugh.

"Barnett Grantham?"

All around the table ten sets of eyes turned to a man standing behind her husband. He wore a shapeless black suit, white shirt, dark tie.

"They're feeding the security staff in the kitchen," Kate Grier Flutterman said, as if referring to farm animals. She was a cochair of the event. Lily noticed two similarly dressed men flanking the one who'd spoken her husband's name.

"Did you want something?" Barnett said, his torso twisted to face the men.

"My name is Jay DiGregorio, from the Federal Prosecutor's Office. We have a warrant for your arrest. Please come with us."

"What?"

Lily looked at him, then at the three men, and then, unaccountably, at the Temple of Dendur.

"What is going on here?" Barnett asked. One of the men who hadn't spoken placed a hand on his shoulder.

"Get your hand off me!"

"Come with us, please," Jay DiGregorio said. Beginning at their table and radiating outward, a wave of silence unfurled to the far corners of the room. "We don't want to use the handcuffs."

"What?"

"What are the charges?" Alan Flutterman said. "I'm Alan Flutterman of Flutterman, Petrovsky & Wald."

"He'll be charged downtown," Jay DiGregorio said. "You can meet us at Foley Square."

"Down—I'm not his attorney," Alan Flutterman said quickly.

Jay DiGregorio's two colleagues all but lifted Barnett out of his chair by his elbows.

"Take your hands off me this instant!" he said. "I demand to know what the charges are." Lily had to wince. Even under the circumstances—arrested in front of all of New York society—Barnett was overdoing the dignified-under-pressure bit.

"Let's go," Jay DiGregorio said. "You have the right to remain silent. Anything you say may—"

"Barnett, what's going on?" Lily said.

"Call Morton Samuels."

Looks were exchanged around the table. Morton Samuels was the most famous lawyer in New York, or the most famous lawyer who hadn't yet stooped to appearing on CNN to punditize about the latest high-profile murder. Morton Samuels would *never* appear on CNN, which was one of the reasons he was so highly regarded among the Temple of Dendur set. Lily and Barnett knew him socially. Nevertheless, she felt a tremor of dread, for summoning Morty Samuels while being read your rights was akin to calling for a priest on one's sickbed.

"I'll come with you." She grabbed her purse and stood up.

"You can meet us downtown," said Jay DiGregorio.

"Call Samuels!" Barnett shouted as he was led from the room. His voice already sounded faint and distant.

Instinctively she reached into her purse for her cell phone, but as she turned it on she realized she didn't have Morton Samuels's home phone number.

"Does anyone. . . ."

She glanced around. She was the only one standing in a room of five hundred people. No one spoke. No one moved. She brushed a strand of hair from her forehead, *that* strand. She'd call Nanny and ask her to look up the phone number. But first she needed to make an exit.

"It's some sort of mistake," she said to the people at her table, all of whom nodded energetically. "We'll be back for dessert!" She smiled gallantly. They smiled back dubiously.

Her heels clattered on the slate floor as she crossed the enormous room as quickly as possible without appearing to be fleeing. The instant she left the room, voices erupted behind her, growing louder and closer like an approaching tornado. She began to run.

Five

News happened to other people, Peggy had always thought, which is what made reading the Metro section of the *Times*—full of sordid murders and unfathomable budget cuts and water mains erupting through the asphalt like daffodils in the spring—not merely tolerable but a guilty pleasure. There was reassuring satisfaction in the daily reminder that while the city she'd always lived in continued its slow, inevitable decline, her own world hummed along quite unaffected, even impervious. Dinners were served in restaurants, theater curtains rose at eight, cash machines never ran out of crisp twenty-dollar bills, buses chugged up and down the avenues, diseases were diagnosed and cured or succumbed to, the mail arrived, the phone rang, *The New York Times* was dropped outside her door each morning at six-thirty precisely. Scanning the Metro section was like reading about some distant, never-to-be-visited land where the government was always on the verge of falling to anarchists—*Thank God I don't live there!*—so spotting Lily's name among the murder and mayhem was startling to say the least.

"Oh my God!"

Monroe Gimmel, sitting across from Peggy at the small kitchen table, peered at his wife over the top of the business section.

"What's wrong?"

"They've arrested Barnett." She pointed to the small article in the Metro section. "He was arrested last night at the Metropolitan Museum—*the Metropolitan Museum*—on charges of diverting millions of dollars from company funds to private accounts."

"Why would he do that? He already makes a fortune."

"It says that arresting him in public like that was a way of sending a message. Poor Lily. She looked so lovely last night."

"What kind of message?"

"He's being taken to Rikers Island pending a bail hearing later today." Rikers Island. It sounded so hopeless, so final. They might as well have sent him to one of those dank, rocky prisons off the coast of France full of debauched aristocrats with long, greasy hair and rotten teeth.

The phone rang.

"Maybe it's Lily," she said as she picked up the receiver, though she feared it might be a reporter.

"Peggy? It's Lucinda Wells. We have an offer!"

At seven-thirty that morning, Lily caught a glimpse of herself in the gilt Louis XV mirror in the lobby of 913 Park Avenue. She fully expected to be shocked by what she saw, and in fact she was shocked—she looked fabulous. Her hair had come undone a bit, but the coif that Alexandre had constructed earlier that day—no, yesterday—had a bit of dishevelment built in. Her makeup was intact; she hadn't cried once all night, even when that dreadful man, Jay DiGregorio, had advised her, as she was leaving the police station, once they'd finally sent Barnett to Rikers Island, to take the subway home, since the Justice Department would soon begin confiscating every last cent they had. His exact words: *every last cent they had.* She'd managed a dismissive chuckle for the prick, and then had a vision: all their wealth transformed into piles of pennies, neatly housed in those brown sleeves she'd enjoyed filling up as a child and exchanging for dollar bills at the First National City Bank on Eighty-sixth Street and Broadway. How many fifty-cent rolls would it take to equal what they were worth? she found herself wondering. She imagined stacks and stacks of them piled in one giant pyramid in the center of the Sheep Meadow in Central Park. A pile of pennies as big as the Ritz.

She applied lipstick and smiled gallantly at the mirror. It was important not to look too haggard for the children. Thank God she never cried. There were moments over these last hours and, occasionally, over the past years, when she sensed that a good, long cry would feel as restorative as a massage or a hit of pot or one of those purgative therapies her friends raved about. But she invariably stopped herself just before actual tears appeared, responding to a vague but deep-set fear that once she started, she'd never be able to stop. She'd just cry until her body was as shriveled and flat as a prune. It had happened once . . . well, almost happened. That week Larry kept calling, she cried every time the phone rang, even before Peggy came in to say, for the eightieth time, that he was on the phone and was desperate to speak to her. Tell him I'm not home, she'd said between sobs. Look, Peggy had said, finally. Either talk to the poor boy or stop crying. You're going to dry up like a prune.

Hah! Every fear, every insecurity, in fact every mental path, straight or twisted, led back to Peggy, and always had.

She was positive the elevator man looked at her strangely when he greeted her with his usual "Morning, Mrs. Grantham." Had he read something in the paper or seen something on the news, or was he just responding to the way she was dressed, the fact that she was returning home, alone, at seven-thirty in the morning? It occurred to her that she would be the focus of a great deal of unwanted attention in the coming days. Barnett would be returning home that afternoon, she'd been assured by Morton Samuels, who'd shown up at the prosecutor's office several hours after she'd called him. Perhaps then the whole incident would be forgotten. Not by her, of course. She'd sensed, even as Barnett was being dragged from the Temple of Dendur, that the arrest would have life-changing consequences.

She unlocked the door to the apartment and shut it with unnecessary force, hoping the sound would announce her return and bring the children running. After a long, lonely moment, one of the worst in a long, lonely twelve hours, she went to the kitchen and found Sophie and William eating breakfast. Sophie was in her school uniform. William had on a polo shirt and khakis; his school had abandoned uniforms a year earlier, reluctantly acknowledging that the blue blazers and maroon striped ties, both emblazoned with the school crest, had become virtual "come and get it" signs for gangs of young thugs who regularly descended from poorer neighborhoods uptown to pick the kids clean of their lunch money, personal audio equipment, and, in one incident that was still talked about throughout the Upper East Side, a brand-new pair of custom Nike high-tops. Nanny hovered nearby.

"Hi, Mom," both children said between slurps of cereal.

She'd told Nanny that Mr. Grantham had been called away on a business emergency and that she'd had to accompany him to the airport and wait with him for his flight to depart. Pretty feeble, but she wasn't about to tell Nanny Griffen, who sashayed around as if she were first cousin to the Queen of England, that her employer was spending the morning in jail, Rikers Island, no less. They'd all find out soon enough. Perhaps Nanny already knew. She had cast a rather pitying look at Lily when she first saw her, and was even now looking at the children with a wistful smile, as if they were impoverished orphans.

"How was everyone's night?" Lily asked gamely.

The children shrugged, their most prolific response these days.

"Where did Dad go?" Sophie asked.

"Cleveland" sprang from her lips. "He has a client there."

"You must be real tired."

She sounded almost sympathetic. At fourteen, Sophie affected a world-weary sophistication that seemed at odds with her sweetly pretty appearance, like a child playing dress-up, and looked particularly ludicrous on school days, when Sophie was made to wear the Sacred Heart uniform: blue plaid dirndl, matching skirt, starched white blouse. Sacred Heart (actually, Convent of the Sacred Heart, but Lily, though she hadn't set foot in a synagogue in decades, could never bring herself to even *think* the full name), one of the best girls' schools in the city, had been Barnett's idea (his mother and several cousins had gone there). Peggy had been mortified ("I tell my friends she's in private school and hope they'll leave it at that"). Sophie had inherited Lily's dark hair and dark complexion and Barnett's aqua-blue eyes and strong profile. Lily never tired of looking at her.

"I'm exhausted," Lily said.

William was his sister's physical opposite. With Lily's dark eyes and Barnett's fair complexion, he looked delicate and pensive, though he was neither. At fifteen he was the star forward on Trinity's soccer team and, judging from the number of calls he received at night, he was popular and gregarious.

"Eat up," Nanny said from her post by the kitchen sink. "We're running a bit late."

"Is your homework done?" Lily asked, asserting maternal control. They both nodded, their second most prolific response.

"They were done by nine sharp," Nanny said.

She would not acknowledge that. Watching the children eating a balanced breakfast, she felt depressingly superfluous—her kids didn't need her, the party last night had bubbled on without her, Larry Adler had recovered from her tragic rejection and, infuriatingly, hadn't gone completely to pot . . . in fact he looked better than she remembered him.

Now, how had that last thought crept in?

"I think I'll change," she announced to no response, and headed to her bathroom, where she washed her face and put on a long bathrobe.

"Bye, Mom," William said from the doorway to the bedroom. Sophie stood just behind him.

"Come in," she said. "We need to talk about something." They stepped into the room, urban Sherpas shouldering enormous, bulging backpacks. One good poke would send them both tumbling backward. "Your father isn't in Cincinnati."

"He's in Cleveland," William said.

"Well, yes. I mean, no. Last night . . ." In a brief, lucid moment she'd realized that they might hear something at school. "Daddy was arrested."

William cocked his head with a one-eye half-squint and lopsided half-smile, his habitual gesture for *Huh?*

"But it's okay, really. Everything will be fine. Please don't get upset," she said, as if they'd erupted into sobs of remorse. "He should be home today."

"What did he do?" Sophie asked.

"He didn't *do* anything. He's *accused* of taking money from one of the funds he manages."

"Why would you steal your own money?" William asked.

"It's not his money. It's money that people and companies give him to invest for them. He's done very well for them over the years. It's absurd to think he'd risk everything to—"

"But the market is terrible now," Sophie said anxiously. "Like, it's down over a hundred percent."

"Idiot, how can it be down more than a hundred percent?" William said.

This seemed to injure Sophie more than the news that her father was locked up. And since when did fourteen-year-olds follow the market? At fourteen the only market Lily knew was Gristedes on Broadway, and she wasn't exactly a socialist, even back in the seventies.

"So he's in jail now?" Sophie's voice caught on the word *jail*.

"But he should be back today. We've hired the best attorney that—" *That money can buy*, she almost said, but what kind of lesson would that send? She felt briefly gratified at the appearance of tears on Sophie's cheeks, then a surge of pity. She opened her arms. Sophie winced, causing Lily to wonder if she regretted that the proffered limbs, so balletically elegant in a sleeveless gown, weren't a tad more maternally fleshy. But she stepped forward after a short hesitation and Lily closed her arms tightly around her.

"It's okay, sweetie," she said. With one hand she gestured for William to join the family hug, but he stepped away with another cocked-head, eye-squinting, half-smiling *huh*. "Everything will be fine, you'll see." Immediately Peggy's voice began throbbing in her head like an incipient migraine—*No kinahurras, Lily*—and she regretted her reassuring words. Youthful buoyancy was fine for Barnett—for all Gentiles, Peggy would say, and why shouldn't they skip through life happy as clams, no one ever tried to wipe *them* out? But Lily should have known better than to utter a line like "Everything will be fine." You might as well throw open your window and shout out to the world, "Come and get me!"

Guy was at his desk in his office when Lucinda Wells called to say that the Gimmels had made a counteroffer. Henry Delano, his CFO, was with him.

"We're burning through way too much cash, Guy," he said.

"No more than last month. We knew breakeven wasn't until Q4 next year."

"But we were counting on a secondary. In this market that may not be possible."

Guy rubbed his eyes. He always experienced fatigue first as a steady pressure behind his eyes, as if his body were trying to eject worn-out parts. He tried to concentrate on Positano's burn rate. Last night he and Rosemary had been up very late talking about the apartment at 218 West End Avenue, he fantasizing aloud about life in such abundant, well-lit, and well-located square footage, she agonizing over the price and the prospect of going into debt and then, inevitably, complete financial ruin. He'd initiated sex to put an end to it all and, tired as he was, rose manfully to the task. They were both just twenty panting seconds away from a mutually satisfying conclusion when one of the twins began to cry, joined shortly by the other. "Don't stop," he'd moaned into Rosemary's ear. "Don't stop," she'd echoed moistly into his neck, but he felt her stall a second later and almost immediately he sensed that his moment had passed, too.

"Fuck," he said. The crying had escalated into a duet of anguished howls and hacking moans.

"I'll go," she said.

He must have fallen right to sleep, for when he awoke the next morning, priapically ready, despite fatigue, to resume where they'd left off, the boys were in the bed with them and he had no memory of their arrival.

"Fuck." It was his last word of the previous day and the first of the present one. Bad sign. The boys were curled up between him and Rosemary, Patrick's head at her breasts, Edward's at her stomach. Like a small litter, he thought, taking him down a notch further. His morning erection looked immense and inappropriate next to their sleeping, pink innocence. He cupped it as he got out of bed, dressed quietly, picked his way through the mine field of baby gear that lay between the bedroom and the front door, stumbling only once, in the narrow hallway, over an unopened package of disposable diapers the size of a Volkswagen, and left.

"We need to make cuts," Henry was saying.

"Cuts? We're growing at seventy-five percent a year."

"Revenues. *Run-rate* revenues. Our costs are growing even faster."

"What about the MyJob contract?" Positano had a bid in with the Internet's hottest job site. Automatic, "personalized" e-mails would, if Positano got the job, be zipped off to all applicants acknowledging their interest in a given job and promising them a response within a specified time. The contract would propel their growth rate into the triple digits.

"It's not a contract, it's a bid," Henry said.

CFOs were professional bad-news givers, he decided, grim reapers who hunched over spreadsheets for hours on end to reach the inevitable and profoundly gratifying conclusion that there wasn't enough free cash to fund operations. Whereas entrepreneurs, people like him, were optimists at heart. You had to be, to start something in a world as competitive and fast-changing as this one. If you didn't believe that tomorrow would be better, bigger, *richer* than today, you . . . you kept your head down, banging out code in the veal farm, collecting your inadequate check every other week, dutifully making your inadequate retirement contributions. Or you became a numbers man, a treasurer or controller or CFO—he never did understand the difference, though Positano now had one of each—whose role in life was not merely to plan for the worst but, secretly, to relish it.

"The secondary is definitely off?" he asked. In precisely sixty-seven days—six months after the IPO—Positano's lock-up period would expire; the company, and its executives, would be free to sell shares to the public— assuming the public was interested.

"Not in this market," Henry said with predictable gloom. "A lot of investors feel burned by Internet companies. We were lucky to get off the IPO."

"We're not a dot-com."

"But our customers are, and if they don't have money, then neither do we—at least that's how the market sees it. Kashkin's report claims that seventy-five percent of our business is from dot-coms."

"That's bullshit." Ron Kashkin was a research analyst with Lehman Brothers who "covered" Positano's sector, Internet services, issuing long, turgid reports on Positano and its competitors. Guy had nothing but contempt for Kashkin and his kind, though they most often concluded their "analyses" with buy recommendations or the even more desirable and almost as ubiquitous "strong buy." These "analysts" didn't really contribute anything to society. They created no jobs beyond employing legions of hardworking, minimum-waged Central Americans to tend to their Hamptons lawns and pools. Instead, they devoted their careers to studying a handful of companies the way an English professor focused on Dickens or Wordsworth, the difference being that a sell-side analyst like Kashkin made in a week what a Dickens or Wordsworth scholar made in a year, if he was lucky. Another difference: Charles Dickens, lucky soul, didn't have to kowtow to Professor So-and-So, while Guy and Henry spent what seemed like half their time catering to Ron Kashkin and his counterparts at other firms, supplying them with financial results and revenue models, dropping everything to take their calls, flying around the country to speak at their conferences, and all for a single, fuck-all-else purpose: to prop up the company's stock price. The bottom line wasn't the bottom line. It was the stock price.

"Let's have Kashkin into the office when the MyJob deal is announced," he said.

"*If* it's announced."

"Right." He picked up the ringing phone, grateful for the distraction.

"It's Lucinda Wells. Are you sitting down? The Gimmels came back with a counteroffer. Two-point-two-five. I think we have a deal."

"Let's split the difference," he said. "Two-point-two." He was gratified to see Henry's eyebrows arch disapprovingly.

"It's a plan," Lucinda said. "We'll need to move fast. This market is white hot."

"At least something is." He clicked on his browser's *Refresh* button. In less than a second Positano's updated stock price appeared. Down another eighth. How refreshing.

"How quickly can you arrange financing?"

"Goldman has given me their complete assurance that I can have the necessary financing in twenty-four hours. I don't anticipate any problems." He invariably lapsed into starched syntax when talking about Goldman Sachs. Henry crossed and uncrossed his legs.

"I'll call the Gimmels ASAP. Let me have your cell."

He gave it to her despite strong misgivings—Lucinda Wells was clearly a person to whom one didn't give one's cell number lightly.

A while later, restless, he wandered into the cafeteria, not particularly hungry, though it was almost lunchtime. The Positano cafeteria had been painstakingly designed to resemble an old-fashioned diner, complete with round, vinyl-covered stools lined up along a counter, booths with jukeboxes, and a blackboard that listed the blue plate special in colored chalk. It was amazingly authentic, down to the kitschy uniforms on the servers, and had cost a small fortune (another use of proceeds). But prospective employees loved it, back when they were still hiring and you needed every edge possible to lure talented people. Free coffee and sodas? Of course. Subsidized lunches? Definitely. Ping-Pong and foosball? Jacks for openers in Internet land. Stock options? *Duh.* A cheery replica of a fifties diner? Now you're talking. *This place is way cool, so retro it's cutting edge.*

About a dozen employees were in the diner when Guy entered. Most were staring up at the television suspended in a corner of the room. He knew without looking that it was tuned to CNBC, the business channel. A TV in the cafeteria tuned silently to CNBC was another thing you had to have to attract and keep talented people.

Of course, everyone in the room knew who he was, the CEO. They looked at him, briefly, smiled deferentially, and turned back to CNBC. The way they stared up at the silent box, faces paralyzed with concern, reminded him of his parents watching their black-and-white RCA after Robert Kennedy and Martin Luther King were shot, that same bottomless sadness tinged with dread. A fellowship of anxiety. Well, the NASDAQ _was_ down another twenty-four points.

His cell vibrated. He slipped it out of its belt harness.

"Guy speaking," he said.

"It's Lucinda. We have a deal."

A collective moan erupted.

He glanced up at the TV in time to see "POSI" glide off the right side of the screen trailing a red "-⅜."

Six

Barnett hunkered down in the study the moment he got home from jail.

"Don't you want to shower?" Lily asked him. Rinsing off would top her to-do list after spending most of the day at Rikers Island. But Barnett merely removed his tuxedo jacket and bow tie, which he'd kept resolutely knotted all night, asked Consuela for a cup of coffee, and turned on his computer. He seemed disinclined to discuss the situation. Well, he wasn't much for discussing things in the best of circumstances.

She allowed him an hour of privacy before joining him in the study. He was on the phone, nodding more than talking. Though he made no gesture of encouragement, she took a seat in front of the mahogany desk and waited. Lack of sleep had darkened the soft flesh beneath his eyes, and his hair had acquired a murky sheen overnight. He'd never been what you'd call handsome, but Lily had always found his confidence and self-possession attractive. He seemed to need nothing that he couldn't provide for himself, which was appealing to her—she, who had always looked to others for satisfaction. He'd been raised in Greenwich, the son of a lawyer who was himself the son of a famous investor, Ben "Sell 'Em" Grantham, who, on the eve of the 1929 stock market crash, had not only liquidated his entire portfolio but sold short, thus making an obscenely huge fortune just when everyone else was losing their shirts. Gradually, however, the "Sell 'Em" Grantham fortune dissipated, and during his sophomore year at Trinity College in Hartford, Barnett was forced to apply for a scholarship, a terrible humiliation for the scion of an illustrious if notoriously opportunistic dynasty. After a quick MBA from Wharton, Barnett began to make his mark on Wall Street, eventually cofounding Grantham, Wiley & Zelma with two friends from b-school. Lily had met him, at a share house party in East Hampton, just as the firm was beginning to flourish. At the time, he lived in a soulless one-bedroom apartment in a Second Avenue high-rise: white walls, framed art posters, dhurrie rugs, a giant "entertainment center" housing an unfathomable tangle of audio and video equipment, and, opposite the platform bed, a large photograph of blue-blazered, bow-tied Sell 'Em holding aloft his baby grandson. She lasted there for a year following their marriage, then they bought the place at 913 Park.

It was ironic, really, that Barnett had been arrested at a charity dinner. He hated those events, despised any venue that involved the display of wealth, and high-end charity functions were nothing if not opportunities to flaunt one's assets. He liked making money for its own sake, for the dick-stiffening thrill of outearning his colleagues on the Street by a percentage point or two—and perhaps there was the goal of restoring stock-picking luster to the Grantham name. His idea of a fun evening was helping the kids with their math homework, then reading a stack of investment research reports in bed, impenetrable documents cluttered with zigzagging graphs and bar charts marching ever upward to the right. Once a week, usually a Monday night, when they were least likely to have plans, he'd toss aside his investment reports and place a firm hand on her right breast, indicating that sex was desired. He wasn't an adventurous or particularly passionate lover, but, as with investing, he was perceptive and determined and squarely focused on long-term results, which was a good thing, as Lily was slow to warm up.

She was the one who'd launched them on the charity circuit. She'd spread around Barnett's money judiciously, at first latching on to less popular causes where she could make a quick splash—a charity that spayed stray cats (tickets to dog events were more coveted), an organization that offered scholarships to needy culinary students. It wasn't until she'd reached the highest echelons of the charity world (major art museums, opera and ballet companies, cancer of non-icky organs) that she stopped to wonder why it had been so important to her. And the answer came to her at once: She desperately needed to be popular, to feel accepted. All her life, from elementary school at P.S. 87 through Mount Holyoke, she'd homed in on the most popular group and then set about infiltrating it like a CIA mole. New York Society, as it was called, was just one more clique for her to pry open with her winning smile and protean conversational skills and Barnett's growing pile of money. Why she'd felt the need to run with the popular set was something she never understood, not even after two forays at analysis, the first with a harsh Freudian on Central Park West who sent her fleeing after only a few months, the second with a more user-friendly Jungian over on Lexington with whom she'd remained for nearly two years. Neither had managed to penetrate her need to be popular, let alone alleviate it. In fact, winning over the second analyst, convincing him that she was more than a shallow socialite, perhaps even attaining the status of Most Favored Patient, had been an almost obsessive goal. How she'd studied his face each time he opened the door for her, searching for some indication in his expression or his flat "Come in, please" that now, at last, after hours spent listening to the dreary, uninteresting problems of dreary, uninteresting people, his Most Favored Patient had arrived, his day was made, an entire career—perhaps an existence—justified. Even therapy, for her, was a popularity contest.

"Tell me what's going on," she asked Barnett.

"I didn't take any money," he growled.

"I know you didn't."

"However," he added slowly, and her stomach heaved, "there *is* money missing, about three million dollars. Our auditors discovered the gap a few months ago."

"Did they tell you about it?"

"They told Wiley and Zelma. Who told the Feds."

"But why not you?"

"Apparently my signature appears on certain unspecified documents having to do with the unauthorized withdrawal of funds from various unspecified investment accounts."

The lawyerly diction was not a good sign.

"What?"

"It's ludicrous. Why would I steal money from my own firm?"

Because it isn't really your money, she didn't say. *It's money that people have given you to turn into more money, which you haven't been particularly successful at lately.*

"The thing is . . ." She steeled herself. "The thing is, the Feds have frozen all of our accounts. You see, they haven't been able to locate the missing three million dollars. They know it's not where it should be, but they haven't found out where it actually is. They think I have it stashed somewhere, and that by denying me access to any other funds, I'll eventually have no choice but to use the stolen money, at which point they'll pounce."

"When you say 'frozen our accounts' . . ."

"We can't withdraw from our brokerage or savings accounts." He jabbed a key on his computer and a pattern of numbers appeared on the screen. "Not that there's much to freeze, not these days," he said in a quietly bitter voice.

"What?"

"You may not have noticed, *darling,* but this hasn't exactly been a great time in the market."

"I'm aware of that." Even Sophie was aware of that. "But we never invested in Internet stocks," she said. "You avoided them like the plague." She swallowed. "Right?"

"Well, I did avoid them like the plague, but eventually the pressure got to me. Every day another investor calling to ask why Grantham, Wiley & Zelma was making a pitiful twelve percent a year when investment houses run by teenagers with pierced eyebrows were pulling in three times that . . ."

"But that's the *firm's* money," she said quietly. "*Our* money—"

"Is invested with the firm. You can't expect me to invest my clients' money one way and ours another, can you, Lily?"

"I guess not," she whispered. "But the bubble burst a while ago . . . haven't you been on the rebound since them?"

"No one's *rebounded,* no matter what you hear. No one's making money in this market. I've been suspended from the firm, without pay. The children's tuition is paid up for the rest of year, thank God, though we have to make a down payment for next year soon, and we have enough in checking to cover the maintenance on this place for a few months . . ."

"A few months?"

"We'll rent out the house, which should cover the mortgage on it and the taxes and leave a bit for household expenses. Apparently the rental market in the Hamptons is still strong. At least something is. As for the mortgage on this place . . ."

"Since when is this place mortgaged?"

"I unlocked a portion of our equity in the apartment six months ago."

"Unlocked? Barnett, this is our home."

"You're beginning to sound like your mother."

"Who happens to be selling her apartment for two-point-two million dollars," she said, beginning to shout. "Free and clear!"

"All of this is temporary, Lily, we just need to ride it out," he said in the voice you'd use to tell a child that the ride to Grandma's house would be over soon. "Once the charges are dropped, I'll be back on salary, and by then the market should be on the rebound."

"By then? When exactly is this expected to be resolved?"

"All I need to do is find the missing money." Stupidly, they both glanced around the room, as if stacks of hundred-dollar bills might be stashed behind the sofa, the wing chairs, the yards of leather-bound books on the burled-walnut shelves.

She wished she could be more sympathetic, but the truth was, Barnett never seemed to want sympathy or support . . . or anything much from her. True, she'd always liked that about him, but now she didn't know quite how to behave.

"How long, Barnett? I mean, how long can we hold on with no income coming in, with all our expenses piling—"

Nanny appeared in the doorway, as if to remind them of one significant monthly expense.

"Excuse me, I'm so sorry," she said in a tone that lacked all remorse. "If you don't need me, I thought I'd run a few errands and then pick up Sophie on the way back."

"Fine," Lily said.

"We don't need *her* anymore," she said as soon as Nanny left. "We haven't needed a nanny for years. We could let her go."

"That's ridiculous. Who would make sure the children got off to school on time, who would . . . pick them up from school . . . who would . . ." He shrugged, out of ideas.

"I would."

He smiled indulgently. "We're not that desperate yet." He clicked the *Refresh* button on his browser and sighed—rather despondently, she thought—at the updated market statistics. "They've blocked my access to the firm's intranet. I can't see how our portfolios are doing, I have no way to monitor inflows and outflows."

"We could have a part-time sitter, then," Lily said.

"We can't give up Nanny, especially now. It's important that we disrupt our lives as little as possible, especially where the children are concerned." He swiveled in his chair to face her. "And that includes you, Lily." He gestured for her to bend over and combed back her hair with his fingers. "I think we can still afford an appointment at the hairdresser."

Later, in the park, she discovered a bird's nest in an oak tree on the eastern edge of the Rambles. She waited several minutes for the female to return, a plump towhee, rather drab, its feathers dusky grays and browns. The towhee settled into the nest after a few wing flexes and then all but disappeared into the surrounding twigs and fluff, as nature had intended when she gave the males the showy plumage, the women the dreary housedresses.

While the towhee warmed her eggs, Lily tried to concentrate on what was happening in her life, sensing the need to formulate a plan of action, but she found she couldn't get very far. What if Barnett didn't get his position back? What if he went to jail? Apparently most of their wealth had disappeared a while back with the Internet bubble. What then? She could go back to work . . . but at what? *As* what? She'd raised millions of dollars for hospitals and museums and animal shelters in the past ten years, but she couldn't very well throw a charity ball for herself and the children. She felt quite useless, forty-two years old and unable to help herself or her family.

You're a very lucky girl.

Barnett's mother, Grace, had uttered those words in the library of the Granthams' enormous but deteriorating Greenwich home shortly after Barnett proposed. Grace, who'd succumbed to heart failure several years later, was a stout, large-breasted matron whose white hair, piggy-pink complexion, and bosomy warmth concealed an encyclopedia of prejudices: blacks, Jews, Hispanics, the poor in general, the newly rich, foreigners who weren't British, immigrants, Democrats, homosexuals, chemo patients who eschewed wigs, cabdrivers. To spend time with Grace was to discover entirely new categories of despisable people. "Barnett and I are both lucky to have found each other," Lily had managed to say, then found Barnett in the backyard chipping golf balls. She repeated Grace's comment and started to cry, causing Barnett to shank a Titleist into the crumbling swimming pool. "You're rich and Protestant and you come from . . . from . . . this . . ." She waved at the twenty-room Georgian Colonial, ignoring the peeling paint on the black shutters and the overgrown shrubbery and the cracked flagstones on the terrace. Inside, the deterioration had progressed to within six months of Miss Havisham territory. But even the seedy decline seemed classy to her Upper West Side sensibility, like the slight fading on old Oriental rugs. "I'm the lucky one," Barnett said. "You're all I ever wanted."

How had he avoided all of Grace's prejudices? she'd long wondered. But lately she'd begun to think that Barnett wasn't so much free of prejudice as uninterested in or perhaps unaware of the qualities that differentiated people. Companies, to him, were distinct, some to be embraced, others shunned. People were all of a piece, not equal so much as indistinguishable.

The towhee twitched her head from side to side, taking stock, and, feeling secure, retracted it. Lily lowered the binoculars, stood up, and began to head for home. But after a few steps she stopped and came to a quick decision. She turned around and headed west.

Seven

Rosemary had been meaning to straighten up the apartment all morning, but when the doorman buzzed to announce Lloyd Lowell's arrival, she had only seconds to make the place look presentable. The morning had simply . . . vanished, as mornings tended to do when infant twins were involved. Mornings, afternoons, evenings, nights. Nights were particularly elusive. In the master bedroom she used her foot to rake various items of dirty clothing into one pile, then scooped it up with both arms, pried open a closet with an elbow, and hurled the pile at the back wall. The doorbell chimed. What next—the dishes in the kitchen? The towering archive of unread newspapers on the living-room coffee table and floor? The pungent diaper pail? The bathroom?

The doorbell rang again, disrupting her mental triage. She ran to the boys' room and hoisted the bag of diapers from the can. It weighed as much as she did. How was it possible for two tiny creatures to produce so much crap? What was truly astounding and depressing was that the entire stinking mess of it had originated in her breasts. She twisted the bag and tied a tight, odor-blocking knot at the top. Guy commented proudly on the heft of the diapers every time he emptied the container. "Can you fucking believe the weight of this?" he'd ask dumbstruck friends and family, holding the diaper bag aloft. Then he'd sling it over his shoulder like a macho Santa and head for the garbage chute. Rosemary opened the boys' closet and a stack of unopened baby gifts tumbled out, two of everything. She heaved the bag into the closet, kicked the boxes back in, and managed, barely, to close the door.

As she caught sight of herself in the hall mirror on the way to the front door, hair disheveled, eyes unmade-up, the shoulders of her shirt encrusted with the twins' regurgitated milk, she realized she'd overlooked one important task. The doorbell rang again, an angry, throat-clearing sound that lasted several impatient seconds. On second thought, too late for a makeover. All she could do was smooth back her hair and, inhaling deeply, zip and button her pants.

"You look wonderful," Lloyd told her after they hugged.

He sounded wholeheartedly insincere but it buoyed her nonetheless to be complimented on anything other than milk production.

"So, where are they?" Lloyd asked. *"Where are they?"*

He might have been inquiring after a Lalique vase or Tiffany lamp, the way his lips puckered in anticipation. Lloyd was the head of Atherton's decorative arts department, and her boss.

"Sleeping, thank God," she said. "I'll show you if you promise not to wake them up."

She led him into the living room, where both boys were rocking in their electric swings, serenaded by the purr of the motors. Lloyd squeezed her arm. He hadn't seen them since visiting her at Mount Sinai.

"How old?" he whispered, ever the appraiser.

"Sixteen weeks."

"I can't decide which one I like better." He glanced back and forth, a deliberative finger touching his bottom lip. "I guess I'll have to take the pair." His decision made, he followed her into the small kitchen.

"I couldn't find a sitter, so I thought we'd eat here," Rosemary said.

"Perfect." Lloyd looked elegant and put together, as always, in a light-blue shirt tucked into charcoal gray pants. He was tall and very thin, with a narrow, equine face, deep-set blue eyes, and full lips that were his most expressive feature. After working for him for five years, Rosemary could read those lips like a user's manual. She'd present him with a Gallé vase she'd found, or a piece of old Cartier jewelry, and would know exactly what he thought of it by the way his lips squashed to one side *(Don't waste my time),* puckered *(Let's take a closer look),* or curled inward, all but disappearing *(At last, we've found our catalog cover).*

He brought her up to date on his tireless exploits in New York's upscale, downtown gay community. They gossiped about the office while she decanted several small plastic containers of salads from Zabar's into bowls. She set them down on the small table in the hallway, from which she cleared a month's worth of mail. As they ate they talked about the impending spring sale for which she'd done most of the research and written the catalog copy before beginning her maternity leave.

"You should come," he said.

She told him she'd try but she knew she wouldn't. She'd only left the twins twice with a baby-sitter, once for a follow-up with her gynecologist, the other time for dinner at a restaurant with Guy. Both times she'd felt breath-shortening pangs of anxiety. Hailing a cab, ordering wine, walking home holding hands with Guy—what did any of this have to do with who she was, now that she had two tiny boys to look after? It wasn't guilt at leaving the twins that unsettled her (how could she feel guilty about something that gave her so little pleasure?), it was a strong feeling that she had changed fundamentally that evening in Mount Sinai Hospital, and that any replication of her old, pre-twins life was fraudulent, somehow. Or at the very least amateur play-acting.

"I do need to know that you're coming back to work," Lloyd said. "You can hedge on the date, but I must have your word that you're not going to bail once your leave is up."

"I'm coming back," she said. "It might be a bit later than planned—the boys were on the small side at birth and I'm kind of hoping—"

"You don't have to explain, just don't leave me in the lurch six months from now."

"I won't," she said. It was equally hard imagining herself back at work and imagining herself *not* working. Depending on her mood and the twins' disposition at the moment, one or the other seemed a cruel fate.

"It's just that I've been burned so often in the past," he said with a tragic sigh. "Our business attracts so many debutantes—I mean, who even knew such creatures existed anymore? Pretty blond girls from Duke and Skidmore with barrettes and pearls who swear they'll come back to work directly from the delivery room, and then call up, tearful, three months later and whine that they can't leave little Spencer for one moment, they never thought they'd become so *attached*. And Cliff or Roger or Trip is so busy at Morgan Stanley or Goldman Sachs, where, by the way, he makes enough to support a family of forty, they'd never see each other if they both were working. But trust me, they knew all along they weren't going to mix a career and *motherhood*, as they inevitably refer to it. A few years at Atherton's is the ultimate preparation for childbirth, you see, like one very long Lamaze class."

She smiled and debated whether to defend her barretted and pearled colleagues, at least a few of whom were quite serious about their work.

"How's Guy?" he asked before she could decide.

"Busy."

"It's all I can do to keep from checking Positano's stock price every five seconds, I sometimes wish they'd never invented the Internet. Guy must be beside himself."

"It's not about the stock price, it's about building the company."

"Oh, of course." He spooned cold shrimp in dill sauce from the bowl onto his plate.

She'd persuaded Guy to give Lloyd five hundred "friends and family" shares when Positano went public. He'd been able to buy them at the offering price of $15 a share—without the directed shares, he'd have had to buy them on the open market, and since they closed their first day of trading at $28 a share, Guy's gesture (hers, really) had netted Lloyd a tidy profit. It had been the best first-day performance of any post-bubble IPO, a fact heralded in numerous news articles. But as the stock continued to climb, he'd become a bit obsessed, lavishing on Positano's share price the kind of attention he usually reserved for a piece of vintage Lalique. At one point he had a fifty-thousand-dollar profit. Now he was back to where he'd started. They all were—well, not Guy, actually; as a company insider he'd been able to purchase his shares for less than a nickel apiece.

"I told you to sell," she said. But no one sold, it seemed. Not her parents, who were "friends and family." Not even their friends who weren't "friends and family" but bought anyway, paying retail. Not the individual investors around the country who used to send Guy e-mails filled with gratitude and praise (one happy shareholder had sent him a fruit basket), and now lobbed e-mails at him filled with expletive-laced invective and histrionic tales of financial distress. What were they thinking, investing their kids' college funds in a company with barely any revenue and big losses, a company named after the town where its CEO had spent his honeymoon? Hadn't they learned anything in the nineties? Guy's shares were locked up by law, but not theirs. Was everyone crazy?

"The company is strong, though, right?" Lloyd asked.

"Growing like a weed. There's some big contract coming—" She stopped herself before treading further on treacherous ground. "Well, Guy is very optimistic."

"What kind of contract?"

"I'm pretty sure I could go to jail if I said anything more."

"To me? Who would make the connection? I sell tchotchkes for a living."

"I'm Caesar's wife now, I need to be above suspicion. Having to keep quiet about this kind of thing drives Guy crazy. If he could, he'd stop people in the street to talk about how great the future is for Positano. He'd be grabbing the beggars in front of Zabar's and telling them to take their coins out of the coffee cup and put them into Positano stock. But he can't. There are all sorts of rules and regulations about fair disclosure and forward-looking statements and conning homeless people into investing their last dimes."

"A big contract for a company Positano's size . . ."

He hadn't listened, no one did anymore. No one at Atherton's made much money, but they'd always taken a perverse pride in that. Their customers had truckloads of money but no taste, while they were paupers but rich in taste—the universe was a benign place. Then, sometime in the nineties, as the NASDAQ began to take off, everyone, it seemed, was getting rich, not just boring old plutocrats in baggy Brooks Brothers suits but cool people in jeans and T-shirts. And not just rich but private-plane-and-art-collection rich. Gratifyingly, many of them had lost it all when the bubble burst, but plenty had cashed out, and suddenly it wasn't so easy or satisfying to deprecate the rich—the rich were exactly like them, only they had money. Fast, easy money. They'd sweep into the showroom at Atherton's, aggressively grungy, clutching a bottle of water in one hand, their assistants checking off items in the catalog as if circling dishes on a Chinese take-out menu. It drove a lot of people crazy, including Lloyd. It was one thing to kowtow to dyspeptic Vanderbilts and Mellons; half the time these people were selling, anyway, to raise money for taxes or the tab at Betty Ford. You could almost feel sorry for them, which was always reassuring. But these new people in stained T-shirts and running shoes were at once so studiously unpretentious and appallingly arrogant. Somehow they seemed less deserving of stupendous wealth than the fifth-generation Rockefellers behind whose backs they'd always snickered. So when the opportunity to get in on the ground floor of Positano came along, even in a small way, Lloyd snatched it.

It was a shame, really, because one of the things she'd loved about the auction business was its complete separation from what she'd always thought of as the real world. Oh, money was a big part of it, naturally, but ultimately it came down to spending hour after hour with rare objects that only a handful of people could appreciate or even desire. Her specialty, and Lloyd's, nineteenth- and twentieth-century decorative arts, was particularly obscure. Old lamps, strange-looking vases, garish jewelry, candlesticks, de-canters, bowls—there were perhaps a few dozen people who focused on this area at the professional level, and she'd always liked that. She felt comfort-ably isolated, ensconced in a world all of whose inhabitants she knew well. And then along came the NASDAQ, the great leveler, offering everyone, even decorative arts specialists, the pipe dream of easy riches, and suddenly her world wasn't so comfortably isolated. The sudden dive in the NASDAQ only intensified the sense of desperation. The chips they played for were changing. Once, discovering a rare vase or chandelier was the ultimate objective—a small bonus might follow, enough to buy a pair of fake Mission chairs at Pottery Barn. Now the chips were big-time money, fast, over-the-counter money. Everyone was in the game. A certain innocence was gone—strange to think of the glitzy world of art auctions as innocent, but that's how she'd always seen it.

"I sometimes wish Guy had never started Positano," she said. "We were a lot poorer back then, but happier."

"*Please,*" Lloyd said with a roll of his eyes. "Everyone always pines for simpler times, it's part of being filthy rich, like complaining about taxes or the help."

"I never see Guy anymore."

"It's just a stage. Once the company is more established, he'll hire people to run it and then you'll be complaining that he's always underfoot."

"I suppose you're right. Did I tell you we're moving? At least we're hoping to move. We put an offer in on a co-op on West End."

"So much for the simpler life." He gave the narrow, dark foyer a slow, puckered-lip evaluation. "Does this new place have an *actual* dining room? Because if you have an *actual* dining room in New York, then it is in incredibly bad taste to complain about *anything*, ever. Your life is perfect. End of story. Shut up."

All the way from Central Park to the West Side, Lily fully intended to visit her parents. She hadn't dropped in on them, unannounced, in years, but lately, since Barnett's arrest and the impending sale of her parents' apartment, she'd been seeing somewhat more of them. However, when she reached her parents' corner of West End Avenue, she turned around. Two blocks later she entered the Broadway Nut Shoppe.

Larry was standing behind the counter, as she'd hoped he would be, but what struck her immediately, what caused her to freeze just inside the front door, was how little, if at all, the place had changed since she'd last been inside over two decades earlier. The same unfinished wood floor. The same glass-front display cases along the right, crammed with containers of fresh chocolates and nuts and other forbidden treats. The same glass shelves along the mirrored wall behind the counter, brimming with boxes and tins of candy and nuts. The same smell, a salty-sweet blend of roasting nuts and chocolate. She felt at once comforted and disturbed that this narrow slice of New York had never changed. Everything and everyone changed over time, for better or for worse. They'd redone all the bathrooms in their apartment fifteen years ago, six in total, and already tiles were cracking in places, the finish was coming off the polished brass fixtures, the mirror in the master bath was silvering in one corner. Fifteen years ago she'd assumed they'd never have to touch the bathrooms again. But at forty-two she already understood the cruelest lesson of age: Time chipped, cracked, yellowed, abraded, wrinkled, shrunk, scuffed, rusted, tore, frayed, loosened, stiffened, buckled, coddled, grayed, thinned, thickened, weakened, and silvered—all with a ruthlessly democratic disregard for wealth, character, or quality of fixture.

What made the Broadway Nut Shoppe exempt?

"May I help you?"

She almost missed the irony in his voice. "No, I'm . . . oh, hi."

He stood behind the counter, at the end closest to the front door where the glass display cases were highest, revealing only his shoulders, neck, and head. She was struck a second time by his youthfulness. He was her age, which meant he was Barnett's age, but he looked a generation younger. This, too, was a bit disturbing. Perhaps the fountain of youth was not a bubbling spring somewhere in Florida after all but a narrow candy shop on the West Side.

"I was in the neighborhood," she said. He motioned for her to join him at the far end of the store, where the only thing between them would be a long, waist-high counter and the old NCR cash register.

"That's better," he said when they were face-to-face again. "Look at you."

She did just that, courtesy of the mirrored wall behind him. The long walk from the Rambles had taken its toll. A halo of frizzed hair ringed her head, sweat glistened unattractively on her face and neck, the collar of her shirt had gone limp. Larry, in contrast, looked cool and relaxed in a crisp white oxford shirt and blue jeans.

"You've been bird watching," he said, pointing to the binoculars around her neck. "I wouldn't have thought there'd be much to see on Broadway, other than pigeons, of course." His smile revealed slightly crooked teeth.

"I was on my way to . . ." She didn't want to lie about why she was there, nor did she completely understand, or care to find out, what an honest explanation might be, so she changed the subject. "This place is exactly the same."

"Since my father died I've contemplated renovating the store, but I never quite get around to it. I think maybe I'm allergic to change."

Or ambition, she thought, and immediately regretted the unkindness.

"It looks just as I remember it."

"Close your eyes," he said.

Surprising herself, she obeyed. A few moments later she felt something on her lips—not his mouth, thank God. Something small, very thin, and hard. He pressed it between her lips. She smiled with recognition and opened her teeth to let it in.

"Just one nonpareil," he said as she ran the tip of her tongue over the dotted surface of the candy. "Every day after school for three years, my father offered you whatever you wanted and you always asked for a nonpareil, but just one. He never could get over that."

"I'm a creature of habit," she said.

"No, it was that you only had one. I mean, you were the proverbial kid in a candy store and you had just one, every time. That was amazing self-control for a teenager."

The semisweet chocolate melted across her tongue. She wanted to swallow but felt a thickening at the back of her throat that was only partially chocolate-induced. She was going to cry. Confused and embarrassed, she turned away, as if to examine the display on the opposite wall. Thankfully, the front door opened and a very old woman entered the shop. She walked directly to the counter in front of Larry.

"One pound, mixed nuts, unsalted," her savior said, depositing what looked like a half-dozen plastic bags from various local merchants on the counter. Larry walked to the nuts section and began scooping. The old woman followed him step for step from the other side of the counter and leaned so close to the case, her breathing fogged the glass.

"Don't give me all peanuts," she croaked. "Last time I couldn't find a single cashew or filbert."

"It's all mixed together," he said as he continued scooping.

"When you pay for mixed nuts you want mixed nuts," she said with a confirming nod, examining the scooping process so closely, she might have been watching a pharmacist mixing her heart pills. He placed the small bag on the scale.

"One pound exactly. That'll be six ninety-five." He took the bag off the scale and added a few more nuts.

"What was that?"

"I gave you a few extra," he said.

"Why?" she demanded.

"Because you're such a pleasure to serve." She looked at him doubtfully, then followed him as he headed back to the counter, still watching intently lest he remove anything from the bag now that it had been weighed. She dug into her purse, paid him the exact amount, gathered up her plastic bags, and left the store. Lily had managed to collect herself during the transaction, though she still couldn't fathom why the single nonpareil, or the memory of so many single nonpareils, had unhinged her.

"Customers like her are what make running this place such a joy," he said. "She comes in the same time every week, orders the same thing every time, warns me not to shortchange her, then demands to know why I gave her extra nuts for free."

"Why *do* you give her extra, then?"

"Like I said, I'm allergic to change."

"That's kind of obvious," Lily said, looking around.

"Is that why you dropped me, because I wasn't going to change?"

Did he *have* to bring that up again?

"Who can remember what was going through one's head then? That was over twenty years ago."

He nodded, but his expression told her he wasn't buying. She did remember, of course, and he was right about her motivation. Even at eighteen she had created a fully imagined life for herself, and a candy store owner allergic to change just didn't figure in it.

"I remember what was going through *my* head at the time," he said. "I was destroyed. In my head I always imagined the rest of my life with you. When you stopped returning my calls, it was like you had died. Suddenly I had to rethink everything."

"We were just kids, we would never have worked out in the long run." she said. "God, I can practically hear the violins."

"I read about your husband. This must be a difficult time for you."

"We're coping," she said, then sighed. "Barely." She glanced at the door, hoping to be rescued by another customer. Why didn't she just leave? "He's innocent, of course, my husband, it's just a question of some missing funds. Once they turn up . . . look, I really have to go," Lily said. "Thanks for the nonpareil."

Larry ducked through the opening under the counter in one impressively agile motion.

"I'll walk with you. I've haven't been out all day."

He flipped the sign hanging on the door from WE'RE OPEN! to BE RIGHT BACK! a typically, and infuriatingly, Victorian touch, she thought. They walked a few blocks together. Absurdly, she felt vulnerable strolling up Broadway with him. What if her mother saw them, or one of her mother's legion of neighborhood spies? How would she explain walking along Broadway with her high-school sweetheart so soon after her husband had been arrested for embezzlement? What *was* she doing, walking along

Broadway with her high-school sweetheart so soon after her husband had been arrested for embezzlement?

"Have you had many serious relationships . . . since?" she asked.

"One serious, several not so serious."

"Tell me about serious."

"Her name was Karen. She was a lawyer at a big firm on Wall Street. She specialized in bankruptcies, only she called them reorganizations. We were together for a few years. She wanted to get married, I didn't. End of serious."

"Why not get married?"

"Karen viewed marriage as the first step in remaking me in her own image. She dropped hints about my selling the store, giving up the apartment, going back to school for something like law or business. And the truth was, back then I thought about doing all those things, too. I just didn't want to change for someone else. Besides, you don't give up a seven-room, rent-controlled apartment—that's asking way too much of anyone. Sell the business, suck it in and go to law school, fine. Give up an eight-hundred-dollar rent? That's insanity."

They were now a block from her parents' building, dangerous territory.

"I need to get back," she said, and before he could say anything else, she stepped into the street and hailed a cab. He held open the door for her but neither said anything as she got in.

"East Side," she told the driver as Larry closed the door.

Eight

"I'll tell you what's criminal. What's criminal is what happened to your daughter. Humiliated like that in front of the whole world."

Lucinda Wells glowered at a crooked painting in the living room of the apartment she was showing to Peggy Gimmel. She straightened it, then crossed the room in two long strides and shoved a small pile of old magazines into a drawer.

"I mean, arresting your son-in-law so publicly. *Why?*" She frowned at a sagging sofa pillow before plumping it with two swift jabs of her left fist.

Three weeks had passed since the arrest. Barnett had a platoon of lawyers working on his case. He was banned from the office, so he was home all the time, which probably explained why Lily was gracing her parents with her presence lately—not that she needed to travel all the way across town to avoid someone in that apartment of hers, you could avoid the entire New York Philharmonic in there if you wanted to.

"The prosecutor felt he needed to make a statement," she said, parroting several of the articles on the incident, including a four-page abomination in *New York* magazine that included snide descriptions and unflattering photographs of Lily that made her out to be a Prada-obsessed Marie Antoinette. The article even had the gall to mention her "humble beginnings in a dreary West Side rental apartment," which infuriated Peggy even more than the implication that her daughter deserved the guillotine. The prosecutor, named Jay DiGregorio (who Monroe, infuriatingly, kept calling Joe DiMaggio), was considering a run for mayor, and a public arrest of a Park Avenue *ganof* could only help his chances.

"If Barnett Grantham isn't safe from the government, who is?" Lucinda asked. "How do you like the view?"

"Not bad," Peggy said, and felt a twinge of pleasure at the way Lucinda's lipsticked smile slackened at her lack of enthusiasm. In fact the view from the nineteenth floor was superb. The Empire State Building, Chrysler Building, and RCA Building (or whatever they were calling it these days) presented themselves in the distance like old friends assembled for a party in her honor. So much had changed, it wouldn't have surprised her one bit to find them hidden by taller, pushier buildings, or simply torn down to make way for something newer. But there they were, just as she remembered them. Fellow survivors.

They were touring the fourth apartment of the day, or was it the fifth? They all began to blur together, these boxy apartments in cold postwar buildings with long corridors that smelled like shoe boxes. White walls without moldings, parquet floors, narrow kitchens without windows. She suspected Lucinda was losing patience with her, but she'd collect a fancy commission from selling the apartment on West End, which had "gone," as Lucinda put it, in one day for more than two million dollars. Peggy had to place a steadying hand on the window ledge at the thought of such a sum.

"It's an estate," Lucinda said as Peggy continued to admire the view.

Of course it was—death was as pungent as mothballs. Peggy had paid so many shiva calls to the apartments of the recently deceased; death was like lingering perfume that soured a bit each day. The worn furniture, the dog-eared books, the clothes hanging in closets and jammed into drawers, the dented pans and unopened cans and chipped glasses in the kitchen, the ticking clocks, the limp towels and the dripping faucets that left lurid blue stains in porcelain sinks—all of these called out for the one who was gone.

"I like this one best," Peggy said, glancing around the living room, trying to overlook the tired upholstery and heavy, faded drapes, the worn carpet, happy grandchildren aging awkwardly from one framed photograph to the next.

"I thought you might," Lucinda said, arching her tweezered eyebrows in a self-satisfied way that made Peggy want to change her mind or perhaps slap her.

"It's fourteen hundred square feet, which is humongous for postwar, BTW. Both bathrooms have windows, which you don't see a lot, either. The kitchen isn't bad—you could spruce it up if you wanted to, Nu-Face the cabinets, some granite, terra cotta for the floor would look nice, but you don't have to."

"Oh, thank goodness."

Lucinda looked at her uncertainly. "A fresh coat of paint, hang a few pictures, not that you'll actually be spending much time here."

"I have a few good years left."

"No, no, no, I didn't mean—What I meant to say was, you'll be at Lincoln Center every night. Listen, my mother's just like you, she's out every night. She'd die to live this close to Lincoln Center."

The thought of anyone bearing maternal responsibility for Lucinda Wells gave her pause.

"How much did you say this costs?" she finally said. Like asking the price of a coat at Loehmann's.

"Nine seventy-five. We'll offer nine forty-five and split the difference. Common charges and taxes together are twelve hundred and change, which is nothing. Did I mention this is a condo? No board approval, a blessing, let me tell you. I had a turn-down last week, nice young couple, money up the wazoo, they both work, traders on Wall Street—or was it M&A? Anyway, you wouldn't believe the money they throw at people down there. I chose the wrong profession, trust me, you kill yourself in real estate and for what? But the board wanted applicants who can manage on one salary, you see, and you can understand their position, what if she decides to have a kid and then stays home to raise it? That leaves one income, and no matter how much he pulls down, one income is more vulnerable than two—I mean, what if he gets canned?"

"Who?"

"I was heartbroken, devastated, truly devastated, and you can imagine how I hated having to break the news to them. I can have you in here in a month."

It took Peggy a few moments to leap from Lucinda's broken heart to her own impending move. A month? But there was so much to do. And where would everything go? She'd need a month just to decide what to take and what to . . . sell? Give away? Throw out? She looked at Lucinda, dressed in a severely tailored black pantsuit that fit her like tight armor, barely rippling when she moved, which was constantly. Her hair was pulled back in an angry fist of a bun. *I can have you in here in a month.* If only she could just go to bed one night at 218 West End Avenue, surrounded by a lifetime's random accumulation, and wake up the next morning in this shiny new place, everything neatly stowed away, but less encumbered, freer, sunlight washing the perfectly smooth white walls, the way she'd always imagined heaven, one endless room, sunny and white, with no flaking paint or cracked moldings. Moving would be a kind of death and then a kind of rebirth, but without the pain and dementia and incontinence. God's favorites die in their sleep—how many times had she heard those words at services lately? Why couldn't God's favorites move in their sleep, too?

"Mrs. Gimmel?"

She blinked and Lucinda Wells came back into focus, Elijah in Prada with keys to the promised land. She wondered, not for the first time, if Lucinda was Jewish. Usually she could spot an MOT from a mile away—Jewdar, her friend Belle called it. They all had it. Even today, when Members of the Tribe had names like Felicity and Clark and Tiffany and, God help them, Christie, she could usually tell. Lily might think she was fooling people with her silky accent and WASPy friends and that name, Grantham, like some town in Connecticut with a village green, and maybe the goyim didn't notice, but a Jew could always spot a fellow traveler.

Although she was having trouble with Lucinda Wells. Somehow she transcended religion, or perhaps her religion was real estate, the great interfaith equalizer. Not that it mattered, of course. But it would be nice to know.

"I forget, where did you say you grew up?" Peggy asked.

"I didn't say. I grew up on Long Island."

"Ah," Peggy said.

"Oyster Bay, actually."

"Oh." She'd have to ask Belle about Oyster Bay, but a town named for a shellfish didn't sound promising. "I'd like to bring my husband here."

"Of course. I could show it to him tomorrow morning."

"I'll check his schedule," Peggy said with a touch of sarcasm that was lost on Lucinda Wells. Tomorrow morning? At seventy-three she was used to a slower pace. You called the doctor on Monday, maybe he could fit you in the following Thursday. Out of fresh oranges? A slow walk down to Fairway, an exploratory squeeze of twenty or so candidates before settling on the perfect half-dozen, a quick check in cheeses to see what they were sampling, a pitted olive from one of the big vats when no one was looking, a leisurely inspection of the deli counter, then the slow walk back home. Half a day for six nice Florida oranges, but who was complaining? Now it seemed she spent more time selecting a brisket than an apartment. Peggy glanced out the window. There they were—Empire State, Chrysler, RCA. Even the Citibank building with that ridiculous slanted top like some kind of appliance was comforting after all these years. Amazing what you could get used to.

On the way out Peggy paused at a console table in the foyer. A large photograph showed an old, large-breasted woman seated on a sofa she recognized from the living room, flanked by a family—her daughter and son-in-law, three grandchildren. They all smiled stiffly in their dresses and suits—she could practically smell the holiday chicken soup or roasting brisket. She was momentarily deflated—what was the point of it all? To live for eternity in a color photograph, first on the console table of your forlorn home, gawked over by nosy apartment shoppers, then on an end table in your daughter's never-used living room in a big house out in the suburbs, still later, if you were lucky, in the home of a sentimental grandchild, and then, finally, inevitably, in a drawer in a house in Oyster Bay, under old diplomas and class pictures, pawed over every decade or so by strangers carrying a few of your genes but with names like Madison and Alexandra and Cody, who would wonder, for the moment it took them to turn to the next picture or document, Who is that fat old woman on the sagging brocade sofa?

And then it hit her. These stiffly smiling people would be the recipients of her $975,000! She studied their faces more closely, particularly the parents of the young children. Their eyes gleamed with avarice.

"Let's offer nine twenty-five," she said, turning to Lucinda Wells. "Not a penny more."

.

Barnett had spent the past weeks sequestered in his study, gazing at his computer screen, only occasionally taking or making calls. Once or twice a day he'd take long walks with no apparent purpose. His phone seemed to ring less often each day, Lily thought, which felt ominous. Her own phone rang less often as well. She'd begged off several events they had planned to attend, to the ill-disguised relief of the hostesses. And new invitations had dried up altogether, except for the ones to charity events: These would continue to arrive as long as they could afford to buy a table (which they couldn't, but no one knew that yet).

Several times each day she entered the study to inquire, with nervous tact, into the status of their situation. "I'm working on it," Barnett would growl without looking up from the computer monitor. Wouldn't he make faster progress by getting out and seeing people, asking questions? He shot her a pitying look. Ever heard of e-mail, Lily? How about these nifty new machines they call faxes?

Other than these brief and increasingly hostile exchanges about their "situation," as they'd begun to refer to Barnett's impending trial and the family's possible homelessness, their interactions had dwindled to mumbled greetings at the breakfast table and chaste good-night kisses in bed. While finding herself an overnight pariah in New York society was unexpectedly liberating, she was growing more and more anxious about the future. How long before the money ran out? Barnett seemed completely divorced from the new realities of their lives. She was the one who put their Southampton house on the market (they found a renter almost immediately). She was the one who arranged a line of credit with their bank. And it was she who arranged for refunds from the various charities to which they'd pledged what now seemed like fantastic sums.

"We could hire a detective," she suggested. "Time is against us, Barnett. I'm not sure you're fully aware of the extent of our monthly—" She almost said "nut," but the word felt ludicrously insufficient for what amounted to basically a flood, a torrent of outgoing funds. In her mind a stream of money cascaded from all twenty-two windows of their apartment, showering Park Avenue with dollar bills like confetti that quickly filled up the canyon between buildings. "Nanny alone costs a thousand dollars a week, which is insane, given the age of the children and the fact that—Will you *please* stop tapping on the keyboard, Barnett? This is serious."

"And so is this," he said imperiously, but at least he'd stopped typing.

She considered him a moment. The scandal had taken its toll. Though he showered every morning, his hair looked greasy and unkempt. He'd acquired dark, veiny crescents under his eyes, and scowling had etched seams that ran south from the corners of his mouth. He'd been eating less but his face looked, if anything, more jowly, his body almost doughy. There were men who could get away with grooming lapses, the handsome WASPs they knew in Southampton whose hair, when they neglected to brush it after a swim at the club, looked tousled rather than messy, men on whom a five o'clock shadow looked insouciant but never seedy. Barnett was a WASP whose appeal lay not in congenital handsomeness but in a kind of willed perfection. It was part of what had drawn them together, she'd always thought, their shared effort at self-creation.

A memory: Shortly after they were married, while vacationing in Barbados, Barnett insisted they rent a small sailboat, just the two of them. When she prudently mentioned his lack of sailing experience, he looked puzzled and a tad put off, as if the ability to tack and come-about had been part of his genetic endowment, along with a strong jawline and the Protestant work ethic. The excursion was a terrifying disaster, the boat almost capsizing a dozen times, the boom nearly taking off their heads as it whipsawed back and forth. Finally a launch was sent by the resort to tow them in. Her legs buckled when she staggered onto shore, but Barnett leapt off the boat like Hernando Cortés laying claim to Barbados for Greenwich, Connecticut. "That was fun," he said jauntily, and she was about to challenge him—indeed, she nearly grabbed an oar to pummel him—when she realized there was no point: Barnett had already transformed what was patently a near-death experience for both of them into "fun."

Which made his inability to find the bright side in his current situation inauspicious to say the least.

"Let's go for a walk," she suggested, still standing in front of his desk. "It'll be fun."

"Fun?"

"We'll go to the park." She almost mentioned the towhee nest. She'd been to the Rambles every day since she'd discovered it. Any day now the three chicks, all beak and eyes, were going to hop off the edge of the nest and, after a terrifying plunge, begin to fly.

"First you want me to work harder, apparently, and then you want me to take a walk. I'm getting mixed signals here, Lily." He pressed an index finger to his temple, as if bleeding a radiator. "I have enough on my mind."

"I want to help, that's all."

His face softened. "Come here, sweetheart," he said gently. He clicked a few keys and took one last, longing glance at the screen as she circled the desk. She placed a consoling hand on his arm. Perhaps some quick afternoon sex would restore his color, not to mention his resolve.

"At least my eyesight isn't going," he said as he brushed the front of her blouse. "You've got a stain, right here."

She withdrew her hand. "I'm going out. Don't forget, you promised William you'd take him to baseball practice today."

"I did?" His eyes drifted back to the computer screen.

"Four o'clock. He knows the place."

Guy had almost forgotten how to knot a tie. Back in the New Jersey veal farm, he'd been too insignificant to have to wear one, and now, as CEO of Positano Software, he *was* the dress code and ties were banished from the office, even when calling on a major client—no one, not even a C-level executive on Park Avenue, trusted a tech guy in a tie. But Rosemary had insisted that he wear one to the co-op board interview and after some debate he'd agreed. He had two: a butter-yellow one that screamed "eighties investment banker wannabe" and a striped one from the Gap that whimpered "loser." He went with loser and, after several false starts, managed to fashion a passably tight knot.

"I feel like I'm choking," he told Rosemary. "Who said beware of any enterprise that requires new clothes?"

"Thoreau. I wonder what he'd say about a board interview to buy a two-point-two-million-dollar co-op."

Just weeks had passed since their bid on the apartment was accepted. Lucinda Wells had been eager to close the deal quickly, preparing an exhaustive "board package" that included their tax returns, statements from their bank, brokerage accounts, letters of reference. It was like applying to college, only Columbia had never cared how much money he made and how much he'd managed to save. Becoming CEO of a public company had made him feel exposed, even vulnerable—suddenly his salary and benefits and options were public knowledge, instantly available to any voyeur with an Internet connection. Worse, he had to watch what he said about the company, lest he be seen by regulators as making "forward-looking statements." Imagine having laws to prevent people from making "forward-looking statements." Where would America be without the forward-looking? (Guy was a Democrat and would remain one, no matter how high Positano's stock rose. But sometimes the government went too far, he was beginning to think.) If going public had made him feel exposed, applying to live in a co-op was a humiliating striptease performed not for mere strangers but prospective neighbors. At least investors didn't care what you wore or whether you smoked or if you had a dog or how many times a month you screwed your wife.

Lucinda had called both of them every day that week, often several times a day, with advice and strategy for the interview. Every possible objection the board might have was raised in advance and dealt with. His salary was on the low side—not unusual for a tech CEO, whose compensation was primarily stock, but a major concern to co-op board members, whose overriding interest was that all residents make their monthly maintenance payments. Lucinda's advice: Tell them that the board, the *company's* board, would be reviewing his compensation in a month, and that he had begun a regular plan of share divestiture. Neither happened to be true, of course. Thorough Lucinda had done her own credit check on Guy and Rosemary and come up with quite a bit of credit-card debt, fifteen thousand dollars' worth, divided among several cards, money he'd needed to get the company started. Lucinda's advice: Be honest (for a change). Regale them with tales of buying computers and office equipment and supplies with personal credit. "You're Steve Jobs and the pathetically tiny junior four you're trying to escape from is the garage in which an empire was founded. They ought to put a plaque on the door."

And so on. Guy wondered if Lucinda ever slept, her feverish brain working 24/7 to prepare innocent clients for the horrors of the Inquisition.

He decided halfway through the preparation process that he hated her. She tried mightily to adopt a commiserating tone with them when discussing the board interview, and she obviously wanted the sale to go through, but in the real-estate war in which they were now engaged, she was clearly a collaborator, working both sides. She might hedge conversations with "I know this is ridiculous . . ." or "This is absurd, however . . ." But she quite obviously bought into the stupid rules and "concerns" of these boards who lorded their power over hardworking people like him, young men (well, youngish men) whose entrepreneurial companies were growing a shitload faster than their arthritic old banks and insurance companies. (Young women, too: Even in his thoughts he was evolving, thanks to Rosemary.) *It's a game,* Lucinda liked to say, *just play by the rules until you're in.* But it was more than a game to her, he felt certain, much more than a game.

Barnett was with William at his baseball practice in Central Park, and Nanny was picking up Sophie from a friend's place on East End Avenue. That left only Consuelo in the apartment; she spent afternoons in her sunless slot of a room behind the kitchen, emerging only to begin dinner preparation at around five. Restless, Lily began walking through the apartment. They'd hired a well-known decorator when they'd bought it sixteen years earlier, and it hadn't changed significantly since then. Lily had added a few chairs, a painting or two, family photographs in every room, but the apartment seemed impervious to her. In a lavishly illustrated feature on the apartment in *Architectural Digest,* their decorator had described the process of doing the Grantham home as a collaborative undertaking with her clients, but she'd been as collaborative as Napoleon, ignoring or scoffing at every one of Lily's suggestions.

She passed by the study, her least favorite room, with its shelves of books-by-the-yard and myriad photographs of Barnett's relatives wielding fishing rods, racquets, golf clubs, and cocktails, but on second thought decided to have a look. It was so rarely unoccupied these days. The computer monitor was black, and there was a disturbing absence of papers on the desk. She would have liked some indication that Barnett was mounting a vigorous defense. She picked up an envelope, which turned out to be a solicitation for an investment newsletter, and as she replaced it her hand brushed the mouse. A faint crackling sound, and then the monitor lit up, startling her. Like the children, she was under orders not to touch Barnett's computer. Consuelo wasn't even allowed to dust it, as if one inadvertent key stroke would erase all their wealth.

Well, there wasn't any wealth to erase, as it turned out.

The browser went right to some sort of financial site. On the left of the

screen was a long list of stock symbols. She was dismayed to recognize several tech stocks—you couldn't buy a candy bar for what some of these losers
were selling for. She opened Barnett's mailbox next and skimmed his in-box
for evidence that he was working on clearing himself. It was surprisingly
empty, and the few e-mails she read were solicitations for still more investment advice. She clicked back to the browser and opened up a list of the
sites he'd most recently visited. The site at the top of the list, the one, apparently, he'd been visiting when she'd reminded him it was time to take
William to his practice, was something called Womanimations.com. She
opened it.

After a few seconds' delay the page loaded. She read a brief warning
about adult-oriented content and then clicked on the words "I Agree,"
thereby attesting to her adult status and desire to view sexually explicit ma-
terial. This took her to a new page consisting of a menu without any sort of
illustration, a commendably spare, even elegant design, she had to admit.
She began to read the dozen or so choices: Anal, Dildos, Fucking . . . The
list, helpfully, was alphabetically arranged.

What the hell, she thought, and selected "Dildoes." She was instantly
greeted with a page of small photographs, at the top of which was a banner
ad for something called Premium Escorts. Each of the photographs showed
a woman, either alone or with another woman or, in surprisingly few cases,
with a man. She clicked on one at random and, in a new window, it filled the
screen instantly—God bless the cable modem. An unfashionably voluptuous
platinum blonde crouched on all fours, glancing back at another woman, this
one not quite as blond, who was inserting a dildo the size of a rolling pin
into her. Lily leaned closer to the screen to discern which orifice the dildo
was penetrating as it moved back and forth, back and forth, at least five or
six times a second. She quickly realized that the same action (and the recip-
ient's blissful, mouth-distended reaction) was being repeated over and over.
This wasn't a video but an animation of a photograph. Thus, the name of
the site: Wom-animations. Clever. Well, cleverish. And boring, though in an
admittedly hypnotic way. How could anyone (how could Barnett?) watch
this sordid little scene for more than a second or two? Or was repetitiveness
perhaps the point, distilling an entire erotic scenario into one infinitely repeated action, eschewing any sort of foreplay and follow-up and, by relent-
lessly focusing on the act itself, freezing time at the very instant of

satisfaction—wasn't this, really, what sexual participants, or at least men, longed for?

Lily considered this and a variety of related issues as the two women continued to thrust and react, thrust and react. For example, was Barnett into dildos? And if so, why hadn't he ever mentioned it? (Well, thank God he hadn't, but still.) Or did he patronize the anal page? Or the fucking section? Shouldn't she know this about the man she'd been sleeping with (albeit it rather conventionally) for seventeen years? Thrust and react. Thrust and react. And what in the world did this have to do with finding the missing money and restoring his reputation and their security?

Nothing, obviously. She re-opened the list of Barnett's recently visited sites and explored one, and then another, and then another. All were sex sites, protected by stern but ineffectual warnings, and all began with lists of very targeted options spelled out in clinical detail: Interracial/Anal, for example, or Lesbian/Threesomes. She supposed it must be comforting to learn that you were not alone in your desire to watch a video of a man sliding his penis between the balloony breasts of a bouffanted transvestite (Tit Fucking/She-Men). Or that others shared your passion for watching the amazingly elastic mouth of a sad-eyed woman accommodate two elephantine penises simultaneously (Oral/Two Cocks). Did anyone *(did Barnett?)* want to *do* these things, or was observing them on a computer screen gratification enough?

She found herself disgusted and fascinated. And quickly bored. After fifteen minutes exploring the sites Barnett had recently visited, she could have sworn the same woman showed up in all of them (teased platinum hair, turgid red lips, a figure that took the concept of hourglass to a cartoonish level), doing pretty much the same thing in an inexhaustible number of positions in animations, videos, and still photographs. Each page was festooned with banners advertising escort services and "toys" and the occasional offer for discount plane tickets or low-interest credit cards. She and her family were about to be thrown off Park Avenue while platinum-haired sluts with tits the size of the medicine ball D'Arcy once threw at her abs twice a week were getting rich as Croesus selling banner ads to airlines and banks.

She logged off and sat there for a few minutes. Barnett had been doing nothing to advance his case since he'd been dragged from the Temple of

Dendur. All those hours at his desk, when she'd assumed he been tracking down the missing funds, had been spent instead trolling the Internet for sex. Their money was raining down on Park Avenue like confetti and he was passively jerking off to a multimillionaire with 44D tits who could painlessly give birth to a Lexus. She felt furious and hurt and afraid . . .

. . . and (she could hardly believe it herself) free. In a few short weeks all the ties to everything that was familiar in her life had been cut free, save those that connected her to the children. Her entire life was up for grabs, and now, with no money, their friends deserting them like rats, their reputations obliterated, her husband addicted to online sex, she was free to conduct her life in an entirely new way—or not, as she pleased.

She felt light-headed, giddy with freedom, and wanted to do something right away to acknowledge her new status. But what? A jolt of panic shot through her: Perhaps she wasn't free, just trapped—what was that line from the Janis Joplin song, "Freedom's just another word for nothing left to lose"? Perhaps she'd buy a Janis Joplin CD and blast it through the apartment's state-of-the-art sound system. Picturing Barnett's reaction, not to mention the kids' and Nanny's, gave her momentary pleasure, but playing "Bobby McGee" for the first time in three decades wasn't exactly storming the Bastille. Perhaps she'd buy a dildo, a big, ugly one the size of a rolling pin. Well, perhaps not. She considered logging onto the Internet again to find sex sites that turned *her* on . . . but what would such sites contain? Naked men? Couples? Lesbians? The truth was, on those rare occasions when she surfed the Internet, she searched for sites advertising homes for sale in places like Paris or Santa Barbara or Santorini. Real estate was her porn. How unfair that men could meet their needs so easily—and, with a cable modem, so quickly. She could run away for a while, just disappear, but she'd have to take the children with her, so in the end that wouldn't be running away at all. She checked her watch. It wasn't yet six o'clock. She picked up the phone, dialed information, and asked for the number of the Broadway Nut Shoppe. When a recording offered to call the number automatically, she happily pressed "one" to activate the service, never mind the seventy-five-cent fee, which counted as an extravagance, given their current circumstances. She was free.

Nine

The co-op board interview had been going amazingly well when Guy's cell phone rang and ruined everything. The three board members seemed, if anything, awed by Guy's connection to Positano Software and asked more questions about the outlook for the company's stock price than about Guy and Rosemary's finances or the likelihood of their acquiring a dog (allowed but not encouraged). The interview took place in the apartment of Sheila Ratliff, the oldest of the three. The apartment was stuffy and badly decorated, a classic seven two floors above the unit they were buying (or hoping to). Rosemary had been effusive nonetheless in praising the decor, to the obvious delight of Sheila Ratliff, who must have read in their application where Rosemary had worked and what she had specialized in. ("I must confess, these aren't real Tiffany," she'd said conspiratorially when she showed them into the living room, pointing to a pair of sconces so garishly hideous, even Guy could tell they were worthless.) Sheila Ratliff, about eighty, was short and white-haired, with pale blue eyes and the suspicious, more or less permanent scowl you saw on old women at the checkout in Zabar's, where they watched the cashiers ring up their small purchases with predatory vigilance. The other two inquisitors were men, both in their forties, Guy guessed, probably lawyers, the default profession of the upwardly mobile.

All three threw mostly softballs that evening, although one question nearly tripped them up.

"Do you plan to renovate?" asked Sheila Ratliff.

Guy was about to jump in with an enthusiastic affirmative, perhaps followed by something glib about the state of the Gimmels' apartment, when Rosemary leaned forward and preempted him in a reassuring voice.

"We will be renovating." Sheila Ratliff's expression darkened as she glanced protectively around her untouched living room. "But our first concern will be to preserve the integrity of the apartment. You can't re-create these moldings, no matter how much money you have."

Sheila Ratliff's face relaxed as the five of them dutifully observed the crown moldings along the ceiling. All Guy could see was peeling paint and chipped plaster—he wouldn't hesitate to tear them out and start over.

"So many young couples move in and tear everything down," Sheila Ratliff said. "I saw the plans for one apartment . . . they knocked down every wall, made it into one big room. I think maybe they're planning to bicycle from one end to another."

Guy and Rosemary chuckled dutifully as he wondered if she would have to approve their plans, which would include the removal of several walls.

"Why buy in a building like this in the first place unless you appreciate its bones?" Rosemary asked.

"Exactly!"

"I see from your board package that you're paying all cash," said one of the men, whose name Guy couldn't remember. "But you'll be financed one hundred percent by Goldman Sachs."

"Correct," Guy said.

"That's a lot of debt to service. Almost a hundred thousand a year in interest charges."

"Tax deductible," Guy said, and immediately regretted the way it sounded, so defensive, so *granular,* as they liked to say in the tech space about anything less momentous than a new software release or a secondary offering.

"How will you be servicing the debt?" the other man asked. Guy would have loved to ask both men if they could afford to buy in the building now that even a junior four cost a million-two. They'd probably gotten in during the early nineties, when they were giving away these old places, and now liked nothing better than to harass people like him and Rosemary who were worth ten times their sorry asses. Or was it all really just financial voyeurism?

"The board—Positano's board"—everyone smiled—"will be reviewing my compensation at its next meeting. Given our recent performance . . . revenues up nearly a hundred and fifty percent this year . . ."

"Run-rate revenues," one of the men said.

Christ, everyone was an accountant all of a sudden.

"Given our recent performance, I'm confident they'll approve a significant increase in overall compensation."

"Your Positano holdings were used as collateral," one of the men said.

"Correct."

"The board is a tad concerned about its recent performance."

A *tad* concerned? Guy hadn't put in a good night's sleep since the stock peaked at $73 in February. The twins slept more soundly.

"The market's been tough on everyone," he said with strained airiness.

"Yes, well, given the size of your holdings, I don't think we'll have a problem. You can always sell shares to cover your obligation."

Guy nodded, though he'd sooner chop off a finger than sell shares for something as *granular* as servicing mortgage debt.

"Would you mind taking a look at an old vase?" Sheila Ratliff asked Rosemary. Like a physician, Rosemary was often pulled aside at social events and asked, in an anxious, discreet voice, for her professional opinion. Everyone had an old vase or washstand or Barbie doll, invariably worthless, that they were convinced could finance their children's college education or a house in the country.

"I'd love to," Rosemary said.

Home free, Guy thought as the two women left the room. Well, not free . . . two-point-two million, in fact. Then his phone rang.

Larry had suggested the restaurant, and the moment Lily walked in, she knew why. La Mirabelle, on West Eighty-Sixth Street, was a throwback to the seventies—pastel paint, lots of chrome, beveled mirrors covering the walls. She and Larry might have gone there on a date had either of them been able to afford even a modestly priced French meal back then. Even the clientele looked like they'd hit their prime during the Nixon years; she nervously scanned the room for Peggy and Monroe before taking her first breath inside the restaurant.

He was at the small bar drinking a beer. He wore a nicely pressed work shirt, khaki pants, loafers—West Side dress-up. She doubted he'd changed much since the seventies, either, but he looked handsome and comfortable.

They exchanged identical, slightly awkward "hi's." An older, heavyset woman with a lilting French accent escorted them to a small table all the way at the back of the half-empty restaurant, as if sensing something clandestine about their meeting. They opened menus without speaking.

"French comfort food," he said, and she nodded: boeuf bourguignon, coq au vin, coquilles St. Jacques, duck à l'orange. She hadn't seen so much cholesterol on a menu in decades. She was starving.

They ordered and talked about food and France and other safe topics and then, more dangerously, about things that had changed and things that hadn't. She noticed a few people staring at them . . . at her, rather. She was often photographed for the *Times* Sunday Styles section, wearing something expensive, fingers clasping the stem of a wineglass, talking animatedly through a tooth-baring smile, always, instinctively, playing to the camera's ubiquitous presence.

"Why'd you call?" he asked.

She hesitated before answering, opting not to mention the role of dildo-wielding lesbians in bringing her to the West Side.

"Because I could."

"Huh?"

"I suddenly realized that I'd been following a whole set of rules that didn't really apply to me anymore. Maybe they never had."

"Rules?"

"Well, you need a lot of money, for starters. I realized a long time ago I was never going to make much on my own. I mean, I had no head for business, I still have trouble figuring the tip on a restaurant check, so rule number one became 'Marry well.'" This was more revealing than she'd intended. Was it too late for the lesbians? She sipped the house red wine he'd ordered for them. "I know that sounds terrible."

"No, it doesn't," he said quickly.

"Yes, it does, even to me. I took the easy way out. And once I'd succeeded, once I'd married well, I realized you have to live in a certain way, in a certain type of building in a certain neighborhood. You hire a certain decorator, invite certain people, go to certain parties. I worked so hard to follow all these rules that I forgot it was all voluntary."

"Where the hell did you learn these rules? I mean, we both grew up on the West Side before all the investment bankers moved in and started renovating. I thought your place was as grand as it got—I mean, you had wall-to-wall shag in every room. How did you even know this other world existed?"

"I read about it in magazines, I suppose," she said, but then a memory began to take shape. "I met this girl once, in Central Park. We were both ten or so. She was with a nanny who wore a white uniform and a navy blue cape. Her name was Lizbeth Sampson, not Elizabeth but Lizbeth. Those missing syllables seemed absolutely fraught with significance to me, like her nanny's little white cap or Lizbeth's perfect little sweater set with embroidered violets. We played together while my mother and the nanny looked on. She told me she had exactly one hundred stuffed animals and every single Barbie outfit made—Enchanted Evening, Guinevere, Pajama Party, all of them. I was dazzled. She seemed so confident and satisfied. Lizbeth insisted that I give her nanny my telephone number, and the next day she called—the nanny called—to invite me over to her place on Fifth Avenue.

"Lizbeth lived like a little fairy-tale princess. The Sampsons had the only apartment on the top floor, like a secret castle up in the sky. A man answered the door. I thought it must be Lizbeth's father but it was a servant, I eventually realized. Lizbeth appeared and I said good-bye to my mother, who seemed very reluctant to leave. We walked down a long hallway to Lizbeth's room, which was everything I'd imagined it to be. Beautiful stuffed animals everywhere, a canopy bed, pink walls with these incredibly realistic birds and flowers painted on, so it seemed as if she lived in the middle of an enchanted forest. There was a view over Central Park, of course. I'd never seen the park like that before, from twelve floors up, so neat and orderly, as if it were her own little backyard.

"I don't remember what we did that afternoon, I only remember that when the man who wasn't her father appeared to tell us that my mother had returned, I was devastated. I pleaded with Peggy to let me stay. She said we had to go, but she also asked Lizbeth if her mother was home. When she heard that she was out, she asked Lizbeth to show her the apartment. Lizbeth took us to a huge living room, a dining room, a library. 'What, you don't have a kitchen?' my mother asked. Lizbeth said she wasn't supposed to go in the kitchen while dinner was being prepared, which I thought was the height of sophistication. Peggy made a point of poking her head into every closet and bathroom. In the master bedroom she walked over to one of the windows and admired the view while Lizbeth and I bounced on the enormous bed. Suddenly I was aware of a woman standing in the doorway, beautiful and stern faced.

"'Mommy!' Lizbeth shrieked, and rushed over to her. Or maybe she said 'Mummy.' Lizbeth introduced me to her mother, who seemed tense and suspicious. I'll never forget how dressed up she looked, the way her hair seemed to form a perfect blond halo around her head. I looked over at the window but my mother wasn't there. A second later she emerged from the bathroom. I heard the words 'Even a bidet' from her mouth, then both women gasped. It was an excruciating moment—if this were the movies, one or both women would have dropped a glass and it would have shattered. 'This is quite a place,' my mother said. Even at ten I could tell this was completely unsuitable. I don't think Mrs. Sampson acknowledged what my mother must have intended as a compliment. She wasn't the least bit gracious, my mother pointed out later on the crosstown bus. I felt Mrs. Sampson's disapproval so strongly as she led us silently back to the front door. I knew I'd never be invited back. I remember thinking how old my mother looked— she had me when she was in her late thirties, which practically made me a medical miracle back then. And how dowdy, too, with her sensible wool sweater and sturdy skirt and low-heeled shoes.

"I think that was when I realized that there was a whole other universe right here in New York, where people talked quietly and dressed up for play dates and lunches and decorated their apartments like museums and stayed away from the kitchen while dinner was prepared. My mother showed me a photograph of Mrs. Sampson in the *Times* that Sunday, and after that I started looking for her every week. I discovered this new in-crowd of beautiful, sophisticated people who seemed to do nothing but attend parties in beautiful clothes. And I realized that I wanted to be in those photographs, and eventually I learned what I had to do to get there, the rules I had to follow."

Their waitress arrived with steak au poivre for Larry, a glistening duck à l'orange for her. She dug in.

"What's amazing to me," Larry said, "is that you bought right into that world. Instead of sympathizing with your mother, you took Mrs. Sampson's side."

"In some stupid way I wanted to earn her respect."

"And not your mother's?"

"Maybe I figured I'd never get that. Anyway, once I'd managed to infiltrate the Sampsons' social circuit, I kept an eye out for Lizbeth, but she never appeared. Then a few years ago I read somewhere that she'd become a doctor, a heart specialist, I think, and lived somewhere in the Midwest."

"How did that make you feel?"

"At the time, confused. It seemed so unlikely, it seemed almost wrong, somehow, to turn out so unexpectedly. I couldn't quite figure out how you went from princess on Fifth Avenue to cardiologist in Detroit or wherever."

"And now?"

"Now?"

A chill breeze of sadness blew through her. She shrugged and concentrated on the duck, which was gamy and succulent and would require a month of lunges to work off. They said little, in fact, over the rest of the meal, but the long silences were surprisingly comfortable. Later, walking along Columbus Avenue, toward his building, he took her hand. She pulled away.

"I'm sorry," he said. "But I thought . . ."

"Don't be sorry," was all she said. But she felt adrift, as if she'd entered a strange new country and not just another neighborhood. She needed to get her bearings, and that meant being alone, at least at that moment. She touched Larry's arm, a tentative gesture from which she retreated immediately, then stepped off the curb and hailed a cab.

Guy walked into the foyer to answer his cell phone, leaving the two male board members in the living room. His phone's little LCD screen read *Private.*

"It's Derek."

He didn't respond, hoping, illogically, that Derek would hang up or be struck dead by a heart attack or meteor shower.

"Don't tell me you don't—"

"Of course I know who you are."

"And I know who you are. The CEO." Derek gave each initial its own smarmy emphasis, making Guy's precious title sound like an adult cable network.

"What do you want?"

"I hope you're not this impatient with all your shareholders."

"My shareholders don't call me at eight-thirty at night."

"This one's different."

Derek Ventnor's voice was deep and resonant. It suggested someone tall, husky, self-confident. In fact, Ventnor was short and wiry—scrawny, actually. He was in his late forties and any self-confidence he had was badly misplaced.

"What the hell's been going on?" Ventnor asked.

"I don't know what you—"

"Positano's stock is down seventy-five percent. I can't fucking believe it. I've never been through anything like this."

He sounded whiny and petulant, as if the collapse of Positano Software—the collapse of its *stock price*—were some petty ordeal he'd been needlessly put through, like having his car towed from a legitimate parking space. When the stock was in its ascendancy, investors universally felt it was their financial acumen that was behind its rise, as if they had collectively willed it to levitate (and maybe, in a way, they had). When it started to decline they were suddenly clueless innocents at the mercy of incompetent executives.

Guy launched into his new mantra. "The entire market has been weak, especially technology stocks. Investors with a long-term horizon—"

"Easy for you to talk long term. You didn't put your shares up as collateral when they were selling for sixty-seven dollars. Now they're down to fifteen bucks and I'm getting margin calls. You gotta do something."

"Wait a minute, you borrowed against your Positano shares?"

"Easiest money I ever made. I put the proceeds in a bunch of stocks my broker recommended. They doubled, they tripled. Then they went straight to hell. Now my broker's calling me every goddamn hour wanting me to send cash to cover the spread. I mean, *cash*. He wants fucking cash."

Imagine wanting something as *last year* as cash!

Rosemary and a beaming Sheila Ratliff passed him in the foyer and went back into the living room. The vase had presumably turned out to be "very special, though it's nothing I've ever seen before"—Rosemary's stock appraisal, affording her enough wiggle room to avoid ever having to actually take it on consignment at the auction house. As she walked by she shot him a get-off-the-phone-and-make-nice-with-these-people look.

"In my opinion, these cellular telephones are a curse," Sheila Ratliff huffed as they sat down.

"Look, if you borrowed against your Positano stock, it's not my concern," Guy said. "I never suggested you invest in Positano in the first place."

"I was 'friends and family,'" Ventnor said bitterly. "Remember?"

How could he forget? Ventnor was not his friend and, thank God, he certainly wasn't family, but he'd gotten the biggest allocation of directed shares, fifteen thousand in all, at the offering price of $15. When they closed on opening day at twenty-eight, he had a quick profit of $195,000. At their peak of just over $70 a share, Ventnor's stake was worth over a million dollars. But that wasn't enough for Derek Ventnor, a gazillion percent profit in under a year. He'd borrowed against his holdings to buy shares of the next Positano. It was never enough for anybody.

"What do you want from me?"

"I need cash." Guy felt something clutch inside him, just south of his rib cage. "Not the whole thing, just fifty thousand dollars."

"I don't have it."

"You have three million shares," Ventnor said. "Three million two hundred and twenty-five thousand shares, to be exact."

Ventnor probably kept Positano's registration statement on his nightstand, consulting it for consolation, like the Bible. Or maybe he jerked off to the option tables and income statements, visions of double-digit profit margins stiffening his dick. He knew to the dime what Guy was worth, his salary and bonus plan, where he'd worked before Positano, where he'd gone to school, the fact that he'd allocated 280,000 shares to a trust fund for the twins.

"Shares aren't cash," Guy said.

"Then sell a few."

"It's not that easy. The lock-up period isn't over and the SEC—"

"Fuck the lock-up period and fuck the SEC, okay? I don't want to hear about the SEC, you understand?" Ventnor sounded more affronted than truly angry, as if the Securities and Exchange Commission were responsible not only for his recent financial reversal but also for his receding hairline, diminutive stature, and failure, thirty years ago, to get into the college of his choice. Guy glanced into the living room. Everyone was watching him.

"I have to go."

"You can't get rid of me," Ventnor said. "You needed me, back then, back when you were a nobody, a total schmuck. Now you're Mr. Big Shot, Mr. CEO. But you wouldn't have three million two hundred and twenty-five thousand shares if it weren't for me. You'd still be out in the swamps of Jersey, writing code."

"I'm eternally grateful," Guy said, though in fact he was thinking yearningly of the veal farm at that moment.

"I know where you work!" Ventnor shouted.

Guy clicked off the phone and walked back into the living room.

"Sorry about that," he said, trying to suppress a nervous quiver in his voice.

"Not a problem," one of the men said. He stood up and the others followed suit. "We won't keep you any longer, other than to say that we don't see any reason why you and Rosemary wouldn't make wonderful neighbors at 218 West End Avenue."

They shook hands all around as Guy tried to marshal the requisite enthusiasm. What would the board think if they knew what that phone call was all about? Well, they might be impressed to know he'd been conferring with one of the Internet's most successful entrepreneurs who also happened to be one of Positano's largest individual shareholders. Of course, Derek Ventnor wasn't selling books or airline tickets. Derek Ventnor was dealing in flesh, and like virtually all Internet pornographers but unlike many legitimate online businesses, he was actually making money.

And still he needed cash, fifty thousand dollars of it. Even successful pornographers were short of cash—what was the world coming to?

. . .

Peggy waited for the elevator to take her up to the sixth floor. It wasn't even ten o'clock. Thank God the play at Lincoln Center had been short, and no intermission, either—the producers didn't want to risk mass desertion, the play was that bad. No intermission equaled lousy play—she went to enough theater to have seen this formula prove itself time and again.

She pressed the call button a second time. The elevator was taking a long time on eight. Perhaps it was a board meeting in Sheila Ratliff's apartment. Despite the early hour, Monroe would be asleep already. He hated the theater, everything about it; the prices, the lack of legroom, the shouting, most of all the shouting. "On the stage, they can't say 'Good morning' without shouting like drill sergeants," he always said. "Gives me a migraine." She was happy to leave him home and go with a friend, as she had tonight. The play had been about an older couple getting evicted from their rent-controlled apartment in the Bronx. Depressing, but then most plays lately were about old people or gays, all of them facing death. Well, look at the audience, gay men and old women, Jewish widows, mostly, who subscribed to every theater company that had a mailing list. Death made for good drama, she supposed, which explained all the old people and gays, though in her personal experience death was about as dramatic as a leaking faucet.

She gave the call button another good poke. In their new building there were three elevators, thank God. Speaking of which, she hadn't even begun to think about moving, much less *do* anything about it. In a way she still couldn't believe it. She imagined that some nights, returning alone from the theater, she'd instinctively head back to 218 West End. She'd waltz right in, head straight for the bedroom, as she always did, and catch some young couple going at it, the attractive woman sitting bolt upright, on top, like the women always were in the movies, head thrust back, riding her partner like a wild horse. *Oh, excuse me,* she'd say, *I forgot I don't live here anymore.*

She blushed at her own nutty thoughts and tried to remember the last time she and Monroe had had sex in that room—or anywhere, for that matter. Well, let's see, Johnson was in the White House . . . or was he still vice president? Joking!, as Lucinda would say. She blushed again. The elevator finally opened.

"You don't have to be so mysterious about it," an attractive woman was saying to an attractive man. They both looked mid-thirties. She wore a dark pantsuit over a white blouse, had a nice figure, though a bit more zaftig than she probably liked. He had on a suit and tie—nice to see that for a change.

"I'm not being mysterious. It's just work."

"You spent fifteen minutes on the phone, you almost blew our board interview to take the call, then you came back into the room looking like you'd seen a ghost, and now you won't tell me what it's about."

The *buyers,* Peggy thought, pressing the call button to keep the doors open.

"It's complicated," the man said as they headed to the front door.

"Don't patronize me, Guy."

"I'm not . . ."

And that was all she heard. Energized by this bit of surveillance, so much more intriguing than anything she'd just heard at the theater, she finally entered the elevator and pressed the button for six. So that's where the two-point-two million dollars was coming from. They didn't look like the source of so much money, but you couldn't tell anymore. Nor, for that matter, did they look like they'd be going at it much in the bedroom, not if they always fought like that. Still, she smiled as the elevator rose, imaging them in her and Monroe's bedroom, furnished just the way it was, shtupping like teenagers on top of the chenille spread.

Ten

Lily waited until late the next morning to confront Barnett. By ten o'clock he'd been at his computer for three hours, the kids were safely at school, and she'd been amply fortified by strong coffee and a half hour of exercise. She'd fired D'Arcy as an economy and found that she could replicate on her own most of what he'd been doing with her. She couldn't, of course, hurl a medicine ball at her own abdomen, but she didn't, unsurprisingly, miss that part of the regimen, and her abs were surviving without it.

She entered his study without a word. He jabbed at the keyboard and the monitor went blank.

"What are you doing?" she asked.

"Working."

"On what?"

"On finding the missing money, clearing myself."

"What does HornyNymphets.com have to do with finding three million dollars?" He started to speak. "Answer me, Barnett. Do you think the money was stolen by a horny nymphet? Or was it perhaps taken by a cum-eating slut or an anal whore?"

"You've been snooping."

Snooping. It was so like Barnett to reduce her panic over the unfolding disintegration of their lives to a silly, Nancy Drew–ish word like *snooping*.

"You haven't been doing one thing to help yourself, to help us. You've been sitting in here jerking off for weeks."

"That's ridiculous, utterly outrageous."

"Don't start with the upper-class indignation. This is serious, Barnett. I don't know how much longer we can afford to stay here. If you did take that money, you can talk to the lawyers and maybe—"

"No!" His face crimsoned. "I did not take that money."

"I know you didn't," she said, mustering all possible conviction. "But we can't afford to sit back and wait for the government to figure out who did."

"The government? *The government is going to help us? Is that what you think?*" His voice had acquired the shrill, maniacal lilt of a cornered mad scientist. "Lily, the government isn't looking for the money. They're convinced I have it in an offshore account. Mort Samuels called yesterday, he said *the government* is thinking of revoking my bail."

"What?"

"I'm being uncooperative, apparently. I know where the money is, but I'm not telling them. Ergo, uncooperative. Ergo, back in jail."

"Oh, no."

"I can't spend another minute in jail, I simply can't," he said, a bit melodramatically, though perhaps such a sentence couldn't be uttered any other way.

"Then why aren't you doing anything?"

"Because there's nothing to do," he said. "No one at the firm will take my calls. I keep thinking I'm overlooking something, but I don't have any clues."

"You could have told me, you could have told me instead of sitting here staring at these . . . these women and . . . Barnett, do you *like* these things?"

"I don't know what—"

"Dildos and anal sex and . . . and black women. I mean, you never said anything all these years. I can't do much about my race, but if I thought you really and truly wanted me to—"

"Lily!" He jumped up. She stepped back.

"I feel I don't really know you, that's all."

"That's completely absurd, absolutely ridiculous."

More WASP indignation.

"It's not ridiculous. You've retreated to some sort of sick fantasy world when there's so much to do."

"There's nothing to do." His shoulders unsquared, as if to drive home the point.

He looked pathetic. She'd gotten used to thinking of Barnett as a doer, a man of action, someone in complete control of his destiny (and, by extension, hers). But had he ever been such a character? He'd spent his days buying and selling stocks on the computer, leaving his desk only to seduce wealthy investors and pension fund managers over lunch and dinner at well-reviewed restaurants.

"Let's work together," she said. "All that money can't simply evaporate. There's got to be a trail . . . we'll find it together, starting now." She dragged a chair next to Barnett. "Okay, where do we start?" she said, and though she regretted her own Nancy Drew–ishness, she felt confident that what Barnett needed above all was a bit of encouragement.

"There's nothing to do," he said slowly, barely moving his lips. "You don't seem to get it. You never get it. The government has its target, and they're very happy with their target. Their target is rich, or so they think, their target is well known, their target's wife is out every night in a new dress that costs as much as they make in a month. No one is on my side."

"I am," she said.

"What can *you* do?" he said with such contempt she found herself short of breath. What she could do was gape at him, paralyzed. "You see, you can't do a damned thing for me. You never could."

Still speechless, she wondered briefly, perhaps absurdly, if this was about sex after all. He seemed so petulant, so adolescent in a legs-shaking-under-the-desk kind of way. What if, all these years, she'd encouraged him to plunge a giant black dildo into whatever orifice he pleased, would he now be turning to her for succor instead of turning *on* her, as if *she* were somehow responsible for his downfall?

"And now I'm going to prison," he said petulantly. "What can you do about *that*, Lily?"

She stood up and, while fleeing, slammed her thigh into a corner of the desk.

"Fuck."

"You see, you can't do anything, Lily. You can't do anything. No one can. I'm going to jail, Lily, and you can't do anything about it."

She left, but not before his fingers resumed tapping on the keyboard.

. . .

For Guy, last night had been troubling on two levels. First, the call from Derek Ventnor, and then Rosemary's anger at his refusal to discuss it. Once they were back in their apartment, Rosemary stopped questioning him about it. Actually, she'd stopped speaking entirely, which made the cramped confines of their apartment seem even crampier. There was nowhere to hide from her silence.

"I think that went well," he said as they undressed in the bedroom. "We should get an official answer tomorrow." He climbed on a chair. "But I'm sure we're in." He lowered the top of the room's only window a crack and squeezed an old camp blanket in the opening, then fanned it out to block the light from the street lamp just outside. *Blinds for the bedroom window* had been a recurring and unresolved theme of their marriage for several years, along with *going to the theater more often* and, more recently, *letting the twins cry themselves to sleep.*

She nodded.

"You really hit it off with that Ratliff woman," he said, jumping down from the chair. "Once we move in, she'll probably treat you like her in-house *Antiques Roadshow,* lugging down every tchotchke in her apartment for you to appraise."

She offered the tiniest of nods.

They were both naked as they performed the final ablutions of the day: tooth-brushing, face-washing, peeing. Strange, to be so comfortably naked and simultaneously not on speaking terms. Marriage in a nutshell, he supposed, intimacy and hostility in perfect balance. Her body had altered visibly since the twins' arrival, though in clothes it looked unchanged. She'd once been thin and small-breasted; now she was less thin, though hardly fat, and her breasts had acquired a heft that still surprised him. They practically never had sex anymore, or so it seemed after five child-free years of near-daily fucking. But most nights he cupped her breasts before kissing her good night, happily awestruck by their new heft. He watched her from the bed as she brushed her teeth in the tiny bathroom, the vigorous movement of her right arm sending tiny ripples through her buttocks (she approached dental hygiene as she approached every task, as if it were a daily battle requiring relentless application). The truth was, his body had changed more than hers postpartum. He ran his hands over his midsection. Even in his senior year in college, when a bout of mono had sent his weight below one-fifty, he'd never had visible abdominals, the coveted six-pack. One of the disappointments of his life: He'd never felt his own abs except behind a layer of intractable fat. Now that layer had thickened and tended to soufflé over the elasticized tops of his boxer shorts, leaving a zipper imprint around his waist when he undressed at night.

Rosemary began flossing with the vigor of a violinist attacking a Hungarian scherzo. Despite everything (Ventnor's call, Rosemary's hostility, and of course Positano's sagging stock price), he found himself aroused. How long had it been since he'd simply watched her, naked, brushing and flossing? That probably counted as quality time. He idly stroked himself, thinking that a quick fuck would do more to ease the tension between them than any conversation. That had always been the way with them. Nothing short of sex ever fully dissipated whatever tension was building between them—no wonder things had been edgy since the twins' birth. Funny how the sweaty abrasion of two bodies, the desperate insertion of one organ into another, the panting climax, could have such a restorative impact on a relationship, so much more effective than talk or flowers or even therapy at working things out. That was how it would happen tonight, he thought as he flung off the covers to expose his jutting olive branch.

She deposited the used floss in the toilet and turned, facing him.

"Oh, for God's sake," she said, eyeing his peace offering. "You really are clueless, you know that, Guy?" She grabbed the covers and flung them back over him.

"Darling . . ." he said quietly as she joined him in the bed.

"The boys will be up in five hours, Guy. If we're lucky. Go to sleep."

Guy held no secrets from Rosemary, never had, so it confused him, that night and the next morning, his reluctance to tell her about Derek Ventnor. All he'd have to do is tell her who and what Ventnor was and the chill between them would thaw instantly. She'd understand what he'd done, and what he had to do now.

But he couldn't. When they'd first met, Rosemary had been a successful appraiser for the most prestigious auction house in New York. She was beautiful, had a graduate degree in art history from Barnard, knew the ten best restaurants in New York at any given moment in time and had been to most of them. From the perspective of the Jersey veal farm, she was untouchably sophisticated. All he'd had in his column was what one old girlfriend had called a swarthy handsomeness—and that only went so far with women. Eventually the basic dreariness of his life kicked in like a recurring rash and at that point most of the women he'd met got second thoughts. Rosemary had seen something else in him, intelligence and charm, he liked to think. And then, almost overnight, he'd gone from code-writing frog to high-tech prince. He didn't want her to know that her prince was beholden to a porn king.

Henry Delano knocked on his always-open door and entered his office.

"Our stock's on hyperdrive," he said, crossing the big room to Guy's desk. A giant angel fish seemed to follow him, moving with an unfishy lack of urgency from one end of the big tank to the other. "Two million shares traded already this morning, up to nineteen and change."

"Wow." Positano's stock was very thinly traded, which was one reason it was so volatile. "The right direction, at least."

"There's a rumor floating in one of the chatrooms that someone's buying us out. You haven't been talking to anyone about selling, because—"

"Fuck no." Give his child up for adoption? He'd sooner shut Positano down.

"Well, someone's buying. I'll speak to our transfer agents to see if they know who it is."

He started to leave, pausing to tap the tank. Everyone did that; there must be something fundamentally reassuring about watching a dozen tiny, helpless creatures lurch into a frenzied panic at the mere touch of one's fingertip.

"Listen . . . I got a call last night from Derek Ventnor." Henry walked back toward the desk and sat down. "The asshole put his Positano stock up as collateral for a margin loan and bought a boatload of loser stocks. All underwater now. He needs cash to make a margin call."

"Let me guess, he wants it from us."

"Fifty thousand dollars."

"Out of the question."

"I don't think we have a choice."

"Look, when we went public we had no choice, we had to allocate him the directed shares. The IPO's a dicey time in a company's life cycle, you can't afford anything unsavory or the investors won't bite." Henry looked pleased with his little metaphor. "Now that we're public, investors aren't going to dump us because of Ventnor, they can't afford to. Anyway, he's not as important to us as he once was."

"I'm speaking next month at the Merrill Lynch tech conference in Boca. Our IR firm worked overtime to get me on that agenda. I don't exactly like the thought of standing up there, knowing that everyone knows about Derek Ventnor."

"So fifty thousand dollars is the price of speaking at that conference?"

Guy frowned. Financial types were so depressingly, predictably literal. "It's the price of holding my head up in front of my peers. Anyway, I'm not so sure there won't be legal implications if Ventnor goes public. We didn't exactly highlight him in our prospectus." In fact, Positano's S-1 document for the IPO had made no mention of Ventnor or his company.

"We could check with legal."

"Legal" was a lawyer, one person, a quiet, bookish woman named Hilary Hillman who'd forfeited a lucrative partnership in a major corporate firm after the birth of her third child in order to, as she'd put it, downsize her professional commitments.

"No, I don't want Hilary or anyone else involved. I need some sort of check that Ventnor can cash but that can't be traced back to us."

"Christ, this is Mafia shit, like paying a bribe."

"Don't forget, we have the MyJob contract coming up. It's down to us and Vignette Software. A dead heat. They're looking for a reason to go with one company over the other. I don't want to give them Ventnor. How soon can you get me a check?"

His cell phone chirped from its holster on his belt.

"It's me."

Why wasn't there a law that only spouses were allowed to begin phone conversations with that line?

"Hello, Lucinda."

"I just heard from the board. You're in!"

"Great."

"Maybe you didn't hear me, I said the board accepted your application."

"And I said 'great.'"

"There's great and there's great. You're not having second thoughts. . . ."

"Of course not. I'm in the middle of something."

"Oh, well . . ." She seemed flummoxed by the concept that something might be more important than being accepted by a co-op board. She probably interrupted quadruple bypass surgery to tell the doctor that his application had been accepted. "We'll talk later," she said. "You'll want to get your financing ducks in a row ASAP. And start looking for a contractor. You'll want to submit your plans to the board before you move in. Okay, G2G. Congrats."

"So," he said to Henry after reholstering his phone, "where were we?"

"I can get you a check this afternoon. I'll have to work out who to make it payable to. . . . You going to messenger it over?"

"Make it out to cash. I'll take it over myself."

"I wouldn't recommend that. The less you have to do with that scumbag—"

"I need to make it clear that this is the last time."

After Henry left, he called Rosemary.

"I just heard from Lucinda. We're in," he said.

"Great." He heard his own lack of enthusiasm echoed in her voice. At least she was speaking to him, though admittedly she couldn't just nod over the phone.

"Maybe we should go out and celebrate tonight."

"I'll never get a sitter on short notice. Oh, I hear them waking up now. Bye."

He hung up, thinking that he'd have to find a way to seduce her that night; he didn't think he could endure the cold war another day. He could also tell her about Ventnor, which might be easier than trying to coax her into sex. He glanced at his computer screen. Positano was up a full point on heavy volume. Something was happening. A jump in a company's stock price was like a rising fever, nothing alarming necessarily but an indication that something more serious might be going on. Positano was running a fever, no doubt about it. He clicked over to his digital calendar and saw a solid mass of yellow covering all the remaining hours of the day—meetings, back to back. He added the words "find contractor" to his to-do list and minimized the calendar to a small icon at the bottom of the screen. Then he picked up a pencil and tossed it at the tank, whipping the fish into an utterly gratifying frenzy.

Eleven

Peggy knelt before the dresser in Lily's old room, grimly resolved to begin throwing things out in order to successfully downsize from seven spacious prewar rooms to four smallish modern ones. She opened the bottom drawer and decided to segregate the old clothes into two piles: one earmarked for Goodwill, the other for keeping. The first thing she pulled out was Lily's sweatshirt from P.S. 87. The fabric felt age-brittled. Lily would probably want her to give away the sweatshirt, but who would want it? Might as well hang on to it. Next out of the drawer was a peasant blouse, once white, now a sickly ivory. The embroidery still looked good, little tulips and daffodils trailing across the shoulders and chest. Lily had practically lived in peasant blouses in the seventies, though they made her appear perilously top heavy.

Peggy paused to contemplate her daughter's breasts. Where had they gone? She'd been so zaftig, teenage boys had flocked to her like filings to a magnet, making dopey conversation as they stood in the foyer and gaped at her chest. Now she barely filled out a b-cup. Between West End Avenue and Park Avenue she'd lost a good twenty pounds, ten in each breast, apparently. Peggy sighed and held up the capacious blouse. Had she been overly critical of Lily's figure, back when she had one?

Enough. You could make yourself nuts second-guessing how you raised your child. She folded the blouse and placed it on top of the sweatshirt.

Twenty minutes later the drawer was empty but the Goodwill pile con- tained only one item, a pair of thick wool socks. She eyed the tall pile of keepers with a sense of dread. What had she been thinking, selling the apart- ment? She began stuffing the clothes back in the drawer, thinking of that self-storage place on Amsterdam Avenue. But she couldn't bear the thought of condemning Lily's things to a commercial storage place, or her things, for that matter. That defeated the whole point of keeping things, didn't it, not to mention the bugs and rodents and thieves she felt sure had the run of the place.

She closed the drawer and stood up. She'd make lunch and then figure it all out.

"Tuna fish okay with you, Monroe?" she said as she passed the guest room-slash-trading floor. The markets were open, so she didn't expect an answer. In the kitchen she'd just opened the tuna when the phone rang.

"It's just me," said Ruth Greenhill in her usual way.

"How are you, Ruth?"

"I've finally turned the corner."

"I'm glad to hear it," she said, hoping Ruth was recovering from a cold and not something dreadful like cancer, which would call for further explo- ration. It was getting harder and harder to keep up with her friends' ail- ments, not to mention those of their husbands.

"How are you holding up?"

"I'm fine," Peggy said, wondering if Ruth was referring to the impending move or to Barnett's legal crisis.

"The newspapers have finally dropped the story, which is a blessing."

And no doubt a disappointment to you, Peggy added silently. "Well, there isn't anything to write about."

"It's probably just a bookkeeping error. Last week at the cash machine I asked for sixty dollars and got just forty, two twenty-dollar bills. I made quite a stink, let me tell you, but the bank insists I got what I asked for."

"What did the receipt say?"

"The receipt? The receipt said it gave me forty."

"So what's the problem?"

"But I asked for sixty."

"Then you should have asked again, for twenty."

"But it was the bank's mistake, not mine."

"Maybe you pushed the wrong button."

"What button? You tap on the screen. I don't trust these new models with the screens you touch."

Conversations with Ruth often drifted along unanticipated but deeply regretted paths.

"At any rate," Peggy said firmly, "I'm having an awful time sorting through everything for the move. I just can't seem to throw anything out."

"I know what you mean. When Walter was alive and we—"

"Yes, well, that was a long time ago, and you never had a place as big as ours to begin with." With Ruth Greenhill it was always best to take firm control of the conversation. "And I'll tell you what else is bothering me. My friend Natalie, who you don't know, Ruth, told me that these young people, they move into an old place like ours and rip out all the moldings and tear down all the walls and replace the kitchen and the bathrooms—"

"Your place is immaculate, mint condition."

"Triple mint, actually. Our broker told me. Sounds like an ice cream flavor, I thought, but it's what buyers look for. But even triple mint's not good enough. Everything has to be new." She ran a finger along the front of a metal cabinet, as smooth as polished nails. "I just hate the idea of all of this ending up in a Dumpster on West End Avenue, after all the years I've taken care of it. People picking through my cabinets and whatnot like vultures."

"Like when you die," Ruth said unhelpfully.

"I took a peek at an apartment upstairs, in the same line as this one, while they were still working on it. Nothing was the same—the dining room was a bedroom, the guest room was a den, the kitchen was in the hallway, the hallway had these rounded walls . . . I tell you, I got lost in my own apartment."

"But it wasn't your apartment."

"I understand that, Ruth," she said.

"It must cost a small fortune to redo these apartments."

"But what's a small fortune these days? The people buying our place, I don't know about her, but he's the founder of a computer software company. He's paying all cash. Monroe was so impressed he bought a hundred shares."

"What's the name of this company?"

"Positano Software." Ruth repeated the name slowly, as if writing it down. "*You're* not thinking of buying it?"

"Listen, people say these Internet stocks are about to turn around, and if this person can afford to move your kitchen into your guest room and make your corners round, he must know something. Walter always said investing isn't rocket surgery, you know."

"Whatever you say, Ruth. Just keep a little aside for food and shelter."

"Well, of course I will, I wouldn't think of—"

"Was there some reason you called?"

"Just to see how you were holding up."

"Well, I'm fine. I'll call you in a few days."

She hung up and made two tuna sandwiches on rye, which she placed on the kitchen table.

"Come and get it, Monroe," she called. He didn't respond, which meant either the market was up a lot or crashing through the floor. She walked to the guest room and found him slumped over the keyboard.

"For heaven's sake, Monroe, it's not even one o'clock."

She crossed the room and touched his shoulder.

"Monroe?"

She shook his shoulder. He didn't move. Above him, stock prices marched obliviously across the screen. For a moment she took that as evidence that he was still alive.

"Monroe, wake up!" She shook him harder, then put a hand to his cheek, which felt warm, thank God. Still, he was obviously unconscious. "I'm calling an ambulance," she announced as she left the room.

Back in the kitchen, she dialed the emergency number and was disconcerted when a Caribbean baritone answered with "What city, please?" Damn. But then again, in her entire life she'd never once dialed either 411 (which cost seventy-five cents, last she checked) or an ambulance, thank God.

She hung up, took a deep breath, and dialed 911.

Guy pressed the button marked *Ventnor Place* on the small, dilapidated console outside a run-down four-story building on East Twenty-ninth Street. A man's voice through the rusted intercom asked who it was, and after he shouted his name, a loud buzzing unlocked the front door. He climbed two dimly lit flights of stairs and found that one of the two doors on the second-floor landing was partially open. He entered the apartment. A tiny vestibule led to a very narrow room straight ahead, once the bedroom, presumably, and a slightly wider main room to the right. In the former bedroom, atop two long desks constructed of unpainted plywood boards placed on filing cabinets, sat an array of computer equipment—monitors, keyboards, processors, a scanner, a printer—all connected by a dense linguini of cords.

Guy saw Derek Ventnor in the other room and was immediately struck by how ordinary he looked. They'd met several times before, of course, in Positano's earliest days, but since then Guy's memory had recast him from the blandly unmemorable figure before him into a villain of Shakespearean stature, Iago and Richard III and the all-too-appropriate Shylock rolled into one snarling, invincible monster. Guy couldn't help feeling a twinge of disappointment at Ventnor's short stature, his pathetic comb-over, and his bulbous midsection, contained, just barely, by a stain-flecked white T-shirt. The only thing remarkable about Derek Ventnor was his forehead, a ledge of rippled flesh that cast his face in gloomy shadow.

Ventnor motioned for Guy to join him in the larger room, where Guy refused his offer of a handshake. His intention was to hand over the check, deliver a short speech to the effect that this would be the final payment, and then be out of there. Although he should have anticipated what would be going on in the room, he was startled speechless by what he saw.

At the far end of the room, beneath two windows whose shades had been drawn, a naked woman was listlessly administering a blow job to a naked man. He was lying on his back on a twin bed, eyes closed, hands clasped behind his head, as if napping in a hammock, while she knelt between his splayed legs and went about her task with a steady if unenergetic rhythm. Only the occasional groan from the man indicated that he was awake and deriving pleasure from the exercise—that, and an impressively durable erection. Whether the woman was deriving any satisfaction was hard to tell, as a glistening mass of long, platinum hair swirled around her face as she bobbed up and down, like seaweed undulating in a strong current.

Capturing the action, if you could call it that, was a single video camera on a tripod positioned about six feet from the bed.

"They're our most popular performers," Ventnor whispered, smiling parentally. "We pick up a dozen new subscribers every time we feature them."

Guy glanced at a monitor connected to the video camera. The two figures filled the entire screen. Jar lamps mounted to the ceiling cast a clinical light on the performers that was only partially softened on the screen.

"And our regulars never miss them. Apart from their obvious physical charms, they've got a chemistry going that burns right through the fiber optics."

Remarkably, the woman managed to devour her partner's entire shaft, eliciting a long, shuddering moan from its owner.

"Tracy and Hepburn," Guy said softly. He couldn't see the woman's face, but her body's lush "charms" were quite evident. As she bent over her partner's groin, as if in supplication, her swollen breasts grazed the tops of his thighs. And the man's erection, re-revealed when she came up for air, had a similarly outsized charm. But the two had about as much chemistry as a surgeon and an anesthetized patient.

"Our average subscriber logs in right at the start and stays with us for the full hour," Ventnor continued in the resonant hush of a golf commentator. "All I can say is, thank God for Viagra." He gave Guy a collegial nudge on the shoulder and checked his watch. "We're just about winding up the hour now."

Guy glanced back at the male performer, still magnificently tumescent after a full hour. Ventnor should get Pfizer to sponsor his Webcast.

"I brought the money you asked for," Guy said as he removed the check from his pants pocket. "But this is the last payment, period."

Ventnor took the check and glanced at the monitor of a laptop sitting atop a small computer desk.

"Our viewers are getting impatient for the finale," he whispered. He tapped the screen. "The spelling in these messages . . . it's a crime. Then again, it isn't easy typing with one hand." He winked at Guy, scribbled something on a piece of paper, and held it up to the performers, clearing his throat to get their attention.

Start fucking now, read the admirably economical message.

The actors turned briefly to read their instructions, then got to work. The woman detached herself from her partner, shimmied forward a few inches, raised herself up a bit from her knees, and then lowered herself easily onto her Viagra'd companion, whose position and expression had changed not at all in response to the new procedure.

"Excellent, just fantastic." Ventnor was showing far more interest in the proceedings than either of the two participants. Guy wondered if drugs or boredom or perhaps both were responsible for their apparent lack of interest.

"We pioneered audio in sex cams," Ventnor whispered. "Most of our competition still don't have it. We get a twenty percent premium over other sites, and it's mostly the audio."

"Did you hear what I said?" Guy asked. "This is the last payment, and by the way, it's a loan," he added pointlessly, knowing he'd never see a dime of it back.

"We've come a long way, you and me," Ventnor said, glancing at the check before slipping it into his back pocket. "Your software, it's a fucking miracle. Every time we get a new subscriber, automatically he's logged into our Get-ItLive dot-com database with all his preferences recorded."

"Preferences," Guy snorted.

"Anal, dildos, feet—nothing kinky. Our customers are mostly vanilla, you come right down to it."

Anal, dildos . . . Guy spent his days meeting with senior banking executives to discuss how to track and monetize preferences for fixed or variable loans, or consulting with e-commerce honchos about how best to acknowledge and capitalize on preferences for fiction versus nonfiction, overnight versus regular delivery. But his first customer, the one whose patronage had been instrumental in getting Positano launched, was happily—and, almost alone among Positano's customers, profitably—tracking men's preferences for anal versus dildos.

"With your software, we maintain a community. Men from all walks of life, with different interests—fucking, oral, interracial—they all come together at GetItLive dot-com."

"It's a small world after all."

"I know what you mean. We got twelve thousand subscribers currently at nine ninety-five a month—you do the math."

Guy did the math as the woman clasped her hands behind her head, arched her back, and began to moan. Almost a hundred thousand a month times twelve months, that was a million-two . . .

"One million two hundred thousand," Ventnor whispered. "And I run it all myself. No secretarial help, no producer or director, just a part-time accountant to make sure I'm kosher with the IRS. You think it's easy dealing with that much money?"

"Your performers work for free?"

"Practically," Ventnor said. "You'd be surprised the talent you can get for a couple hundred bucks an hour."

The talent was becoming uncharacteristically verbal, signaling an impending climax.

"Right on time," Ventnor said, checking his watch. "Our subscribers like that we're prompt on both ends. They schedule their whole day around us. We know this thanks to Positano. We send out automatic evaluation e-mails after every show. You know, did they want to see more oral, for her to maybe sit on his face longer—you missed that, right before you came, her signature move. Real-time feedback is fucking incredible. We do a show every two hours, starting at four in the afternoon and ending at midnight on weekdays, so we can't wait until the next day to know what's turning our clientele on. Our competition's just a mouse click away."

Guy heard the same Web clichés every day from his own clientele.

Ventnor checked the laptop to do a bit of on-the-fly market research and scribbled new instructions based on the latest feedback from his clientele. He thrust the paper directly in front of the male performer: *Pull out for climax*, it read. He rejoined Guy at the other side of the room.

"Look, during the IPO, we couldn't let investors know that our biggest customer was . . . was this." Guy pointed to the writhing performers. "They wouldn't have touched us. But you're not our biggest customer anymore, so—"

"Damn straight we're not. We get Positano for free."

Free software had been Ventnor's first bit of extortion.

"Exactly my point," Guy said. "You're not important to us anymore."

"But here you are," Ventnor said, giving his back pocket an affectionate pat, "check in hand."

Guy thought of the upcoming MyJob contract. Needless to say, Ventnor Place was not on the reference list submitted to MyJob or any other client. He could just imagine how Ventnor's reference would go: *Positano? Terrific fucking company. With Positano, we can really understand our clientele. How else would we have known that three-quarters of our customers wanted the chick on top when she comes?*

"This is the first and last payment, Ventnor. We're not generating cash the way we were a few months ago, and even if we were, I'm through dealing with you."

"That's bullshit about the cash. Your burn rate is two million a month. You got sixty million from the offering four months ago, and even with your stock in the toilet you could pull off a secondary, no sweat." He stepped a few feet closer to the performers, careful not to get in front of the camera, and whispered, "Jeremy, you're lying there like a lox. Pump up the volume, okay?" Back at Guy's side, he added, "Viagra works miracles on the dick, but you still gotta show some enthusiasm. That leaves twenty-eight million in the piggy bank."

Beware the pornographer with a business head—that should be lesson number one in every New Economy manual. Ventnor's employees dutifully shifted into high gear, the man by emitting a steady stream of *ohbabyyeah-babydon'tstop*'s his dick re-exposed for the world to see—as the world had requested—while his partner launched into a series of rhythmic, high-pitched squeals.

"You won't get another cent from me," Guy said.

"Let's wait and see what happens to Positano stock. Fuck's going on over there, anyway, how come the stock went to hell?"

"Everyone keeps expecting the nineties to happen all over again. They *want* them to happen again. They remember when the bubble inflated, not when it burst. Anyway, where you choose to invest your money is none of my business."

"Fuck that. I *am* your business. You were two days from oblivion when I answered your two-bit ad. Christ, I've seen classier ads for penis enlargers in the back of *Hustler*."

With nothing more than a few thousand lines of code to his name and not a single customer, Guy had borrowed money on his credit card and placed a half-page advertisement in a few Internet magazines. A week after the issues hit the stands, he hadn't gotten a single response and was ready to give up when Ventnor called.

"It wasn't just the money, either," Ventnor said. "I practically developed your FastResponse product, which had more kinks than my freakiest customers."

He had a point, not that Guy was going to acknowledge it.

"How many hours did we spend back then, working out all the bugs? You had the basic framework, the theory, but I had a real-world application. You think your customer at Merrill Lynch would have spent all that time with you? Not fucking likely. Can we at least *pretend* we're getting off on this?"

It took Guy a few seconds to realize that the last statement was not directed at him. It took the performers a few seconds as well to crank it up a notch.

Ventnor chuckled quietly, shaking his head. "Can you imagine what Merrill Lynch would say if they knew that the software they use to respond to inquiries from millionaire geezers clipping coupons in Florida was originally developed to respond to horn dogs who wanted a little more anal in their life? Probably the same client base, now that I think about it."

"I don't want to argue with you, I just want to make it clear . . ." The woman let loose a piercing shriek that elicited a thumbs-up from Ventnor. ". . . that I'm not handing over any . . ." Two more shrieks, even louder than the first. ". . . any more money. You can call *The Wall Street Journal* and tell them all about our relationship, I don't . . ." The shrieks were coming at close intervals now, with Ventnor waving his arms at the couple like Leonard Bernstein inciting the New York Philharmonic to a crescendo. ". . . a lot of Internet infrastructure companies have adult entertainment clients, some of the biggest names . . ." A sudden pounding from above shook the camera—on the monitor it looked like the woman's climax was causing a minor earthquake. Ventnor shoved his middle finger at the ceiling. "Just trying to make an honest living, *neighbors*," he hissed. Guy tried to remain focused. ". . . Akamai, Inktomi, Veritas—you think these companies don't have customers like . . . like . . ." Shrieks from the woman now merged with the steady pounding from above. ". . . like this . . . this enterprise of yours . . ." There was abrupt silence as the woman turned off like a stalled car and the upstairs neighbor relented. ". . . even today these companies have market caps of . . ." She massaged her breasts as her partner began stroking himself. ". . . of billions of dollars, and everyone knows that when they started out . . ." An anguished gasp accompanied Jeremy's remarkable money shot, which brought his eyebrows into play.

"Range like that, the guy could play center field for the Yankees," Ventnor said. "And you notice, no condoms? Our clientele doesn't want to see condoms, ruins the fantasy. So we have our performers tested. *Suck some face*," he whispered to the couple.

The performers obligingly waged a desultory sword fight with their tongues.

"Okay, it's a wrap," Ventnor whispered. The performers got up from the bed with uncharacteristic energy. "Slooowly," the director cautioned, then turned to Guy. "Our clientele goes ballistic when the performers race off camera like they can't wait to take a crap."

"I gotta get out of here," Guy said. He felt a new depth of unease in the bizarrely impersonal postcoital atmosphere. "As far as your relationship to Positano is concerned, consider it finished."

Ventnor took a wad of money from a pants pocket and gave a hundred-dollar bill to each performer, who accepted their payments silently as they continued to dress. The man's chemically enhanced erection, Guy noted, showed no sign of deflating, even as he maneuvered it into a pair of tight jeans.

"Be back by six forty-five sharp," he said.

Guy knew he didn't want to leave with them. He couldn't begin to imagine what sort of small talk he could manage with two people who'd just fucked in front of him and a virtual audience of who knew how many pay-per-viewing freaks.

"I'm serious, Ventnor, I don't want to hear from you again. And if I do, not only will I not pay you anything, I'll go to the authorities."

"Get your stock back over thirty bucks and you won't hear from me," Ventnor said. "Meanwhile, I got margin loans up the wazoo, and if I need cash, I know where to find it."

Guy saw no point to responding to what was, after all, just another disgruntled shareholder, and headed for the door.

Twelve

Lily didn't miss Barnett until dinnertime. She'd spent the late afternoon in Central Park with William, who had a baseball practice, and had managed to slip away for a half hour of bird watching in the Rambles, where she'd witnessed a flamboyant blue jay plunder the nest of a dull, frantic English sparrow, sending two eggs crashing to the ground before absconding with a third in its beak. She went to the Rambles for peace and quiet but found drama, anyway. With birds as with people, the story never changed: The strong beset the weak, the fancy tormented the plain.

"Where's Daddy?" Sophie asked that evening. She stood tentatively in the hallway just outside the master bedroom.

"He must have an appointment," Lily replied.

"Like he ever has appointments anymore."

"Well, things have changed." Lily tried to sound optimistic. "Is this hard for you, sweetie?"

"Not really." She stepped into the master bedroom, however, indicating a willingness to face further questioning.

"Kids at school don't mention your father's situation?"

"We talk about it all the time."

"Really?"

"Mary Katherine says that her father said that people like Daddy never go to jail. They just write a check to the government or whatever. Alison says her father told her that it's all one big cat-and-mouse game."

Lily imagined a daisy chain of charming bedtime scenes in cozy children's rooms up and down Park Avenue, fathers and daughters intimately discussing the Granthams' legal predicament.

"Well, it may not be that simple," Lily said. For one thing, she did not add, any check they wrote to the government would bounce into orbit. "But it will work out one way or another, and I'm glad you're handling it so well."

"Yeah, well, I mean, you know . . ." Sophie raised and lowered one shoulder. "Are you doing okay?"

"Me? Of course, sweetie." Sophie looked unconvinced. "Why do you ask?"

"You seem different, that's all. Like you don't . . . you know, care as much."

"Care?"

"About, you know, how you look and stuff."

Lily raised an involuntary hand to her head and felt an unfamiliar swelling of hair behind her ear. She was weeks overdo for a cut.

"It's not just your hair. I mean, I never saw you with your shirt not tucked in."

Lily stole a quick glance at her waist. "I was in the park . . ."

"Like that ever made a difference before? I'm not saying it's bad. You look, you know, kind of younger this way. Cooler. Almost."

"I do?"

"Like, before? You always seemed so, you know, like . . . stiff. Marnie's mother told her you'd commit suicide if your hemline was the wrong length."

Lily tried to recall if she knew Marnie's mother and what the implications were of being considered suicidal over hemlines.

"I mean, you're my mother, so it wasn't, like, *wrong* to look like, you know, formal. But now you're like . . ." She completed the thought with another one-shoulder shrug.

Nanny was next to check in.

"It's just that I made pot roast, and it's going to dry up if I don't serve it soon," she said from the bedroom doorway.

They'd fired Consuelo as an economy measure and had tried to axe Nanny as well, but she'd had a complete and utterly unexpected meltdown at the prospect of unemployment. There were plenty of positions for a skilled child-minder with good references, as Nanny must have known. But not with these children, she'd wailed, exhibiting a depth of feeling for William and Sophie that Lily had never suspected. They'd allowed her to stay, at a reduced salary, on condition that she chip in with the cooking and cleaning.

"Fine, we'll eat now."

"Shall I put a plate in the oven for Mr. Grantham? So it will be nice and warm when he gets back."

Nanny's voice and attitude could make the most innocuous statements sound fraught with accusation. Something about "nice and warm" seemed vaguely reproachful . . . or was it the "when he gets back," which seemed laced with sarcasm?

"Good idea."

"I'll gather up the children."

"Yes, gather them." Why had they so easily given into Nanny's histrionics? Hadn't she mentioned a sister living nearby she could stay with until a new position materialized?

Barnett's absence was not mentioned during the quick dinner in the breakfast room, but by eight-thirty Lily was worried. She wandered restlessly from room to room, joined periodically by the children, who kept asking where their father was. She longed to confide her anxieties to them, but what exactly would she say, that she'd discovered their father spending his entire waking life surfing sex sites on the Internet, and that he may well have flown the coop in embarrassment? Did *she* believe that?

The doorbell chimed at nine-thirty. She hurried to the foyer.

"FBI," came a male voice from behind the front door.

She unlocked the door. Two men stood outside, both in dark suits. She thought she recognized one of them from the Temple of Dendur.

"I'm Jay DiGregorio, from the Federal Prosecutor's Office," said the familiar one. "And this is Special Agent Sammet, from the FBI. I believe you are Mrs. Grantham?" She nodded. "Mrs. Grantham, do you know where your husband is?"

She shook her head and let out a long, slow breath. If Barnett were dead, he wouldn't have begun that way.

"May we come in?" the other man, Special Agent Sammet, asked. Though he looked no older than thirty, his hair was as white and lustrous as ermine. Jay DiGregorio appeared to be about ten years older, and his scant remaining hair was gray. Both men had thick, sinewy necks that strained against buttoned white collars. They looked fit and predatory.

"Where is my husband?"

"May we come in?"

"Tell me where he is."

"We have a search warrant," said Special Agent Sammet, removing a document from his jacket pocket. She declined to take it and stepped aside to let them in.

The two men entered the foyer.

"Your husband boarded a plane for London this afternoon, Mrs. Grantham," said DiGregorio as he gaped brazenly at the decor. "He left the country using his own passport."

"Well, why wouldn't he?"

"Exactly. Unfortunately, we didn't confiscate his passport." DiGregorio's frown dug angry dimples into his jawline.

"Why is Daddy in London?" Sophie asked. She and William stood on either side of Lily.

"The British authorities have no record of him checking into a hotel," said Special Agent Sammet. "Do you have any friends in London, Mrs. Grantham?"

"A few, but we never stay with them."

"I'd like their names and contact information."

"But why are you—"

"We don't think your husband is still in London, or in England for that matter," said DiGregorio. "We assume he transferred at Heathrow to someplace without an extradition treaty with the U.S."

"He ran away?"

"He's supposed to check with our office before any travel, even within the country," said Special Agent Sammet. "He didn't."

"But he . . ." He didn't check in with her, either.

"He didn't tell you," said DiGregorio quietly. She shook her head. "We'd like to see what he took with him, check his computer . . . it might help determine his whereabouts."

She was paralyzed by conflicting emotions: hurt, anger, isolation, confusion. Part of her thought of calling a lawyer, another part wanted to say, *What the hell, ransack the apartment for all I care, it won't be ours much longer.*

"This won't take long," Special Agent Sammet said. "Which way is the master bedroom?"

She led them down the long hallway and pointed out Barnett's closet, which, along with her closet and dressing area, had been converted from a guest bedroom. Barnett's suits, dozens of them, hung with grim precision on a long rod, his shirts nestled neatly on a column of specially designed shelves, exactly two shirts to a shelf, his shoes in custom-built, size 8½ slots. He'd spent days designing the closet. After Lily showed guests the living room, the dining room, the children's rooms, Barnett would take them into the master bedroom and proudly fling open the double doors of his closet. *Behold the dazzling order of my life. Nothing is beyond my control!* It seemed unthinkable that he'd leave all that behind, almost as hard to accept as his deserting the family.

"What was here?" Special Agent Sammet asked, pointing to a large empty shelf.

"A suitcase," she said. Then she noticed a few missing shirts, a missing sweater or two. In the precisely ordered closet, the absent items left painfully obvious holes, each as unexpected and unsettling as a missing front tooth. "There are clothes missing, and . . ." She glanced down. "Shoes."

Both children gaped at the empty slots in the closet as if they foretold a parlous future, which perhaps they did.

"We'd like to see his computer," DiGregorio said. When Lily ignored him, distracted rather than uncooperative, he took the warrant from his colleague's hand.

"I don't care what you do," she said, barely mustering the breath to speak. She led them back down the hall to Barnett's study, the children following closely. DiGregorio sat in Barnett's leather chair while his colleague stood behind him. Lily and the children watched from the other side of the desk.

If she needed any proof that Barnett was gone, perhaps for good, she had only to look at the two men at his desk, violating his sanctum sanctorum. After a few minutes she circled the desk.

They were opening, perusing, and quickly closing documents.

"What exactly are you looking for?" she asked.

The men didn't respond. Sophie and William joined her to watch. Di-Gregorio closed a Word document and clicked on the Internet icon. After a half-second there appeared some sort of financial page crammed with numbers. The two men exchanged glances, then DiGregorio clicked on the address box to see which sites Barnett had recently visited. He clicked on the most recent address. The screen jumped to a page called Expedia. Special Agent Sammet leaned closer to the monitor.

"What's that?" Lily mouthed to William.

"Travel site," William whispered. He spent half his life online.

DiGregorio clicked around the Expedia site for a few minutes, then went back up to the address bar and clicked on the second address from the top. After the briefest pause a new screen appeared, this with a small gray box at the center. As the five of them watched, the gray box gradually gelled into an image, like a developing Polaroid. Two people, on a bed, having sex. In a corner of the box was a digital clock, ticking away time in hundredths of seconds.

"Sophie, William, out!"

They stared open-mouthed at the screen. She, too, couldn't turn away. The quality of the image was awful, and the performers moved in sudden, jerky jumps (one moment, a hand clutched a shoulder; the next, it was squeezing a buttocks . . . how did it get there?), but the amateurish nature of the show enhanced its immediacy. The two performers looked thoroughly bored, the man on his back, the woman sitting on him, his cock presumably siloed within her. Both men were working hard to suppress smiles. Lily heard a man's voice from the computer's speaker, an off-camera whisper that nonetheless seemed louder than the performers' pathetic attempts at moans. "Pump up the volume, people," it said. "You look like a couple of loxes."

"GetItLive dot-com," Special Agent Sammet said. "I read somewhere it's like the tenth or twentieth most popular site on the Internet."

"Can we leave this?" Lily said. "That isn't my husband there on the screen, as I'm sure you realize."

"Mommy!" Sophie punched her hip.

Special Agent Sammet opened the address list again, but this time Lily wasn't going to wait to see what Barnett had been up to. She didn't have to.

"Let's go," she said, grabbing an arm of each child.

"We're going to take this with us," Special Agent Sammet said, patting the computer tower under the desk. "We have experts downtown who can—"

"Take it," Lily said. Soon enough it would all be gone, everything.

She led the children back to the bedroom, where they all sat on the bed. None of them spoke for a while, but they all held hands, tightly.

"What's going to happen to us?" Sophie said quietly. Both children stared at her, more innocent and vulnerable than they'd looked in years, which was some consolation. Barnett's desertion had made them children again.

"I don't know," she said. The phone rang. Sophie and William looked at her anxiously. Jay DiGregorio appeared in the doorway. She picked up the bedside cordless.

"Hello?" she said without the slightest expectation that it would be Barnett, calling to explain everything.

"Lily, it's Mother. I'm at the hospital."

Thirteen

Lily sat up abruptly, convinced she was about to be run over. But it was only the alarm clock signaling six-thirty A.M. with the harsh, rhythmic cawing of a reversing truck. She groped for the clock on the coffee table in her parents' living room at 124 West Sixty-seventh Street, wondering, as she did most mornings, if the clockmaker had considered a range of sounds before settling on the hacking bark of a truck backing up. She finally found the clock and smacked the *Off* button. After six weeks she still awoke each weekday convinced that she was being run over or attacked or dive-bombed or blown up. It was just one of many things about her new life in her parents' new apartment that she hadn't gotten used to, having to start each day with the conviction that she was about to be dead.

She rolled herself out of the crevasse at the center of the sofabed's ancient mattress. White morning light shone through the large, curtainless windows, illuminating a room so crammed with furniture, it still startled her each morning, as if gremlins had set up a consignment shop while she slept. Peggy had thrown nothing out, given nothing away. Instead, she'd shoehorned seven large prewar-sized rooms of furniture into four small postwar rectangles. Since moving in with her parents that August, Lily had tried many times to talk her mother into divesting at least a chair or end table, but

Peggy always had a very specific justification for holding on to everything. *Your aunt Marion gave me that when she sold the place in Bayside. Your father's parents bought that for their apartment in Forest Hills, I couldn't think of giving it away, ugly as it is.* There's barely room enough for the people in this place, Lily would say. *Well, we'll just have to cut back. Which one of us are we going to give away?*

Peggy's pack-rattiness had only worsened with Monroe's heart attack in the spring. She seemed desperate to hold on to the past. Monroe had made what the doctors called a full recovery, but his spirit was badly damaged. The only thing that interested him anymore was his pill-taking regimen. If Peggy was even a half-minute late with a pill, he'd begin calling for her in a voice so feeble, it wouldn't have made it beyond the den in their old apartment; at 124 West Sixty-seventh Street, of course, Monroe's gargling whispers could be heard perfectly well in each of the apartment's wallboarded rooms, and probably in the neighbors' apartments as well. *There's nothing wrong with Monroe that a ten percent rise in the NASDAQ won't cure,* Peggy would say wistfully. But Lily doubted even a new bull market would reenergize him.

She navigated an obstacle course of chairs and tables and sealed moving cartons and, safely in the small foyer, headed to the kids' bedroom. Life as she'd known it had ended abruptly in late July, when federal marshals appeared at 913 Park Avenue and removed anything that wasn't nailed to the tenth floor. It had struck her, even as it was happening, as a fitting end to the first half of her life. A tasteful auction of the furniture and paintings she'd acquired sixteen years ago on the not-to-be ignored advice of her decorator, a leisurely search for more modest accommodations—this was not to be her lot, and in a way she was grateful. There could be no pretense about her circumstances, not with the way things had turned out, not with everything she owned displayed on the sidewalk, half of New York (well, *her* New York) gaping in delighted horror at the dismantling of her life. Without so humiliatingly public an end, she might have tried to cling, pathetic and desperate, to her old life.

And it wasn't as if she hadn't been warned. Bring us the missing money and we'll leave you alone, the Feds kept telling her, deaf to her insistence that, even if Barnett had taken the money, which he hadn't, she'd be the last person to know its whereabouts. Then why did he flee? they wanted to know. They seemed completely unwilling or unable to accept the notion that a woman her age, in this day and age, could be so completely ignorant of the family's household affairs. Sadly, she shared their incredulity. We'll take everything you have unless you lead us to the money, they warned. My husband mortgaged the co-op without telling me, she'd say. He invested in dot-coms while insisting that he was playing it safe. He lusted after lesbians with giant strap-on dildos but never so much as allowed me on top during our Monday-night "vanilla" sex, as it was referred to, sneeringly, on his favorite Web sites. Do you really think that if he actually stole three million dollars from his partners and clients he'd tell me?

Both of the children's schools had refused them scholarships, since as far as they were concerned, she and Barnett had at least three million dollars stashed away—just ask the government! The building's co-op board had sent a registered letter informing her that she had to vacate the apartment by July 31—not only had she been unable to pay the monthly maintenance, but the bank was about to foreclose. That same day, July 31, Peggy and Monroe had vacated their rambling apartment at 218 West End Avenue for a claustrophobic box on West Sixty-seventh Street, which lent an air of ironic perfection to the moment: She would be moving in with them on the very dawn of their own, albeit voluntary, downsizing.

She entered the children's room. William had dragged a dresser to the center of the room and piled it with art books salvaged from Park Avenue (the Feds, apparently, were not interested in coffee table books, though they had dragged away the coffee table itself), where it formed a privacy screen between his half of the room and Sophie's. She rapped on the door frame.

"It's six-thirty," she said quietly. Their classes at the Booker T. Washington High School began at 7:45 in order to accommodate the swelling enrollment of largely non-English-speaking immigrant children. The children stirred. She went to the kitchen and made a pot of coffee. Abandoning the apartment and the East Side, sharing a small room at their grandparents' place, leaving private school, enrolling at Booker T. Washington—Sophie and William had greeted the prospect of each new adjustment in their lives with strident protests and frequent tears, but once faced with the reality of their new situation, they were remarkably complacent. For her part, Lily had found that, after twenty long years hoisting herself up the greasy pole, the well-lubricated slide down was almost exhilarating. Money brought choices; lack of it eliminated them. There was something undeniably soothing about not having to constantly decide among a galaxy of temptations and opportunities. She recognized, of course, that her parents shielded her from true destitution, but she also exulted in a strange new freedom—emancipation from decision making. Co-op gone? No choice but to move in with Peggy and Monroe. No money for tuition? Easy—enroll the children in the local public school. Oh, how she'd agonized, a decade ago, over which private school to send William to, how she'd labored over those applications and plotted her admissions interview strategy, from what clothes to wear to which names to drop. Such concerns seemed almost quaint now. In August, she'd simply walked over to the Booker T. Washington High School on West Eighty-fourth Street, which she'd attended before transferring to Bronx Science (though it had been called, more reassuringly, the Felix Frankfurter School back then), wearing a white cotton sweater over old khaki slacks, and filled out a one-page form. The Booker T. Washington High School didn't care who the children's grandparents were or what their parents did for a living or if they had any special talents or even if they spoke English.

Sophie and William, both dressed for school, wandered into the window-less dining area as she was finishing her first cup of coffee.

"What would you like for breakfast?" she asked, as she did every morning.

"Eggs Benedict," William said. "With sausages and home fries."

"Funny. Frozen waffle or a bagel?"

"Western omelet," he said, unsmiling. "On second thought, make that an egg-white Western omelet with dry toast."

William's adolescent sullenness, which had been until recently altogether normal if hard to tolerate, had metastasized into overt hostility. There were so many potential causes (father gone, friends gone, money gone), she had difficulty even thinking about how to deal with it. She turned to Sophie.

"Waffle or bagel?"

"Waffle, please."

In place of her old uniform, a dirndl and plaid skirt, Sophie now wore a tight, nipple-defining T-shirt, baggy jeans, and the clunky, square-toed pumps of a Tenth Avenue streetwalker. Dropping the uniform had been the one aspect of their new situation that Sophie relished, that and the steep reduction in homework. But even in her new grunge/hooker ensemble her inherent sweetness shone through.

Lily went to the narrow kitchen and placed two frozen waffles in the toaster, making a mental note to expand her breakfast repertoire to include an egg dish.

"Well, at least we get to eat breakfast together without doing homework," she said cheerfully as Sophie and William ate their waffles. "Last spring you'd both have your noses in a textbook, worried to death about some test."

"Is that supposed to make us feel *good*?" William asked.

"I always thought you both had too much homework," she said.

"Funny, you never mentioned it at the time," William said.

She looked down at her coffee cup, but not before catching a sympathetic— or was it pitying?—glance from Sophie.

"I told you back in August, if you're not happy at Felix . . . at Booker T. Washington, we can look into applying to private schools for the January term. By then—"

"Yeah, right," William said. "By then Daddy will be back and we'll be rich again."

"By then," she said evenly, "the government will have found the missing money and we'll be able to apply for a scholarship. I don't think we should pin our hopes on . . . on recovering . . . everything."

"I don't mind school," Sophie said quietly. "I don't feel so, like, you know . . ." She swirled a piece of waffle in a puddle of syrup and slurped it down.

"So pressured?" Lily asked hopefully.

Sophie nodded. "And the kids aren't bad. I mean, it's weird, feeling different all the time. But I kind of got used to that in the last six months. Now I'm different because of who I am and not what my father did."

Lily started to say something but felt overcome by relief and admiration.

"You're a girl, it's different," William said.

"It *so* isn't different," Sophie said.

"It *so* is, you just don't get it."

"How is it different?" Lily asked.

"Girls don't get beat up," he said.

"Oh." Though it was only 6:45, and having awakened to the conviction that she was being crushed by a reversing truck, she observed that the day was, amazingly, sliding even further downhill. "Do you get beat up?" she asked William, who shrugged. "Well, do you?"

"Not really."

"Not really? William, either you are getting beat up or you're not."

"Some of the guys say things."

"What kinds of things?"

"Stuff."

"What kind of stuff?"

"About being rich and stuck up."

It was almost laughable—they'd been evicted from Park Avenue for being broke, and now William was tormented for being a rich kid. True, an air of hygienic preppiness clung to him despite the new environment. He had a pampered look, with Barnett's smooth, almost opalescent complexion, and also his father's blue eyes, so pale they seemed too sensitive for any light stronger than a table lamp in a men's club.

"What do you do when they tease you?" she asked.

"Ignore them."

"Good," she said, but she worried that she should be encouraging some other behavior: Challenge them, rebut them, complain to the principal.

What would Barnett have advised? she briefly wondered before reminding herself that he'd fled the country rather than face his accusers. She recalled an incident five years ago—or was it fifty?—when several people at a catered dinner they'd thrown had come down with food poisoning. While she'd made anguished phone calls of apology to the afflicted guests, Barnett retained high-profile lawyers to sue the caterers, pursuing the case beyond all rational hope of financial recompense. At the time, she'd thought him principled, even noble. But all he'd done, really, was hire proxies to get even and, more important, to clear his name, each subpoena and deposition calling attention to his own blamelessness. And the caters, now defunct, had been just starting out; the Grantham dinner party was their big break.

"Have they . . . have they actually fought with you?"

"Not yet." The waffle gone, he swirled the remaining syrup with his fork.

"Do you think they will?"

He stood up abruptly. "Look, it's okay, okay? There's nothing you can do about it, so let's just pretend I never brought it up. You're good at pretending, right? We all are, right?" He left them at the table.

She looked at Sophie, who shrugged. Lily was about to ask if she knew anything about William's troubles at school, and perhaps if she knew what he meant by being good at pretending, when she saw Peggy padding across the living room toward them.

"Some racket," she said, cinching the belt of her floor-length bathrobe around her narrow waist. Her honey-blond hair swept back from her face and held in place by a headband, wearing open-toed slippers with one-inch heels, she exuded a hard-edged, Joan Crawford glamour. She walked past them to the kitchen, poured a cup of black coffee, and joined them at the table.

"I just can't get used to not having the *Times* at breakfast," she said, as if in response to a question. "I called twice already to complain. At 218 West End we always had the paper at six o'clock sharp, rain or shine. I used to hear it hit the floor outside our apartment as I was walking to the kitchen. You could set your watch by it. Now it's seven o'clock, seven-thirty, last week it was eight—can you believe it? It's old news by the time we get to read it."

Lily nodded, having endured a version of this rant every morning for six weeks.

"I have a bridge game at noon," Peggy said. "I'm meeting Belle Kanter for dinner at six, then a concert with Arlette Wander at Alice Tully. Belle couldn't get a ticket, she always leaves things to the last minute. Do you think you could watch your father for me?"

Lily sighed. Peggy was not only more glamorous than her but busier.

"Actually, I have to be somewhere today."

"No kidding."

"I want to talk to Barnett's partner about his situation."

"His situation?" Since Barnett fled, Peggy rarely uttered his name, and when one of the children or Lily referred to him, she squinted and pursed her lips as if he were some notorious criminal or fugitive Nazi.

"He isn't returning my phone calls. I'm getting no information from the Feds. I need to *do* something. He won't refuse to see me if I show up."

"No? Maybe it's better to put this behind you."

"Put it— Mother, we're broke, I'm sleeping in a pullout sofa in your living room, my husband is an international fugitive from justice. I need to find that money so I . . ." She sipped coffee.

"Finish."

Lily finished silently. She needed to find that money to reclaim their old life. But was that possible? Was that even desirable? Her needs had telescoped radically in recent months: her own bedroom, decent schools for her children, enough money to put food on the table without turning to Peggy every time she went shopping.

"Can't you just turn Chapter 11 and start over with a clean slate?"

"He didn't steal that money, Mother. I wish you'd accept that."

"Of course he didn't. He abandoned his wife and children in their hour of need, but God forbid he should be a thief."

She'd awakened convinced she was being crushed by a truck, had learned that her son was being threatened at school, and now her mother was urging her to declare bankruptcy. Lily craned her neck to see the clock over the kitchen stove. Not even 6:55 A.M.

"Nanny can watch Daddy while I'm out," Lily said.

"Your father won't like that."

"I'll be here most of the time."

Nanny had refused to be fired. "I'll be deported, I can't go back, I simply can't," she'd whined, as if England were Afghanistan and she'd be forced to wear a burkah the rest of her days. "Keep me on part time at least, I'll live with my sister up in Washington Heights. I'll take half my old pay, just don't sack me altogether."

"It's hard to believe we have a nanny at our age," Peggy said.

"Think of her as a housekeeper with a British accent," Lily said.

"We don't need a housekeeper. I can vacuum the entire apartment without changing outlets. If I thought I needed help, I'd have kept my girl when we moved."

Her "girl" was a sixty-eight-year-old Ecuadorian.

"I just wish she wouldn't wear that white uniform. Your father thinks she's a nurse, which makes him anxious. And those white shoes. And that accent."

"She's British."

Peggy harrumphed. "She's lived here since VE Day. You'd think she'd drop it after all this time."

"It's an accent, not a hairstyle."

"You're funny. She looks down her nose at me every time I ask her to do something. Who does she think she is, Julia Andrews looking after the little princes?"

"It's *Julie* Andrews, but I think you mean Mary Poppins."

"That's what I said."

"No, you said— Forget it, I have to check on the children . . ." *Before I kill myself or you.*

"She's always underfoot, follows me around the apartment with those white shoes that squeak like mice on the parquet—not that there's a whole lot of privacy here even when she's not around. Some days I think I'll jump out the window, if only I could figure out how to open the damn things."

Fourteen

Guy wanted to be present when the wall came down. He'd arranged his entire week's schedule around the event, which Victor Ozeri, the contractor, had assured him would take place promptly at nine o'clock on Tuesday.

Of course, even at this very early stage of the renovation, he had learned that "promptly" was an astonishingly elastic concept for Victor Ozeri. Phase I of the renovation, which involved ripping out and carting away bathroom fixtures, kitchen cabinets, appliances, crown moldings, base moldings, floorboards, floor tiles, linoleum, ceiling fixtures, and radiator covers, had gotten off to a bad start when the Dumpsters hadn't arrived on schedule. Unfortunately, by the time Ozeri had shown up at ten, his crew of small but improbably strong Peruvian men had already begun moving things down to the street. Rather than haul it back up, they'd left what was essentially the entire Gimmel kitchen on the sidewalk—cabinets, appliances, countertops, hunks of black and white linoleum—drawing a five-hundred-dollar fine from New York City's Sanitation Department. That fine had sparked their first disagreement, with Ozeri claiming that Guy and Rosemary were contractually obligated to pay all ancillary expenses, Guy arguing, reasonably, that since Ozeri had forgotten to order the Dumpsters, the fine was his responsibility. "I can't work this way," Ozeri had said in a histrionic whine that had become all too familiar. "If this is how it's going to be."

Guy had paid the fine rather than risk losing the most sought-after contractor in Manhattan, reminding himself that five hundred dollars was a pittance compared to the renovation's total cost of $250,000. But after that small defeat he saw his influence with Ozeri melt away as new skirmishes were fought and lost. Ozeri was late for every appointment, at first by fifteen minutes, then by a half hour, and then, just two weeks into the project, by an hour or more. He never apologized, and Guy kept his mouth shut. He'd had to beg Ozeri to take the job, even after agreeing to a ten percent up-front "signing bonus." A mere six weeks into the project and they were, somehow, nine weeks behind schedule.

Guy had spent an uncharacteristically relaxing morning in their old apartment with Rosemary and the twins before heading over to 218 West End Avenue. Lucinda Wells had sold their apartment quickly and had negotiated for them to remain in it for two months, by which time the renovation of the new place was supposed to have been sufficiently advanced to allow them to move in. With no end in sight, he'd begun looking for temporary quarters.

He arrived at the building at 8:45. Out front, two Dumpsters brimmed with the wreckage of apartment 6D. Upstairs, four workmen were engaged in ripping out the remaining vestiges of the Gimmels.

"When do you think you'll get to the living-room wall?" he asked the man in the kitchen, who was hacking away with a chisel at yet another layer of linoleum on the kitchen floor. A few more layers and Guy had no doubt they'd find fossils and arrowheads.

"When Mr. Victor get here," the man said.

"He said start without him." A look of horror came over the man. "He told me explicitly that he wouldn't have to be here."

"Last job, we take down the wrong wall," the man said. "I think the whole building will fall on top of my head."

"You took down a bearing wall?"

The concept of bearing walls had become central to Guy's life. As their architect had explained whenever Guy made a suggestion for reconfiguring the apartment, bearing walls held up a building and couldn't be taken down or weakened in any way, no matter how inconveniently located they happened to be. Inevitably they were located between two spaces that Guy wanted to combine.

"This time we wait for Mr. Victor." The workman resumed chipping at the floor.

Guy went to the living room and called Ozeri, cell phone to cell phone.

"Your men won't start without you."

"Bullshit, tell them I said they could start."

"Apparently they took down the wrong wall on the last job."

"They told you that?"

"Funny, you never suggested we call those owners for a reference."

"Okay, listen, I'll be right over."

Right over could be anywhere from ten minutes to a week.

"I can't stay long."

"You don't have to be there."

"I want to."

"Whatever floats your boat. Listen, have the markets opened?"

"It's only nine o'clock."

"Right. How's Positano going to do today? You think it's a bargain at nine and change?"

His beloved company had been marked down to the price of a movie ticket. Any lower and he'd be hearing from Goldman Sachs about selling shares to pay down the loan he'd taken for the apartment.

"I can't talk about the company's stock price. And how would I know what it's going to do?"

"Insiders always know before the rest of us," Ozeri said, a touch irritably. "Thank God we didn't do that deal I suggested, huh?"

The deal had involved granting him Positano stock options instead of his contractor's fee. People seemed to think a company's CEO could dole out shares of stock like Rockefeller handing dimes to children. If Positano hadn't tanked, he wouldn't have been surprised if his dry cleaner had asked for stock in lieu of cash. No one seemed to understand that ownership was a finite thing, that each newly issued share diminished the value of the originals. No wonder the market was going nowhere.

He got off the line and corralled the three workmen in the living room.

"This is the wall that's coming down," he said, giving it a firm rap with his right fist. The wall felt dauntingly solid.

"We wait for Mr. Victor," said the man from the kitchen.

"Victor said start."

The three men exchanged glances that Guy took to mean, *This tall gringo with too much money thinks everyone works for him.*

"We have other work now," said the kitchen man.

Guy flipped open his cell and pressed *Redial.*

"Tell your men to start," Guy said when Ozeri answered. He handed the phone to the kitchen man. A conversation ensued in Spanish.

"Okay, we start," the workman said, handing Guy the phone.

The men left the room and returned moments later with two menacingly large axes and a sledgehammer. After some discussion in Spanish among them, they gathered at the center of the wall.

"Mr. Gorbachev, tear down this wall," Guy said.

"*Qué?*" asked one of the workmen.

The kitchen man, apparently the foreman, gestured for Guy to step back. All three put on plastic goggles. The foreman, looking as if he were about to execute an innocent man, raised the sledgehammer above his shoulders.

"Wait!" The men turned to Guy, the foreman with a gratified I-told-you-so expression. "I'd like to take the first swing."

The sledgehammer felt ridiculously heavy, and when he hoisted it overhead, it took all his strength to keep the tool from continuing its trajectory and crashing into his lower back. He put everything he had into the first swing, feeling not only the heft of the sledgehammer but the full symbolic weight of what he was doing. He was staking his claim to this space, felling the first tree, as it were, to build his cabin.

The head of the sledgehammer all but bounced off the wall, as if repelled by it. Guy staggered back. When he regained his footing he saw, with dismay, that his colossal effort had resulted in an unimpressive dent in the wall—the sort of damage a toddler might inflict with an errant throw of a toy fire engine.

"Let's try that again," he said with a collegial smile for the workmen. This time his effort sent several deep cracks zigzagging along the wall, and a gratifyingly large chunk of plaster fell to the floor.

All three workmen began to clap. One of them patted him on the back. He heard what sounded like congratulatory expressions in Spanish. But as he handed the sledgehammer back to the foreman, he suspected they were mocking him, or at least patronizing him, and when the foreman, a good head shorter and at least fifty pounds lighter than Guy, practically broke through to the next room with his first whack, his suspicion was more or less confirmed.

His cell phone chirped *Für Elise* between the third and fourth blows.

"Guy here."

"It's Henry."

"Can I call you back in a—"

"I have news."

Inevitably bad. A narrow shaft of light glinted through from the next room, but the transcendent moment was lost.

"What is it?"

"I just hung up with an inspector at the SEC. There's an investigation—"

"What?"

"Just before the MyJob announcement there was a spike in price on unusually heavy trading volume. They want to know why."

"Nice to know the government has nothing better to do than keep an eye on Positano Software."

"This stuff is easy to track. A computer spits out a variance report at the end of every trading day. Any security that doesn't behave is called to the attention of a—"

"I understand. We looked into it ourselves. No one at Positano was involved."

It was all so ludicrous, given that the stock's price, which had spiked in the trading days leading up to the announcement of the MyJob contract, had wilted within a few weeks, and then given back even more. There had been no corresponding spike in volume as the stock slid in value, so whoever had tried to take advantage of inside information—assuming such a person existed—had lost his or her shirt along with everyone else who owned Positano. Vice was its own punishment.

"The SEC wants to know everyone involved in pitching the MyJob account."

"Half those people don't even work for us anymore."

The MyJob contract had been a hollow victory. The company had decided to use Positano's solution at the very moment its business was peaking. They'd cut back their commitment dramatically just weeks after the contact was announced. Positano had laid off one-fifth of its workforce.

The workmen had managed to squeeze a hacksaw through the small opening in the wall.

"Doesn't matter to the Feds. We'll have to talk to everyone who was involved, find out who may have told someone who told someone. There were four full trading days between when MyJob told us verbally we had the contract and when we announced it publicly. That's when the stock spiked, and that's the period the SEC is looking into."

The men had cut out a near-perfect square of plaster. One of them pulled it from the wall and dropped it into a waiting wheelbarrow. As Henry discussed strategy for dealing with the investigation, Guy imagined laboring alongside the Peruvian workmen, prying blocks of plaster from the wall, transporting them down to the street, repeating the process until the wall was gone. Nothing at Positano had been as satisfying lately as personally removing the wall, piece by piece, would be. He'd step back, physically spent but mentally charged, and survey his creation: space. Raw, problem-free, non-SEC-regulated space. An invigorating void that asked nothing of him. Every decision in recent weeks involved cutting something: ad spending, R&D budgets, head count. How much can we cut without inducing coma? was the prevailing theme. He lived in triage hell. Even his sex life had withered in lockstep with Positano's market cap.

The foreman was having difficulty prying a large block of plaster from the wall. Guy made excuses to Henry and hung up. He grabbed one side of the block and pulled along with the foreman. When the block was almost free the foreman said, "I got it."

"No, I'll do it." Guy positioned himself at the center of the block, flexed his legs like a mighty Russian weightlifter, gripped the bottom edge, and lifted. Perhaps he'd take the day off and help out at the apartment, let Henry—

A spasm of hot pain sizzled from deep inside his left butt cheek down through his left leg and almost to his ankle. Instinctively he released the plaster, which fell to the floor, barely missing his feet, and smashed into several smaller chunks.

He felt as if someone had shoved a hot poker into his ass and twisted it all the way down through his leg.

"Chew okay?" the foreman asked.

Guy had heard that burning pain in the left arm meant heart attack. What about the left leg? He managed to nod while preparing for imminent death. Was there time to call Rosemary and apologize for his recent inattention? Perhaps the twins could hear his voice one last time. A call to Henry Delano, firing him.

"*Conjon,* the floor," the foreman said, pointing to a small crater in the parquet. "Chew tell Mr. Victor this is not us who fuck up your floor."

Taking the tiniest bit of comfort in the fact that he wasn't dead, Guy promised to do just that, then limped slowly to the front door, his left leg completely stiff and burning painfully from the inside. He heard a chorus of Spanish whispers behind him.

Manny Zelma, one of Barnett's partners, greeted Lily with forced warmth in the small but tasteful reception area of Grantham, Wiley & Zelma on the sixteenth floor of 11 William Street.

"Lily, what a surprise," he said.

"You haven't returned any of my calls," she said, ignoring his outstretched hand.

Zelma's smile soured. He was about Barnett's age, mid-forties, but a foot shorter. His head was precariously large for so small a frame, but his features were bunched tightly in one small area about halfway down, leaving large, uninterrupted planes of smooth, pink skin. Barnett had called him The Mole, a reference to the bunched features as well as the smooth, pink skin, which appeared never to have seen sunlight. And perhaps it hadn't. Manny was the brains of the firm, the partner who had developed the financial models the rest of them used to buy and sell stocks. While Barnett had entertained clients at restaurants and golf courses, Manny tapped away at his computer in his corner office, pausing only to chirp instructions to a crew of similarly pale, nervous grinds. While Lily sipped white wine at gala benefits in hotel ballrooms, always remembering to smile for the ever-present *New York Times* photographer, right foot angled outward, in front of the left, Manny's wife, Cynthia, cooked dinner for her four sons in Short Hills, New Jersey, keeping a plate warm for her husband, who rarely arrived in time to dine with them. Lily saw Cynthia and Manny once a year, at the firm's

Christmas party, where they regarded her, she felt, as a benign alien from another planet—precisely the way she had always regarded them.

"I wasn't aware that you had—"

"Cut the bullshit, Manny," she said, surprising both of them. "I left three voice messages."

He hiked up his khaki pants, purchased, perhaps, at Gap Kids, and cleared his throat. Manny was so skinny his body seemed not quite up to the task of holding aloft his outsized head.

"My hands are tied, Lily. I'm not free to discuss this . . . situation with you."

"Can we speak somewhere private?" she asked, nodding at the receptionist, who glanced away.

"I'm afraid there's someone in my office right now," Manny said. Behind him, the firm's glass-walled boardroom sat patently empty.

"I need to clear Barnett of these charges, since he obviously isn't doing anything to help himself."

"I would have thought helping Barnett would be the last thing on your agenda."

"Don't be stupid. I need to help myself and my children. Once I find out who took that money, I'll have access to his partnership interest and then—"

"Barnett took it. There's no doubt in anyone's mind."

"We don't have a cent, Manny. If Barnett took the money, where is it?"

"Wherever he is."

"No, I don't believe that."

"Lily, the man abandoned you and the kids. Next to that, stealing a few million dollars from his partners is hardly surprising."

How could she explain to him that, for Barnett, abandoning his family was more in character than stealing from the firm he'd built from scratch and loved at least as much as his children?

"Anyway," Manny was saying, "what do you think he's living on, wherever he is?"

The question had plagued her since Barnett's disappearance. She couldn't imagine the grandson of Sell 'Em Grantham sleeping in fleabag hotels, much less on the sidewalks of whatever city he'd landed in, as appealing as those images might be.

"You must have records, files, *something* I could look at. I know my husband's signature, I know his handwriting. If you'd just let me see the documents in question—"

"That's impossible, Lily. My hands are tied."

"Stop saying that." He quickly clasped his hands behind his back.

"We've been under a lot of pressure these past months," Manny said. "The markets are flat at best . . . no one's making money . . . I was insulated to some extent, but Barnett couldn't pick up the phone without hearing from an irate pension fund manager or foundation trustee."

"Siphoning money from the firm would only make things worse. Barnett's not *that* stupid." Spineless, cowardly, perverted, but never stupid.

"Sometimes the pressure gets to you. You do things that aren't necessarily in your best interests. And don't forget, our compensation is tied to the markets. You have a very expensive lifestyle—the apartment, the house in Southampton, private school tuition, household help, the—"

"We've cut back," she said, a monumental understatement. Given that they were living rent-free, a welfare check could cover their monthly nut.

"You need to put this behind you."

"Not until I find out who took the three million dollars from the firm. And I can't do that without your help."

"I'm sorry, Lily, my hands—" He shoved them in his pants pockets. "I can't help you."

No one could. It was perhaps the biggest difference between her current life and her former one, bigger than sleeping on a pullout sofa in her parents' living room, bigger than finding herself dropped from the invitation lists of all the charities she'd raised so much money for, bigger than sending her kids to a school whose only entrance requirement was no weapons. It was the sense, the *reality*, of being on her own. In the past people lined up to help her (though their motives, she now realized, were anything but altruistic), but now, with no money and no husband—translation: no way to reciprocate— she was truly, definitively, terrifyingly on her own.

"Good-bye, Lily," Manny said. "And good luck."

The 104 bus was pulling into the Eighty-second Street stop when Peggy decided not to get on. She'd returned to her old neighborhood, which was only fifteen blocks from her new one, to do some shopping. So much had changed in her life—Monroe's deterioration, the new apartment, Lily and the kids moving in—she needed a little continuity. She wanted to see 218 West End Avenue, just a quick once-over before heading back to her new home in a modern high-rise that looked as if one stiff breeze could send it toppling onto Lincoln Center, which they were talking about renovating anyway, even though it seemed like just yesterday it was built. But as she approached the building she caught sight of the doorman, Afternoon José, as everyone called him (there was a Night José, too, and a José who worked the service elevator), and decided she couldn't face him just then. He'd ask her about Monroe and Lily, whom he'd known since she was a baby, and what could she say that wasn't completely depressing? The one had lost his health, the other her husband. And what if he asked why she was back—what would she say? That she wanted to make sure the building was still standing? He'd think she'd lost her mind, like those old women you saw on the streets pushing shopping carts full of rags and empty boxes, telling anyone who'd listen that they'd been abducted by aliens or Elizabeth Taylor. So she turned back toward Broadway, and that's when she saw her kitchen, right there on the curb. Her cabinets, range, refrigerator, dishwasher, even her sink, for God's sake, all piled in a huge Dumpster. She stepped closer and saw jagged slabs of black and white linoleum. Dizzy, she grabbed on to the side of the Dumpster, filthy as it was. Why? Hadn't Lucinda told her the apartment was in mint condition? Triple mint. Why pay two-point-two for an apartment and then just throw it all— Wait, that sink, and that medicine cabinet . . . the second bathroom, also discarded. She glanced around. What if someone in the building recognized this cast-off rubbish as her precious kitchen and bathroom, which she'd kept immaculate—*triple mint*—for thirty-nine years? Frieda Brand in 12B, who'd renovated a perfectly nice kitchen two years ago and couldn't stop crowing about how happy she was, you'd think she'd traded in her *ferkrimpt* husband for a new model, please God don't let her see this.

"Get away from here!" she shouted at a homeless man who had begun to poke through her kitchen. "I said get away from here!"

Rheumy eyes considered her from behind a greasy curtain of bangs.

"Help yourself," he said finally, slamming shut a cabinet door. She half expected to hear her good china rattle. "It's all crap, anyway." He trundled off toward Broadway.

She glanced back at the Dumpster. It was like standing over an open casket—horrifying, but you couldn't quite turn away. From the corner of her eye she spied someone emerging from 218 and decided she wouldn't wait around to be pitied. She walked a few yards toward Broadway, stepped off the curb, and flagged a passing taxi.

Fifteen

"Rosemary, this is the one! This is definitely it."

Lloyd gestured to the most unusual—make that hideous—sink in the Il Bagno showroom. A rustic bowl made of what appeared to be hardened porridge sat atop a slab of pebble-studded concrete. The spigot was a sawed-off pipe, the faucets lumps of jagged rock.

"It looks like a goat trough," Rosemary said. "I mean, what's the matching toilet, a slop pail?"

"It's perfect for a small powder room," he said.

"In Kabul, maybe." She found the price tag. "Lloyd, this is . . ." She checked again to make sure she hadn't transposed a decimal point. "This is twenty-six hundred dollars."

He frowned. "You invited me along for my opinion."

A mistake, perhaps, but Il Bagno was located near Atherton's, so a lunchtime consultation with Lloyd had seemed a good idea. His taste was usually impeccable, though apparently it didn't extend to bathroom fixtures.

"Let's take another look at the sink Donald Acheson recommended."

Acheson was the architect she and Guy had retained. His plans specified every detail, down to switch plates, but she and Guy wanted to bless every selection.

Lloyd clutched the rim of the goat trough. "I'm not leaving until you buy this."

She took his arm and pulled him across the showroom to the elegant pedestal sink Acheson has specified.

"What's this model called, *The Scarsdale*?"

"Actually, it's part of the Parthenon Collection, and it's beautiful," she said. "I could be very happy with this in the powder room. Just *having* a powder room will make me very happy."

"*The Parthenon*. You've lost your edge, Rosemary. It's those twins, sucking the taste right out of you. Have you thought of adoption? You know, there are some very nice young couples looking for a set of healthy boys."

"Has Atherton's started a Contemporary Babies department since I've been gone?"

"It's a thought."

"Anyway, this is just four hundred dollars. We're already three weeks late and way overbudget."

Lloyd dismissed her concerns with a shrug. "It's an investment, Rosemary."

"I'm not investing twenty-six hundred dollars in something that looks like it earned an S for 'satisfactory' in first-grade art class."

"It's a classic, or will be. And speaking of investments . . ."

"Were we?"

"What's with Positano's stock?"

"Software stocks have been out of favor for a long time. Do you like polished or unpolished brass with this sink?"

"Polished, but I still hate it. I should have listened to my broker."

"You don't need a broker to buy 'friends and family' shares, you— Lloyd, you didn't."

"I did. After we had lunch at your apartment. You implied that the company was on the verge of turning around."

"It doesn't need to *turn around*. But I did mention that there was a big contract in the works. Is *that* why you bought more?"

Lloyd closed his eyes and nodded. "I simply couldn't resist."

I simply couldn't resist. Precisely the phrase he used whenever he blew a month's salary on a piece of vintage Daum glass.

"I shouldn't have said anything that day."

"Please, I bought a thousand shares. No one goes to jail for buying a thou-

sand shares of anything, and besides, I *lost* money. They're going to send me
to jail for *losing* money?"

"You bought a thousand shares?" The stock had been selling at $21
around then. Twenty-one thousand dollars was a huge sum for someone on
an appraiser's salary, not to mention that the stock had since fallen to nine.

"It could have been worse."

"What do you mean?"

He shook his head. "Let's cruise the tiles."

"Lloyd."

"I happened to mention the . . . opportunity to a few coworkers."

"What?"

"Please don't get all moralistic on me, Rosemary. You get that lurid Pre-
Raphaelite coloring on your cheeks and forehead. *Not* becoming. Besides,
this kind of thing goes on all the time."

"This kind of thing? You mean insider trading?"

"If you must call it that. People like you and me, we spend our days—or
you *did*, before the arrival of what's-his-name and what's-his-face—we
spend our days around people who are always having inside information
whispered in their ears. That's how you make it these days."

"That's so cynical."

"That's so the truth. But no one whispers anything in our ears, other than
how much to bid on their behalf for some *objet* they wouldn't know from a
Pottery Barn tchotchke. So when you mentioned that Positano was about to
be awarded a big contract, I had to act."

"And you had to share your good fortune with . . . how many people,
Lloyd?"

"A few."

She glared at him until he fessed up.

"Arthur in Decorative Arts. Susannah in Old Masters. Fred in Greek and
Roman. The Franklin sisters in Near Eastern. Celia."

"From the cafeteria?"

"Her arthritis is getting so bad, Rosemary. How much longer can she
stand there making tuna sandwiches? A small windfall would have liberated
her from hell."

"Oh, Lloyd."

"I've been eating at my desk every day for a month to avoid facing her.

And the saddest thing is, right after we all bought, the stock started climbing. I looked like some kind of hero."

"Well, of course it climbed—half the art world was buying. God only knows how many people your friends told to buy. I'm surprised the SEC hasn't called you."

"But then it fell." He closed his eyes and lips, shaking his head slowly, as if remembering a departed friend.

"Did anyone in the Lloyd Lowell Investment Club happen to sell?"

His eyes opened wide.

"Should we?" He grabbed her arm. *"Tell me."*

"I don't know anything, and if I did I certainly wouldn't tell *you*, Lloyd. This isn't gossip about some widow with late-stage cancer and a houseful of old masters. This is about the law."

"So I shouldn't sell."

She was tempted to tell him to sell just to be done with it, but then, what if the stock went up? Sometimes it was hard to resist the thought that life had been much simpler when they'd been poorer.

"I don't know how *I'm* going to come back to Atherton's, now that half the people I work with have lost money on Guy's company."

"It's me they blame. You're the wealthy wife."

"Oh, great, that makes me feel so much better."

"Any idea when you're coming back? It's been *forever* . . ."

"Soon," she said. "I was hoping to wait until the renovation's finished."

"That could be five years from now."

"*So* glad I invited you along."

"Face it, Rosemary, it takes longer to gut-renovate a New York apartment than it took to build the Panama Canal."

"We'll be done by the end of the year."

"What year? Don't answer. Just promise you won't keep me hanging and then tell me you can't bear to leave the twins with a nanny."

"I promise."

"Good, now let's look at tiles."

Lily entered the Broadway Nut Shoppe and, finding it empty, headed to the back room. Larry was hunched over his desk in the tiny, windowless office.

She felt briefly disoriented: Was this Larry or his father—both tall, lean, narrow-shouldered men with sandy hair invariably in need of a trim, both partial to white or blue oxford shirts? She hadn't been back to the Shoppe since moving in with her folks six weeks earlier. Too much going on to add another complication. But that morning a visit to Larry had suddenly struck her as the opposite of complicated, a return to a familiar, simpler place.

"Hello," she said from the door.

"I'll be right with you," he said without turning around.

"Take your time. Remember when we screwed on the floor in the living room, how when we were done we noticed the boy across the street staring at us through binoculars?" He turned around so fast she caught him mid-flush. "Remember?"

"You walked over to the window and pressed your breasts against the glass."

"I think the boy fainted."

"I think he died. Happy."

"The youngest documented case of cardiac arrest."

"You were a bad girl."

"And then I became a good girl," she said with unintended wistfulness.

He just stared at her and she found herself tempted to say something stupid and embarrassing like "And now I want to be bad again." She resisted, but he must have sensed what was on her mind, for he stood up, placed his hands on her shoulders, and kissed her lips.

The phrase *melted in his arms* sprung to mind, less because she felt suddenly weak with desire and relief and perhaps even happiness, all of which happened to be true, than because she felt her life, her *old* life, melting away like grime from an old pan. The moment was so fraught with import, at least for her, that she had to force herself to concentrate on the physical. His lips on hers. His hands squeezing her arms. The press of his hips, the smell of him, musk and chocolate, distantly familiar.

She heard the front door squeak open and bang shut.

"I have to go," she said.

"Where?"

He'd always asked questions for which anyone else could plainly see there were no answers, or no answers required.

"I have errands."

"Can't they wait? I haven't seen you in months, and now you swoop in here, stir things up, and then fly away."

He kissed her again. This time she found herself trying to recall when she and Barnett had last kissed, really kissed, standing up. Standing-up kisses were so much more erotic than in-bed kisses, which she suspected Barnett had always viewed as a series of small down payments on fucking. Standing-up kisses were their own justification.

She parted her lips just enough to allow his tongue to slip between them. Why couldn't she just lose herself in the moment? *Focus.*

"Is there anybody here?" came an old woman's voice from the front.

"Yes!" He was breathing heavily. "I'll be right there."

She followed him to the store, where a very short old woman with wispy white hair was already haranguing him in a scratchy, high-pitched voice.

"I just wanted to know when you got these nuts in. The last batch I got from you were so stale I almost broke a tooth, so I . . . oh!"

Lily's presence shut her up her momentarily. She glanced back and forth between Lily and Larry, as if sizing up a conspiracy of stale-nut vendors.

"The nuts arrive fresh each week, Mrs. Dickson."

"So you say."

Lily edged around her and headed for the door, marveling that even owners of candy stores had to take shit from customers. Was there no shit-free profession?

"Wait," Larry said.

"I'll . . ." She couldn't quite finish: *I'll call? I'll stop by? I'll go get my diaphragm and be right back?* So she merely waved with her back turned and left.

Peggy returned home to find Nanny (did she have an actual name, or had *Nanny* been inscribed on her birth certificate in response to the patently obsequious and servile nature she'd exhibited right there in the delivery room?) perched on the living-room sofa watching television. She sat forward, back rigid, legs crossed at the ankles, as if she weren't merely watching a soap opera but serving tea to a visiting delegation of royals.

Peggy put down her bags in the hallway and went directly to the master bedroom, where she found Monroe sleeping on top of the bedcovers. Since returning from the hospital, he slept like a hibernating bear. When she managed to get him into the shower (once or twice a week was all she had the energy for), she was surprised he hadn't grown a coat of winter fur.

"Did Mr. Gimmel have lunch?" she asked Nanny once she'd put away her shopping.

She turned away from the television just long enough to chirp, "He didn't say he was hungry."

"It's three o'clock. I think you might have assumed he was hungry for lunch at some point." She often heard an uncharacteristic formality in her voice when speaking to Nanny; next thing she knew, she'd be smoking fags and knocking up her husband to serve him bangers and mash, whatever the hell that was.

"Preparing meals for Mr. Gimmel is not part of my job responsibility."

"Preparing . . . responsibility . . ." Peggy grabbed the remote and flicked off the television. "What exactly *are* your *job responsibilities*?"

"Looking after the children . . ."

"The *children* are fourteen and fifteen, and they're in school all day."

". . . preparing their meals, doing their laundry."

"How about housework?"

"I was getting to that. Tidying their rooms." She squeezed out a tight smile. "I mean, *room*."

"I think you could find time to pitch in and help out with . . . with everything. I have my hands full taking care of Mr. Gimmel, and now with three other people in the apartment . . ."

"I watched him today."

"You . . . you watched television while he slept."

"I don't think you fully understand the proper role of a professional nanny. Perhaps you and Mrs. Grantham should have a talk." This last was delivered with a patronizing gentleness that made Peggy want to pummel her pink head with the marble obelisk Lily had bought on one of her European trips, an object whose purpose, until now, Peggy had never quite grasped.

"Oh, we'll have a talk all right," she said, and left the room. Unfortunately, the new apartment, barely adequate for a close-knit family of dwarves, was much too small to comfortably contain two full-sized people who loathed each other. She heard the television spring back to life the moment she left the living room, and even from the bedroom, with the hollow plywood door closed, she could hear the hushed, soap-operatic babble. She collapsed onto the bed, hoping to awaken Monroe—he'd listen to her complaint, even if he wouldn't respond. But he continued to hibernate despite her commotion, a circle of glistening dribble pooling on the pillow near his mouth.

Sixteen

Guy raised a sliver of foie gras–filled ravioli from its bath of silky beef consommé to his mouth. He tasted and felt nothing, as if his mouth were novocained. And this was no ordinary foie gras, if there was such a thing as ordinary foie gras. This was foie gras from Restaurant Daniel, and it cost twenty-eight dollars for a trio of three ravioli the size of postage stamps. He took another bite. Still nothing.

It wasn't his taste buds. If only it were that simple. It was the company—not *his* company, though the state of Positano Software was worrying enough to numb all five senses. It was the company at the table, five men, including himself, Positano's largest shareholders and most influential directors. These were the venture capitalists who had invested in Positano when it was still a private company. The dinner was a quarterly ritual.

And it wasn't that he didn't like the company. The four men—Dan Radakovic of Sycamore Partners, Marc Gaiman of Sunrise Investments, Alan Norbertson of Greystone Ventures, and Pete Tallyrand of Apex Unlimited—were intelligent, perhaps brilliant. *Visionary* was the sobriquet most often applied to them in fawning articles, and all articles about them, even post-bubble, tended to fawn. Only the Colombian cocaine trade generated a higher return than these men had delivered to investors over the past decade. Their success was the stuff of investors' most lubricious dreams, obscene returns that could be calculated only in exponents: a thousand percent in two years, fifteen thousand percent in four years, 10^4 percent in seven years. A mere (choose any small denomination) invested with (pick any one of their firms) back in (insert any year prior to 1990) would today be worth more than the GNP of (name any smallish African country)—this was the gist of most articles written about these men. When Guy had approached them five years back, he'd been genuinely impressed by the incisiveness of the questions they'd asked about Positano's product and business model. They had zeroed in with laser acuity on both the company's shortcomings (a single product with only a handful of installations) and its opportunities (first-mover advantage in what everyone agreed was a huge fucking market). Just having them as financial backers had given him a huge credibility boost; more important, they'd introduced him to their other portfolio companies, several of which had become Positano's earliest customers. Synergy, it was called at the time, when the fortunes of these businesses were on the rise and one plus one equaled at least three. (Today, with returns dwindling to nothing, and *survivability* the watchword of the day, what had once been labeled synergy was now referred to, in the financial press and among increasingly pesky regulators, as double dealing.) On the IPO road show, Guy noticed that when he got to the slide with the logos of the four venture firms, investors nodded, eyebrows arched, pens began scribbling on the covers of prospectuses. *If it's good enough for Sycamore, Sunrise, Greystone, and Apex, I'm in!*

But these quarterly dinners, which had once had a celebratory, self-congratulatory spirit, had become more and more gloomy. The fact that they were invariably held in one of New York's most expensive restaurants only heightened the gloom, underscoring a "Let them eat cakiness" that Guy found increasingly hard to swallow. Literally. He so despised these events that he couldn't taste the food anymore. His suggestion to hold the meetings over sandwiches and sodas in Positano's boardroom, however, fell on horrified ears.

"We're concerned that you're burning through cash too quickly," said Marc Gaiman of Sunrise. Gaiman was a portly thirty-something with a bushy mustache and beard. He was fond of floppy bow ties and houndstooth check jackets, always with a silk handkerchief flouncing from the breast pocket, and he smoked a pipe whenever he could, and whenever he couldn't, as in Daniel, he held it in his plump, manicured fingers, amusing himself and irritating everyone else with incessant reaming and tamping. Based in Burlingame, in Silicon Valley, he got away with a studiedly Victorian affect because he'd been the nineteenth employee of Cisco, a status worth about fifty million dollars in stock, most of which, following retirement at age thirty, he'd pumped into Sunrise Investments and promptly quintupled. With that kind of wealth you could look like Prince Albert's gay footman and still get your calls returned.

"We've reduced our monthly burn by twenty-four percent," Guy said. Henry Delano had spent most of the day in his office, prepping him with the numbers he'd need to survive dinner.

"Black at CSFB thinks you'll run dry in nine months," Gaiman said.

Ray Black "followed" software stocks for Credit Suisse First Boston. Every fall since the bubble burst, he released a list of companies that he felt would need new capital to survive. The Black Death Watch, it was called, and its predictions had proven uncannily prescient. Positano had been on the most recent list.

"He's maintained his 'buy' recommendation," Guy said. He took a sip of the Côte de Rhône that Gaiman had ordered for the table on the solemn advice of the sommelier.

"Everything is a buy for them," observed Dan Radakovic of Sycamore Partners. "A lot like my wife."

When the dutiful chuckling subsided Guy felt the unamused heat of four pairs of eyes.

"We're still ramping up," he said. "We're in growth mode. We've laid off twenty percent of our workforce, and that was painful. A lot of those people were with us from the beginning. They were counting on their options to pay for their first house, their kids' college tuition, their . . ."

Guy registered the blank expressions of his investors, for whom layoffs were just another financial strategy, like issuing warrants or pre-paying taxes, men for whom human sacrifice would be an acceptable means of achieving positive cash flow.

"If we cut any deeper, we'll hit bone. The fat is gone from Positano Software."

"Twenty percent," Radakovic repeated. He swirled his wineglass before a lit candle and observed the swishing Côte de Rhône with such anxious intensity, he might have been expecting it to explode or, at the very least, reveal tomorrow's NASDAQ close. "Twenty percent. Alan, how many heads did FizzGig chop last month?"

FizzGig was a hot Web design firm. Make that formerly hot. Alan Norbertson's firm had been an early-round investor, along with Radakovic.

"Half," Norbertson said. At fifty he was the elder statesman of the group and an éminence grise of sorts in Silicon Alley, just forty or so blocks south of Daniel, where he was widely considered an expert on the content side of the technology business.

"Half!" Radakovic said, as if this were news to him. No company would axe fifty percent of its workforce unless its financial backers had ordered it. FizzGig (NASDAQ symbol FIZZ) had gone public five years ago at $15, shot up to $36 the day it priced, and peaked at $248 eighteen months later. The last time Guy looked, it was trading at a buck seventy-five, barely enough for a tall drip at Starbucks. "Half is tough, but these are tough times."

For some of us, Guy wanted to say. Radakovic and Norbertson had sold big chunks of their holdings in a secondary six months to the day after FizzGig's IPO, about a million shares each at $165.

"We've looked at every single Positano employee," Guy said.

"How about R&D?" Radakovic asked.

"We told the Street we'd have a new release early next year. We won't make that if we cut anyone in research. Don't ask me to eat our seed corn." Guy cringed, but as no one at the table seemed disturbed by his use of the New Economy cliché, he decided to lay on another one. "We've plucked all the low-hanging fruit. The next big sales won't come as easily without a new release and a crack sales team."

Waiters deposited plates of artfully arranged entrées before them. Guy glanced at his selection, two tiny, gleaming squabs nestled on a pillow of truffled mashed potatoes, their spindly legs thrust defensively in the air, and felt his stomach heave.

"How about administrative support?" asked Norbertson, a forkful of scarlet lamb loin dangling before his parted lips.

"We already laid off half our back-office staff," Guy said. He attempted to pierce one of the squabs with a fork, sending it sliding across his plate as if revivified and splattering droplets of dark truffle sauce on his shirt. "Believe me, if I could cut anyone in administration, I would in a second."

"Guy," said Pete Tallyrand. He raised his nearly empty wineglass, and for a brief, hopeful moment Guy thought he might be proposing a toast to the hardworking, visionary CEO trying to hold together, nay *grow*, his company following a disastrous technology downturn that would have overwhelmed a less talented, persevering executive. Instead he thrust his head back and flung the remaining wine into his gaping maw. "We're worried that you're too close to the situation."

"Sometimes an outside perspective is beneficial in situations like these," said Radakovic.

Guy heard someone utter "forest for the trees" but had already retreated to a panic zone in which once-unimaginable scenarios played across his mind. Were they thinking of replacing him? Holy God, half the tech companies on the NASDAQ were run by professional managers, many of them former management consultants, while their founders, the true visionaries, were shunted aside in satellite facilities and given titles like Chief Technology Officer or the egregious Director of Innovation, rarely invited to key meetings or cc'd on important e-mails. Once in a while he saw these castoffs at investor conferences, on those occasions when they were allowed out in public, skulking on the periphery of meeting rooms and cocktail parties like parents of child stars, trying to look engaged but pitifully aware that, though quite wealthy, they'd been rendered obsolete once they'd weaned their prodigy—never mind the difficult pregnancy, the excruciating labor, the long, lonely nights when it was just them and their offspring, beset by fatigue and insecurity. If Guy ever doubted that it wasn't all about the money, he had only to think of these set-aside founders, latter-day Croesuses all of them, but utterly miserable.

". . . PriceWaterhouseCoopers or Lansdale, Bucks & McKinney. Is that acceptable? Guy?"

"I'm sorry, I . . ."

"Dan was suggesting that we retain a consulting firm," Alan Norbertson said. "We were thinking of either PriceWaterhouseCoopers or Lansdale, Bucks & McKinney. I had good experiences with Deloitte & Touche, too."

"Are you sure they haven't merged?" Guy asked. "Picture the letterhead:

'PriceWaterhouseCoopersLandsdaleBucksMcKinneyDeloitte&Touche.' "
When this elicited shrugs rather than smiles, he added, "A joke. I was making a joke. Actually, I feel that we're executing on our strategy just fine. All we need to do is ride out this recession—have they declared it a recession yet?—and then when the recovery happens, we'll be back to double-digit growth, triple digit, if the recovery is as robust as some people, economists, are predicting."

"We'd like to send over a consultant," Tallyrand said somberly.

Guy noticed that his was the only plate with food left on it.

"A fresh set of eyes," Radakovic said.

"Lansdale, Bucks & McKinney worked miracles over at Periforma," said Norbertson.

"Miracles?" Periforma Software Solutions, which enabled companies to file highly complex regulatory forms online, had cut three-quarters of its staff and shuttered all but one of its offices before being sold to a financial printing company in Long Island City. "The only miracle is that Lansdale, Bucks & McKinney, to cut costs, didn't line up Periforma's management team and execute them by firing squad."

"We'd just like to send someone over to have a look," Radakovic said, waving to a hovering waiter. "Who's ready for dessert?"

"Just give me three months," Guy said.

"Are you finished?"

Fortunately, this was uttered by a busboy. Guy nodded and the squabs were taken away.

"We have no choice, Guy. These are tough times."

"I hear the rhubarb tart with crème fraîche is out of this world."

"Tough times call for tough measures."

"Last time I had the trio of chocolate desserts."

"When the going gets tough . . ."

"Too bad we didn't order a soufflé when we sat down."

"Just hear what the consultants have to say, Guy. We know you'll be impressed."

Seventeen

Lily caught her reflection in the brass elevator doors of 11 William Street. Dark glasses despite the late-night hour, silk scarf wrapped around her head and tied under the chin, gray flannel trousers, midcalf raincoat, hands shoved in the pockets as if clutching a pistol. Greta Garbo as Ninotchka, she thought, briefly gratified, though in fact her right hand clutched the plastic card that Barnett had been issued for after-hours access to the office, but never mind.

After signing in with the night attendant, careful to write so illegibly that only a pharmacist could read the signature, she checked her watch: 11:45.

A single overhead light cast a milky fluorescence over the windowless reception area on the sixteenth floor. She slid the access card into a slot in a small gizmo beside a glass door and heard a dull click as the lock disengaged. She stepped inside for the second time in as many days, doubling the total number of visits she'd ever made to the office, having made a point of avoiding the grubby source of the funds that had financed the co-op, the house, the dresses, the vacations, the charitable donations, the household help, the everything else that had constituted her lifestyle.

Zelma's office was vast—his desk seemed a tennis court away from the doorway—and furnished with the same generic antique reproductions with which Barnett had filled his office. Every horizontal surface was piled with paper: reports, magazines, newsletters, brochures, prospectuses. One of Barnett's tech investments, she'd found out after his disappearance, had been a company that facilitated online document management. PaperFree.com, it was called. No wonder they'd lost every penny. If Zelma's office was any indication, the paperless society was just another investor pipe dream, right up there with the perpetual-motion machine and male birth-control pill.

She began searching his desk, having no idea what exactly she was looking for. What she did know was that the Feds and Zelma were keeping her completely in the dark—as had Barnett, for that matter. She needed to know more about the charges against her husband, and since no one was telling, she'd been forced to go looking.

His desk yielded nothing of interest, so she turned to the long credenza behind it. The office was lit by the pale, blue-gray light from thousands of windows of the surrounding skyscrapers, giving her the uncomfortable feeling of being trapped inside a black-and-white TV. She felt at once nakedly vulnerable and reassuringly invisible, suspended in a dense, twinkling grid.

She was beginning to despair at finding anything relevant when she came upon a file labeled simply *BJG*. She immediately thought of the monograms on the dress shirts Barnett had made for him at Sulka. Their luggage had been similarly monogrammed, as had the towels in the guest bathroom, the small, tasteful sign at the end of the Southampton driveway, their formal stationery. Their entire joint existence had been branded *BJG*—why hadn't that bothered her all those years?

The file contained few papers. There was a printout of an e-mail sent to all employees announcing Barnett's "leave of absence." She scanned several copies of letters from the Federal Prosecutor's Office detailing the charges against Barnett. One line that caught her attention read "We launched our investigation in response to a request from senior Grantham, Wiley & Zelma management." The only other papers of interest were a series of photocopies of canceled checks. These were company checks, made out to numbered accounts, in very large denominations: fifty thousand dollars, seventy thousand dollars, one hundred and sixty-five thousand dollars. The dates on the checks spanned six years. The backs of the checks had been photocopied as well, revealing that they had been deposited at a variety of banks in Switzerland, the Cayman Islands, and Belize. The signature on the front of the checks was unmistakably Barnett's.

Damn him. He'd signed those checks, dozens and dozens of them. And now he was doubtless trotting the globe, from Switzerland to Belize, visiting his accounts, while she slept on a pullout couch with a mattress manufactured by a sadist during the Civil War.

Later, with an envelope containing photocopies of the checks tucked under her left arm, she left the building and walked quickly along William Street toward the subway. The sidewalk was deserted; downtown Manhattan felt spooky at night, all gated stores and empty lobbies, as if abandoned not for the homeward commute but due to panic or plague. Two blocks from the subway station she thought she heard someone behind her, but when she turned there was no one.

A block later she heard footsteps moving closer. This time, when she turned around, there *was* someone—a tall, stocky man in a long dark coat with a wool cap pulled over his forehead. Nothing alarming about him except the way he seemed to look away from her, down and to his left, even as he seemed to be walking straight at her. She turned back and focused on the subway stop half a block ahead.

Suddenly he was right next to her, and then she felt him tugging at the envelope.

"Stop that!" she yelled. Still glancing down, making it all but impossible to identify him, he made another grab for the envelope. This time she cradled it to her chest, protecting it with both arms, and began running to the subway. She fully expected to feel a hand on her shoulders, if not a knife in her back. But she heard rapid footsteps heading south; she briefly turned and saw him running away. Just then a yellow cab appeared at the corner. She jumped into the street and flagged it down.

Inside, she caught her breath and tried to make sense of what had just happened. It seemed unlikely that a random pickpocket had targeted a manila envelope. So he had been following her, and wanted those check photocopies. Who was it?

At Fourteenth Street the taxi ran a red light and almost collided with a sanitation truck.

"Are you trying to get us killed?" Lily said as she strapped on her seat belt. Her second brush with death that night.

"You are kidding me? Please, sit back and enjoy the ride, okay? I will handle the driving." The driver's accent was formal Indian mixed with lilting Caribbean.

His weary, patronizing tone reminded her of Barnett whenever he'd deigned to respond to her inquires about the family finances. *Sit back and enjoy the ride, okay?*

The fare came to just over fifteen dollars. Though she had a twenty in her wallet, she gave him a hundred-dollar bill—a handout from Peggy—without apology and was surprised and disappointed when he made change without protest: four twenties and a five.

"I'd like a receipt with your medallion number," she said. Not that she had any intention of reporting the driver to the Taxi and Limousine Commission. She just wanted to piss him off.

"You see, solid as a rock."

Victor Ozeri rapped an enormous knuckle on a portion of the dining-room wall next to the kitchen door.

Rosemary heard the dull, architectural plan–destroying *thump* of flesh making contact with an unmovable object, in this case a support beam in her new apartment at 218 West End Avenue.

"No way we can move the door four inches. Not unless you want the building to come down on top of us."

Ozeri grinned—inappropriately, she thought. Falling buildings were no longer a laughing matter, if they ever had been. He seemed to delight in delivering bad news—or was it rather that bad news was the only kind he dealt in? Did contractors ever call clients to tell them a job was progressing ahead of schedule and under budget? Were floor tiles ever easier to remove than anticipated, paint faster to dry than expected, appliances delivered early and with all necessary parts? Or were contractors like those saintly doctors you read about who dealt only with the terminally ill, delivering bad news as dispassionately as a weather forecast.

Ozeri was at least six-five and so barrel-chested and bandy-legged, he looked like he, and not the building, might topple over. His head was a geography of outsized features: huge, deep-set boulders for eyes beneath an unbroken thicket of eyebrow, a long, craggy arête of a nose jutting from a pale, undulating desert of hairless cheeks. Though he towered over most people, he positively dwarfed his workmen, most of them shortish South Americans who regarded him as if he were a large, frisky dog.

"But we were assured the door could be moved," Rosemary said. The use of the passive voice disguised the fact that she couldn't recall precisely who had done the assuring. Their architect? Ozeri? Or Guy himself, who had spent a good two hours one morning pounding, with proprietary zeal, on every wall in the apartment to determine which ones could be safely obliterated, until the downstairs neighbors had complained to the doorman?

Ozeri rapped the wall again. "You were mis-assured," he said, his lips curling into a smug grin.

She retrieved the architect's plans from the double stroller, which was parked just inside the front door, and in which the twins slept soundly. Back in the dining room, she unfurled the plans on the radiator.

"If we can't move the door," she said, "then we can't put the Sub-Zero over here. And if we can't put the Sub-Zero over here, it has to go there, which means the breakfast area—"

"Which means there is no breakfast area."

For want of four inches, a breakfast area is lost—Rosemary leaned against the wall until she realized it was caked with plaster dust.

"Can't you just . . ." She brushed off her sweater, but the plaster dust seemed to have bonded with the angora. "I don't know, shave a few inches off the beam?"

He shook his head and rapped the offending section of the wall.

"Please stop doing that," she said, rubbing her temples at the first dull throb of a headache. "What are we going to do?"

The opening bars of Beethoven's Fifth trilled from Ozeri's waist. In one practiced motion he unholstered his cell phone and flipped it open. While he consoled what was clearly a deeply distressed client, she went into the kitchen and looked around. Without appliances and cabinets the room looked smaller than she remembered. How were they going to squeeze in a table and chairs? In one corner she saw a small patch of linoleum that had somehow eluded the workers' efforts to strip the floor down to the original plywood under-floor. She counted five layers of linoleum and thought wistfully of her mother's holiday au gratin potatoes. Along the ceiling, moldings had been ripped off, leaving angry scars. Capped-off pipes jutted pointlessly from the wall, wires hung limply, awaiting connections. Strange, that one had to completely destroy a room in order to improve it, the way a cult breaks down a target's emotional stability, removing all positive memories and associations, in order to begin constructing the desired mental framework. Moving the door had been such a small thing next to the tectonic shifts their architect had proposed for the rest of the apartment. Entire walls had already been destroyed, and new ones would be constructed—of plaster, of course, not Sheetrock—with rounded corners, gently contoured recesses, and big swaths of opaque glass blocks here and there to channel sunlight to places in the apartment where nature and the building's original layout had not heretofore allowed it to penetrate. (Guy had particularly liked this part of the plan, ingeniously illuminating the dark kitchen by what he probably viewed as redirecting the course of the solar system.) Floors would be re-parqueted to eliminate clues to the apartment's earlier configuration, new moldings installed to seamlessly gird the new, more open spaces. With such grand transformations in the works, moving the kitchen door four inches to the left had been too small a detail to pay much attention to.

She speed-dialed Guy's office on her cell phone and left the kitchen while it rang. But the open expanse of the apartment, where formerly there had been discrete and, she now felt, cozy rooms, left her feeling small and vulnerable, so she retreated back to the problematic but hearteningly four-walled kitchen and left Guy an urgent message.

"Look, we could push that wall out six inches," Ozeri said as he reholstered his phone. "Or we could just rip it down and install an island, a California kitchen like the one I put in 12D."

There was something unsettling about the way Ozeri breezily proposed destroying walls that had been in place for seventy-five years. Her education and professional life had been dedicated to appreciating the past, maintaining it.

"I'm guessing you never met a wall you didn't want to tear down," she said.

"They begin to quiver when I enter a room."

"Doesn't anyone ever ask to you leave things alone?"

His face darkened. "Where would I be without these old rabbit warrens?"

"These *rabbit warrens* worked just fine for a lot of people."

"Maybe, maybe not. Tearing down walls is the new status symbol."

"It is?"

"It's a sign of wealth. If you're strapped for space but you can't afford to move to a bigger place, what do you do? You make one bedroom into two, you put up a wall! Say you need a home office but can't afford an apartment with a library. You put up a wall in the living room to make two small, cramped rooms out of one. But if you've really arrived? Ah, now you buy a place with more rooms than you need and start combining them. Two small bedrooms become one big master suite. A guest room becomes a closet. A walk-in closet becomes a central-air-conditioning hub. Now we're talking luxury."

"But the architects who designed these old buildings, they had a reason for what they did."

"And the people who are buying them today have their reasons, too."

"I wonder if the people who move in after us will put the walls up again. Restoring apartments to their original floor plans will be the new luxury."

"Speaking as a contractor, that would be just fine with me."

He smiled broadly but Rosemary was vaguely discomfited by the thought of walls going up and down in Manhattan apartments like hemlines.

"We have cabinets arriving on Wednesday," Ozeri said. "I need to know where they're supposed to go."

Rosemary promised to let him know once she and Guy had consulted their architect.

Eighteen

"What's this?" Peggy asked the morning after Lily's raid on Grantham, Wiley & Zelma, waving a piece of paper.

"It's a dry-cleaning receipt."

"I can see that. From a place over on Lexington Avenue. What's the matter with the cleaners here on the West Side?"

"It's from before," Lily said. *Before the sky fell.* "Check the date."

"Well, you better go and get it, otherwise they'll hit you with a storage charge. Celia Krasnow had to pay over twenty dollars last year in storage, even after she explained to that nice Chinese man at the Belnord Cleaners that she'd been in the hospital and then rehab for six weeks after her stroke."

"I don't really need—"

"Well, truth be told, her speech *is* a little slurred, and I don't think that Chinese man speaks very good English, either. Maybe he didn't understand that she would have picked up her cleaning if only she could have. And don't get me started with the Spanish at Gristedes."

Lily was still too rattled by the attempted mugging the night before to argue. She'd called Jay DiGregoiro at the Federal Prosecutor's Office first thing that morning. He hadn't been impressed by her story. File a complaint with the city, he'd told her. See how far you get.

. . .

She'd never been to the Savoy Cleaners on Lexington Avenue—Consuelo had handled that aspect of her former life. Behind the counter stood a surly-looking man of about fifty, with unruly black hair and narrow, wary eyes that widened with distaste when she handed him the ticket.

"This is three months old." He had an accent—Eastern European?—that sharpened *old* into *ault*.

"We moved."

He continued to study the receipt, shaking his head as if reading positive biopsy results.

"I hope I can find this one."

And she hoped he couldn't. He disappeared into a hanging garden of plastic-sheathed garments.

"Lily?"

"Hellohowareyou!" she said as she tried like mad to recall the name of the attractive, well-groomed woman standing before her.

"Veronica Selig," the woman said. "Rachel's mom?"

Rachel had been Sophie's good friend at school. She might have met Veronica Selig at Parents' Nights, or perhaps not. People she didn't know recognized her all the time; she'd been a minor celebrity, after all.

"Of course. How is Rachel?"

"She's great. And Sophie? Where is she at school this year?"

"Washington," Lily said quickly, turning to see if the dry cleaner had returned with her dresses.

"D.C.? Is she boarding?"

"No, actually it's Booker T. Washington, on the West Side."

"Oh!"

Veronica Selig had never moved in Lily's circle. Like many of the non-working wives of law partners and doctors and investment bankers, she would undoubtedly have known who Lily Grantham was, having seen photos of her in the *Times* and elsewhere. And she undoubtedly had followed the expulsion of Barnett Grantham from the Temple of Dendur and had perhaps seen in the *Post* (the New York *Post*) the photo of the Granthams' household belongings waiting on the sidewalk in front of 913 Park Avenue to be loaded into a moving truck bound for a federal depot in Maryland.

"I'd heard that you moved," Veronica Selig said lightly. "Rachel would love to hear from Sophie."

"I'll pass that on." Lily had encouraged the children to keep in touch with their old schoolmates, but both seemed determined to make a clean break. She didn't know which hurt more, the idea that they were embarrassed about their new circumstances, or that their old life had never really meant all that much to begin with.

"Here, I got them for you."

Lily turned to the counter and nearly swooned at the site of her black Saint Laurent dress, with the bias-cut neckline and exquisite beadwork along the bodice, a relic from her former life. Behind it was a maroon Oscar de la Renta. It seemed unthinkable and also painfully real that less than a year ago she'd not only worn Oscar de la Renta, she'd lunched with him. She wanted to tell the man to keep the dresses but there was no turning back. She handed him two twenties, which he held up to the overhead light after removing his glasses.

"Is not good," he said. *Ees nod goot.*

"What do you mean?"

"Is counterfeit." He placed the unwanted twenties on the counter.

"You must be kidding."

"The stripe says five dollars—these are twenties."

"Really?"

"Is fake."

"That bastard," Lily whispered, thinking of last night's cabdriver. *Sit back and enjoy the ride.* She had only six dollars left in her wallet, six genuine dollars in addition to the two other no-doubt-fake twenties.

"I'll have to get more cash and come back," she said, stuffing the fake twenties into her jacket pocket.

"Come back before tomorrow or I will have to start adding storage." *Storatch.*

"Here, I'll lend you the twenty," offered Veronica Selig with, Lily thought, a trill of amused pity.

"Thank you so much, but I'll just go get more cash and come back."

"Don't be silly, you can send me a check. We're still at 680 Park."

Lily felt her face flush as she backed away from the counter.

"No, really, I'll just get more cash and be right back."

She even tripped over the door saddle on her way out.

Instead of cash, the ATM on the corner of Seventy-third Street and Lexington Avenue disgorged a receipt imprinted *Insufficient funds*.

If the current chapter of her life had a title, that would be it: "Insufficient Funds."

Peggy returned exhausted from her errands. She still hadn't adjusted to the new neighborhood and was beginning to wonder if she ever would. It wasn't exactly a practical location, she was discovering. Within a few blocks of her apartment were a huge Barnes & Noble bookstore, a Victoria's Secret, a Virgin record store, something like six Gaps (Baby Gap, Gap Kids, just plain Gap Gap . . . any day now, they'd open an *alter kaker* Gap), and a string of Starbucks. Which was all well and good if you happened to be in desperate need of a book, negligee, or latté, but what if you just needed a couple of nice Florida oranges and a seeded rye? You had to get on a bus and head for Fairway. Imagine, getting on a bus for oranges and bread!

So even a quick trip to the deli had become a major undertaking, and as Peggy entered her apartment, she looked forward to lying down for a few minutes before making lunch. Then she saw Nanny What's-her-name and Monroe in the living room, side by side on the sofa, staring numbly at the television like a miserable old couple.

"What are you doing?" she said, still holding the plastic Fairway bag.

Both heads turned with obvious reluctance from the screen.

"I'm folding the children's laundry," Nanny said.

Peggy hadn't noticed the ridiculously small pile of clothes on the coffee table, one day's worth of laundry. She felt contradicted and foolish.

"Monroe, you're not even dressed."

He glanced down at his pajamas, then back at her.

"Why, are we going somewhere?"

She thought she saw a smile crack Nanny's pasty face.

"You shouldn't allow him to sit around all day in his pajamas," Peggy said.

"That's not—"

"I know, that's not your job. Your job is to do a load of laundry every single day, if you could call a handful of underwear a load, which accounts for fifteen minutes of your precious time."

Nanny placed one of Sophie's tiny tank tops on the small pile and lovingly smoothed it.

"On Park Avenue we had a laundry room in the apartment. Now I spend half my time in the elevator, traipsing back and forth to the basement."

"On Park—" Peggy had a fleeting but enormously satisfying vision of swinging the oranges-and-bread-laden Fairway bag at Nanny's face. "Monroe, get dressed. And you . . ." She couldn't think of anything useful for Nanny to do. The apartment was clean, the children's laundry done (and she certainly wasn't going to ask Camilla Parker-Whosit to hand-wash *her* underwear). *Kill yourself with a bread knife* was a tempting suggestion, but she wasn't sure she could take any additional disobedience in her own home. On the way to her bedroom, if you could be "on the way" in a dark and narrow six-foot-long hallway like the one that connected the apartment's two bedrooms, she heard noises from behind the closed door of Sophie and William's room. She stopped and listened. Perhaps it was only street noise. Though they lived on the sixteenth floor, a constant din found its way through the apartment's large windows, a continuous hum, one long, undulating chord of car engines and horns and the beeping of reversing trucks and footsteps and conversations and barking. Sometimes at night, lying awake in bed, listening, she thought she knew what it must feel like, or sound like, to live underwater, the tiny movements of billions of fish uniting into a giant, deafening roar. But this wasn't street noise coming from Sophie and William's room. She rapped on the door and opened it.

At first she was aware only of frantic movement, as if she'd disturbed a colony of giant mice. But it was only Sophie and another person, a boy, leaping from her bed, more or less clothed, thank God.

"Grandma!" Sophie said as she took a giant step away from the boy.

"What are you doing home?" she asked, though she well knew the answer.

"It's lunchtime and we— This is Paco."

He was about Sophie's height, Hispanic-looking, very thin, with dark eyes and dark, close-cropped hair. His baggy blue jeans clung perilously to the bottom of his narrow hips, exposing a swath of white underwear with the letters *2(x)ist* stitched in blue on the waistband. She squinted: If he had an erection, which she strongly suspected, it would have to be frightfully large to make itself known behind so much denim.

Sophie's getup was equally disturbing: loose jeans and a skimpy T-shirt, squared-off shoes with clunky platform heels that forced her to move with a stilt-walker's slow, knee-lifting strides. In the front closet her old school uniforms hung like clothes for a giant, old-fashioned doll.

"Does your mother know you're home?" Peggy asked.

"She's here?" Sophie's eyes widened.

"She's out. Not that there's room for her, anyway, with the crowd we always seem to have. I just thought she should know that you and your . . . you and Paco were coming home for lunch."

"I always came home for lunch at Convent."

Peggy winced at the C-word, though she had to admit she missed the blue plaid dirndls and pristine white blouses and the plain shoes that didn't look like they belonged on a circus clown or hooker.

"Yes, well, this is different."

"How?" Sophie squinted one eye and shook her head while thrusting it forward, a familiar gesture from her extensive repertoire of nonverbal insults.

"Everything's changed," Peggy said. "You lived in a different world, a safer world."

"That's ridiculous."

"You used to live in a very homogenous community. Now there's a lot more going on and you need to be more careful."

"That's true," Paco said.

"This is, like, the West Side, not Baghdad."

"No, really." Paco stepped closer to Peggy, who almost, but didn't, back away. "My cousin, the one I was telling you about, Soph? He's, like, bad news, you know, holding up kids for their lunch money and shit and roughing them up on the way home from school. When I tell him, Ray, leave this neighborhood alone, you know? You don't, you know . . ." He glanced uncomfortably at Peggy. "You don't, like, do it where you sleep, you know? Like, go over to the East Side, okay, where they have, like, more money and shit. And he's like, no way, they got more cops over there and the mothers, they have these patrols and shit going on, they wear these orange, like, T-shirts over their clothes and they stand on the corners and stuff with whistles and cell phones."

Peggy didn't know what to make of Paco's story, which seemed to support her side of the argument but in a decidedly unsettling way. And she couldn't help returning to the waistband of his boxer shorts: What in heavens name did 2(x)ist mean? What sort of statement was it sending out from that dangerous region? Best to change the subject.

"What did you have for lunch?"

Sophie glanced quickly at Paco.

"Nothing, we were just . . ."

Peggy didn't need or want to hear what they were just.

"I'll make you sandwiches," she said. "Tuna fish okay?"

Five sandwiches, she thought as she walked to the kitchen. Two cans. Well, she couldn't very well make lunch for the entire household and exclude Nanny, satisfying as that would be. She could ask Nanny for help, of course, but that would mean having to stand side by side with her in the narrow, windowless kitchen, like stewardesses in an airplane galley. Anyway, she wouldn't be much use. Didn't the English slather butter on their sandwiches? Imagine buttering bread and then slapping on roast beef, pale, fatty roast beef at that. She'd make the five sandwiches herself and try not to think about how her life had gone to hell in a handbasket since leaving 218 West End Avenue.

Nineteen

"You need to ramp up your strategy for monetizing Positano's intellectual capital."

Guy nodded with what he hoped was a thoughtful I'll-take-that-excellent-idea-under-consideration expression, not the stop-slinging-the-tired-clichés look that more accurately reflected his thinking. It was important that the consultant, Sumner Freedman, leave with the conviction that Guy was paying attention. Though he affected a collegial, we're-in-this-together stance, Sumner doubtless reported back to the board at regular intervals, and never with news that put Guy in a favorable light.

"Positano spends over three mil a quarter on R&D, with only one new release planned this year and next." Freedman, who looked about twenty-five, with straw-colored hair, pinkish skin, and very faint blue eyes, had the pasty, watery good looks of the severely overbred. "A lot of companies would pay top dollar for that intellectual capital. You could outsource your software engineers for two, three hundred dollars an hour easy."

Is that, Guy wanted to ask, *the best that your phalanx of consultants could come up with—turn Positano's best and brightest into code-writing whores?* The mood at the company, which had been deteriorating in lockstep with Positano's stock price, had turned almost suicidally dismal with the invasion of the suit-and-tie-wearing Lansdale, Bucks & McKinney consultants, armed with cell phones and Palm Pilots and laptops and calculators and Black-Berrys and the unshakable conviction that they knew better how to run Positano than the people who actually worked there.

"We'll never get off another release if we start renting out our engineers."

"With all due respect, you'll never get off another anything if you don't start getting your P&L in shape. We're talking the s-word here."

For some time, *survivability* was breathed among tech firms the way *plague* had been whispered in fifteenth-century Europe. The s-word could send employees fleeing for their professional lives, impel suppliers to demand cash on delivery, cause analysts to downgrade a stock to the deceptively innocuous-sounding "hold" rating, which investors easily recognized as code for "Dump this crap with all due speed." More to the point, the s-word could aggravate sciatica in an anxious CEO. Guy shifted in his chair but couldn't get comfortable. He should have left demolition to the experts. He turned to the tank and was pathetically reassured to see that Positano's marine life, at least, was surviving.

"We could sell the rainbow tetras to Le Bernardin," he said. "They'd make very nice appetizers."

"I don't think . . . Oh, I see. Ha-ha." Freedman attempted a smile, but his tight, fine-featured face seemed ill-equipped for the job.

"I will not go into the outsourcing business," Guy said. "That's not what I had in mind when I founded this company . . ." He paused to let "founded" sink in. Freedman was a Wharton MBA who'd worked for Lansdale, Bucks & McKinney his entire "career." Guy suspected the only thing he'd ever founded was the New Canaan chapter of the Young Republicans. "It's not what I have in mind now. We're a software company, a solutions provider."

The opening strains of *William Tell's Overture* signaled a cell call.

"Guy speaking."

"It's Ventnor. We need to talk."

"So talk." Guy glanced at Freedman, who was doing his best not to look put out.

"In person. Tomorrow night. Eight o'clock. The McDonald's on Seventh, across from Penn Station. One other thing—bring a check, ten grand." The line went dead.

"The CEO of one of our largest customers," Guy said, reholstering the phone. "It's not easy being mission critical." This was meant as irony, albeit feeble irony, but Freedman nodded earnestly and waited a few thoughtful seconds before speaking.

"That phone call brings up another point. In reviewing your management structure, we find that too much hands-on operational control is centered at the top. With you, actually. My colleagues are putting the finishing touches on a new org chart that puts more day-to-day management in the hands of a chief operating officer."

"We don't have a chief operating officer."

"Yes, well . . . that's another thing we're going to be recommending."

"Let me get this straight. Our overhead's too high, we need more layoffs, and you want me to hire a COO at what, a buck seventy-five a year?"

"The candidate we have in mind would run you more like two hundred thousand a year, plus options, of course. And benefits."

"We'll never find someone who knows the business and—" Something in Freedman's expression . . . he was so pallid, Guy thought he could see blood pulsing through the capillaries of his cheeks. "You?"

Freedman cleared his throat. "I think I could bring some operational structure to the company, an external, objective perspective that could—"

"You're twenty-five years old."

"Twenty-eight, actually. But that's besides the point, really. I've led engagements with dozens of the top software, infrastructure, and content companies."

William Tell overtured and Guy again answered without checking.

"Guy? Guy? Can you hear me? It's Rosemary."

"I can hear you."

"It's a nightmare, Guy. One of the capped-off pipes in the second bathroom leaked, and before anyone found out, it had dripped all the way down to the third floor. I have six of our new neighbors in our dining room, or what used to be the dining room, ready to lynch me. You have to help."

"That may not be possible."

"They're going to kill me. I'm not talking figuratively here, Guy."

"I'm in a meeting—"

"Please, Guy. I can't get Ozeri to return my calls and they want answers."

"I'll see what I can do." He clicked off. "Family emergency," he said.

"I completely understand. And I firmly believe that family always comes first."

"I'm sure your parents will be gratified to hear that." Guy stood up and headed for the door.

Lily was unaccustomed to using a bus pass, so it took her several tries to get it properly in the slot, attracting contemptuous glances from the passengers in the seniors-and-disabled seats at the front of the M79 crosstown bus. A harsh beep drew her attention to the digital readout, which flashed *Insufficient fare*—another chapter heading. Even her MetroCard was out of money. She foraged in her purse for change but came up twenty cents short. By then the seniors and disabled appeared to be on the verge of mutiny, so she stepped off the bus and, as it abandoned her at the corner of Lexington Avenue, realized she had no choice but to walk home.

A drizzle began just as she entered Central Park, and by the time she reached her (or rather, her parents') apartment, she was soaked, chilled, aching, and deeply resentful of the entire world and its every inhabitant, beginning with her mother, who met her at the door and, ignoring her patently desperate condition, assaulted her with the news that Sophie had been discovered with a young man in her room. "And I don't think he's a Rodeph Shalom boy, either." In the living room Nanny launched into a lengthy complaint about Peggy's attitude as Lily searched in her one chest of drawers for dry clothes, ignoring the drone of an afternoon soap opera. Unable to locate the sweater she was looking for, she slammed the drawer shut and went to her parents' room. Monroe was propped on the bed, a magazine on his lap, sleeping. She found Peggy's pocketbook and took out forty dollars. In the elevator on the way down she retrieved from her purse the taxi receipt from last night.

The global headquarters of MTS Taxi Corporation turned out to be a small house in the Richmond Hill section of Queens, one Van Wyck Expressway exit short of JFK Airport. The house was identical to countless others on the street, which was identical to countless other streets she'd once been vaguely aware of from the leathery comfort of a hired Town Car en route to JFK. Narrow, two stories high, it had a three-step cement stoop leading to an awninged door. In front was a neatly tended patch of grass about the size of the Laver Kirman in her old living room. A short driveway led to a one-car garage in back. In front of that garage sat a yellow taxi, a splash of garishness in an otherwise colorless neighborhood.

She'd expected a fleet of cabs and wasn't sure what to make of the fact that MTS Taxi Corporation was apparently one person with a medallion. For that matter, she wasn't sure what she was doing there at all. The attempted robbery on William Street, then the rejection of her twenty-dollar bills, ATM card, and MetroCard had shattered something—her sanity, perhaps—that had, remarkably, remained intact through bankruptcy and Barnett's desertion and moving in with her parents. She'd been propelled from the West Side of Manhattan to Richmond Hill, Queens, still soaking wet and now bone-chilled, by pure breath-shortening, stomach-tightening, altogether brainless rage. A more sensible course would have been to report the counterfeit twenties to the police—or, wiser still, to ignore the whole situation. Getting caught passing counterfeit money was the kind of story she could have dined out on for weeks, back when she dined out.

The man who opened the door looked Indian or Pakistani, which jibed with the accent she recalled from last night. He was in his early thirties, she guessed, about five-seven, of slight build but with a round, fleshy face that overwhelmed his small, dark eyes.

"Were you . . . were you driving your taxi last night . . . in Manhattan . . . about midnight?"

"Why do you want to know?" His right hand gripped the edge of the open door.

She recognized the surly tone.

"It *was* you. You drove me from downtown to the West Side."

"That may be true."

"I gave you a hundred-dollar bill and you gave me back four twenties. They were fake, counterfeit." She started to reach into her bag for the evidence, then thought better of it. His hand slid off the door and now hung at his side, balled in a fist. "All the twenties are at home, with my family, and . . . and I left instructions that . . . that if for some reason I don't come home, they should . . ."

An enormous plane shuddered overhead, making conversation impossible and casting a slow-moving, foreboding shadow over the entire street. She saw *Air France* written on the side of the fuselage and felt a pang of nostalgia—not long ago she would have been at the window of such a plane, one of the front windows, looking down at row after row of tiny, identical houses and wondering idly who lived in them and what they did and whether the noise of landing planes drove them crazy. Now she knew.

"People give me twenty-dollar bills all the time," the driver said once the plane was gone. "I don't check to see if they are counterfeit or not."

"People don't give you *four* fake twenty-dollar bills. One twenty, maybe, but what are the chances of four separate people all giving you fake twenties?"

"From the airports many people pay me with twenties."

She hadn't thought of this, though she clearly should have, and the notion that he might be unaware that he was passing counterfeit money deflated her somewhat. She'd blown thirty-eight dollars on the cab ride out to Queens . . . for what? The driver looked at her as if she were pathetic or crazy or both.

"I'll report you to the taxi commission," she said.

"That is your prerogative. Would you like me to give you the telephone number and address to make it easier for you?"

She almost said yes just to annoy him. Instead, she turned and headed toward the street.

"Would you like a lift back to the West Side?" he called out after her in a Caribbean-inflected Indian accent that turned every line into inappropriately cheerful iambic pentameter. "I go on duty in twenty minutes, you could be my first fare of the day."

Insufficient funds! she almost called out as she headed for the corner, unsure where the nearest subway station was. Perhaps she'd follow the trail of landing jumbo jets all the way to the airport and take a shuttle bus home. Then she changed her mind and hurried back to the driver's house—she'd get his full name after all if only just to piss him off. The taxi was locked, however, and she was unable to read anything through the closed windows. She was about to resume her trek across Queens when she saw the driver dart across the small backyard and enter the garage through a side door. There was something furtive about the way he scampered from the house to the garage, glancing behind him. A moment later a light went on inside.

A row of small, square windows in the main garage door had been covered from the inside by cardboard, but the corner of one piece had curled up a bit. She peeked through this opening and saw the driver pull a sheet off a computer setup and large printer.

He's printing money, she realized. He's printing money!

And suddenly the whole crazy world seemed so much simpler. Barnett had always made the financial system, and his exalted role within it, seem impossibly complicated, as if he were some sort of MBA'd alchemist turning rumors and calculations and educated hunches into gold. But money wasn't complicated at all. Certainly not to the driver and, as of ten seconds ago, to her.

You simply printed it!

She went to the side of the garage and opened the door.

"Oh my, good grief, why did you come back now?" he lilted.

Is this the face that launched a thousand ships?

She stepped into the garage and nearly swooned from the vinegary smell of ink.

"MTS Taxi Company has a new partner," she said, proffering her right hand. "I'm Lily Grantham."

"I hope you filed your plans with the City Housing Authority," said the man from 4D.

"And got board approval," added 3D, a woman.

Guy nodded yes to both of his future downstairs neighbors.

"How about insurance?" asked the third member of the welcoming committee, an elderly man whose apartment, 5D, was directly below theirs.

"We have insurance," Guy said. "And I'm very sorry for the inconvenience."

"Inconvenience?" said 3D, a thickset woman in her fifties who cradled a tiny white dog tight against her breast. "My bathroom ceiling is on my bathroom floor. I never heard such a crash. We thought . . . we thought the building was coming down." She gave the dog a consoling head pat.

"Our insurance will take care of that," Guy said, hoping it was true.

"I don't know why you didn't leave the bathtub where it was in the first place," said 3D. "Whoever heard of moving a bathtub?"

This evoked frowns and shrugs from all of his neighbors, and a bottomless sigh from 4D.

"Moving all those pipes around is asking for trouble," said 5D.

"We've never had a problem with the tub where it was meant to be," said 3D.

"We're dividing the bathroom in two," Guy said. "A full bath and a powder room."

"Powder room?" said 5D as all three glanced around, awestruck, as if Guy had announced the discovery of a fourth dimension, right there in 6D.

"How in hell are you going to fit two bathrooms in?" asked 4D, a stocky man of about seventy whose face was hardened in a scowl of paranoid belligerence.

"We're incorporating the hall closet to add space," Rosemary said. Guy rapped on the soon-to-be-eliminated wall that separated the closet from the bathroom.

"Then . . . then where will you put your linens?" asked 3D, cosseting the little dog to her breast.

"We're opening up the big closet in the second bedroom to the hallway," Guy said.

"But then there won't be a closet in that room," 5D said. Her neighbors nodded approvingly at her grasp of D-line architecture.

"We're adding a full wall of closets," Rosemary said.

"But won't that make the room kind of small?" asked 5D. "What's the point of moving into a place and making it smaller?"

"The overall footprint of the apartment remains the same," Guy said.

"Footprint?" said 5D with a suspicious glance at the floor.

"And we're opening this bathroom, the full bath, into the second bedroom."

"So even though it will be smaller, it'll have its own bathroom," Rosemary added.

Guy couldn't believe they were justifying their renovation to a bunch of people, none of whom had paid more than fifty thousand dollars for their apartments, who clearly regarded moving a towel rack as tampering with God's unfathomable design.

"The point is, we're very sorry for the damage our crew has done," he said. Turning to Rosemary, he added, "Speaking of which, where are they?"

"They left as soon as this came to light."

"Probably fled the country," 5D said.

"Back to Ecuador or Bolivia," added 3D.

"Or Colombia," whispered 4D. This elicited ominous nods from his neighbors.

"I don't know," said 5D, "it all seems like a lot of effort for a powder room. And what happened to your kitchen? I didn't see it when I walked in."

"It's . . ." Guy decided not to go there. Now that the doorway between the kitchen and dining room was determined to be unmovable, he himself wasn't sure exactly where in the apartment the kitchen would end up. If they canceled the kitchen renovation and instead ordered in three meals a day for the next thirty years, they'd easily come out ahead financially, not to mention psychically. "Let's go find the super and see about cleaning up the mess downstairs."

"You're the fellow from Positano Software," said 5D as they waited for the elevator. "My son put me into Positano at fifty-seven," he said, as if recalling his committal to a nursing home during the Eisenhower administration. "What the hell happened?"

"It's a tough market."

"First the stock market, and now my ceiling falls down. What's next?"

"I wish I knew," Guy said, though he might have replied "Outsourcing programmers" or "A new chief operating officer."

Or the simpler, more descriptive, and invariably accurate "Nothing good."

Twenty

Mohammed T. Satywatti, proprietor of MTS Taxi and part-time counterfeiter, dropped Lily Grantham off at her building (or rather, her parents' building) opposite Lincoln Center.

"Now, don't forget," she said before leaving the back of his cab, "I told my parents about getting the fake twenties from you, and I told them where I was going today, and I told them your name and medallion number, so if anything happens to me, they'll know exactly who to blame."

"Good grief, I am not going to murder you, if that is what you are suggesting to me. But maybe if you don't leave my cab soon, I will reconsider."

"And as soon as I get upstairs, I'm going to write everything down," Lily continued from the backseat. "How you distribute the bills through other cabdrivers around the city. Then I'll put the paper in a safety-deposit box but leave instructions with my parents to open it up in the event anything should happen to me." It occurred to Lily that a counterfeiter might have no problem murdering not only her but her parents. "And I'll leave instructions with friends, people whose names you don't even know."

"Now I am seriously considering killing you. Please get out before I do something that both of us will regret."

He seemed disconcertingly mild-mannered for a criminal: small of stature, gentle of voice, with an attitude more weary than threatening. He had a wife and four young sons in Guyana and was saving money (well, printing it) to send for them.

She finally left his cab but decided not to head home just yet. She walked across the street to a Banana Republic, grabbed the first thing see saw, a tan cashmere sweater, and brought it to the counter.

"Eighty-nine dollars plus tax," the cashier said.

Fighting an urge to flee so intense it caused her legs to tremble, Lily handed over five freshly printed twenties, her very first handiwork. During the long drive in from Queens, Mohammed had warned her not to pass off fake twenties at small retailers like the dry cleaners. "They always check because when they take the money to the bank to deposit, they get stuck with it. But at big chain stores no one really cares because no one is accountable." The advice fell on receptive ears: Lily felt vaguely better about foisting bogus twenties on a big company like Banana Republic than on a small-business owner. In any case, she imagined the counterfeit twenties circulating endlessly through the economy, acquiring legitimacy and value as they purchased groceries and clothing and packs of cigarettes and movie tickets, bouquets of flowers and bottles of wine and packages of condoms. Her shiny new twenties were tiny pebbles tossed into the great economic pond, sending out ripple after ripple of financial satisfaction at the nation's cash registers.

When the cashier handed her four dollars and seventy cents in change—real money, she noted—as well as a bag containing her new sweater swaddled in tissue paper, she felt a shiver of guilty pleasure and knew she couldn't go home (to her parents' home) just yet.

As Lucinda Wells led her through the empty rooms of the former Grantham apartment on the ninth floor of 913 Park Avenue, Rosemary felt like a tourist in one of those English stately homes reluctantly opened to the paying hoi polloi. Wasn't there something fundamentally wrong in gawking at the lapsed extravagance of the newly impecunious? Their contractor, Victor Ozeri, had suggested the expedition. He'd handled the Grantham renovation many years earlier, and when Rosemary had voiced her qualms about how their architect's choice of kitchen countertops (gray honed granite) would go with their cabinets (butter cream–painted walnut), he'd recalled installing a similar configuration for the Granthams. She'd mentioned the idea of calling the Granthams to Guy, who immediately recognized Barnett Grantham as a former Positano shareholder who'd sold his stake at a sizable loss. Later, during a phone call with Lucinda about a mortgage issue, Rosemary had mentioned the Grantham kitchen.

"It's my exclusive!"

"They're selling?"

"Not *they*, the government. Didn't you read what happened? It was all over the papers."

"Current events stopped the day the twins were born."

Lucinda sighed her bottomless disappointment and immediately began recounting the Grantham saga in breathless, schadenfreudian detail, finally getting around to the real point of the entire narrative: Thanks to the lobbying of the husband of a second cousin, who worked for the Justice Department's New York office, Lucinda Wells had been given an exclusive on the Grantham apartment.

"Trust me, it's not an easy sell," she told Rosemary in the apartment's foyer. "Scandal means bad karma, and the feng shui's all fucked up. Still, at nine-point-five, someone'll bite."

The foyer was the size of an old-fashioned bank lobby, and about as cozy, with a marble floor as shiny-white as freshly Zambonied ice. The walls were glazed a luminous burgundy. A gnarled wire dangled from the ceiling where a lighting fixture had been removed.

"*Architectural Digest* ran ten pages on this place," Lucinda said. "I've never had a client bag that much real estate in *AD*. The article said it took eight coats of paint to get the walls like this—you paint it on, then sand it off, then paint it on again, etcetera, etcetera, etcetera." She tapped the wall with a pink fingernail as incandescent as the burgundy glaze. "I don't know, it feels *très* nineties to me. Everyone I show it to agrees. They bring their decorator along on the second walk-through, even before the husband, and the decorator always says the same thing—these burgundy walls have to go, the white marble floor, yuck, we'll have to install new moldings, and what if we moved the doorway to the dining room just a foot to the left to let more light into the foyer? Suddenly it's a gut renovation and for nine-point-five that's a turn-off in any market. You want to see the whole place, or just the kitchen?"

Before Rosemary could answer, Lucinda was heading for the living room. She had on a dark gray pantsuit in some rich, shiny new microfiber that looked like it could withstand a napalm attack. Her thick, glossy brown hair framed her face like a headdress. The heels of her stiletto-toed boots, which Rosemary thought she'd have trouble getting over the twins' tiny feet, clattered irritably as she crossed the room.

"All the public rooms face the Avenue," she said, tapping a window with a fingernail. "The light's not bad for Park Avenue, especially in the morning."

"Well, for nine-point-five, you can't expect afternoon *and* morning sun."

"You're catching on."

Rosemary followed her dutifully from room to room, wondering if it wouldn't be wise to leave a trail of rice. She'd come to think of their new apartment on West End Avenue, scene of a near-riot by neighbors earlier that day, as palatial, and compared to the place they were living in now, it was, but it could easily fit into the "public rooms" of the Grantham's former abode. In New York there was always something better than what you had, something just beyond reach; the moment you'd finally climbed to the top of the ladder, still panting from the effort, someone would haul up a new and taller ladder right next to you. New York was a city of parallel ladders getting taller and taller and taller.

"The master bedroom," Lucinda announced as she crossed the large room. A king-size bed had left four deep footprints in the cream wall-to-wall carpet. "They converted a bedroom into closets and a dressing area. Did you know he was having an affair?"

Rosemary gasped.

"It shocked me, too."

But the gasp was for Lily Grantham's vast closet, an Escher-like configuration of mahogany shelves and drawers and hanging racks and shoe slots that could comfortably display the merchandise of a Banana Republic.

"A client told me. Everyone knew except Lily herself—surprise, surprise. She wasn't someone in their crowd, the girlfriend. Wall Street type, I wasn't told the name."

"Did she leave the country with him?"

"Well, no one's missing! It looks like mahogany but it's really the aromatic wood from some rain-forest tree that's practically extinct now. They paid a fine for importing it, a few thousand dollars, I think, but that's what people did back then."

"Back in the nineties."

"Today everyone's sooo eco-conscious. Anyway, this will all have to come out, and Barnett Grantham's closet, too. His shoe slots were made for a man's size eight-and-a-half, not an inch to spare—one of my prospective buyers had her decorator measure them—and how many men have feet that small, or will admit to it?"

In the kitchen Rosemary quickly reassured herself that honed gray granite countertops went beautifully with butter cream–painted walnut cabinets. She liked the pewter cabinet pulls and drawer handles, too.

"Where is Lily Grantham now?" she asked Lucinda as they waited on the private landing for the elevator.

"In a postwar closet near Lincoln Center with her parents. I sold them the place. In fact, the Gimmels, who you bought from? The Gimmels are Lily Grantham's parents."

"No kidding?" Rosemary almost added, "What a coincidence," but of course it was nothing of the sort. Lucinda, it seemed, had her expertly manicured hands in every move in the city. Rosemary pictured her angled Gepetto-like over the island of Manhattan, working the strings as people jumped from apartment to apartment, climbing one ladder, skidding down another, or leaping across the bottomless chasm of failed expectations to an even taller ladder to begin still another hopeful ascent to the top.

"How's the reno going?" Lucinda asked.

"Slowly, very—"

"You could move. Cut and run. I could get you two-point-eight like *that*. Throw in a few shekels and I'll have you in a comparable place already done over. You'd have to move uptown a few blocks, but so what?"

"Move?"

"The market's up thirty-five percent since you bought, haven't you heard?"

"No, I—"

"Right, you're in art. Most of my clients—most of the world!—they read the real-estate section first on Sunday, before the news. Before the business section! I mean, who needs scandals and deficits and stocks going nowhere when the place where you put your head down at night is gaining value every single day without your having to do a thing about it?"

"But it's just paper."

"Get out of here, it's real estate. *Real* estate."

"It's insane."

"And paying ten-point-five for a swatch of canvas that some alcoholic threw paint at isn't? You can't sleep on a painting."

"Where do *you* live?" Rosemary asked as they got into the attended elevator. Funny that the subject of Lucinda's own living arrangements had never come up before.

"Me? East Seventies, rent-controlled junior four, doorman, views, don't ask me what I pay, you'll be sick."

Guy wrote a check for ten thousand dollars payable to Derek Ventnor, put it into a plain envelope, and addressed it to Ventnor Place. The check was drawn on a new account he'd opened up to pay for the purchase and renovation of apartment 6D at 218 West End Avenue, which had been funded by a two-million-dollar loan from Goldman Sachs, with one hundred thousand shares of Positano Software as collateral. Earlier that day Kristin Liu had called from Goldman with the delightful news that, because of Positano's recent plunge (to just under seven bucks a share), he would have to put up an additional thirty thousand shares. He had six million shares in all, so this was only mildly alarming, the movement of paper from one account to another, although he couldn't help but think that paying for something—an apartment, a renovation, a bribe to a pornographer—with a currency that was more or less constantly being devalued could not, in the long run, be a good thing. Just ask the Argentineans. He'd actually sunk so low as to resurrect the idea of a zero-cost collar with Ms. Liu, a concept that he'd scoffed at only months ago. "That might be difficult to do right in the current market environment, but I'll bring it up with my managing director at our next staff meeting," she'd said. Goldman-speak for *No fucking way.*

Ventnor had margin issues of his own, he'd informed Guy, and if he went down, so would Positano. Guy knew he shouldn't make another payment to Ventnor, but he didn't have the energy, much less the time, to figure out what else to do. Positano was pitching a major new customer—the largest online magazine subscription company—and couldn't afford any kind of negative publicity. Even after laying off a tenth of the workforce, Positano was burning through two million dollars a month, which meant that the IPO proceeds, which only last year had seemed like a bottomless cookie jar of funds, would be depleted in six months, after which he'd either have to sell out or . . .

He got up and crossed his office to the tank. A sharp rap on the glass startled one giant tetra, but the other fish merely regarded him with logy disdain. He'd been rapping on the tank a lot lately.

Lily unbuttoned her blouse and wished she'd had the foresight to turn off the overhead light. How long had it been since she'd undressed in front of a man other than Barnett, who had seldom looked up from his research reports as she disrobed at night? Between breaking up with Larry at nineteen and marrying Barnett at twenty-five, there had been several men, but her body had been flawless then and undressing had been part of the turn-on for her, the bestowal of the prize. Now, despite all the squats and crunches and missiles launched at her abdominals, it was something to be gotten through.

Larry seemed to feel no such qualms. He undid only the top two buttons of his oxford shirt and pulled it over his head, as if he couldn't wait to be naked. Well, he was a man—men could go to seed and it didn't seem to matter, though he looked, she had to admit, wonderful, a bit fleshier than the last time they'd been undressed together, but the basic structure was still intact: tall, long-legged, narrow-shouldered and -hipped, a bit furrier now at the chest and thighs but his back, thank God, was smooth.

It had started with a chaste kiss in the Broadway Nut Shoppe (to which she'd hurried from the Banana Republic—fruits were the theme of the day, apparently). "When do you close?" she'd whispered to him. It was the money at work, the fake money, *her* money. She felt reckless and powerful and anxious and horny as all hell.

"Twenty minutes." When she frowned, he quickly added, "Actually, we're closing early today."

He flipped the hanging sign on the front door to WE'LL BE BACK SOON as she walked to the back room. When he rejoined her, her blouse was off.

"Now, this brings back memories."

Back then, Larry's father would occasionally leave then alone in the Nut Shoppe after school while he went down the block to the bank. Within moments they'd be naked in the back room, Lily's back pressed against the wall, Larry's hands cupping her ass, drawing her up and into him; five minutes later they'd be back behind the counter, dressed but still panting.

He unfastened her bra, loosened her belt, unzipped and unbuttoned her pants, then pulled them and her panties down in one smooth movement. She almost lost her balance.

"Sorry, I don't mean to rush you, but it's not like twenty years ago," he said. "I need to strike while the iron is hot."

She glanced down at his iron, which was unquestionably hot, and hurriedly kicked off her pants and panties.

Peggy was watching the remaining moments of the *McNeil-Lehrer News Hour* (as she still thought of it, even though one of them, McNeil or Lehrer, she could never remember which, had left the show years ago) on the small television in her bedroom, her sole remaining zone of privacy, when Lily knocked on the door.

"Okay if I come in?"

"Wait, I'll get dressed," Peggy shouted, then added, "Monroe, you old goat, get off me and put some clothes on."

"Oh . . . I'll come back."

"I was joking. Come in."

Lily entered looking tentative. Did her daughter really imagine they were having sex? It was gratifying to be thought sexually active at seventy-six, even by one's daughter, but Lily's obliviousness to her father's deterioration was unsettling. The man could hardly move his bowels without assistance— did Lily really think he was up for sex, no pun intended?

"I was wondering if you'd had dinner."

"You-know-who fed the children some sort of gristly stew with the mashed potatoes dumped right on top."

"Shepherd's pie," Lily said.

"Well, she didn't offer us any, not that I would have touched it."

"I thought we might go out for a bite."

"Out?"

"My treat."

"Did you win the lottery?"

"I think I can still afford to take my parents to dinner once in a while."

Peggy forced herself not to respond. Only that afternoon Lily had raided her pocketbook for forty dollars. Now she seemed like a different woman.

"What happened to you all of a sudden? Where have you been all afternoon, robbing a bank?"

"Oh . . ." She glanced away, but an embarrassed smile pulled at the edges of her mouth. "I was in the park. There was a beautiful grosbeak . . ."

"We used to know a Grosbeak from temple," Peggy said, rather than point out that Lily's binoculars had never left the apartment. One thing about living in a bunker; it was a cinch keeping track of everything and everyone. "Well, okay, but just the two of us. I don't think your father's up for a night out."

Twenty-one

Rosemary felt disoriented as she surveyed the dinner menu at Hoyle's. Braised beef cheeks, pan-sautéed skate on polenta, roasted free-range quail. Hoyle's had been her regular haunt during most of her career at Atherton's, famous for the spicy inter-table art-world chitchat and bland food, but the menu had completely changed in her eight month absence.

"I don't recognize any of this stuff," she told Lloyd. "What happened to the meat loaf?"

"That menu was older than most of the stuff we sell," Lloyd said. "Anyway, the chef died and they—"

"Eddie Garnett?"

"At the stove, with his hand on a sauté pan. Heart attack, apparently. They found him covered with béchamel sauce. I mean, who even wants béchamel sauce anymore?"

"He made creamed spinach when I was pregnant, just for me."

"Anyway, *merci* buckets for coming, you know how Esme Hollander adores you."

Rosemary put down the menu.

"What does she have?"

"I don't know. She's being her usual mysterious self, stringing us along for a free dinner. Don't you hate it when rich people act cheap? It's so discouraging."

Thrifty Esme Hollender appeared a few minutes later. She was one of the those tiny, quiet, ancient women, invariably swaddled in layers of jackets, sweaters, and scarves and laden with bags and packages of unfathomable content, who somehow manage to cause a commotion when entering a room, emanating, like a small child, the prospect of overturned china and raised voices.

She took several wrong turns in the large and crowded dining room, having peevishly waved off the maître d's offer of an escort. She found their table after a slow tour of the restaurant and proffered a pink cheek, which Rosemary dutifully pecked. It felt like fine calfskin. Lloyd aimed for the same cheek but Esme, getting up on tippy-toes, reached around his neck, her arms still burdened with bags, and directed his lips directly onto hers.

"You're looking well, Esme," Lloyd said when he'd extricated himself, a gash of scarlet lipstick across his mouth. As she unburdened herself of the bags, he discreetly napkinned his mouth.

"I *feel* well," she said, lowering herself into the chair with a long, aspirated sigh. "Where's the waiter with my drink?"

A waiter appeared almost instantly with a glass of sherry, half of which she took care of in one swill. She was a small, birdlike woman in her eighties, always fussily coifed like a First Lady from an earlier era, with skin so smooth and almost translucently pale, she brought to mind some exotic, milky species, newly discovered in a rain-forest cave, that had never seen sunlight. She had on her usual getup: a floral-patterned silk dress, pearl choker and earrings, and a watch encrusted with so many improbably large diamonds, it was a miracle she could hoist the sherry to her lips.

Esme was the daughter of the late Frederick Packard, who'd invented an obscure valve or gauge that was still an indispensable part of the internal combustion engine. His autobiography, published in the 1950s and entitled *The Importance of Unimportance,* became a Bible of sorts for people on the make in the postwar boom. Rosemary had trudged through it while courting Esme Hollender. She learned that one had a lot more pricing control and security in making a small, "unimportant" component of a much larger entity, such as an automobile engine, than an important one. After the book's publication, the U.S. Patent Office was briefly flooded with applications for newfangled gaskets and grommets.

Frederick Packard's only child, Esme, was plain in every sense, but she had a large enough fortune to attract a presentable, if reputedly homosexual, husband, who devoted his life to satisfying his obsession with art glass. Neither Esme nor her two grown children had much interest in the stuff, so when Alden Hollender died four years ago, Esme had contacted Atherton's for an estimate of the collection's potential worth. She was staggered to learn that Alden's folly might attract five million dollars at auction, but she'd been coy about letting the collection go, ensuring an uninterrupted flow of obsequious attention and free meals from Lloyd Lowell.

"I've brought you something!" she said with a coquettish lift of her penciled eyebrows.

"Reeeally?" Lloyd's tongue made a quick tour of his lips. "Might I see it?"

She reached for a small shopping bag on the floor, but the arrival of the waiter distracted her. He recited the day's specials, took her order for another sherry and Rosemary's for a club soda, and left them alone.

"I can't help thinking I'm betraying Alden, even contemplating selling the collection."

According to art world scuttlebutt, Alden had betrayed her with half the call boys in New York. Rosemary wondered if Esme didn't perhaps have designs on Lloyd himself, another homosexual with a keen eye for art nouveau.

"And then there are the children. They grew up surrounded by these things. So much beauty . . ." She smiled wistfully and drained her sherry just as the waiter arrived with its replacement.

The "children," two "private investors" in their late fifties living off vastly diminished trust funds set up by their grandfather, had contacted Lloyd, separately, to enlist his aid in prying the collection from their mother.

"You could donate a few pieces to the Met in their names," Rosemary suggested, not for the first time.

"You look tired, Lloyd," Esme said, placing a hand on his. "What's been keeping you up nights?" She pursed her lips provocatively.

"The art nouveau market's red-hot," Rosemary said, doing her part to steer the conversation back to the mission at hand.

"There's no sense of tradition anymore," said Esme. "My father wasn't much of a collector, but I treasure the few things he left me. He was too busy building his business to dwell on aesthetics. Have you read his autobiography, *The Importance*—"

"You mentioned a vase . . ."

"Oh, yes." She reached to her left, but once again the waiter appeared, this time to take their food orders. Esme glanced at the menu and ordered a Porterhouse steak with truffles, by far the most expensive item on the menu. She'd leave Hoyle's with all but two bites packaged in a doggie bag.

"Vase?" Lloyd said the moment the waiter left them.

"No thank you." Esme raised her sherry glass. "I'm still working on this one."

"VASE!" Lloyd pointed at the bag on the floor.

"Would you like to see it now?"

His jaw pulsed with frustration.

Esme picked up a plain shopping bag, but the two sherries had apparently weakened her grip. Rosemary dove for the bag and managed to catch it just inches from the ground. Inside, she saw a luminous profusion of colored glass: green and purple leaves, lilac and white flowers, a lemony yellow background.

"Not my cup of tea at all," Esme said as she signaled the waiter for a refill.

"Is it . . ." Lloyd took a deep, steadying breath. "Signed?"

"There's some bit of raised writing on the bottom. Begins with a *G*, with an accent at the end. French, *je pense*."

"Gallé," Rosemary said.

"That's it! Think it's worth anything?"

"We'll have to examine it carefully," Lloyd said, his voice already thick with desire.

"Well, examine it." Esme gave the bag an unnerving thwack with her right hand.

Rosemary didn't dare pull out the entire vase, not in Hoyle's. It could break, for one thing. Even more risky would be exposing it to the voracious dealers in the room. If it really was Gallé, they'd follow Esme home and propose marriage to extricate it from her.

"Safer to wait until I'm back at the office," Lloyd said as Rosemary rewrapped the towel around the vase. "Emile Gallé was a well-known glass designer in the later part of the nineteenth century. He's considered a European Tiffany. We'll call you as soon as we've done a full appraisal."

The rest of the meal was torture. Lloyd barely touched his fish—his only hunger now was for the vase. If the piece was in fact by Emile Gallé, and if the entire vase was in the same condition as the section he'd seen, it would pay for a hundred meals with Esme Hollender. A Gallé vase in fine condition could be the centerpiece of the winter or spring sale. And once Esme saw how much the vase went for, she'd almost certainly let Atherton's have the rest of the collection.

"I'll call you in a day or two with our appraisal," Lloyd told her on the sidewalk.

"Perhaps we should set up a lunch to discuss it," she said as she tottered to the curb. "Or maybe another dinner."

Lloyd hailed her a cab and saw her into it.

"Phillips had an eighteen-inch Gallé vase in their spring show," he told Rosemary as the cab took Esme away. "It went for two-sixty," he practically whispered.

"Amazing."

"There's still a lot of money around," Lloyd observed with a sigh. "Speaking of which . . . I got a very curious phone call from a mousy-voiced man from the SEC of all places."

Rosemary knew right away where this was headed. "Positano?"

"He said they're looking into all purchases of Positano stock on certain dates. Including the date I bought, which was right after our take-out lunch in your hallway–slash–dining room."

"Did he say why?"

"He was completely unhelpful. I told him I've lost my shirt on Positano, wished I'd never heard the name—I'm sorry, Rosemary, but it's true. He wasn't exactly sympathetic."

"What did he want?"

"A list of people I know who either work for Positano or do business with Positano or who know people who work for or do business with Positano."

"That would be me."

"I spoke to a lawyer friend. He told me that it was highly unlikely I'd be sent to jail for losing money."

"Jail?"

"Insider trading, my dear. All of our best customers are doing it."

Rosemary couldn't quite manage a smile.

"I need to talk to Guy about this."

"Probably a good idea."

"It's the last thing he needs, something else to worry about. His board of directors is trying to ram a new chief operating officer down his throat, our renovation is behind schedule and way overbudget—"

"New chief operating officer? Is that a good thing or a bad thing?"

"Guy hates having someone else to—"

"For the stock price."

"For God's sake, Lloyd."

"Don't get all exasperated on me, Rosemary. How much longer can I go on living in a rent-stabilized studio? I keep waiting for real-estate prices to go down—I mean, everything else has."

"It's a very nice studio."

"Don't patronize me, Miss Powder Room. Real estate keeps going up while my savings move in the opposite direction. I used to think I'd schlep out to Brooklyn if I had to or even Queens. I mean, *Queens.* The way things are going, I'll end up commuting by plane from Syracuse. Not to mention I was counting on Positano for my retirement."

"You're thirty-six."

"Which is seventy in gay years."

"I need to get home." She flagged a cab and got in. As it drove off she watched Lloyd cross Madison, taking small, cautious steps and cradling the vase as if it were a newborn.

Ensconced in a prime booth at Chez Nous, Lily discreetly opened her purse and gave the plump wad of counterfeit twenties a reassuring squeeze.

"Let's order a bottle of wine," she said.

"A glass of Chablis will be fine for me." Peggy hadn't stopped glancing around the restaurant from the moment they'd been seated, her expression an unflattering mix of squinting distrust and pursed-lipped hostility. "I always figured this place would look . . . fancier. You read about this one and that one eating here."

"No one looks at anything but each other."

"Still, the carpet looks older than your father. Would it kill them to spring for new window treatments?"

Lily had felt a frisson run through Chez Nous as she entered, her first appearance there since Barnett's arrest. None of her friends were there that night, if *friends* was the right word for people who hadn't bothered to call her since the trouble began, much less invite her anywhere. But she recognized a few faces, and knew from the wave of averted glances and lowered cutlery that trailed her to her table that she'd been recognized as well. Jake, the maître d', had sat them at a prominent booth just beyond the bar area, a gesture not of loyalty but of provocation: He'd always relished the minor humiliations he was able to inflict on New York's social grandees, and seating the impoverished wife of a fugitive—out with her mother, no less—at a table of honor would put several noses out of joint.

Lily took a sip of the good Chardonnay she'd ordered and, surprising herself, cooed with pleasure.

"It's *that* good?" Peggy sniffed her glass before tasting the wine.

"I'm just glad we came. I used to feel so tense coming here, like I was presenting myself for a panel of judges each time I walked in. Tonight I really didn't care."

"Then why did you ever come here?"

"To prove that I could make the judges like me."

"You were such a confident little girl, so pretty, and an A student. I don't know why you always felt you had to prove something."

Lily observed her mother drinking wine, blissfully unaware that she might have played even a small role in forming Lily's craving for approval. She'd been an A student because Peggy viewed A-minuses as only marginally less tragic than teenage pregnancy.

"Let's order," she said. "The Dover sole was always tolerable."

Peggy hadn't fully realized how much wine she'd had until she set off for the ladies' room. The floor rose to meet her feet with each step, like that time on the *Caribbean Princess* when they ran into a storm off the coast of Belize. She spread both arms to keep her balance. How silly she must appear—how embarrassed Lily must feel, watching her lurch along, and she *was* watching, Peggy felt certain, always on guard for the poor choice of word or fork that would betray the unsophisticated roots from which she'd sprung like some sort of genetic mutation. Inside the bathroom, one stall was occupied. She entered the other one. A good evening, all in all; she'd forgotten what fun Lily could be. How long since they'd had a meal together, just the two of them? Too long. Nice to be out with someone who hadn't yet qualified for Medicare, talking about things other than grandchildren and prescription drugs and how this store or that one overcharged. A flush from next door, then the sound of someone else entering the small bathroom.

"How have you been?" A woman's voice, naturally.

"I've been wonderful. You?" Another woman's voice. Both had that silky lilt Lily had picked up somewhere between high school and Park Avenue.

"Did you see who's sitting in the first booth?"

"I almost choked. I'd heard she'd moved away."

"Only to the West Side. Who's that she's with?"

"Must be her mother."

"Who knew she had one? I think she's put on weight."

"Well, some people eat under stress. I'm the opposite. I lost five pounds planning the leukemia benefit."

"You should write a book, *The Leukemia Diet!*"

"You're *terrible*. I'm surprised she'd come back here. I mean, everyone knows about her husband."

"One of his former partners called Seb and practically begged him to keep our money in the firm."

"I meant the girlfriend, not the money."

"Did you know her?"

"No one did. But Seb saw her photograph in the *Times* a few weeks ago, on some business matter. Francine Sparkler, one of those severe-looking finance types, all business until they get into the bedroom, and then they're all about 24/7 blow jobs and positions that would give Olga Korbut a hernia."

"Stop."

"Listen, after Seb came back, I lost seven pounds just from the . . . I mean, we were at it all night, two, three time a week, and it wasn't like the old days, when I could just lie back and wait for him to be done. And that was on top of the weight I lost while he was gone."

"The Cheating Husband Diet."

"I mean, these girlfriends *do* things. They have to, I suppose. Where were we? Oh, Francine Sparkler. Apparently, she used to advise Barnett on what stocks to buy. But Seb's attorney's partner is now her attorney, and one hears things."

"Like what?"

"Oh, just that the Feds have been all over her, thinking she knows where Barnett is. I hear they're convinced she's sending money to him, wherever he is."

"I thought he absconded with the millions he took from the firm."

"Well, that's one theory, I suppose. The other is that she's supporting him. Still, I miss her in a way, Lily Grantham. You could always count on her at parties to keep the conversation moving. And the men liked her. If you put her at their table, they were less likely to whine about having to stay till after dessert."

"No one could laugh at a bad joke like Lily Grantham. Seb always used to say that she . . ."

The silky voice dissolved a second before the door closed. Peggy got right up and left the bathroom, neglecting even to wash her hands.

"Francine Sparkler," she mumbled as she made her way back to the table.

"Are you feeling okay?" Lily asked when she sat down. "I was about to go after you."

"Francine Sparkler."

"Who?"

"I'll tell you in a minute. First write the name down. Francine Sparkler."

The McDonald's near Penn Station was half full. No, it was half empty, Guy decided as he waited for Derek Ventnor to arrive. The lighting bathed the mostly solo diners in a sallow gloom, a great equalizer, in a way: Everyone—black, white, Asian, Hispanic—looked identically jaundiced, members of one race: the depressed.

Was he depressed? Mentally Guy tore off a piece of foolscap and drew a line down its center. On the left he drew a plus sign and under it wrote "marriage, twins, Positano, new apartment." Then, on the right column, he drew a minus sign and wrote, after a long hesitation, "marriage, twins, Positano, new apartment." He reviewed the right column from the bottom up: The renovation was a nightmare, Positano was running on fumes, the twins, after several weeks of sleeping through the night (if "night" could be defined as the fidgety interval between the end of the eleven o'clock news and 5:15 A.M.), had recently formed a perfectly synchronized and very noisy partnership whose sole objective was to keep their parents in a constant state of bleary-eyed consciousness, and he and Rosemary, thanks to all of the above, had slipped into a mostly silent, occasionally bickering, and completely sexless . . . *relationship* seemed too positive a word—more like détente.

And yet if the right-hand column essentially negated the left, that didn't add up to depressed, just . . . equilibrium? Survival? Just getting through the day, the week, the month, the year—an animal or bird doing whatever it took to survive, over and over and over again.

"My man!" Ventnor looked right at home in the sickly gloom. "You're not eating?" he said.

"I prefer Burger King," Guy said.

"You should have said something." Ventnor shrugged and toddled off to the back of the restaurant. He returned several minutes later. "You bring the check?" Ventnor asked as he began to unwrap a half-dozen Styrofoam and paper containers.

Guy handed him the ten-thousand-dollar check and added the name Derek Ventnor to the right column of his mental foolscap, which tilted the scale decisively toward "depressed."

"I have this friend," Ventnor said as he deposited the check in his shirt pocket. He went at his burger, consuming nearly half of it in one raptorous bite, his mouth dilating impressively to accommodate the intake. "Actually, he's more of a colleague," he added through a mouthful of burger and roll.

Guy felt a surge of nausea at the thought of what a "colleague" of Ventnor's might want.

"He runs a Web site, one of the top twenty most-visited sites, in fact."

It seemed unlikely that Ventnor's colleague was Jeff Bezos.

"A porn site?"

Ventnor made a "duh" gesture.

"He's having trouble scaling." He aligned three plastic packets of ketchup, ripped off their tops in one brutal movement, and squeezed the contents onto a pile of waiting fries. "At a certain point you gotta monetize your traffic or you're just a destination with no revenues. This fellow, he showed me his books the other day, you wouldn't believe the churn he's got."

"I'm sure your astute advice is precisely what he needs to turn his business around."

"I've given him a few pointers. But the thing of it is, we're talking a gay site. Not that my friend is gay, don't worry. But gay is where the bucks are. More disposable income, no kids, and they have more time to surf the Net without worrying that the wife is gonna catch them whacking off to beaver shots when they said they were planning the family vacation on Expedia. And then you have the closet cases, married guys who live out their fantasies on gay sites. I've thought about getting into gay myself—not the straight gay scene, as in two women performing for men, I already got that covered—I mean the gay gay scene, as in two men. Or three men or twenty men or an army of men—group scenes are very big in that world, you know. And they got toys you wouldn't believe." Ventnor crammed a fistful of ketchupped fries into his mouth. "So here's the thing."

Guy braced himself mentally and, gripping the edge of the table with both hands, physically.

"My friend, he spends like half his time sending e-mails to his clientele. He sends each one himself, it's a friggin' nightmare. And his click-through rate is like less than five percent. I told him about Positano and he's big-time interested."

"I'll send him a brochure."

"See, that's what we don't need in this instance. I already sold him. He's ready to sign a license agreement. My point being, I'd like a commission."

"We don't pay third parties a—"

"Fifty percent."

"Out of the question."

"I listened to your second-quarter conference call on the Internet a while back. Even with a fifty percent commission, you'll make money on the deal. Your gross margins are, like, seventy-eight percent."

Positano's gross margins were precisely seventy-eight percent. Wasn't the Internet a wonderful thing? Not to mention the SEC's new full-disclosure policy, which meant that anyone, even a greedy pornographer, could listen in on a company's quarterly earnings call with analysts. What used to be a clubby quarterly ritual was now a spectator sport, all in the interest of fairness. The notion that Ventnor had been listening to him recite Positano's second-quarter numbers and business strategy was profoundly creepy—no doubt two of Ventnor's performers were fucking in the background as he cheerily talked up the company's prospects for margin improvement.

"We don't pay third-party commissions," he told him again.

"I'm not your typical third party. If I decide to make our relationship public—"

"Twenty-five percent," Guy said. His head rang with the creaking and groaning of his principles giving way.

"Fifty."

"Thirty."

"Fifty."

"Thanks for being flexible."

"Listen, porn is what the Internet's all about. You'll never make it unless you figure that out. You think AOL and Yahoo are any different? They're portals to sex sites. Okay, so there's eBay and a few travel sites, but trust me, while the wives are selling shit from the attic on eBay, their husbands are looking at pussy . . . or dick."

Guy stood up. "Who do I send the contracts to?"

"To me. I'll handle everything. Hey, I gotta earn my commission." Ventnor's smile drove Guy's spirits, already depressed, to a new, NASDAQ-style low.

"Send me an e-mail with the details," he said, and walked away.

Twenty-two

Francine Sparkler lived on Lexington Avenue on the seventh floor of exactly the sort of undistinguished white-brick building from which Lily had rescued Barnett twenty years earlier, a fact that, in Lily's eyes, made his betrayal all the more bitter. She doubted Francine would let her up if the doorman announced her, so she whisked right by him to the elevators. If you looked unthreateningly affluent and projected an attitude of blithe entitlement, you could breeze by most Manhattan doormen in the larger, more impersonal buildings.

"It's Lily Grantham," she shouted through the closed door of apartment 7R, in response to a surprisingly husky "Who's there?"

"Leave me alone."

"Trust me, you don't want to have this conversation with me out in the hallway," Lily shouted, though in such a large, soulless building it was possible that the resident of Apartment 7R had never exchanged more than cordial greetings with the occupants of Apartments 7A through 7Q, let alone cared that they knew she had been the mistress of an international fugitive.

"Go away."

Her voice faltered over the two words. Encouraged, Lily banged a fist on the door and pressed the doorbell several times with her other hand. The door opened.

"I have nothing to say to you," Francine Sparkler said. "I've told the U.S. Attorney everything I know."

Lily didn't know what to focus on first, the fact that the Feds had already spoken to Francine—meaning the U.S. government knew her husband had been fucking her long before Lily did—or the fact that the object of her husband's . . . call it lust . . . was a plumpish woman not much younger than she. She had steeled herself for a hard-bodied, age-inappropriate vixen— and found herself nonplussed by the flaccidity of her competition. In cheating on her, Barnett had traded down both in location and looks.

Francine was a small woman, but Lily doubted anyone would call her petite. A mass of ringletted hair flounced from the top of her head, adding crucial millimeters to her stature. Her face was pretty enough, with the smooth, unlined skin that was the one benefit of pudginess. She had on a cream silk blouse and dark linen pants—there was probably a matching Ann Taylor jacket draped over a chair in the bedroom, since she looked like she was about to leave for work, Lily having arrived, following a sleepless night contemplating the latest horror to beset her, at eight in the morning. It was difficult to imagine her making million-dollar decisions on Wall Street, let alone making love to Barnett. She exuded neither competence nor sexuality.

"If you came here to stare at me, fine. Now go away." Roused from her unkind musings, Lily lunged inside.

"I really don't care what you and Barnett were up to," she said. As if to undermine her own words, she glanced with undisguised curiosity around the living room, which opened directly from the small foyer. Wheat-colored sofa with matching love seat, fabric blinds in a neutral tone, framed Impressionist posters, new Oriental carpet. A generically comfortable environment. She'd been betrayed—she, whose apartment had nailed ten pages in *Architectural Digest*—for a doughy investment banker and a shrine to Crate & Barrel.

"Can I offer you a *tour*?"

"Oh . . . I was just . . ." The mistress had a sense of humor, at least. Was *that* part of it? Or did she enthusiastically offer up her "third input," in the quaint locution of one of Barnett's favored Web sites, Ass-ettes.com? Was she perhaps handy with a dildo?

"You're making me very uncomfortable."

"Yes, well, as I was saying, I really don't care what you and Barnett . . . did. I just need to find him."

"I don't know—"

"Don't misunderstand me. I don't care if I never see him again." She paused, struck—in fact, almost exhilarated—by the truth of that statement. "He left us, my children and me, without a penny. We lost everything we had."

"So I've heard, but I don't know where he is."

"When I learned he had fled the country, I thought, No, that's not like him. But when I learned, just yesterday, that he'd been . . . with you . . . I realized that running away was precisely like him. He was a rat. I just never knew it."

"He hated the dishonesty. He was on the verge of telling you when . . . when he had to leave."

"Telling me? Are you saying he was about to—Wait a minute, when he *had* to leave? He didn't *have* to do anything."

"He didn't have to fall in love with me," she said quietly.

"Oh, please."

Francine crossed the living room and sat heavily on the wheat Crate & Barrel sofa. After a few moments, Lily joined her, choosing the matching love seat. Love seat! Good Lord. Feeling a choking panic coming on, she ran her hands along the nubby fabric on which, no doubt, Barnett and Francine, fleshily naked as Rubens satyrs, had engaged in sexual gymnastics worthy of a Web site. Rubenesquemiddleagedsexcontortionists.com.

"When exactly did you . . ."

"Mornings, mostly, and sometimes at lunch. There are new hotels downtown that we—"

"When did you first *meet?*"

"Oh." Francine blushed. The Brontes would have described her as "handsome," Lily supposed, with her flawlessly milky complexion and dark, "spirited" eyes. "Three years ago, at the CS First Boston High Yield Conference."

"That must have been very romantic."

"We had a lot in common," Francine said quietly. "We talked about everything."

"Junk bonds, default rates, discounted cash flows." She offered a smug smile.

"Passion, fears, dreams."

"Passion, fears, dreams," Lily repeated. *Barnett had those?*

"I miss him terribly."

"So do—"

So do I, she almost said, competitively.

"He was terrified he'd be arrested, and for something he didn't do."

The mistress is always so credulous, Lily thought. It must be part of the turn-on for the man.

"Three million dollars is missing. There are checks, drawn on client accounts, with his signature on them."

"Anyone with practice can forge a signature."

Don't lecture me *on forgery,* Lily was tempted to say.

"The man I knew never stole a dime. But the man I knew would also rather kill himself than go to jail for something he didn't do."

"But he didn't kill himself, did he? He ran away."

"He was right," Francine said under her breath.

"About what?"

"About you."

"What do you—"

"About your not loving him, not understanding him, not respecting him."

"How dare you?" Lily said with all the indignation she could muster, which, even to her own ears, wasn't much. (When stripped of dignity, was it even possible to exhibit indignation?)

"He said you used him, that you wanted a certain place in society and saw him as a stepping stone. I used to see your picture in the Sunday *Times,* even before I met Barnett. You were always referred to as Mrs. Lily Grantham, or sometimes even Mrs. Barnett Grantham, but Mr. Grantham was never in the picture. Literally *and* figuratively."

Well, *he* wasn't wearing ten thousand dollars of couture. *He* hadn't been eating like a prisoner of war all week to fit into it.

"I introduced him to half his clients at those parties. He wanted to go."

"That's not what he told me."

"You were his mistress. You'd believe anything."

"You didn't know him."

"I won't argue with you," Lily said, and proceeded to do just that. "I was married to him for sixteen years. We have two children together, a history."

"You had more time with him than I did, that's all. A few nights before this whole scandal broke out, we were cooking together and he told me that he'd always wanted to learn to fly a plane. We decided that when . . . when we were together, we'd take lessons."

"You cooked together?"

"He was a magician in the kitchen. We had very few evenings together, and when we did we always ate in."

"How discreet." Not to mention inexpensive. No wonder Barnett had been smitten.

"He loved to make halibut with a fennel sauce. It was our . . ." She glanced demurely at her lap.

"Your what? Oh, for Christ's sake . . ." Lily had to look away to avoid either laughing or doubling over in horror. Halibut with fennel sauce had been their aphrodisiac. She'd never known Barnett to make toast, much less get a hard-on from fish. Clearly, it was time to regain control of the conversation, and then get out of there.

"Where is he? You must have heard from him." Half of her hoped that Barnett had been in touch, the better to track him down and recover the money. The other half desperately wanted him to have stiffed his mistress as well as his family. God, she was tired of shouldering so many conflicting emotions.

The mistress's eyes began to water unbecomingly, and when tears finally spilled over onto her cheeks, she made no effort to wipe them away. Lily handed her a tissue from her purse. The mistress shook her head, shedding teardrops onto her lap.

"Dry yourself off, for heaven's sake."

She took the tissue and dabbed at her face.

"So he hasn't been in touch with you, either. Well, at least you know where you stand."

"He'd call if he could."

"I imagine there's phone service wherever he is. But if it helps to believe that . . ."

"They might be bugging my phones, watching me. He can't take the chance."

"He could face his accusers like a man."

"He was being railroaded."

"His investments were in free-fall—I don't suppose he told you that."

"They were down an average of sixteen-point-three percent for the year on the day he left," she said through sniffles. "That's net return, after fees. We talked about it the Saturday before the scandal, when he came here for lunch. He brought two bags of produce"—*sniff*—"from the farmers' market on Union Square and made pasta niçoise. It took forever to prepare"—*sniff*—"because he parboiled each vegetable separately before tossing them with the linguini."

Lily could scarcely picture Barnett striding through the Union Square farmers' market in his weekend uniform of polo shirt, freshly pressed khakis, and penny loafers, as disdainfully incongruous as a khakied colonial emissary in a Moroccan casbah. She certainly couldn't picture him tossing individually parboiled vegetables into linguini.

"We talked about the market that day and he seemed so optimistic, he was sure everything was going to turn around. We talked about the possibility of hedging with index futures and shorting ETFs."

Shorting EFTs . . . was *that* what Barnett had missed, not her *third input* but hot talk of index futures and hedging strategies?

"He radiated such confidence. He would never have stolen from his own firm or his investors."

"But things haven't turned around. We'd be broke now even if he hadn't left, so stealing a few million dollars wasn't such a bad idea after all."

"I wish you'd go."

Though she hated to give the impression of obedience, Lily stood up. As she crossed the living room she couldn't help glancing into the kitchen. She pictured Barnett in that narrow, windowless space, parboiling beans and broccoli from the Union Square farmers' market while his mistress looked on admiringly, breaking the comfy silence only to whisper sweetly of index futures and net returns.

The mistress remained on the sofa as Lily let herself out.

Guy and Rosemary hired a sitter and went to inspect their new apartment.

"I guess this qualifies as a date," Rosemary said as they walked in early-evening darkness along West End Avenue. "So tell me, Guy, what is it you do?"

"I'm the CEO of a software company!" *We enable porn sites to communicate more effectively with their customers, straight and gay, vanilla and kinky.* "How about you, Rosemary?"

"I'm on leave from Atherton's, where I specialize in decorative arts."

"I hope that's not a maternity leave, because I don't date women with baggage."

Rosemary took his hand. "Is everything all right, Guy? You seem miserable, but you never say anything." She decided not to mention Lloyd's call from the SEC, which would take Guy down even further. It was bound to blow over, once the government realized Lloyd had *lost* money on Positano.

"Business sucks."

"Let's talk about it."

"You don't want to know."

She retracted her hand and they continued in tense silence. Five minutes later they entered 218 West End Avenue. Inside the apartment, Guy fumbled for the light switch and felt a cruel letdown when he finally managed to find it.

"Nothing's changed," he said. "It's just how we left it last week."

They toured the empty apartment in dejected silence. The kitchen floor had not been laid, which meant the cabinets and appliances had not been installed. The gashes in the ceiling where the wall had been taken down between the living room and guest bedroom had not been plastered, which meant that painting could not begin. None of the plumbing in any of the bathrooms had been touched, so of course none of the new fixtures were installed, much less the new tiles. Toilets and tubs and unopened boxes of Italian ceramic tile waited in the hallway outside the guest bathroom like women at a Broadway intermission.

"Victor gave me his word that everything was on track," Rosemary said when they regrouped in the kitchen.

Guy unholstered his cell phone and speed-dialed Ozeri's number. After one ring he got his voice mail.

"Can we fire him?" Rosemary asked when Guy hung up. "We still owe him a lot of money."

"But we've already paid him fifty thousand dollars. If we walked away now, he'd still have our fifty thousand dollars and we'd have to start over with someone else."

"Lucinda said we could sell the apartment for something like a six-hundred-thousand-dollar profit. All that money and we never even moved in. It's like someone's paying us just for existing."

"That's real estate," Guy said. "But we're not selling."

"I was going to measure the windows in the boys' room for shutters tonight. Seems pointless now."

"You might as well. We have the sitter."

Rosemary went to the bedroom they'd earmarked for the twins and took a measuring tape from her purse. Something on the floor near the window caught her eye. She bent down for a closer look. It was handwriting, etched in a corner of the parquet floor, which had until a week ago been covered by rust-colored wall-to-wall carpeting. She blew away the plaster dust that coated every surface of the apartment and read the inscription: *Lily and Larry, 5/25/75 and forever.*

She called Guy and showed him the inscription. "She must have pulled up the corner of the carpet and secretly done this."

"Nineteen seventy-five . . . Lily must be the Gimmels' daughter."

"She wanted to leave something behind, something permanent about their love."

"Nothing's permanent in a New York apartment, not the walls, the plumbing, the wiring, and certainly not the floors." Most of the apartment's floors were slated to be sanded down to raw wood and polyurethaned, though in the foyer their plans called for removing the seventy-five-year-old parquet and replacing it with honed slate.

"We can't just . . . remove this," Rosemary said. "She must have been bursting with love, and wanted some way to commemorate it."

"Never fear, at the rate Ozeri's going, Lily's inscription will last another quarter-century."

"Lily Gimmel became Lily Grantham, a society figure until her husband got caught up in a financial scandal."

"Well, her parents just became overnight multimillionaires, thanks to us."

Rosemary frowned. "I wonder if she and Larry did in fact manage to last forever. Larry Grantham . . . the name doesn't sound right. I don't think that's the guy she married."

"Probably just a high-school crush."

"I suppose." Rosemary licked the tip of her finger and rubbed it across the inscription, clearing away a film of dust. Guy knelt beside her.

"We could add our own inscription, once all this work is done."

"I like that idea."

He wrapped his arms around her and they kissed.

"As long as we have the sitter . . ."

"I was thinking the same thing."

"There's some sort of canvas sheet in the other room," Guy said.

He led her to what their architect called the "great room," a newly-vast space formed by the demolition of the wall that had once separated the living room from the guest bedroom. On one end, an expanse of built-in cherry bookshelves had been installed, an absurd bit of progress amid the otherwise moribund renovation—the cabinetmaker had insisted on delivering the bookshelves in order to clear his workshop for the next project. Though it must have fundamentally shaken his sense of cosmic order to complete even one small facet of the job ahead of schedule, Ozeri had blessed their installation. In the opposite corner of the great room Guy found the canvas sheet, which would one day protect the floors from dripping paint, assuming that day ever arrived, and spread it on the floor. Rosemary undressed as far from the uncovered windows as possible.

"Let's fuck in every room tonight," Guy whispered into the pregnancy-deepened gorge between Rosemary's breasts. "Including the bathrooms."

"I'm not sure my back could take that," she whispered.

He rolled off her, onto his back, and pulled her on top of him.

"Better?"

"Hmmm, much."

"God, I'm so freakin' horny, Rosie," he said as she began gently gnawing at his nipples. "How long has it been?"

"How old are the twins?" Slowly she worked her way down his arched midsection and took his hard cock in her mouth. He felt thrillingly exposed, there on the floor of the great room—*the great room!* They were having sex on the floor of the great room! *His* great room! The greatest great room in the greatest city in the greatest country in the world! He imagined the scene Web cast to horny browsers around the world, a million hands gripping

mouses and dicks as they watched, lustful, perhaps even jealous of the passion, the vigor, and (among Manhattanites, at least) the square footage.

"This is so fucking hot, Rosie. Oh, God, Rosie, don't stop." He let his
head loll to one side. "Oh, God."

She moaned in sympathy. "Oh, God."

How could he have missed it? The center portion of the bookshelf unit,
an enclosed cabinet with precisely calibrated compartments for the fifty-
two-inch flat-screen television, the TiVo, the VCR, the DVD, the tuner,
the equalizer, the CD player, the DVDs, the videotapes, and the CDs, was
misaligned.

"Oh my God," he moaned.

"I know, I know, oh . . . I want you, Guy. *I want you.*"

The enclosed cabinet should have been centered along the wall. But one
corner of the wall had a sixteen-inch build-out that concealed a steel riser.
Instead of accounting for this anomaly, the cabinetmaker had simply centered the unit between the built-out corner and the other corner. The entire
unit, fifty-five thousand dollars of tongue-and-grooved cherry, was off-
center by a hideously obvious sixteen inches.

"What's the matter?" Rosemary asked from a distant region of his now-
motionless body.

He turned from the misaligned cabinets to Rosemary, who held his withered prick in her hand.

"The bookshelves," he said. "They're all wrong. Don't you see, the center
unit is too far left."

"Oh, Guy." She refocused her attention on his dick, but to no avail. She
rolled off him with an exasperated sigh, stood up, got dressed, and stomped
out of the not-so-great room. Guy put on his clothes and looked for the architect's plans, which might reveal who was responsible for the misaligned
bookshelves, which would have to be rebuilt at someone's expense.

"Rosie, have you seen the blueprints?" he said when he found her in the
twins' room. She was kneeling over the inscription in the corner. "Have you
seen the plans?" he repeated when she didn't answer. Then he noticed that
she was crying. He placed a consoling hand on her shoulder, which she
shrugged off. He headed for the bathroom off the maid's room, which contained the apartment's only working toilet and was, in fact, the only room

not affected by the renovation. It was tiny but in decent shape, with faded wallpaper that Rosemary had pronounced charming. Midway through a long, urgent pee (at least his dick was good for something) a water bug the size of a hamster skittered across the wall facing him. Startled, he stepped back, spraying the wall, but not the water bug, with piss. Now even the maid's room wallpaper would have to be replaced.

Twenty-three

When it came to Nanny, Peggy constantly surprised herself with what she was learning to tolerate. The drone of the afternoon soap operas from the living room—Nanny's precious "stories." The meagerness of the meals she prepared for the children: slices of turkey breast as thin as plastic wrap, tiny scoops of pallid "mash," two or three flaccid string beans, which the children sensibly ignored, despite Nanny's braying encouragement to "Eat your veg, dears." The way she vacuumed the entire apartment in under five minutes, idly sashaying from room to room as if in the arms of a dance partner. Peggy supposed she should be grateful: The only chore Nanny volunteered for was "hoovering." And who knew British was such an irritating language?

But tying up the phone flicked her tolerance right over the edge.

"You know, you really should try to restrict your phone calls to one or two a day," Peggy said, reasonably, shortly after the kids had left for school, followed closely by Lily on one of her mysterious new "errands."

"They're local calls," Nanny replied with that insinuating accent that turned a simple word like *calls* into a multisyllabic whine. "I do have a life, you know, apart from looking after the children and whatnot."

What kind of life? Peggy wanted to know. Having made an unavoidably close study of her over the past several months, she'd come to realize that

Nanny wasn't nearly as old as she seemed—perhaps only fifty, or even late forties, though she dressed and acted like she'd been looking after Queen Victoria's children.

"I'm expecting a call from . . ." Peggy futilely racked her brain for a plausible name. "It's an important call."

"You might consider call waiting."

Blood surged into her head.

"On Park Avenue we had three phone numbers, plus dedicated lines for the children's computer and Mr. Grantham's."

"Well, *we* have just one line here on Broadway," Peggy said.

"Then there will be tie-ups. If I have to ring my sister, I'm going to use the telephone. I'm sorry, but that's the way it is. Now, I'll just get back to tidying up."

She left Peggy in the kitchen to resume "tidying up," which, apart from "hoovering," involved nothing more strenuous than flitting about with a feather duster. Later, Peggy heard her on the phone in the living room, talking, as she always did, in a conspiratorial hush. She picked up the bedroom extension and was about to inform Nanny that she needed to use the phone when she realized that her presence on the line had gone undetected.

"I'm thinking of sheer white for the curtains," she heard Nanny whisper. "I like to imagine them billowing in the breeze when the windows are open in the warm months."

"You're such a romantic, Caroline," came a man's voice.

Caroline. So Nanny *did* have a first name.

"I want it to be all light and sunny, not like this place I'm in now. We're up on the sixteenth floor and you might think we're in a church basement, it's that gloomy."

Peggy couldn't help glancing around the bedroom. The queen-size bed, on which Monroe was napping, was covered with the ivory chenille spread she'd had in the old place. The headboard was upholstered in a matching fabric. She'd had the drapes from her old room refitted to the new windows, and recalled the name of the color even after thirty years: burnt sienna. *Classic* and *elegant* were the words she'd use, perhaps even *timeless*, though Monroe, with his open mouth and spittled chin, did add a gloomy touch. Still, you couldn't include him as part of the decor, even if he moved as infrequently as the mahogany highboy he kept his underwear and socks in.

"There's nothing gloomy about you, Caroline." His voice was American, quite deep, and laced with a gruff innuendo.

"I don't know how much longer I can stand it here. She's always underfoot."

I'm *underfoot?* Peggy almost shouted into the phone.

"We can't afford to have you leave now," the man said. "Just be patient and keep your eyes on what we're working toward."

"A white settee and matching armchairs," Nanny said dreamily. "All clean and crisp."

"And impractical."

"Okay, then, white sailcloth slipcovers. When they get soiled you just pop them in the washer."

"I can't wait."

"And I better get off. She's been wingeing about the phone. Next thing the old bitch'll be on my case about using the loo too much."

"Just keep your eyes on the prize, Caroline. And I'll keep my eyes on your luscious ass."

"That's enough from you."

"I'm sitting here imagining your lovely ass—or should I say arse—billowing in the breeze."

"Right, I'm hanging up."

Peggy waited until the line went dead before clicking off. The overheard conversation had raised many intriguing questions, and inflamed her in numerous ways, but at the moment she felt an overwhelming need to survey Nanny's behind—or should she say arse? She found her in the living room, daintily flicking the feather duster at the bookshelves like Rembrandt applying the finishing touches to a portrait.

"Did you want something?" Nanny inquired, turning around.

"Oh, I . . ."

She was at a loss for words, surprised and inexplicably unsettled to realize that Nanny did, in fact, have a perfectly formed heart-shaped derriere. *Luscious* might be an overstatement, but how had she missed the fact that Nanny was rather well put together?

"Are you all right, Mrs. Gimmel?"

"Don't forget to dust the windowsills," she said through fixed lips, achieving the desired lady-of-the-manor lockjaw, and fled the room.

"Do you ever feel . . ." Lily shook her head and ran an X-acto knife along the sheet of paper.

"Do I ever feel guilty?" Mohammed was making faint pencil marks on another sheet to guide her blade, working with a diamond cutter's close concentration. "I feel guilty that I ever allowed you to become involved with me. I feel guilty that my income is now half what it was."

"That's not what I meant."

"You should talk to my wife in Guyana. She was planning to bring the children to New York next year. Now she's not so sure."

"So *I'm* supposed to feel guilty?"

"There is fortunately an easy cure for your guilt. Get out of my life."

Lily felt a curious letdown. She'd come to enjoy the hours spent in the garage with Mohammed, making money. It hadn't occurred to her, though clearly it should have, that he resented her presence.

"I happen to know you've upped production since I came on board," she said.

"There's a limit to how much I can safely print. I do not want to get greedy and flood the market with these bills. That might attract attention."

"Yes, well, a counterfeiter wouldn't want to get greedy."

"I beg your pardon?"

"Anyway, you admitted last week that it was immigration issues, not money, that was keeping your family from joining you."

"If they were Arab terrorists, the government would let them right in, no questions asked," Mohammed said. "Unfortunately, we are middle-class Guyanese, of Indian descent." He spoke very fast, words butting up against one another, at least to her ears, with a lilting accent that ended each sentence, even complaints about her presence, on an optimistic upbeat.

"They could come over for a visit and just stay. That's how . . ." That's how Consuela had come from the Dominican Republic.

"Good grief, do you think I would allow my children to enter this country illegally?" he said as he took a sheaf of papers from the printer tray, each printed on one side with the front of four twenty-dollar bills. He inserted the paper back into the printer to print the reverse side and sat in front of the computer to type in instructions. "I will not have my children living illegally. Anyway, I want a bigger house. This place is unacceptable."

Lily had been inside only to use the bathroom, and it hardly struck her as unacceptable compared to what she imaged his wife and sons were accustomed to in Guyana.

"I don't know what kind of place your family is living in now," she said, "but this wouldn't be so bad for them."

"You wouldn't bring your children here."

"I'm living on a pullout sofa in my parents' home."

"Even so."

He waited for her to draw the X-acto knife lengthwise across a sheet of twenties.

"I am putting most of my income"—he looked at her and smiled—"into the stock market. By the time next year comes, I will have more than enough to buy a proper home and then I will send for my family. I would like them to live in Manhattan. When they think about New York, they think about Times Square and the Empire State Building. Not"—he nodded toward the small garage window and the vast sprawl of Queens beyond—"this."

"You can't count on the stock market, Mohammed. Not anymore."

"I study it closely. This is not gambling for me, it is science."

"That's what my husband used to say before he fled the country. Do you just bring piles of twenties to your broker?"

"Don't be absurd. You see, I drive a taxi, a cash business. Who can tell how much cash I bring in each day, a temporary bachelor who works 24/7? Every Friday morning I bring my cash earnings to the bank and make a deposit. I pay taxes, too. Everything legitimate. Hand me that pile of fresh twenties, please."

"But doesn't the bank check the money?"

"Perhaps, but as you know, I make a lot of change in my cab, at the local stores. By the time Friday rolls around, most of my cash is legitimate."

"You must miss your family very much," she said a while later.

"We talk often during the week, and we chat all the time online. I fool myself into thinking I am a part of their lives, even after being away for five years. Then I receive a photograph and I don't recognize my boys, they are like strangers to me. The oldest has a shadow of dark hair over his lip. Soon he will be a man. I wonder if they will know me when they finally get here."

"I think not recognizing your own children is part of being a parent. Mine can walk in a room after being at school all day and I think, Who is this person?"

"Sometimes I think they resent me for being here. They think I am living like Jerry Seinfeld and drinking at the Cheers bar every night while they squeeze into three rooms with bad plumbing and no air-conditioning."

"Take it from me, parents who live with their kids aren't always so wonderful."

He looked at her sympathetically and she was almost encouraged to continue along this line. But she wasn't quite ready to review her shortcomings as a parent with Mohammed Satywatti.

"You should get the bath ready for these," she said, waving a sheaf of new twenties. Soaking the newly minted bills in a milky liquid, the exact formula for which Mohammed refused to divulge, made the bills feel stiff and coarse, more like the genuine article. She suspected the bath was nothing more than starch and water, but Mohammed made her leave the garage while he concocted it. The alchemic mixture prepared, he allowed her to dip the bills, stir them around a bit, then hang each one with a paper clip on a wire to dry. Making money was quite labor intensive. Who knew? as her mother might say.

Later, walking toward the subway stop, stacks of fresh twenties lending a satisfying heft to her Prada tote bag, Lily was sure she spotted a familiar face duck into a corner bodega. A tall, sandy-haired, Nordic-looking man in an area inhabited almost exclusively by Guyanese. As she swiped her Metro-Card, noting with pleasure the $220 balance, she decided he was the same man who'd tried to take the envelope from her on William Street on the night she'd broken into Barnett's old office and first met Mohammed.

Rosemary hired a sitter for two hours and spent Thursday afternoon in the library on the second floor of the Metropolitan Museum, just off the Medieval Courtyard. The Met's nineteenth-century decorative arts collection wasn't extensive—the Victoria and Albert's was far better—but she couldn't very well fly over to London, as appealing as that might be, to research the provenance of a vase that her boss was resolutely convinced was genuine. Rosemary had misgivings, which she would not share with Lloyd until she had proof. She hadn't been to the Met since the twins were born and hadn't realized, until she stepped inside the grand hallway, how much she'd missed it.

The library in particular was a favorite spot, a quiet sanctuary where people pored over books on African tribal masks and Qing Dynasty porcelain with the hushed seriousness of wartime cryptographers. She had gathered a small pile of books on decorative glass, which lay before her on a table.

She'd seen the vase only once since the dinner with Lloyd and Esme, when her suspicions had taken root. Trying to fall asleep that night, she focused on the vase, but pleasurable thoughts of a successful winter auction quickly gave way to wakeful anxiety. At first it was the signature, on the bottom of the vase rather than the side, as was customary for Gallé. Her philosophy had always been to let the object authenticate the signature, rather than the other way around, so she'd tried to overlook the fact that Emile Gallé, unlike contemporaries Louis Tiffany, René Lalique, and the Daum brothers, almost always acid-etched his signature on the side of objects. What about the piece itself?

She opened the first book, a Gallé catalogue raisonné, and began flipping through it. She found much that looked familiar. Glass designers seldom subscribed to the "less is more" theory, adding spirals, beads, and molten bits of glass while the object was still hot, always trying to stretch the bounds of what could be done with glass, with results that were sometimes of dubious aesthetic value. Gallé in particular liked to lay it on thick, literally and figuratively. He was a master of cameo glass, layering different hues of glass one on top of another, then carving a design through the layers. It was a tortuous process, but when done well could result in dazzling sculptural works that appeared to have been carved from luminous marble. Esme's vase was a prime example of cameo glass—or was it? In the nineteenth century, some glass designers, particularly in Bohemia, coated objects with molten colored glass and cut through the transparent surface to the clear metal beneath. Although she hadn't caught it over dinner at Hoyle's, Rosemary sensed later that Esme's vase might have been produced using the Bohemian method, which would destroy the Gallé attribution.

The peony pattern of Esme's vase appeared frequently in the Gallé catalog, which meant nothing, really. A counterfeiter would hardly choose a unique motif. But on Esme's piece, the peonies seemed a bit overused; Gallé, for all his showmanship, was careful to balance gaudy blooms with restrained foliage, all achieved by etching through different colors and textures of applied glass. Esme's vase was a riotous tangle of peony blossoms with very little foliage—it seemed designed to attract attention, and perhaps a high price, rather than earn aesthetic merit.

And then there was the provenance. Or, rather, the lack of one. A quick late-morning call to Esme had yielded no new information. "Alden never shared his passion for art glass with me," she'd said. "He never . . ." Esme fell silent, doubtless contemplating other unshared passions. "He'd bring these lamps and vases and . . . what do you call those perfume bottles? He never called them perfume bottles."

"Flacons."

"Yes, he'd bring . . . bring those home, too, and he never said where he got them. I had no idea that information would be important. Now I feel just terrible." She sounded quite despairing.

"We'll figure it out," Rosemary had assured her. But now, flipping through the catalog, she wasn't so sure. Perhaps if she could examine one or two other Gallé pieces in Esme's collection, and authenticate those, she'd feel more comfortable. She retrieved her cell phone from her bag and headed outside to call.

Guy reviewed the software license for Studseekers.com. Normally he'd have someone in legal take care of this—well, there was only one person in legal now, down from three. But the fewer people who knew that Positano's Fast-Response would be facilitating an online community of horny gay men, the better. He also wasn't eager to have anyone else know that he was providing the software at cost. Bad enough to be in the porn business. But to be losing money in the one reliably profitable niche of the Internet was truly mortifying.

His eyes wandered over to his computer screen. Positano's stock price continued to sink; at the current price, one share would just cover a vente cappuccino at Starbucks or two minutes of X-rated downloads at Studseekers.com. If only he could resist checking Positano's price, but it was a bit like taking your temperature when sick: There was an irresistible fascination in watching your fever rise, even if there wasn't much you could do about it.

"Hey, bro." Sumner Freedman charged into Guy's office and slouched into a chair in front of his desk.

"I'm not your brother."

"No, it's an expression!" When Guy failed to acknowledge this, he added, "Whatcha up to?" Sumner had a distressing habit of ambling into Guy's office and asking what he was up to.

"Giving away our software," Guy said as he slid the Studseekers.com contract under other paperwork. Sumner laughed with inappropriate gusto. "You're too funny, Guy."

"I have a meeting uptown in twenty minutes," Guy said. The meeting was with Victor Ozeri, at the new apartment, to discuss the mis-positioning of the built-in cabinets.

"Who with?"

Guy took a long, slow breath. "What can I do for you, Sumner?"

"Well, here's the thing." Sumner cleared his throat. "The board has requested a monthly management update. You know, new contracts, prospects, follow-on engagements. I wanted your help in putting it together."

"Aren't I giving the presentation?"

"Not exactly." Sumner stood up and walked over to the tank. "They've asked me to present. The feeling is that I'll be more objective." He tapped the tank with an index finger, and when this failed to elicit a response from its occupants, he rapped his knuckles on the glass.

"Don't do that." Sumner turned around. "It's not good for the fish." Sumner's brows furrowed contemplatively, as if the fate of Guy's tropical fish might be another thing he'd want to brief the board on. He shrugged and retook his seat, immediately assuming his customary slouch.

"I'll handle the PowerPoint, but I'd like your input. I'll be rehearsing on Wednesday, and I'd appreciate your feedback at that point."

"We'll present together," Guy said.

"The board wanted me—"

"Fuck the board. This is my company."

"It's not your company, Guy. The board represents sixty-five percent of shares outstanding. Shares that are worth about eighty percent less than a year ago."

"Our comparables are down ninety-three percent."

"We're aware that Positano has marginally outperformed its peer group."

"*We?*"

Sumner waited a few moments before responding.

"No one can sell Positano's software better than you, Guy. We . . . the board wants to free you up to spend more time in front of the customer."

"Why not make me director of sales, then?" *And chop off my balls while you're at it.*

Sumner stood up and headed for the door. "Our only interest—"

"*Our?*"

"—is the success of this company. No one stands to benefit more when the stock turns around than you."

"Go to hell," Guy muttered.

He couldn't tell if Sumner heard him, and didn't much care. His hand moved instinctively to his mouse. He clicked on *Refresh* and saw that Positano had moved up an eighth, meaning that in the ten minutes of Sumner's visit, his net worth on paper (on screen) had increased by $360,000. It seemed like a trade-off of sorts: ten minutes with a pasty-skinned, Wharton-educated, jargon-spewing, fish-torturing asshole in return for $360,000. In fact, he felt cheated.

Twenty-four

Lily easily recalled the address of Forsling, Creighton & Samuels from the invoice-bearing envelopes that arrived regularly from the firm, which she tossed, unopened, into the trash. She hadn't called ahead for an appointment with Morton Samuels, fearing that he'd insist on payment before agreeing to see her.

"You should have called for an appointment," he greeted her in his office after she'd waited for twenty minutes.

"Would you have seen me?"

He squeezed out a pained smile and gestured for her to sit on the sofa. She noted the framed photographs of Samuels with his celebrity clients, all acquitted of white-collar crimes of which they were universally believed to have been guilty. After closing the door he sat in an armchair.

"Tell me what's happening," she said.

"With your husband's situation?"

"No, in Glocamora."

Another pained smile. "Nothing, I'm afraid. You can't do much for a client who doesn't communicate with you." Samuels had a lean, vulpine face and slender legs, but his stomach was inappropriately large. He was in his late fifties, divorced, and shortly before Barnett's arrest had begun showing up on the charity circuit with an assortment of much younger and quite

beautiful women who were attracted to a man with the gaunt face of a prisoner of war, the belly of a late-term-pregnant woman, and the bank account
of a Colombian drug lord.

"You haven't spoken to Barnett?"

"I'm not even sure I'd take his call."

"Did you know he had a girlfriend?"

"I . . . yes, I knew."

"How . . ."

"I can't recall. It was just something one knew."

"'Just something one knew'? Like, only order oysters in months with *r*'s
in their names? Never wear white before Memorial Day? Barnett Grantham
is fucking Francine Sparkler?"

"I'm not sure anyone knew her name."

What must everyone had thought of her, the proverbial, the literal, last to
know? Was it time to recast her memories of the past two years, replacing
Lily Grantham, *stylish wit, indomitable raiser of funds for worthy causes*, with
Lily Grantham, *laughingstock*?

"She's not with him," she said. "I went to see her."

He shook his head, frowning.

"Lily, you need to move forward. You need to put everything behind you,
including his affair, what he did to his firm—"

"Did to his firm? You're his lawyer, for God's sake, and you think he's
guilty?"

"He fled the country."

"Because he was being framed, he was facing a jail term for something he
didn't do." Though she was more or less convinced of his guilt, it seemed
important to argue for his innocence in the presence of his attorney.

With a pitying, almost patronizing smile he shifted over to the sofa. It
took every bit of her willpower not to shift away from him.

"Innocent men have an almost visceral need to exonerate themselves."

"When have you ever represented an innocent man? Anyway, the only
visceral need Barnett had was staying out of jail. He wouldn't have lasted a
day behind bars."

"Yes, well, I'm not sure he's much more comfortable in Zug."

"Where?"

"Oh. I thought you knew. Zug is a town in Switzerland, very nice, and the lowest tax rates in the country, not that Barnett has to worry about taxes. Apparently he's living in some sort of *pension*." *Ponh-si-onh*—his French pronunciation, though laughably off-key, hardly conjured images of suffering.

"Tell me something, Morton. Why do offshore banks have to be in places like Switzerland and the Caribbean? Don't they have enough goodies there for the naughty rich? Why aren't there offshore banks in Ghana and Romania and Iran? I mean, if you're going to steal money from your partners, shouldn't you have to suffer just a teeny little bit when you go to pick it up?" She took a deep breath. "Are you sure he's in . . . *Zug?*"

"The firm has an office in Geneva. We have several clients in and around Zug."

"You should set up a *ponh-si-onh* for your clients. L'Hôtel On-the-Lam."

Samuels coughed. "In any case, Barnett's been spotted."

"Doing what?"

"Going about his business. Despite what you might think, he lives very simply, even austerely. Still, he must have some source of income . . ."

"Well, he's hardly living like someone who ran off with millions of dollars."

"Lily." Samuels gently squeezed her knee with a bony, liver-spotted hand—she thought, a touch regretfully, of the ball-and-claw legs on the twelve Chippendale dining-room chairs she'd once owned, bought at auction at Atherton's. "Don't do this. Don't carry a torch for a man who left you and your children high and dry. A man who cheated on you, cheated his partners, cheated his clients."

"How can you talk about *your* client this way?"

"Ex-client. I've moved on, Lily." So did his hand—up her leg. "Now you need to move on. You're a charming woman, still quite attractive . . ."

The "still quite attractive" hit a nerve deeper than talon gripping her leg.

"If he's no longer your client, then hand over your files on the case." She gently pushed his hand off her leg. "I'll need to find alternative representation."

"You don't need representation, Lily." His took her left hand in both of his. "You need a life."

"When I find out who took that money—"

He released her hand and reached around her back.

"Let it go," he said, pulling her toward him. "It's time to move on." His breath was like the first stale whiff from a long-unopened closet.

"Let me go." She shoved him away and stood up.

"I think we're done here," he said in a flat voice. Checking his watch, he added, "I have a three o'clock."

"I want my husband's case files," she said.

"I'm afraid it's firm policy not to give any paperwork regarding a case to the client when there's an outstanding invoice."

"Don't give me policy, Morton. You *are* the firm."

He crossed his legs, exposing a patch of hairless, marbled flesh above his sock, and checked his watch again.

"How much do we owe?"

"Somewhere north of three thousand."

"I don't have that. As you of all people know, the government took everything. Just give me the files. What's three thousand dollars to you?"

"Two hours' work," he said with a grim smile.

"Exactly. To me it's a fortune, to you it's a rounding error."

"It's the principle."

"Principle? You're a lawyer, Morton."

"This conversation isn't leading anywhere."

"Okay, what if we settled on half, fifteen hundred? Fifteen hundred dollars for the files and we're through."

"We don't negotiate our fees."

"Fifty cents on the dollar, Morton. It's better than nothing."

"I'm sorry, it's the—"

"The principle, you already mentioned that." She plopped down in the chair facing him and crossed her legs.

"My three o'clock . . ." he said.

"Go right ahead and have your three o'clock. I don't mind the distraction. I have no plans, I never have plans anymore." She picked up a thick legal book from the coffee table and began thumbing through it. "Plans cost money. I have no money."

He considered her for a few moments, and it was all she could do not to flinch.

"Fifteen hundred, then," he said at length.

"I thought you'd see it my way." She reached into her pocketbook, took out a thick wad of bills, and began dealing twenties onto the coffee table, counting out loud.

"Lily, what are you doing?"

"Two hundred and sixty, two hundred and eighty . . . I'm paying you, Morton. Three hundred. Three hundred and twenty . . ."

"This is . . . this is ridiculous."

"Four hundred and eighty, five hundred . . ."

He became increasingly agitated as she continued to count. Well, the sight of so much cash was unnerving, she knew, though God knows she'd gotten used to it. Suddenly the entire foundation of a class act like Forsling, Creighton & Samuels seemed like nothing more than an elaborate mechanism for generating cash. For Samuels, watching her count out twenties must have felt like having to visit the pitch-dark and sweaty diamond mines from which had been excavated the diamond ring he'd given his latest trophy slut—it didn't glisten quite so brilliantly once you knew where it came from.

"How much longer will this take?"

"Eight hundred and twenty, eight-forty, eight-sixty . . . Relax, Morton, it's only money."

"Where did you get this?"

"I printed it myself . . . Three hundred sixty, three hundred eighty . . . It's surprisingly easy to print money, you know."

"You've become sarcastic and mean-spirited and vulgar."

"Fifteen hundred!" she said cheerfully. She slid the pile of twenties over to him. "Would you like to count it?"

He frowned as he got up, then went over to the credenza behind his desk and returned with a thick manila folder.

"There wasn't much paperwork, as it turns out. Barnett left the country before we'd gotten started, and of course the matter never went to trial." As he spoke, his eyes never left the pile of twenties.

She took the folder, reached around his neck, and pulled him close to her, pressing against his bulbous stomach. "Morton," she whispered in his ear. "Now that this is all behind us . . ."

"Yes . . ." Lust moistened his eyes.

"I don't have many . . . resources. I mean, I pay my legal bills in cash— how pathetic is that? But you, Morton, you're a powerful man . . ."

"I can help you, Lily . . ." His breathing was accelerating. If it wasn't for his protruding midsection, she had no doubt she'd be able to feel his stiffening prick.

"I've lost everything and you're a powerful man . . . so what you did before, groping me, was disgusting. Unforgivable. You're an asshole, Morton. A total scumbag."

He started to move away but not before she landed a solid knee to his groin. He bent over from the waist, moaning.

"I'll tell your secretary to send in your three o'clock," she said as she left his office.

"You know that phrase you only see in the crosswords, 'at sea'?" Peggy asked her friend Gert Goldman. They were sitting at the tiny kitchen table in Gert's apartment in Peggy's old building at 218 West End Avenue. Gert had invited her for lunch, which invariably meant dry tuna sandwiches and iced tea from a mix, always served in the kitchen. The only time Peggy had ever sat in Gert's dining room was during a shiva call following Ed Goldman's death from liver cancer ten years earlier. Gert had had platters sent over from Zabar's. The second and last time would be after Gert's passing, Peggy thought with a mental sigh more for the awful inevitability of things than for Gert herself, who could be infuriatingly obtuse.

Gert squinted dumbly. "See what?"

"'At sea,'" Peggy said. "The definition is always something like 'lost' or 'adrift.'"

"I see."

"No, Gert, it's *at sea*," Peggy said. "It always seemed like one of those pointless expressions you only find in the crosswords, like erne, a seabird, or Eero, some architect's first name. But just this morning I realized it perfectly describes how I feel lately about our new apartment."

"What does?"

"*At sea.*"

"I see."

Peggy bit into her sandwich rather than continue along what would surely be an increasingly meandering and ultimately dead-end conversational trail, and immediately added a mouthful of iced tea to lubricate the chalky tuna.

She doubted Gert used a teaspoon of mayonnaise for an entire can of tuna and was tempted to say something but, after all, Gert was eighty-two, so there seemed little point. Achieving the proper ratio of mayo to tuna was a new trick that old dog would never learn.

"Maybe in time I'll settle in, but with Lily and the children living with us, it's not easy. And their Nanny, *so-called*—don't get me started."

She waited for Gert to solicit more details but, ever infuriating, she chose that moment to be silent, so Peggy moved on.

"Monroe's completely helpless. I have to take him to the bathroom, help him get dressed. And the worst part is, I suspect he's really capable of doing these things by himself, he just doesn't want to."

"Depression?" Gert breathed the name of humanity's latest scourge the way people once whispered "cancer."

Peggy nodded. "First the stock market, then the heart attack. I'm thinking of getting him a prescription."

"Fred's on Zoloft," Gert said. "And Andy takes Lipitor."

It irritated Peggy no end that Gert blithely assumed she would know who Fred and Andy were—though in fact she knew them to be Gert's sons-in-law, lawyers both. (That she had confused matters by injecting a cholesterol drug into a conversation about depression only added to her irritation.) She would never presume to mention Lily without the qualifying "my daughter," and Lily had been famous, in a way, and was now almost notorious. Just last week the *Times* had run an article on prominent fugitives, in the Sunday Styles section, of all places, and Barnett had been featured. The article suggested he was in South America, but Lily seemed to think he was in Switzerland, though she wouldn't say how she knew. She kept so many things secret lately.

"Of course, Monroe doesn't think he's depressed. Maybe depressed people never think they are, it's part of the problem."

"Maybe *you* should consider an antidepressant."

"What are you talking about? I'm not depressed."

"How do you know, you just said—"

"I know what I just said. How about some more iced tea? My mouth is parched."

"What are your plans for the holidays?"

"I can't even begin to plan," Peggy said as Gert scooped a teaspoon of powder into her glass. "Monroe's in no condition to go to temple, and Lily hasn't been inside a synagogue since she married Barnett. As for the kids, I doubt they even know what Rosh Hashanah is. Yesterday I heard my grand-daughter's boyfriend, Paco—yes, Gert, P-A-C-O—I heard *Paco* say that their school was going to be closed for Rosh Hashanah's birthday."

Of all the disturbing aspects of Lily's retreat from the life she'd grown up with, her abandonment of Judaism had been most painful for Peggy. Plenty of mixed couples raised their children Jewish. At temple nowadays you saw Asian wives and black husbands and kids with mix-and-match features wearing yarmulkes and no one batted an eyelash. The temple's monthly newsletter proudly announced the Bar and Bat Mitzvahs of "Aaron O'Sulli-van" or "Christy Schwartz." "William and Sophie Grantham" would hardly have stood out. But Lily had shown no interest in being Jewish, which was a shame. She'd been such a diligent Hebrew-school student, chanting her Torah portion so beautifully at her Bat Mitzvah, everyone thought she could have had a career in music. And for what?

"I'm spending Rosh Hashanah with Charlotte and Fred, and Yom Kippur with Marlene and Andrew." Gert plunked a glass in front of Peggy. "It's all I can do to keep everyone happy over the holidays, they all want me with them."

"You have such problems."

"It's true," Gert agreed. "Char called first this year, but naturally I—"

"Do you have a spoon? There are iced-tea crystals floating in my glass."

"I thought I gave it a good stirring," Gert said, handing a spoon to Peggy.

Having succeeded in diverting Gert from the topic of her exemplary daughters and devoted sons-in-law, Peggy turned to a more pressing issue.

"Lily has a new source of income. Somehow she always has money lately."

"Everyone has savings."

"Not Lily. She used to borrow bus fare from me. Now she's taking cabs."

"Cabs are so expensive lately, have you noticed?"

"That's not my point, Gert. Where is she getting this money from? I thought you might know something."

"Me?" Gert put a hand to her breast, as if she'd been accused of funneling money to Lily. "How would I . . ."

"Because of Ed."

Ed Goldman had been a tax accountant with one of the big firms. The

Times always quoted Ed when it ran an article about millionaires hiding money "offshore."

"Do you think Lily might have a secret account somewhere—Switzerland, say—that Barnett set up for her?"

"Ed always said that setting up foreign accounts was easy, and you could earn all the money in those accounts you wanted without paying a dime in taxes. The hard part was bringing the money back into the country. If you don't set it up correctly, the IRS will take everything you earned and then some. Barnett may have set up an account for Lily somewhere offshore, but when she went to access the account, she'd have to be very careful. Has she been making a lot of overseas calls?"

Peggy didn't think it worth pointing out that since Ed had died the Internet and e-mail had replaced long-distance calling as a means of moving money around the globe.

"No, but she does disappear quite a bit lately."

"I'd confront her directly. Ask her where the money's coming from."

"I'm just worried about her. She seems so . . ."

"Depressed?" Gert whispered with sympathetic anguish.

"Happy. All of a sudden she seems happy. What the hell does Lily have to be happy about?"

Peggy stirred her iced tea as the two women silently pondered this.

"Speaking of happy," Gert said, "I went to Cecile's funeral on Tuesday. A lovely service at Riverside, three of her friends spoke so beautifully about her—surviving Auschwitz, then cancer. The charity work. Her bridge. Such beautiful eulogies, there was even humor, you know, where you laugh and cry at the same time. I just love when that happens, I really do. I tell you, lately I leave funerals wishing I'd done more with my life."

"Like survive cancer?" Peggy said. "I always leave funerals wishing I had cleverer friends."

Twenty-five

Lily immediately recognized the doorman at 221 West Eighty-third Street, Larry's building, two decades older than on her last visit but still possessing a bemused, inoffensive cynicism, as if his position afforded him a privileged perspective on the droll carryings-on of the human species, which perhaps it did. Every building was home to a hundred dramas—marriages cooling down, affairs catching fire, children rebelling or returning, finances flourishing or deteriorating (Christmas tips being a reliable leading indicator), the inevitable births, illnesses, and deaths—and a doorman with even a modicum of imagination could piece together most of them, weaving a complete narrative from nothing more than the entrances and exits of the players.

"Larry Adler, 5F," she said, surprised that the apartment number sprang to her lips.

He picked up the house phone. "Miss Gimmel to see you," he said with a smile for her benefit. He'd been on duty back when she was, in fact, Miss Gimmel, twenty-plus years ago.

The lobby had changed far less than either she or the doorman, though it had aged, the marble walls and floor acquiring the mottled, yellow tinge of old teeth. The elevator, sheathed in familiar wood-grained Formica, lurched to a halt on the fifth floor, still one of the more terrifying rides in the city. As much as any historical society or neighborhood group, rent control was the great architectural preserver of New York.

Larry looked startled when he opened the door, wearing a white T-shirt, running shorts, and white socks.

"Miss Gimmel!" he said. "I thought it was your mother."

Lily stepped inside the apartment and was submerged in familiarity. The beige carpeting, the mirrored wall facing the front door, the crystal chandelier. She felt herself succumbing to a comforting haze of nostalgia, the way reuniting friends inevitably retreat to bland, dead-end discussions of the past. But she was determined to move forward.

"I was about to go running," he said.

She nodded and stepped around him, placed Morton Samuel's legal files on a familiar mahogany table, its legs sunk a good inch into the thick carpet, as if the beige fibers had grown up like grass around them. She briefly considered a foreshadowy kiss in the foyer but rejected that approach as timidly indirect. Instead, she headed down the long hallway that connected the foyer with the three bedrooms, and turned without thinking into Larry's old room.

"Lily?" he said, following her.

The unexpected sight of a large television and two plump club chairs momentarily fazed her. The room had been converted into a den, probably years ago by his parents, judging by the decor. She recovered quickly and, aware of his puzzled presence just behind her, headed for the apartment's master bedroom. She kicked off her shoes and was unfastening her belt when he grabbed her arms and pulled her to him. When they separated, minutes later, she could barely find her breath. She pulled his T-shirt over his head. He began to unbutton her blouse. They were as hurried and clumsy as they had been two decades earlier, but this time it wasn't desperate hormones and fear of parental discovery that urged them on but a richer stew of needs, equal parts lust and comfort-seeking and the longing to reconnect.

And it was happening in the master bedroom of apartment 5F, of all places! Lily was vaguely aware of the unchanged room as Larry slowly removed her blouse, and she allowed herself to think that she and Larry hadn't changed, either. That thought, which had horrified her for so long, she who was all about willed change and constant progress, now sent a thrill of lusty pleasure down her entire length, beginning at the back of her neck, where Larry had placed a hand that was now pulling her back to him.

Esme Hollender answered the door wearing a voluminous floral caftan that could easily have accommodated two more of her.

"What a pleasant surprise," Esme said, though Rosemary had called ahead. Esme always seemed on social automatic pilot, randomly extracting jauntily delivered lines from a musty repertoire of polite greetings and sympathetic responses. "Won't you come in?" She made a jerky sweeping gesture with one arm.

Rosemary had never been inside the apartment at 700 Fifth Avenue but could immediately tell that, like Esme's caftan, it was much too big for one person. The enormous entrance hall, invariably referred to as a gallery in real-estate ads, opened onto myriad rooms and hallways. It was hopelessly gloomy, and not just because, as Rosemary discovered as she followed Esme into the library, all the apartment's drapes and shades were resolutely drawn against the lovely fall sunshine, blocking what would be a remarkable seventh-floor view of Central Park. An air of what could only be called disappointment suffused the apartment, as if all the French furniture and Oriental rugs and gilt-framed oil paintings somehow knew they weren't quite up to the task of doing justice to the vast space in which they'd been assembled. Esme herself looked small and unimportant in her own apartment, swallowed up in the plush upholstery of the sofa she'd collapsed into. Rosemary sat sideways to her in an armchair.

"To what do I owe this unexpected pleasure?" Esme asked.

"As I mentioned on the phone . . ." Esme looked puzzled and then a touch annoyed. "I wanted to have a look at your full collection of Gallé. It might help us come up with an auction estimate for the vase you gave us."

"Would you like a drink? I think I'll have one, if you don't mind."

She managed to extricate herself from the sofa and crossed the room to a small table crowded with bottles and glasses. She held several glasses up to the dim overhead light before finding a clean one, and filled it halfway with gin.

"What did you say you wanted, dear?"

"Nothing for me," Rosemary answered.

"It's cocktail hour somewhere in the world!" she said, inevitably, as she fell back into the engulfing upholstery with a relieved sigh. She took a deep swallow of gin.

"We have a few pieces right here in the library," Esme said. "There are more in storage." Peering through the gloom, Rosemary made out a few vases on the bookshelves. She stood and crossed the room.

"When do you think you'll be auctioning that piece I gave you?" Esme asked as Rosemary picked up an aqua-blue iridescent vase. She blew off a veneer of dust.

"Our next auction is in four months. Do you mind if I open a shade? I'd like to look at this in natural light."

"Not at all. I used to keep them open, you know, but then I had to let my girl go and it got to be too much trouble opening and closing them myself."

"You never replaced your housekeeper?" Rosemary said, blinking at the sudden infusion of light from the raised shade.

"Well, it seemed easier just to handle the cleaning and whatnot on my own," she said. To Rosemary's skeptical squint she added: "If you do a little every day, it doesn't get ahead of you."

This seemed a dubious claim, given the size of the apartment and the obvious neglect of the library. Beyond the filthy window, Central Park lay before her like a peaceful and orderly Breugal canvas. She raised the other shade.

"My, what a lovely day," Esme said doubtfully, turning away from the onslaught of sunshine.

The vase was a fake. The seams were crudely joined, and the frosted glass, when held up to the light, revealed a faint crazing that never occurred in genuine pieces from the late nineteenth century. She replaced the vase and examined a few more pieces by daylight—a Lalique atomizer, another "Gallé" vase, a Daum bowl. Fakes, all of them, casting the authenticity of the original vase in serious doubt.

"Alden loved his glass," Esme said wistfully. "I never saw the point of it exactly, but *chacun à son goût*, I always say. Well, *he* always said."

"Do you have sales receipts for these items?"

"I used to, but I don't think I kept them. Alden was diligent about giving me invoices. I paid all the household bills during our marriage, you know, just to keep a lid on expenses. He didn't understand money a bit. These vases and perfume jars and lamps cost a fortune, you know. I never could get used to the amounts on those invoices. Shocking, really. Alden hated being kept on an allowance, but it had to be, and I always let him have his way with the glass. It was an investment, he always said. Like money in the bank. How much do you think I could get for the entire collection?"

"Do you recall the name of the dealer?"

She took a deep, contemplative swallow of gin.

"Harold something or other, I can't remember, but it was always the same one, a dealer in Manhattan. I met him a few times, here in the apartment. I don't think he had a proper gallery. A nicely dressed, good-looking fellow." She leaned toward Rosemary and lowered her voice. "A bit swishy, I always thought. The art world, you know."

Rosemary conjured up two alternative scenarios. In the first, Alden, utterly lacking in *goût*, was conned out of a great deal of money by an unscrupulous dealer in fakes. In the other, he and the swishy dealer used patently fake art glass to con Esme out of a great deal of money, getting her to fork over, say, five thousand dollars for a small vase that had been purchased—or perhaps even commissioned—for a few hundred, and then keeping the rest. A simple but clever way for Alden to supplement a stingy allowance.

"Alden bought the paintings, too, you know. He had a connoisseur's eye, he really did. He always said, 'Ezra'—he called me Ezra—'it's wiser to spend a lot of money on something first rate than a little money on something second rate.'" She swirled her ice cubes. "Everything had to be first rate for him," she said a bit sadly.

"The art dealer, was it the same man who sold you the glass?"

"You really are very clever. In fact, he even found us most of the furniture. French, all of it. Do you think Atherton's would be interested? I'd hate to part with any of it, but there's so much to dust, one less commode would hardly be missed!"

"You need to find the dealer's name. Check all your records."

"Sometimes I paid cash," she said very softly.

"Oh, no."

"Henry or Herbert or whatever his name was didn't charge me sales tax if

I paid cash. Do you know what sales tax is on a five-thousand-dollar . . . what do you call those tiny vases?"

"Flacons."

"*Flacons!*" she said, shaking a tiny fist in the air, as if the very Frenchness of the object justified her entire folly. "I saved a fortune paying cash and I won't apologize."

"Still, you should check every drawer in the apartment for his name."

"Will that help the auction?"

"It will help establish the provenance," Rosemary said. Even fakes have a provenance.

On the way out, Esme detoured into the dining room. Running the length of the room was a three-pedestaled Chippendale table (Chippendale-*style*, more likely) on which a small aircraft could have landed. A phalanx of shield-backed chairs, uniformly spaced along either side, called attention to the pointlessly huge room, adding an aura of sad expectancy to the penumbral gloom. It felt less like a private dining room than the boardroom of a long-depleted charitable foundation. Esme stopped before a full-length portrait at one end of the room.

"It's by Paulus von Reiter," she said, looking reverently upward. "Alden bought it on a buying trip to Europe."

"With his dealer, Howard or Harold?"

"It's very important to have expert advice. You'd be surprised at the number of unscrupulous characters in the art world."

The portrait showed a tall, portly man dressed in fancy eighteenth-century garb. It was the sort of safe, goes-with-anything picture prized by decorators. At Atherton's they were dismissed as "Great-Great-Uncle Leopold Portraits," invariably bought in quantity by the newly-rich for the walls of their newly acquired homes, and even when signed by a recognized artist, they were consigned to the basement showroom rather than the auction block.

"You can see the signature, right there. Paulus von Reiter. Alden said there were several Von Reiters in the Metropolitan Museum." She gestured toward the window, beyond whose drawn shade lay that very institution. "I suppose I could let you have it—auction it, I mean." She smiled shyly. "I don't eat in here much anymore. In fact I haven't . . ." She slowly glanced rather sad-faced around the room, as if searching for crumbs, a discarded napkin, some evidence of a recent meal. "When the children visit we eat in the breakfast room, although they don't usually stay for meals. Everyone is so busy these days."

"Atherton's hasn't had much success with"—she squinted at the signature—"with Von Reiter." Rosemary moved away from the portrait and toward the foyer.

"Oh, I see," Esme said, frowning at the portrait, as if the "gentleman," as all unknown male subjects were known, had let her down in a wholly unexpected but quite serious way, perhaps in erotic cahoots with Alden. "I hadn't thought of that."

"Well, it does *look* genuine," Rosemary said with as much enthusiasm as possible, neglecting to add that no one would bother forging a painting by an artist who might fetch at most five thousand dollars in a strong market. "I have to be going. My sitter expires in ten minutes."

"Oh, I see," Esme said, finally turning away from the gentleman. "When will you decide on the reserve for the Gallé?"

"I have to talk to Lloyd," she said. "He'll probably want to speak with you directly." *Want* was not the word Lloyd would use, for it would be unwelcome news he'd be delivering. Alden Hollender and his "dealer" had taken her for a lot of money, and, judging from the state her apartment, and Esme's eagerness to unload even her treasured "gentleman," it appeared she hadn't had a lot to spare.

"Please tell Lloyd to call soon," she said. "I need . . ." Standing in the center of the vast foyer, she turned slowly around on tiny, unsteady feet. As each new room came into view, she appeared freshly panicked, as if she sensed long-standing enemies closing in from every direction. "I need to settle things quickly."

"I'll talk to him this afternoon." Rosemary managed to arrive at the front door before Esme had a chance to point out any other treasures with which she was willing to part, and left after an economical but polite good-bye.

From Lily's point of view, it seemed fitting, somehow, to be reviewing photocopies of checks Barnett had written on the firm's account while she lay in Larry Adler's bed. It had been the writing of the checks, after all, dozens of them, that had set off a chain of events that had led her to her current position—spoons, they had called it back in high school, Larry's long body nestling perfectly into her back, as if their bones and muscles had retained memories of each other's anatomies.

"I think I'm offended," he said. "You're lying here with me, following the best sex I've had in a long, long time, and you're working to exonerate your husband, a man who deserted you and your children. To hell with your husband."

"It's about getting back everything the government took from us."

"Do you need it?"

"I'm living on a pullout sofa in my parents' apartment."

"You've found alternative accommodations." He kissed the nape of her neck.

"Great, I'll go get the kids and we'll move in tonight."

"No problem."

She sighed. "It's not that easy. Nothing's that easy. That was . . ."

"That was what?"

That was always the problem. Larry saw life as a set of circumstances to be accepted. She saw life as a set of obstacles to be overcome. She couldn't decide what to say, and then she became distracted by one of the photocopied checks.

"I need my purse," she said, getting out of the bed. She found it in the foyer and rejoined Larry on the bed. She took out her date book and flipped through it.

"I was right," she said. "This last check, the last one he wrote?" She handed it to him.

"Forty-three thousand dollars. Some check."

"The date it was written? Barnett and I were in Barbados. I remember because the trip was supposed to be for our anniversary, but something came up at the office and we had to delay it a week. This check was written the second day we were away. He wouldn't have written a check while we were in Barbados, he couldn't have deposited it."

Larry began running his hands lightly over her shoulders and back, nuzzling the nape of her neck. Lily flipped through the other check photocopies.

"This one . . ." She turned the pages in her date book. "I'm pretty sure this date was the Friday after Thanksgiving last year. We were in Palm Beach for Thanksgiving."

"How quaint."

"Why would he wait until we were in Florida to write a check? Look, the checks were all deposited in New York banks." She showed him the photocopies of the backs of the checks. According to the Feds, the checks had been deposited in several New York banks, and once they'd cleared a day or two later, the funds had been transferred to offshore accounts.

"And this one . . ." She waved a photocopy at him. "We were on the Prestons' boat in the Adriatic when this one was written. A boat! Who writes checks on a boat in the middle of the Adriatic?"

"Certainly not me."

She frowned. "You don't understand, this is big. This means . . ." What exactly did it mean? Well, that Barnett really was innocent. Innocent of embezzlement, at least. He was still guilty of being a total shit. "Someone waited until Barnett was away to write these checks."

"But what difference would it make to a thief if he was away? You can write a check anywhere."

"I need to find out who had access to the account."

"And I have one important question," Larry said.

"What?"

"Why is it that after twenty years apart, during our few intimate moments together, you and I are discussing your husband?"

"We're not discussing my husband. We're discussing my future."

"It was always about the future with you, even back then. Don't you ever stop to—"

"Smell the *roses?*"

"Go to hell." He swung his feet over the edge of the bed. To a surprising extent they were right back where they'd left off more than twenty years ago, which had felt wonderful twenty minutes ago and now seemed sad and hopeless.

"I didn't mean to sound like that."

Sitting on the edge of the bed, with his back to her, he said, "I can't believe you want your old life back."

"I have two children to support. You don't understand what it's like to be responsible for other people."

"I don't believe it's just about the kids."

"It's also about proving something to myself. I created my life, every aspect of it. I refuse to lose control now." She joined him on the side of the bed.

"Where were we?" she said.

He seemed about to say something, and it wasn't going to be an answer to her question, so she kissed him and pushed him back onto the bed.

Twenty-six

Peggy spotted her the moment she left the elevator at 218 West End Avenue, the pretty young mother pushing the double stroller across the lobby. It was a drearily common sight these days, a beleaguered parent behind an enormous plow of a stroller. They had taken over the West Side, monopolizing store aisles and sidewalks and elevators, often with a leashed dog in tow, as if two children in a stroller freighted with giant packages of disposable diapers wasn't burden enough. Peggy always felt vaguely obsolete as she angled around these sidewalk flotillas, having shrunk a good inch and a half in height while all around her was evidence of growth, younger people taking on kids, pets, and unfathomable new products to tend to them, as if to fill the gap left by her retreating presence.

She hadn't intended to speak to the woman, but as they converged midlobby, she felt overcome by the need to make contact—not so much with the woman herself as with her old life, the one she'd left behind at 218 West End Avenue.

"Are you enjoying the apartment?" she said. The woman looked puzzled. "I'm Peggy Gimmel."

A moment passed before the name rang a bell. "Oh, hi! I'm Rosemary."

"I'm just visiting a friend," Peggy said, regretting the need to justify her presence in what still felt like *her* building. "Are you enjoying the apartment?"

"I'll let you know when we move in, if and when that happens."

"You haven't moved in? It's been—"

"An eternity. We're not even close. I'm meeting Guy, my husband, at the apartment now, with our contractor, our architect, and hopefully the electrician and plumber. Are you settled in your new place?"

"Settled? Yes . . . yes we are." Peggy thought of how remarkably settled in she and Monroe were, two transplanted shrubs already sending out roots in the new soil, despite the presence of Lily and the children and that vile baby-sitter who'd followed them like a stubborn virus. But far from feeling smug about her situation, she felt inadequate. What did it say about her life, that it could be relocated so easily and quickly, without the assistance of a contractor, architect, electrician, and plumber?

"I'm beginning to think we should have left the apartment alone. It was in excellent condition."

Peggy couldn't suppress a smile. "Well, it wasn't always easy to—"

"I mean, we should have stopped at skim-coating the walls, and of course the moldings had to be replaced. Guy thought the kitchen and bathrooms needed redoing, though I felt they just needed updating. It's amazing what you can do with a bit of paint and a few potted plants and pictures to hide the cracks and blemishes. But otherwise the place was immaculate. I don't know how you did it."

Peggy managed a tiny shrug, thinking: What cracks? What blemishes? One of the twins began to stir, its eyes still scrunched closed but its arms and legs flailing as if it were dreaming of tumbling through space. *Replace the moldings?*

"Guy is so busy at his company, and the twins don't exactly allow me a lot of time to play general contractor . . . It's been a very stressful time, as you can imagine."

Peggy couldn't begin to imagine. Rosemary did look a bit harried, though nothing that a good haircut and some makeup couldn't take care of. Young mothers always looked as if they were just barely holding on, even the ones without careers. Perhaps it was a kind of badge of honor, the strung-out new-mother look. Peggy felt certain that she and her friends never let on that they were having trouble coping; it would have been an admission of weakness, though admittedly none of them had a career back then, let alone a general contractor. Had the double stroller even been invented in the sixties?

"Your husband is with Positano Software," she said. "My husband owned stock in it."

"Really?" Rosemary smiled warily, then rolled her eyes. "So does mine."

"We sold months ago, around the time we moved."

"Really?"

"In the nineties you could buy anything and look like a genius. What's it at now?"

"At?"

"Positano stock."

"Oh, I don't really . . . I'm not sure." She flushed, as if she'd been asked to reveal her weight.

"We sold at eleven. I used to check the price every morning after we sold and think, Thank God." Rosemary grimaced and Peggy felt a twinge of pleasure. "I don't even look at the stock tables anymore—what's the point?"

"You'll have to stop by once we're done. *If* we're done."

"That would be nice," Peggy said, though she doubted she'd ever again set foot in 6D. Who needed their nose rubbed in what a contractor and architect and plumber and electrician and six and a half months had done to her old place?

Paint and potted plants and pictures, she thought as she nodded to afternoon José at the door and left the building. Cracks and blemishes.

At least she'd gotten in that zinger about Positano Software. Leave it to Monroe to invest in a New York company named after an Italian resort. Maybe if you were selling leather goods, or olive oil. Okay, so there was that small crack above the sofa in the living room, and maybe one in the guest bathroom over the tub no one ever used. Buildings settle over time, like cakes from the oven, and cracks appear. They hardly justified skim-coating the entire apartment, and you want to talk about cracks? That *fakakta* company of her husband's had more cracks than the sidewalk. Down to one and a half bucks a share, less than bus fare. She checked every morning since selling—of course she did—just to have *something* to feel good about.

Guy entered the conference room at Sycamore Partners, the venture capital firm whose founder, Dan Radakovic, sat on Positano's board, and immediately sensed danger. The board meeting had been called at the last minute.

He hadn't been able to get in touch with Rosemary, who was probably waiting for him at the new apartment. The presence of a tie-and-jacketed
stranger at the head of the large mahogany table couldn't be a good sign.
Grim expressions all around added to a sense of impending doom, as did the
fact that they had obviously been meeting without him. Guy actually sniffed
the air a few times upon entering, like a hunted deer.

"Guy, welcome. Thanks for stopping by on such short notice."

The greeting, from Marc Gaiman of Sunrise Investments, felt perfunc-
tory.

"What's up?" he asked as he sat down.

"Guy, we'd like you to meet Mel Armitrage," Radikovic said, gesturing to
the meticulously groomed stranger at the head of the table.

The name told the story. Mel Armitrage, a former divinity student, was
CEO of Aquinas Solutions, a publicly traded holding company that had cut
a giant swath across Wall Street by buying up small technology companies
and promising to unlock highly profitable synergies among them. The fact
that those synergies had never materialized, and that its stock, once a
headline-making, jealousy-inducing $250 a share, had been marked down to
the price of a small tin of Altoids, hadn't stopped Armitrage from using his
depressed currency to buy up the even cheaper shares of more technology
companies.

"We wanted you to know immediately that we've received an offer for
Positano from Aquinas," Gaiman said.

"Positano's not for sale."

"A very generous offer." In the context of a board meeting to which he'd
been invited as an afterthought, "generous" translated as "done deal."

"The company's not for sale."

"We have a fiduciary responsibility to our shareholders. The offer is a
forty percent premium over yesterday's closing price."

In other words, a nickel over two bucks a share.

"In Aquinas stock, I assume."

A few throats were cleared. These days, selling a company for Aquinas
stock was like being paid with Confederate currency after Gettysburg.

The door swung open and Sumner Freedman blew in on a breeze of
panting self-importance.

"Lehman's lawyers think the FTC won't have a problem with the antitrust issues," he blurted, as if delivering news of an unexpected victory from the front. Then he noticed Guy. "Oh, hey," he said. Guy glared at him. "Maybe this isn't a good time."

"We have every intention of keeping the current management team in place." Armitrage uttered the line in a bored monotone—verbal boilerplate. "And of course Positano's headquarters will remain in New York."

Aquinas was based in Chicago. Of the twenty or so companies it had devoured over the past decade, the management teams of all but two or three had been replaced, and most headquarters had been "consolidated" in the Windy City. Armitrage liked to tell reporters, and anyone else who would listen, that he'd been reading Thomas Aquinas at the seminary in Oak Brook when he'd received a summons from above to start a company—no ordinary company, mind you, but a beacon of prosperity that would create value, untold value, for millions of people. Himself included, of course. Mostly himself. The next day he incorporated Aquinas Solutions and started looking for investors. The first to sign on was the archdiocese of Chicago. Two years later he was the ninth richest man in America and married to a Wilhelmina model, though his reputation among investors was far less saintly these days, his net worth had plummeted, and there were rumors in the tabloids of trouble at home. Still, Armitrage's rise from impoverished seminarian to NASDAQ kingpin remained a New Economy legend, almost folkloric in its power to inspire dreams, his history repeated reverently in the classrooms of business schools and the lunch rooms of veal farms from Palo Alto to Bangalore—and no doubt in the chaste dormitories of seminaries everywhere.

"I reject this offer," Guy said. "We'll be cash-flow positive in fourteen months."

"Guy, Positano is trading at a ten percent discount to cash," Sumner said. Guy turned to him and briefly considered a run at his throat with his Bic pen. He was visualizing blood gushing from Sumner's carotid artery when his vibrating cell phone defibrillated him back to reality. The LCD readout showed Rosemary's cell number. She was probably already at the new apartment, scene of his life's other disaster.

"The entire market is depressed," he managed to say.

"Guy . . ." Sumner began.

"I know my name, putz."

Sumner's right eyelid twitched. "Yes, well . . . we have thirty-five million in cash on the books. Our market cap is thirty million bucks. What the market's saying is that our entire business model, our products and our customers and"—he coughed—"and our management team, our strategy, it's all worth zero."

"Less than zero," intoned Alan Norbertson of Greystone Ventures. Long faces and slowly nodding heads all around.

"What investors are saying is that we're not going to make it," said Pete Tallyrand of Apex Unlimited. "When the cash runs out—which is expected to occur sometime next year—Positano will no longer exist."

"We're offering a lifeline," Armitrage said. "Let's work together to make this happen, not as adversaries." Armitrage had a narrow face, hooded eyes, tanned skin. He was good looking in an unblinking, predatory way: His habit of frequently moistening his lips with the tip of his tongue suggested a lizard eyeing a small insect.

His phone vibrated again—this time it was that pioneer of personalized porn and Positano's most important customer, Derek Ventnor. Despite everything that was happening, or perhaps because of it, Guy had a brief but deeply satisfying image of the four board members butt naked and forced to perform unspeakable acts on one another in the studios of Ventnor Place as millions of horny Webcasters typed in their fantasies. *I wanna see you slap Tallyrand's $500 million ass! Suck that wimp Gaiman's micro-dick, loser! Suck it till the NASDAQ hits 4,000 again!*

"We have a strong pipeline of prospective customers," Guy said. "We can't keep up with the RFPs." Particularly since two-thirds of the sales support staff had been fired.

"Today's investor isn't interested in pipelines, Guy," Norbertson said with paternalistic calm, as if instructing a young child in the rules of baseball. "The market wants cash flow." Guy returned to the far more enjoyable show in Ventnor's studio. *Shove that big dildo up that capitalist's ass! Make his cash flow in buckets!*

"Guy, are you with us here?" someone asked.

"Fuck the market," he said, standing up. "I'll take the company private before I sell it to—" He glanced down the table, suddenly speechless at the prospect of working, however briefly, for the saurian Mel Armitrage. "To him." He thrust a *J'accusatory* finger at Armitrage and headed for the door.

"You'll never get financing for a buyout," Gaiman said. "We've explored every option already."

Guy considered pointing out that if Positano's market cap was less than its cash position, it wouldn't be difficult to arrange financing for a management buyout of the company. Positano's cash would serve as its own collateral. But he was reluctant to interrupt what he felt was a dramatic and principled exit. So he merely flung open the door, which hit the wall with a gratifying bang, and stormed out.

Twenty-seven

"This candy man, he has a wested interest in keeping your husband on the run," Mohammed observed one morning as she hung a fresh batch of newly bathed twenties on the line to dry. Increasingly, Mohammed relaxed in an old patio chair in the garage, smoking cigarette after cigarette while she scanned, printed, cut, washed, and dried. He never seemed pleased to see her, but he'd stopped complaining, treating her like a frequent visitor to be endured, if not enjoyed—a mother-in-law, perhaps. "If you prove that your husband is innocent, he will come back and reclaim you."

"Like dry cleaning."

"Do you want him to come back?"

She avoided asking herself that question, and God knows Larry hadn't gone near it. Barnett had become like a serious illness in remission; no one knew if or when he'd be back, so it seemed best just to avoid the topic and get on with life.

"I want justice," she said after a long pause, but that sounded pompous and hollow. "Well, I want our money back, our things. As for Barnett . . ."

"Do you love this candy man?"

"He's sweet," she said.

"Yes, but— Oh, I see, a joke." He offered a strained approximation of a smile.

"I like to suck on him."

"Good grief, you— Oh, yes, I see, another joke. Perhaps you are awoiding the issue I raised in my question with witticisms. Do you love the candy man?"

"You ask the tough ones, Mohammed."

"We are here, printing money, for which we could go to jail for a long time. Asking tough questions is easy, when you think of it."

"At this stage in my life I don't ask tough questions," she said. "I just do what I have to do."

"But you could do nothing about this inwestigation and your husband will stay in Europe and you will be with the candy man indefinitely."

"I would miss the . . . miss Larry very much if I couldn't see him. Is that love?"

"It is funny when you think of it." He drew on yet another Marlboro, his lean body distending for the few seconds in which he held the smoke. "Our spouses are both abroad. Here I am, risking prison to have money to send for my wife. Your husband ran away to awoid prison. Maybe they should get together to wait and see what happens."

She smiled at the image of Barnett and—

"What is your wife's name?"

"Kassim. She is called Kassie by most people."

"I hope I get to meet her one day."

"Oh, you will, do not doubt it." He smiled shyly at this first admission of an ongoing relationship between them. Otherwise, each time she left him, there was no acknowledgment on his part that she'd be returning. He was like a bad boyfriend in that respect. "I have a photograph."

He handed her a picture from his wallet. Kassie was a small woman with dark skin, long, straight black hair, big eyes, and a broad smile. She sat, legs crossed at the ankles, on a long sofa surrounded by four boys of varying sizes who stared unsmiling at the camera, like a phalanx of bodyguards.

"You have a beautiful family, Mohammed."

He took back the photo and studied it, as if to confirm her comment.

"I hope I am doing the right thing for them," he said.

"Making a better life?" she said, omitting the fact that he was doing so by breaking a big-ass federal law. "How can that be wrong?"

"Yesterday there was a stabbing at the local high school. In Guyana the schools are poor, but the students wear uniforms and no one takes a knife to anyone else. Sometimes I wonder if they are better off where they are."

What a sad state of affairs, when immigrants from Third World countries consider their children safer back home.

"When I wake up at night and can't sleep, I sit on the front steps and smoke a cigarette and worry that my sons will hate me for leaving them. Children do not concern themselves with making a better life. They only want you with them. They do not take the long perspective. And then I think, Will they hate me more when they get here? Will they think it has all been worth it, or will they miss their old life and their old friends? How do you know what is the right thing to do? And Kassie, what must she be going through? At night, in fact all day long, my body desires her, it is like an ache in the joints, what I imagine it feels like to have arthritis in every joint and muscle."

Lily smiled sympathetically.

"It is true, my body aches everywhere from missing her." He held his hands in front of him and observed them clinically. "My fingers, my arms . . . it is like I am not getting some important nutrient or vegetable."

"It won't be long before you see them."

"Do you think she feels the same way?" he said, still studying his fingers.

"I'm sure she does."

He looked at her, brow furrowed. The thought of a wife living a thousand miles away whose body ached with lust wasn't, perhaps, comforting.

"I think I'm done for the day," she said. After flicking off the scanner and shutting down the computer, she removed her apron and hung it on its customary nail, as if she'd just transferred the last batch of cookies to a rack. "Let me ask you something, Mohammed. All the checks drawn against my husband's firm's accounts were written while we were out of town."

"Ah, you are onto that again. It doesn't look good for the candy man."

"Why would that be, Mohammed? Why were the checks written when we were out of town?"

"Because it would be harder to determine that it was your husband depositing them."

"Yes, but Barnett traveled all the time, three or four times a month at least. The checks were written when we were *both* away, which was much less frequent. Why would someone care if *I* was out of town?"

"Could it be coincidence?"

She shook her head. "There were twenty-six checks, written over a period of years. It's as if someone was tracking our movements."

"Perhaps your husband did cash those checks, and wanted to be in a foreign place to deposit them. Holidays with you were a perfect cover."

"He didn't cash those checks."

Mohammed looked at her as if she had said something very stupid and checked his watch. "I must start driving now. The queue at International Awivals will be very long if don't hurry. Let me pay you now before I forget."

She followed him into his house, where he disappeared upstairs, returning quickly with a small stack of twenty-dollar bills.

"Remember," he said solemnly, as he always did, "it is wery important that you don't spend it all in one place."

She smiled as she took the bills.

"My father gave the same advice when he paid my allowance."

"It's a fake," Rosemary said. Lloyd peered at her as if she'd morphed into a faux Chippendale footstool from the Bombay Company. "Everything she owns is fake. Even her husband was a fake, a fake heterosexual. He was running a scam, along with his dealer. They persuaded Esme to buy truckloads of lamps and furniture and paintings, paying top dollar for cheap reproductions. They pocketed the difference."

"What about the cover?" Lloyd asked. "The Gallé was our cover."

They were in Lloyd's twelve-by-twelve-foot studio in Greenwich Village. He'd been renting for a decade, waiting for the real-estate market's widely anticipated crash before buying. Each year for five years running he had managed to put away ten thousand dollars toward a down payment, no small accomplishment for an art appraiser, and each year the cost of an entry-level apartment rose even faster than his savings, first by twenty thousand, then thirty, and so on. It was as if some cruel law of physics (or optics) was in effect: The closer he got to the finish line, the faster it receded into the distance.

"I think Esme is flat broke. Her apartment is way too big to take care of by herself, but I'm pretty sure she can't afford to hire help."

"We're two days from going to press," Lloyd said. "I fought like hell to get the cover. Decorative never gets the cover. It's always *furniture* or *paintings* or even"—he paused to shake his head before uttering the awful truth—"*jewelry*. I mean, jewelry on the *cover?* It's absurd. We're the stepchild of the auction business—*nobody* understands us."

"Lloyd, this poor woman is destitute. She was counting on us to bail her out."

"What are we going to do?" he wailed, propping his head in his hands.

"I suppose we could help her find somewhere else to live." She couldn't help surveying Lloyd's apartment, which could easily fit into Esme's foyer. Lloyd's lanky frame seemed built to the wrong scale for this particular doll's house.

"About the cover!"

"Oh."

"I thought it was tough during the nineties, when pimply yuppies fancied themselves collectors just because they could afford to snort coke off Meissen plates. At least the money was good. Now no one has that kind of money, dot-com money, and suddenly everything real is fake." He unleashed a sigh that sent a visible shudder down the length of his body. "I must have put on twenty pounds wining and dining Esme, and for what?"

His self-absorption and overall lack of perspective were appalling, though hardly surprising.

"I'm going to help Esme work things out," she said. "She can't go on living there."

"I suppose that Lalique vase could work on the cover. But I just know those sharks in Furniture are going to take advantage of this situation to slap some fucking commode on the cover."

The growing pressure in her breasts signaled that the twins were hungry. She'd decanted a few pints of breast milk that morning, but they didn't always take a bottle from a sitter. She was finding it harder to wean them than she'd expected, and much as she'd looked forward to the independence it would bring, she was at least partly relieved that their first small step toward independence was delayed. In the silence that followed Lloyd's commode outburst she felt certain she could hear the boys wailing from uptown like distant sirens. *Bring milk! Bring milk! Bring milk!* Her breasts began to throb. She imagined a daisy chain of babies up and down the length of Manhattan, all alert to her lactating breasts, wailing their hunger and anger. *Bring milk!*

"Where are you going?" Lloyd wailed when she stood up.

"Home."

"You're leaving me?"

"Don't be melodramatic." She slipped on her jacket. "I'm not even on the payroll." She traversed his apartment in two modest strides.

"Speaking of which, when exactly are you planning on coming back?"

"Soon," she said, heading for the door.

"Have you weaned those boys, Rosemary?" He gave her breasts a squinting, pursed-lipped appraisal. "You haven't, have you? You've still got tits like Pam Anderson. I knew it! How will I manage to put out the winter catalog without you? And we have the February auction to think about."

Guy stood in the center of the new apartment's great room and felt small and vulnerable, a leaking dinghy adrift on a sea of soon-to-be-stripped-and-polyurethaned parquet. He'd give anything to have the walls put back up, to feel enclosed and secure. Furniture and window treatments would help, of course. But would the space ever feel cozy? Could a room of such immense proportions ever feel cozy? Oh, how he longed for cozy.

"We're getting there," Victor Ozeri said as he entered the room. Lost in a fantasy of reappearing walls, Guy hadn't heard him enter the apartment. "This is some fucking room we've made for you." Ozeri smiled paternally at the vast emptiness, a reverse alchemist who created voids where there had been architecture.

Ozeri's voice sounded small and muted, as if it had traveled a great distance to reach him. Carpets and upholstery, Guy reassured himself. Carpets and upholstery and lots of big, comfy pillows.

"You'll be moved in by Christmas," Ozeri said. "Lock, stock, and barrel." He clapped his hand and Guy feared the ceiling would collapse on top of them. It wasn't right, tampering with seventy-year-old architecture. Ozeri looked starkly defined against the endless white walls, recently skim-coated at a cost of forty-five thousands dollars and change, the plaster like virgin snow. Ozeri was as vivid as raw meat against the blizzard of smooth white plaster. They'd repaint the walls a soft color, perhaps a pastel. Yes, a pastel, creamy yellow or peach. They'd hang pictures, lots of pictures. Pastel paint and pictures. Pastel paint and pictures, plus carpets and upholstery and lots of big, comfy pillows.

"You don't look well, my friend. Perhaps the paint fumes?" Ozeri crossed the room and opened a window.

The sudden infusion of fresh air and ambient street noise was in fact refreshing. Perhaps that was all that it was, paint fumes interfering with his ability to fully appreciate—tolerate—what hundreds of thousands of dollars had done to the apartment. He reached into his pants pocket and took out a crumpled sheet of paper.

"I have a punch list to go over with you."

Ozeri took the list from Guy, gave it the shortest of glances, as if it were a modest restaurant check, and said, "Isn't it early in the project for a punch list?"

Ozeri was one of those blessed people with a knack for intimidating, browbeating, and even humiliating his employers in just such a way as to make them more, not less, solicitous of him. Somehow, his grumpy condescension caused the Park Avenue titans who engaged his services to bow and scrape to stay in his good graces. Successful auto mechanics and the best-tipped building superintendents had the same talent.

"I'd like to clear these things up," Guy said, mustering his full authority. "In the kitchen, for example . . ." He headed toward the room in question and was disheartened by the absence of footsteps behind him. "Hello? I want to show you something in the kitchen!"

Guy thought he heard a sigh as Ozeri crossed the great room in no great hurry.

"I couldn't help noticing that there's only one wire in this opening," Guy said, pointing to a hole in the wall near the entrance to the kitchen that would, one day that year, if Ozeri was to be trusted, be a light switch.

"Yes, it's a switch for the overhead light."

"What about the under-the-counter lights?"

Ozeri frowned, knitting his eyebrows into a single dark thatch. "Who said anything about under-the-counter lights?"

"They're in the plans," Guy said, though he wasn't sure this was true. He was sure of nothing anymore: his job, his company, his sexual prowess, under-the-counter lighting. He and Rosemary had certainly discussed them with the lighting designer their architect had recommended, but had they actually been specified in the plans?

"And the sconces over the dining area," Guy said. "We wanted to be able to turn them on and off from the entrance."

"Why?" Ozeri frowned and took two giant steps from the site of the future light switch to the site of the future dining area. "There, that is all that is involved. Two steps from the door to the closest sconce, on which we will put a switch. Not too difficult."

"We want to be able to control all the lighting from here."

"Then we'll have to reopen the walls to run the wires. I will have to call back the electrician for a full day at least. Then the plasterer and then the painter. If that's what you want . . ."

The issue, of course, was money. Someone would pay, and if the past months were any guide, he would be that someone. Guy had taken Ozeri's standard contract to his six-hundred-dollar-an-hour lawyer, who had managed to fatten the document from a straightforward six pages of boilerplate to forty-five densely worded pages crammed with contingency clauses and warranty statements and holdback provisions, none of which had, to date, done Guy a bit of good. A simpler, more accurate, and far cheaper contract could have contained just one line: *The contractor always wins.*

"We'll check the specs," he said.

"Of course. If they clearly indicate that the switches go here, by the door . . ." Guy felt a rumbling of defeat making its way southward toward his bowels. Unfortunately, following his urinary desecration of the wallpaper in the maid's bathroom, which had led, inevitably, to the decision to renovate it, there was no longer a working toilet in the apartment.

"Okay," he said, consulting the punch list. "Now, I wanted to ask you about the dining-room door. The way I see it, if it swings open, into the dining room, it will hit the radiator cover."

Ozeri traipsed through the opening that would one day contain a swinging door.

"I think you are right. We will have to move the door two more inches to the right. Let's hope we don't touch the supporting steel in this riser, or we won't be able to do that without bringing down the entire building."

Ozeri grinned ghoulishly, but Guy felt certain that he had already calculated in his mind not only what he'd charge to move the door but also his fee for rebuilding all of 218 West End Avenue, should the structural steel give way. For a contractor, at least, there was no such thing as a bad day.

Twenty-eight

What an unlikely group they made, Lily thought, crowded together in Peggy's small dining area, lack of elbow room forcing them to hunch over the table like paranoid card players. Peggy presided at the head of the small table. Next to her was Sophie, and next to *her*, her boyfriend, Paco. There was pouty, sullen William. Silent, shlumped Monroe. Resolutely upright Nanny, who had stayed for dinner in honor of Sophie's fifteenth birthday, focusing intently on her plate except for the occasional stolen glance at Larry, sitting opposite Peggy in the place of honor, the target of everyone's curiosity.

A few weeks earlier, shortly after Thanksgiving, Sophie had dyed her once-lustrous, naturally auburn hair a sickly, metallic red that flaunted its artificiality. Whatever coloring agent she'd used had leeched all the body out of her hair, so that it hung like old curtains on either side of her face. Her shirt, a bandage-sized expanse of polyester with the word *Juicy* sequined across the chest (a brand name, not an adjective, Lily had been relieved to learn), exposed two inches of pale, adolescent flesh. Booker T. Washington High School forbade belly shirts, so each morning Lily made sure that Sophie's shirt covered her midriff, as that formerly forbidden territory had once been known. But by the time Sophie returned from school, her pants had somehow drifted downward and her shirt in the opposite direction, exposing a generous swath of skin. Lily took some modest consolation from the fact that the midsection that her daughter chose to reveal to the world was pleasingly flat—a few of her friends had tummies that flopped brazenly over the tops of their pants. No sooner had Lily inured herself to the belly shirts, however, than Sophie had appeared at dinner a week or so ago sporting a belly ring, a silver band that, though tastefully simple, caused Lily's abdominal muscles to clench in sympathetic pain and her jaw to clench in maternal disapproval. She'd made a minor fuss over the ring but hadn't insisted that Sophie remove it, because that would have done no good—there was nothing like having your husband desert you, and then moving back in with your parents, to rob you of what little authority you might once have had with your children.

"Lily, these are awesome," Paco said through a mouthful of the roasted potatoes to which Lily assumed he was referring. "There's like this flavor, you know?"

When had she granted him permission to call her Lily?

"Rosemary," she said.

Paco glanced around the table before smiling and pointing to his mouth.

"Oh, rosemary, like the flavor, I thought you meant a—" A poke from Sophie shut him up.

Paco was in the tenth grade at Booker T. Washington High School, but he looked much older than Sophie. He was handsome—ominously so, Lily thought—with lustrously dark skin and very fine features, but she couldn't help focusing on the silver ring through his right eyebrow and the disturbing fact that he never blinked when looking at her, which seemed of a piece with calling her Lily. She'd attempted a mother-daughter talk with Sophie when Paco first appeared on the scene, but Sophie had brushed her off. "Mom, I know about safe sex, okay? I'm not a child." Lily, who had planned to address the pros and cons of *having* sex at age fifteen, not strategies for having it safely, had backed off. She was, however, pleased that Paco's approval of her roasted potatoes had elicited an enthusiastic nod of agreement from Larry. Roasted potatoes was one of the half-dozen dishes in her repertoire, a holdover from the days when she would help her mother prepare seders. She'd also managed to roast a tolerable chicken and prepare string beans without overcooking them.

Nanny looked stiff and uncomfortable at the table, taking tiny, birdlike pecks at her food and saying nothing. Her reticence didn't stop Peggy from casting hateful glances at her, as if she were dominating the conversation rather than doing her best to remain inconspicuous.

"Larry looks so handsome," Peggy had said in the kitchen as she helped Lily serve dinner. "Just like always."

Peggy had always liked Larry. At a time when most Jewish mothers on the Upper West Side dreamed of their daughters marrying doctors or lawyers (while they inured themselves to the idea that their daughters might *become* such things), Peggy had overlooked his lack of ambition and focused instead on his straightforward openness. *He'll never disappoint you,* she used to say, as if that were the highest praise.

Lily wondered if she herself weren't perhaps the strangest figure of all at the table—abandoned by a husband who was on the lam from the federal government, living with her parents at age forty-two, carrying on an affair with her high-school boyfriend twenty-three years after high-school graduation, and strangest of all, risking a long prison sentence by spending three days a week in Queens with a counterfeiter named Mohammed.

"Larry, you still have the best nuts on Broadway," Peggy said, triggering immediate giggling from William, Sophie, and Paco. "What's so funny? It's true. Everyone in the neighborhood loved his father's nuts, too. Oh . . . I see." Peggy frowned. "You'll have to forgive the repartee at the table, Larry." Peggy had become ludicrously coquettish since Larry's arrival. Lily wondered just how unintentional her references to his family's nuts had been.

"Nut jokes were a cross I bore all through adolescence," he said.

"So you and my mom were, like, boyfriend and girlfriend?" William sounded more accusatory than curious.

"All through high school," Larry said.

William turned to her and squinted.

"Yes, Will, I was in high school once, and yes, I even managed to have a boyfriend."

"Not just any boyfriend, a star athlete," Peggy added. "And a top student."

"Then how come you're still at the candy store?" William asked.

"The Broadway Nut Shoppe," Peggy said.

"The 'shoppie,' we used to call it," Lily added.

"The best nuts," Paco guffawed, drawing a thigh smack from Sophie.

"No, seriously, if you were this great athlete and student, how come you're working in a candy store?"

"As opposed to starting for the Yankees?" Larry said with no apparent defensiveness.

"As opposed to . . . I don't know, like working for, like, a company or something."

"I'm sure he had many opportunities," Peggy said. "He *chose* to enter the family business." She lingered over the last two words, transforming the Broadway Nut Shoppe into an enterprise of Wal-Martian scale.

"Well, it wasn't much of a choice, really. My father died during my senior year at Cornell. I took over the shoppie right after graduation, figuring I'd run it until I got a *real* job. But I found I liked it. So I stayed." He glanced at Lily. "I guess I was never all that ambitious."

"Ambition," Peggy said. "Look where it gets you." She gestured first at Monroe, Exhibit A in the Gallery of Failed Ambition, and then at Lily, the gallery's true masterpiece.

"So what are you all saying, I shouldn't bother trying to get anywhere?" William asked.

"That's not what anyone's saying," Lily said, frowning at Peggy.

"You just have to know what you want, what makes you happy," Larry said.

William shrugged and refocused on his food. A shadow of gloomy hostility clung to him lately. Lily had tried to feel him out, but after alluding that one time to being teased by other kids, he'd clammed up. Lily couldn't tell if he was experiencing typical adolescent angst or reacting to having a father who was a fugitive from justice. Whenever she brought up the subject of Barnett, he'd say, "I'm over it, okay?"

"You gotta find your bliss and shit," Paco said, proffering a nod for each guest as he glanced around the table. "Like, if you're not happening with what you're doing, you won't do it good, anyway, am I right? Like, I hate when—"

"That is such bullshit," William said. "Where do you pick that crap up?"

"William!" Peggy said, looking directly at Lily. "Your language."

"You didn't say anything when Paco said *shit*."

"He did not say . . . that word."

"His exact words were 'find your bliss and shit.' You don't forget poetry like that."

Paco couldn't suppress a satisfied grin.

"Let's change the subject," Lily said, and had an unwelcome flashback to countless nights at the Temple of Dendur and other party sites, when she could always be counted on to divert the conversation from uncomfortable topics. "I was thinking we could use a vacation at Christmas."

"Vacation?" Peggy said. "Miss Moneybags all of a sudden."

"See, that's why kids pick on you," Sophie said, addressing William. "You have this attitude."

"What attitude?"

"Like you're too good for the world."

"Too good for *your* world, maybe. Who isn't?"

"Stop it!" Lily said.

"Anyone want to talk about nuts and candy?" Larry asked.

"See, you go around acting like you got attitude," Paco said to William, who was looking resolutely in the opposite direction. "I tell guys, That's my girl's brother, keep your paws off him, you know? We're, like, related or something, almost."

"When hell freezes over."

"And they're, like, that girl you been—" He came to an abrupt halt on a hard consonant that Lily thought might have been a *b* or, more ominously, an *f*. "That girl you been *goin' out with*, that dickhead's sister? Man, you gotta get your head examined. She may be a piece a ass, they say, but her brother—"

"Okay, Paco, we get the picture," Sophie said.

A tense but welcome silence fell on the table, broken by Peggy.

"What are *you* looking at?" Peggy was glaring directly at Nanny.

"Me? Just trying to finish me dinner, that's all," Nanny said. As if to demonstrate the depth of concentration that task required, she daintily speared a piece of white meat, then a section of roasted potato, and finally a green bean and directed the entire shish kebab into her mouth.

"Some of the hotels in the Bahamas are quite reasonable in December," Lily ventured. "You can't count on good weather in December, but that's why it's affordable."

"I've never understood why the British eat like that," Peggy said. "Cramming a bit of everything on the fork at once. It's barbaric."

"*I'm* barbaric? I'm not the one with grandchildren who . . ."

"Grandchildren who what?"

"They had lovely manners when we lived across town."

"That's enough, Nanny," Lily said with recidivistic hauteur. "Let's have a toast to Sophie." Glasses of water and soda and white wine were raised all around. "Happy birthday, sweetheart."

Glasses were clinked and sipped from and set down.

"You ever consider franchising?" Monroe said to Larry. All eyes turned to him in wonderment at this first sign of cognizant life in what seemed like ages.

"Franchising the store?"

"The smart money is saying that franchising is the next big opportunity."

"Monroe, since when has the smart money been talking to you?" Peggy turned to Larry. "He doesn't even watch television anymore."

"Actually, we watch CNBC together," Nanny said. "*Market Watch* at eleven, then the closing wrap-up at four. Don't we, Mr. G.?"

Peggy regarded her with the speechless incredulity of a woman encountering her husband's mistress for the first time.

"*Market Watch* . . ." she managed to wheeze. "The closing wrap-up . . ."

"I've thought about opening a second location," Larry said, "but it's hard enough managing one."

"But that's the beauty of franchising," Monroe said. "People pay you for the privilege of opening a new location. Then *they* run it. Once you have critical mass, you can take the company public."

"That's nuts, Monroe," Peggy said, causing an outburst of giggles from Paco and Sophie. "It's a candy store." She glanced sharply at Nanny, who was gazing fondly at Monroe, as if he were one of her young charges.

"I think Daddy makes a lot of sense," Lily said. It was nice hearing her father utter something other than *It's time for my pill.* "How about it, Larry? Broadway Nut Shoppies from Maine to Texas."

"We could call the company That's Nuts." Larry raised his wineglass. "To franchising!"

Monroe sat up straight and managed to raise his water glass without spilling any.

"I know a chap at E. F. Hutton who can get you the capital you need."

Peggy rolled her eyes. "For heaven's sake, Monroe, there is no E. F. Hutton anymore, they—"

Lily whacked her mother's side, silencing her. She looked at Larry, then at her father, men from her past with, it seemed, new claims on her future.

"To the future," she said, and drank her wine.

"What the hell happened to Hutton?" Monroe asked, glancing plaintively around the table.

"Stay."

Larry grasped her shoulder and gently pulled her back onto the bed.

"I can't," she said. "I'm still a married woman. I can't just walk into the apartment tomorrow morning wearing the same clothes as the night before."

"You're still obeying rules that no one else cares about."

"It just seems wrong. I leave our apartment to 'walk you home' and don't come back until the morning?

"The Lily Gimmel I knew twenty-five years ago didn't give a rat's ass about what anyone else thought. What happened to her?"

"She's long gone."

He looked at her sadly, and when she couldn't take it any longer, she hugged him, thinking how nice it would be to wake up next to him, make lazy, morning love. Even the prospect of curtains on the windows and a real mattress seemed fraught with sybaritic possibility.

"Were you serious about franchising the store?" she asked.

"Would you stay if I said yes? Wait, don't answer. No, of course I wasn't serious." He studied her a beat. "Disappointed?"

She shook her head. "But it was nice to see my father back in the game." She wriggled out from his embrace and started to get dressed. "Maybe we could go away for a few days, just you and me."

"How about next weekend? We could leave Thursday night. There's an inn in northwestern Connecticut I know, you could introduce me to the joys of bird watching. Lily?"

"Oh, right, bird watching."

"What just happened? Where'd you go? You look like you got horrible news."

"Good news, actually. Talking about going away on Thursday . . ." She pulled her blouse over her head. "I was so focused on the dates . . ." She hiked up her trousers and fastened them. "I never paid attention to the day of the week." She stepped into her shoes. "Do you know what this means?"

"What what means?"

"Barnett really was innocent."

"Him again."

"Not him, me. If he's innocent . . ."

"Right, if Barnett is innocent, you're rich again. The fact that he ran away, leaving you and the kids with nothing . . . a minor detail."

"It's not that," she said. She leaned over the bed to kiss him but he rolled away.

"Good luck getting your life back," he said.

"I'm sorry."

"Well, at least this time I get an apology before being dumped."

"Nobody's dumping you."

"I hope everything works out for you. The front door locks automatically when you shut it."

Twenty-nine

"I am thinking this will be our last week together," Mohammed said, pulling on a Marlboro. Lily's X-acto knife made an unintentional detour through the corner of a twenty, rendering it worthless (well, *truly* worthless). "It does not pay to get greedy in this business. We have made enough money."

Lily smiled despite looming disappointment—who would have guessed that counterfeiting was so rich in wordplay?

"I don't agree."

"You have made many thousands of dollars in a few months' time. There are not many professions that pay as well. I have inwested wisely in the securities markets. Now it is time to cash in my chips and send for my family."

A feeling of dread, laced perhaps with panic, fell over her. True, for the past months she'd been making money faster than she could spend it. She'd rented a series of ever larger safe-deposit boxes at a bank branch on Broadway, to which she repaired twice a week carrying an overnight bag plump with packets of twenties. It had occurred to her that amassing so much fake currency was not a good idea. Mohammed had urged her to "get it into circulation," as if her cash horde were a lonely widow in need of a social life. She'd given half of her production to Mohammed to invest through his broker, whose firm, she suspected, was called Ask No Questions Financial Services. When she inquired as to the status of her investments, he'd only say, "Doing wery well, wery, wery well."

Only that morning, emboldened by her revelation the night before, she'd told her mother, who was recounting the horrors of living in tight quarters with "that phony English servant you brought with you," that they would be moving out soon. Nanny, who must have been "lurking" in the hallway, as Peggy invariably referred to her movements around the apartment, had looked stricken when the three women met a moment later in the tiny foyer. Even if her theory about the missing money was correct, it could be years before she got it back. She'd been counting on her regular production of twenties to tide them over in their own place.

"What will you do?"

"I will continue to drive my taxi until the family comes. Then I will inwest full time while we establish ourselves here. And you, Lily?"

He'd never spoken her name before, and it sounded lovely to her ears, with a gentle glissando on the second syllable.

"I think I've figured out who stole the money from my husband's firm."

"So you will be rich again."

"I suppose so."

He smiled broadly. "Excellent. And will you inwite your husband back into your home?"

"I don't think so."

"The candy man?"

"I don't know."

He frowned. Having finished the day's quota of twenties, she turned off the scanner and computer and began to soak the bills in batches of five in the tub of mysterious elixir that Mohammed had earlier prepared.

"You need a plan."

"Did you always have a plan, Mohammed?"

"I have always had this plan, since I can remember."

"This is the first time in my life that I don't have a plan. And it feels okay, which is a bit of a surprise, actually. My entire life has been one long to-do list. Go to college. Marry well. Buy drop-dead gorgeous apartment. Have two children. Get noticed by the right people. Maintain body. It all seems completely pointless now. How is it possible that I could have been completely happy back then but not miss one aspect of my old life today?" She sighed. "Although it would be nice to have my own bathroom again."

"Perhaps you weren't as happy as you think you were."

"No, I was happy. I loved my life. I really did. It was an ideal life in many ways. I just don't miss it."

"I have never for a single instant doubted my plan. Doubts are like drops of water from the floor above. Small things, but if you don't stop them right away, the entire ceiling will come down on top of you."

"But the other day you said—"

"I said I worried that my sons and my wife had doubts. But not me."

"Maybe before all this happened I couldn't admit any doubt or the entire world I'd constructed would collapse on top of me."

"It is better to keep your focus on your goals than your misgivings."

"Unless they're the wrong goals," she said. "Are we really going to just close this down? I'll miss it."

She waited for a reciprocal expression of regret but it never came. Still, she thought she saw a veil of . . . well, not quite sadness, but perhaps wistfulness, briefly dim his eyes.

As Kristin Liu of Goldman Sachs crossed Guy's office, he saw her glance at the tank, as visitors always did. But she looked less admiring this time than pitying, as if the fate of the fish, and perhaps Guy's own lot, were in serious question. It was going to be a difficult meeting. In fact it was going to suck.

Kristin sat on the sofa, Guy in an armchair opposite her. With her long, glossy black hair fanning out across her shoulders like an elaborate headdress, and her groovy eyewear—a tortoiseshell riff on the cardboard glasses once distributed at 3D movies—and her black dress tight as a cowl against her thin body, and her stern, tiny mouth and narrow, impenetrable eyes, she had the aura of a priestess—one who presided over human sacrifices, perhaps. It was going to suck big time.

"It's about the loan," Guy preempted her.

"Exactly," she said, slurring the "ex" into an "ess," a reassuring flaw. She extracted a sheet of ivory Goldman Sachs letterhead from a burgundy leather portfolio. A death warrant? "Last summer you borrowed two-point-two million dollars against your shares in Positano Software. Those shares have now lost 96.6 percent of their value. As a result, we will need additional collateral to keep from triggering default."

"How much additional collateral?"

"Ninety-six-point-six percent of two-point-two million dollars is . . . well, it's over two million."

"I think you know that I don't have anything near that amount."

"You still have three millions shares of Positano stock."

Positano had closed the day before at three cents over a buck. One dollar was the dreaded Rubicon for public companies; cross it and you got a delisting notice from the NASDAQ, thereby entering a bleak purgatory of near-dead companies and technology has-beens. Few ever made it out.

"I'd have to put up two-thirds of my shares."

"Essactly. However, if the price slips below one dollar, we might have to take alternative action."

"I'm guessing that wouldn't be good."

"Our policy is to secure private loans with hard assets when the collateralized share price no longer—"

"Hard assets? We're a software company. We don't have inventory or factories. What are you going to do, cart away our desks and computers?" He stole a quick glance at the tank, whose inhabitants floated obliviously through the preternaturally clear, temperature-controlled salt water.

"Guy, this is a very difficult situation for us."

"My heart is breaking for you."

"There is an alternative, perhaps. There's talk on the street about a takeover of Positano by Aquinas."

"I've rejected the offer." Guy had not spoken to any of the directors since the last board meeting. An ominous silence had fallen over Positano, but he suspected a squadron of frenzied lawyers and bankers was maneuvering behind the scenes to put the Aquinas deal together, with Sumner Freedman, who hadn't spoken to Guy since the deal was presented to him, as their mole inside the company.

"Would Goldman be interested in putting together a management buyout of Positano?"

"Take the company private? I haven't studied your numbers lately, your *corporate* numbers. But my initial reaction is that you're not a candidate for an LBO."

"We have a number of contracts out for bid now—six, in fact. If just three of them—"

"There is no way Goldman Sachs will invest in the enterprise software market at this time. No one is looking to enter this market, Guy."

"Aquinas is."

"Essactly. But that's a roll-up."

As if Positano were an old rug to be shipped off to Goodwill.

"Now, about your personal situation. If the Aquinas takeover comes through, and assuming it's an all-stock deal, we might be more inclined to accept Aquinas stock as collateral. Assuming they offer a reasonable premium over your current stock price."

"There won't be a deal."

"Then we'll have to take Positano stock, assuming it holds above one dollar. We generally frown upon collateralized shares below one dollar. There are legal implications for us if they're delisted."

Six months ago Goldman had thrown money at him. The two-million-dollar loan for the apartment had been pocket change beneath the bulging wad that was his net worth. Guy still couldn't believe it had all vanished, or 96.6 percent of it. There hadn't been one horribly bad day or even one disastrous week for Positano's stock, just an endless, lurching string of small declines. Where did all that wealth go? Rosemary had asked him recently. It can't just disappear, can it? *Someone* must have it, right? She dealt in the world of hard assets, so he found an analogy that worked for her: It's like dropping an uninsured Tiffany lamp, he'd told her. The value isn't transferred. It just vanishes.

"So it's either Positano shares or Aquinas's?"

"Essactly. You'll have to work into the merger docs the fact that a portion of your Aquinas shares will be pledged to us. We can help you with the verbiage."

"I'm sure you can. Are you making a lot of these visits lately?"

"You mean, concerning margin calls?"

"*Essactly.*"

She smiled uncertainly. "Constantly. It's not ess— Not really what I went to business school for."

"And this isn't what I started a company for, either."

She slipped the Goldman letterhead back into the leather portfolio and stood up.

"We need to move quickly. Do you know when the merger is being announced?"

"There won't be a merger."

Her tiny mouth puckered to a perfect pink anus. And to think he'd once found her attractive.

"It might be your best option."

"There won't be a merger."

"Then we'll have to collateralize two million shares, assuming they're—"

"Still over a dollar." Guy stood up abruptly. "I have a business to run."

"I understand," she said.

But he wondered if she really did.

"They're all forgeries," Rosemary told Esme Hollender, deliberately avoiding "fake," which sounded pointlessly harsh. The shades in Esme's library that she'd raised three days earlier had not been lowered, so the room shimmered in bluish afternoon sunlight, exposing a rime of dust on every surface and a crazing of fine wrinkles on Esme's cheeks and forehead.

"Which ones?" Esme asked. "You know, I always had my doubts about that lamp I gave you and Lloyd. Ostentatious, I always thought. But everything else is so much more refined."

"Not just the lamp. Everything. All the art glass, the paintings, even the furniture." Squinting, Esme glanced slowly around as if confronting a roomful of traitors. If only she hadn't brought them that lamp, she might have gone on in happy, trusting oblivion. "Your husband had a very bad eye for value, Mrs. Hollender."

"Bullshit."

Rosemary made a noise between a gasp and a chuckle. "He bought forgeries, very good forgeries that even an expert—"

"Bullshit. He knew exactly what he was buying. I don't know why I let him buy all these . . . these—what do people call them?—these church keys." She cast angry glances at the tchotchkes adorning the bookshelf across the room, then stood up and walked over to them. "I always thought most of this stuff looked like crap, but he rattled off names of fancy French artists and designers and I thought, Who am I to argue with such knowledge?" She picked up a small atomizer, a Gallé knockoff that, if real, would sell for fifteen thousand dollars or more. "I've seen better knickknacks at Woolworth." She hurled the atomizer against the shelf, shattering it.

"Mrs. Hollender, *don't.* Even as forgeries they have some intrinsic value."

Esme grabbed a ruby-red vase and threw it into the fireplace, where it exploded into a hundred pieces, then picked up a small glass bowl that Rosemary just managed to wrench from her hands before it met a similar fate. Apart from trying to salvage what little value these items might have, Rosemary suspected she'd personally wind up cleaning the room once Esme's tantrum was over. Thanks to Alden Hollender's church keys, there was no money left for household help.

"Oh, what shall I do?" Esme wailed.

Esme placed her hands on Rosemary's shoulders and collapsed into her. She was such a tiny bird that even her full weight felt no more burdensome on Rosemary's shoulders than a winter coat.

"Mrs. Hollender, come and sit on the sofa. I'll get you some water."

But Esme clung to her, whimpering softly. Rosemary sidled across the room, dragging Esme with her, and lowered her onto the sofa.

"Nothing he bought ever looked quite right. Once he brought home a Fabergé egg that had a drop of dried glue on the side. He said Karl Fabergé himself had made it for the Empress of Russia. I remember thinking, Would the czar's own jeweler neglect to wipe glue off the side of an egg intended for the Empress of Russia? Wouldn't the Empress have mentioned a drop of dried glue? People were sent to Siberia for lesser offenses back then, you know. Or executed. But I gave him the money he wanted. It seemed easier, somehow."

"Easier than what?"

"Than admitting the truth," she said with quiet misery. "That he never loved me. That he was cheating me, cheating *on* me."

"Have you been able to recall the name of the dealer he worked with?"

"Of course I remember. He was the other woman." She smiled primly. "Henry Something. Henry Becton. Or Harold Becton. No, Harold Brighton. No, wait, it was Frederick Brighton. Or maybe not. I don't have a current address, I'm afraid. Do you think you'll be able to recover anything from him?"

"I doubt it. Your husband was the buyer, and he probably knew full well what he was getting. If he chose to overpay, that was his prerogative."

"Oh, dear."

"You were swindled," Rosemary said. "Perhaps if your husband invested the money he got from you . . ."

She shook her head. "He's been dead ten years. His will left everything to me, and believe me when I tell you, there was nothing." Esme tottered to the drinks table and poured herself several fingers of Scotch. She lifted the glass to her lips but seemed to change her mind, and returned to the sofa empty-handed. "I might as well tell you, now that we have no secrets . . . I'm a bit strapped for funds. It's all I can do to pay the maintenance on this place and buy groceries."

"I'd figured that out."

"Well, I did my best not to let on." Esme cast a brief, longing glance at the drinks table. "I wouldn't have brought you that lamp, only there's an assessment on the building this month, something to do with repointing the facade, whatever that means. It's only for a few thousand dollars, but it was enough to put me in the red. Oh!" She put her hands to her face. "You have no idea how rich I used to be. Filthy, stinking rich. What will my children think?"

No doubt they'll be bitterly disappointed, Rosemary thought, recalling the phone calls they'd made to Lloyd, urging him to sell as much as possible of what they'd assumed to be a valuable collection, never mind their mother's apparent reluctance. And Esme would end up taking the blame, Rosemary felt. She'd done nothing worse than trust a scoundrel, but frail old ladies were such easy targets for resentment, they seemed so out of step with life, so irritatingly awkward about things, especially money, and so incapable, for the most part, of fighting back. And they tended to outlive their husbands, often by decades, which could be very inconvenient.

"You can't keep this place," Rosemary said. "You can sell it, however, then buy or rent a smaller apartment, and live off the interest on the difference." Esme didn't react. "Mrs. Hollender, do you understand what I said? This place is your primary asset now. You need to unlock some of its value to live on." Thank heavens real estate couldn't be forged, or she'd be completely destitute. "Real" estate—she understood the term for the first time.

"Are you sure none of it's genuine?" Esme said, pointing to the bookshelves festooned with worthless glass. "You haven't looked at every single piece. And some of the furniture . . . I mean, that's not your specialty, is it?"

Rosemary shook her head. This was going to be tougher than she'd anticipated.

Lily worked hard to keep at least a half-block's distance between herself and Nanny. She was a fast, impatient walker and Nanny was on the slow side, her arms swinging as she made her way down Broadway.

At Columbus Circle she went into the subway station. Lily waited until Nanny had paid her fare before swiping her MetroCard, which was always amply filled nowadays, thanks to the machines at every station that didn't distinguish between real and counterfeit twenty-dollar bills. (Vending machines that accepted twenty-dollar bills were a counterfeiter's best friend; Lily had a drawer full of loaded MetroCards at home, several lifetimes of prepaid bus and subway travel.) She followed Nanny to the platform of the uptown A train, which thundered into the station a few minutes later, and boarded the car behind the one Nanny chose.

She knew little about Nanny, other than that her real name was Caroline Griffen, that she was born and raised in Essex, England, and had come to New York, after attending some sort of child-care school in England, because she could make twice as much money "minding children" in America as in England. She had worked for a doctor's family on the East Side, a "prominent cardiologist," Nanny had insisted on calling him, until his children were too old for a nanny, and then had found the Granthams through an agency. Lily also knew that, since moving out of their Park Avenue apartment, Nanny lived in Washington Heights with her sister, at the northern tip of Manhattan.

Nanny got off at the 181st Street station, Lily close behind. There was something vaguely thrilling about tailing someone, a mixed sense of power and danger. And with Nanny as the target, the feeling was doubly satisfying, since Nanny knew so much about the Granthams, having spent ten years in their home, while Lily knew next to nothing about her. For example, who would have guessed that Nanny had such attractive legs? She'd switched from white shoes with crepe soles to a nice pair of heeled pumps in the lobby of 124 West Sixty-seventh Street and now she looked taller, even graceful, a navy wool coat concealing the drab blouse she wore tucked into a plain gray skirt, her usual attire.

She headed east on 181st Street, then north on Wadsworth Avenue, making slow, unswerving progress along sidewalks teeming with Dominicans returning from work, among whom Nanny looked like a pale visitor from another land—which is what she was, come to think of it. The December evening was unusually warm, the air dry, the fading light casting a sexy, mauvish hue across the blocks of low-rise brick apartment buildings. In front of one such building Nanny stopped to wrap her arms around a tall man, who had apparently been waiting for her. Their faces remained pressed together in a long, passionate kiss. Lily observed them from half a block away

If Nanny's attractive legs had surprised her, the sight of her children's beloved baby-sitter soul-kissing a man at least ten years her junior—about thirty-five, perhaps forty, Lily guessed—was downright startling. And wasn't he . . . she waited for them to disengage before deciding. Yes, he was definitely the same man who'd tried to steal the envelope from her, the man she'd seen in Queens that day. Lily made a note of the address and headed back to the subway.

Thirty

With Monroe at her side, clutching her arm like a terrified child, Peggy made slow but grateful progress along Broadway. The early evening was unusually warm, the light at once fading and clarifying. The city hesitated between day and night, as if unable to decide between equally compelling alternatives. Monroe had chosen a good moment to step out, after so many months shut away in the apartment.

"We should think about getting a place for Lily and the children," she said. "I don't think I can take so many people living under one roof much longer. Lily mentioned getting her own place, though I can't imagine how she'd pay for it."

"I like that Larry fellow," was Monroe's typically irrelevant response, but at least he was talking. "A good head on his shoulders."

Monroe had become strangely obsessed with Larry Adler since Sophie's dreadful birthday dinner, which had roused him from his post-coronary funk. She wondered, without daring to explore the idea out to its fullest margins, whether seeing Larry Adler caused Monroe to imagine that it was 1979 again, if his mind had convinced his body that the past decades had never happened and he was a frisky fifty-year-old again. Stranger things had happened, if you believed what you saw on the television—people waking up from ten-year comas as fresh as daisies, adults suddenly remembering that Uncle Seymour had molested their five-year-old selves before murdering half the village and burying the bodies by the abandoned railroad tracks, where, wouldn't you know it, the skeletons are dug up fifty years later, just where they were supposed to be. Next thing she knew Monroe would be sidling over to her side of the bed at night, demanding action.

"We have the money from selling the apartment," she said. "We could buy her a small two-bedroom in the neighborhood."

"Marvin likes to say it's easier to run a chain of fifty stores than a single location," Monroe said.

Marvin was Marvin Feldbush, who used to run a national chain of women's clothing stores and had been one of Monroe's biggest customers. Marvin had been dead for at least a decade, the clothing stores were out of business, and the idea that Monroe was still imagining that Larry Adler would expand the Broadway Nut Shoppe into a franchise operation was almost as disturbing as the idea that Monroe might be thinking of reinstating sexual relations.

"I think 'Broadway' has a lot of cachet in Middle America—what do you think, Peg?"

As they continued their slow progress along that very boulevard, the fading sun just visible at the western end of cross streets, where it resisted the final plunge into the undeserving New Jersey horizon, she could only agree.

"They should see Broadway now, out there in America," she said. "Larry would sell out a thousand stores."

"I'm losing Positano Software," Guy told Rosemary on the elevator heading up to their new apartment, as he still thought of it, despite having owned it for five hellish months. As if to punctuate the thought, Patrick, ensconced next to his brother in the double stroller, which they'd only just managed to squeeze into the elevator, decided to stretch his tiny legs, his surprisingly hard little shoe finding the vulnerable mid-portion of Guy's right shin. The whole world was against him, even his infant son.

"There has to be someone with money," Rosemary said.

"Maybe that old lady with the art glass will lend me twenty million dollars."

"If her collection had been genuine, she could have." The thought seemed to depress Rosemary as much as the prospect of losing Positano brought him down.

Inside the apartment they performed what had become a twice-weekly ritual: the inspection.

"The granite is in," Rosemary said cheerfully in the kitchen, always their first stop. "Oh no." She ran her hand along an all-too-obvious seam that cut across the longest, most visible portion of the countertop.

Guy looked at it, then said, "Our kitchen consultant specified that the seam go next to the stove top, where it wouldn't be noticed. I'll talk to Ozeri."

Guy knew that he'd end up either learning to live with the disfiguring seam or paying for a new slab of granite—somehow he'd managed to found a public company that employed, even in its reduced state, 227 people, but he hadn't managed to win a single argument with Victor Ozeri. Because of the glacial pace of the renovation, they'd had to move to a temporary rental in their current building. Ozeri, not surprisingly, had refused to deduct the three-thousand-dollar monthly rent from his contractor's fee.

"Maybe it won't be so bad," Rosemary said as they entered the dining room, where the opening in the ceiling for a planned lighting fixture struck him as egregiously off center.

"So bad? We paid twenty grand for the granite and it looks like shit," he said.

"No, I mean having Positano owned by someone else. You've been under so much pressure, it might be better pleasing one owner rather than a thousand shareholders."

"I don't want to work for someone else. Besides, they'll throw me out on my ass the day the deal is done. It's been Aquinas's MO in ten other deals."

"Then you'll start something else. You'll still have all those shares . . ."

The twins were flailing inside the double stroller, which rocked violently; from the back it looked as though some sort of powerful, feral beast, not two infant boys, had been strapped into it. He hadn't told Rosemary about having to put up two-thirds of his dwindling net worth against the apartment loan. Was he afraid of appearing like a failure in front of her? And if that were the case, if even Rosie needed him to be a big success, at least in his mind, then was *anyone* on his side?

As if heralding an answer to the question, his cell phone chortled. The LCD screen read *Ventnor Place.*

"My man," Derek Ventnor greeted him.

"Your man," Guy replied.

"We hit an important milestone today, Guy. Our five thousandth sub-scriber."

"It's a horny country. Warmest congratulations."

"That's cumulative subscribers—we have some attrition, everyone does."

"Is there something I can do for you?"

In the master bedroom, he saw Rosemary add "crack in crown molding" to her punch list. They'd had every bit of molding replaced, at a cost that now amounted to approximately thirty-five thousand shares of Positano, give or take a few hundred, so even a hairline fracture was unacceptable; 227 em-ployees had toiled for something like six and a half hours for that molding.

"I notice that our stock was up fifteen percent today."

Our stock. Leave it to Ventnor to further cheapen, simply by uttering its name, a stock that had already lost more than ninety-five percent of its value.

"No big deal," Guy said. "It's thinly traded."

"There's no news? Because if this baby is on the way up, I'm buying more. I can bring my average cost down to two bucks if I buy just—"

"Nothing's happening." A lie, of course. Rumors of a takeover had sent the price up two days in a row. The announcement was expected tomorrow.

Rosemary was scribbling furiously in the master bathroom, and he im-mediately saw why. Their plans specified that the floor tiles—off-white, Italian-made, no two identical—be laid on a diagonal, with two-thirds of an inch in between each tile for grouting. The tile men had laid them in straight rows, with minimal space for grouting, upsetting the rustic, Tuscan feeling that their bathroom designer and architect had jointly intended and which they'd enthusiastically bought into (and paid handsomely for, rusticity being staggeringly expensive). Guy left the bathroom before Rosemary was done writing.

"Now I have a question for you," he told Ventnor. "How would you like to buy Positano Software?"

"That's what I was asking. If I were to buy just ten thousand shares at—"

"No, the entire company."

"You're joking."

Of course he was. And yet the notion of a pornographer owning his beloved creation was somehow less horrifying than the notion of that lapsed seminarian taking control and firing half the staff in the name of a "divine rationalization," or whatever bullshit theory he was foisting on Wall Street these days.

"Thirty million dollars and it's yours."

"I don't have *thirty* million dollars." He said this in the manner of a man who, asked for change of a five, realizes he only has four singles.

"Some of your friends must."

"Neville over at Platinum Escorts, he could scratch together thirty mil in an afternoon. He was a first mover on the Internet, and he really gets how to create intuitive user interfaces, but enterprise software? I don't see it."

"Why dirty your hands in enterprise software when you're pimping what, a hundred girls a night?"

"Then there's Hussein at Omarthetentmaker dot-com. Richer than God—like I was telling you, the real money's in gay. You serious about selling?"

"Of course not," Guy said, disappointing himself.

"'Cause if you were to sell, I think I could put together a consortium. . . ."

Guy could only imagine what a Ventnor-assembled consortium would look like, a bunch of greasy middle-aged lechers in gold jewelry and hairpieces taking time out from art-directing beaver shots to pay sales calls on systems analysts in central Tennessee. Or maybe there was something in it, a *truly* rational merger, for a change. *A two-hundred-thousand-dollar license fee includes four years of free upgrades, seventy-five hours of on-site customer support, and five on-site blow jobs from Krystal.* They'd never lose a bid.

"Guy, look at this," Rosemary called from the twins' room after he'd hung up. "They put the air-conditioning vent right in the middle of the wall." Rosemary pointed at the offending orifice. They'd had central air installed at a huge cost, putting a big generator in what had been a closet off the kitchen and running ducts into every room. You could buy a starter home in some of the outer suburbs of New York City for what they'd paid to have central air.

"It looks centered to me," Guy said.

"Exactly. How can we put a picture on that wall? Anything we put there would cover the vent. It was supposed to go under the crown molding and to the right."

"Wasn't that specified in the plans?" Their HVAC consultant, engaged for the price of a triple bypass at NewYork-Presbyterian, had meticulously detailed every inch of heating, ventilation, and air-conditioning. And still they'd end up paying.

She nodded as she furiously added to the punch list, which was beginning to resemble a supermarket receipt. When had they become such perfectionists? Only a year ago the air conditioner in their bedroom had begun to make noises that resembled food being uncomfortably digested by a three-ton rhinoceros and they'd decided to live with it rather than buy a new one at the then-staggering cost of four hundred dollars. After a few days they'd added the dyspeptic air conditioner to the repertoire of urban noises they didn't register anymore: the angry growl of garbage trucks compacting, the beeping of trucks backing up, the exasperated sigh of a bus kneeling to ingest an old person. Now the misplacement of a single vent in the boys' room was cause for torment.

Lily reboarded the express train at 181st Street, and as it hurtled downtown, she contemplated Nanny and her tryst. Why was it so shocking to discover that the woman had a lover, not to mention a sexy, heart-shaped ass, almost as appalling as the firming conviction that she'd stolen several million dollars from her employer? After all, she herself was en route to her own lover's apartment, and hers, unlike Nanny's, would be an adulterous liaison, at least technically (surely marital desertion had its privileges). Wasn't Nanny entitled to a life of her own, apart from taking care of two children well past the age of needing taking care of?

After changing trains, she emerged from the subway at Eighty-sixth Street and headed along Broadway to Larry's place. She'd left him under a cloud of tension last time and was looking forward to clearing things up with some quick, restorative sex.

At Eighty-fourth Street she passed a florist shop and decided to buy a peace offering. As she turned into the shop, she saw a man hesitate, then continue on his way. What caught her attention was his attire—dark, formless suit, white shirt, narrow tie; his grooming, everything about him, including his clipped black hair, identified him as an alien in the land of denim and running shoes—and the fact that he'd been staring at her, of this she was quite sure.

She bought a bunch of tall white lilies with a fresh twenty. Then, as she resumed her walk to Larry's place, she saw the man again, this time heading south, in the opposite direction. He avoided her glance—studiously, she thought. She gave him a few seconds, then turned and followed him.

He turned into the florist shop.

Thirty-one

"You're going to *adore* this place!"

Esme Hollender managed an obedient nod to Lucinda Wells as she and Rosemary were herded into the elevator at 333 East Sixty-ninth Street.

"Thank God you called when you did." Lucinda clutched one of Esme's elbows and leaned toward her, thrusting her sharp breasts into the older woman's startled face. "Can I tell you something? Junior fours in postwar doormen don't come on the market every day," she whispered, as if imparting the secret password to an ancient fraternal organization.

Esme could only re-nod. She looked utterly disoriented, eyes practically unblinking, mouth ajar, one leather-gloved hand busily yanking at the glove on the other. Rosemary began to have second thoughts about the expedition, which she'd set up shortly after discovering that Esme owned one of the world's finest assemblages of fake art glass, with passable collections of fake English furniture, reproduction Oriental carpets, and bogus eighteenth-century portraits.

Lucinda unlocked the door to Apartment 3L and charged in.

"*Voilà,*" she said, posing at the center of the main room, both arms raised, palms up, like a Hindu deity. "How about this light?"

Esme placed a tentative foot inside the apartment and glanced around.

"Southern exposure, the best kind!" intoned the deity.

Rosemary acknowledged, once she had managed to enter the unfurnished apartment behind a very reluctant and slow-moving Esme, that the living room was indeed illuminated by natural light, but it had a phony, grayish cast, like bedrooms in movies after the lamps have been supposedly turned off, leaving the actors still visible through a murky haze.

"Twelve by twenty, top of the line for postwar, size-wise," Lucinda said. As if to prove this point, she walked the length of the room, then the width, stiletto heels percussing the bare parquet floors. She took an ostentatiously deep breath after completing the exhausting trek.

Esme followed the broker's every move with astonished eyes. It was possible, Rosemary realized, to spend a lifetime in New York City and never meet the likes of Lucinda Wells. First, you had to avoid buying an apartment, of course, but more than that, you needed enough money to cushion yourself from the sharper edges of the city, where bargains were offered and purchased and deals proposed and struck. With piles of money you got Lloyd Lowell, fawning and soft-spoken and quick to grab the check. With only a modest hoard, by New York standards, anyway, you got Lucinda Wells, loud and aggressive, her every phrase and gesture urging the merely well off to take it or leave it.

"It *is* generously proportioned," Esme said. The empty room gobbled up her words.

"*What?*" demanded Lucinda, cupping a hand over one ear.

"And you don't often seen a foyer with a window. I like that."

"Did she say 'foyer'?" Lucinda said to Rosemary directly over Esme's shoulder.

"She thinks this—"

"This is the living room, Mrs. Hollender!" Lucinda shouted. "The. Living. Room."

Esme retreated a few steps and glanced around. "You mean this is the—"

"THE LIVING ROOM!" If the room had had a chandelier, it would have trembled. As it was, Esme herself appeared to vibrate.

"We'll offer eight-fifty," Lucinda said at the conclusion of the tour, which took a full three minutes. "A lowball but the apartment's been empty for six weeks. They'll come back with eight seventy-five, we'll settle at eight-sixty and change. I'm assuming you love the place." Inexplicably, they were having the strategy discussion in the apartment's smallest room, its kitchen, which was the size of a Boeing 727 galley, only windowless. "You'll put in new appliances," Lucinda said, perhaps registering the doleful look on Esme's face, though it was hard to imagine Lucinda noticing anything about another person. Esme could have sprouted stigmata right there in the narrow kitchen and Lucinda would have continued extolling the huge number of closets and the extraordinary fact that utilities were included in the monthly maintenance. She rapped the vintage refrigerator with an egg-sized hunk of turquoise attached to a ring on her right hand and stepped closer to Esme. "Trust me, appliances are easy."

"Oh, I see," Esme said, retreating a step.

"I could show you others, but I began with the best in your case. Usually I prefer a slow build—you know, start with drek to lower expectations and work our way up—but I didn't know if you had the . . . stamina for a full day of shopping. Do you want to see others, Mrs. Hollender?"

"No!"

"I didn't think so. Now, about the offer . . ."

"I hope I'm doing the right thing," Esme said in the cab on the way back to her apartment.

"You don't have much choice," Rosemary said. "Anyway, your apartment is too big for one person. You don't need all that space."

"Need? I think I would shrivel up and die in that . . . that shoe box."

"It's got southern exposure," Rosemary said with the dispiriting sense that she was spouting enemy propaganda. "And a roof deck."

"I wouldn't know myself in that place. I'm not an old lady who lives in a small apartment in a new building on Second Avenue. I'm an old lady who lives in a big apartment in an old building on Fifth Avenue. That's who I am."

"You're Esme Hollender, no matter where you live."

"Nonsense. You can't create a life for yourself apart from the place you live. I don't care if it's a palace or a tent. You can't take a plant used to sunshine and force it to live in the shade. It will die. You can't move a penguin to the tropics any more than you can put a zebra in Gramercy Park."

"But we're much more adaptable than animals, Mrs. Hollender."

"Only to a point. The lives we create are defined by where we live, what we choose to surround ourselves with. We accumulate things that are like statements to the world—*this is who I am, this is what I am.* You take all that away, especially at the end of a life, and what's left? All those fakes I've been living with all these years? Nothing could say more about my life. You never met my late husband . . ."

"No."

Her sigh was bottomless.

"My father, Frederick Packard—did I ever tell you about him?" She didn't wait for an answer. "Shortly after he made his fortune, he built a mansion on Fifth Avenue, six blocks from where I live now, coincidentally. We lived in a perfectly nice place near Gramercy Park—I was just a child, mind you, but my mother told me all about it later. Plenty of room for the three of us, plus servants, of course. She never understood why we had to move. My father spent five years of his life building that place, fought like the dickens with the builders, a succession of them, actually, and by the time we moved in, he was quite ill with diphtheria and died a few years later."

Well, at least they'd invented a cure for diphtheria, if not for the more debilitating renovation hell.

"My mother kept asking him why we had to move. Every weekend they'd drive uptown to survey the construction site. 'Why do we have to put ourselves through all this?' she would say. 'Because that's who I am,' he'd tell her, pointing at the new house. You see, Rosemary, we move from place to place, thinking we're improving our surroundings. But what we're really doing is slipping into a new skin."

Rosemary pictured the vast, white great room at 218 West End Avenue, the master bedroom ringed by pristine new moldings, the Italian-tiled master bathroom with its Jacuzzi throne. Her new skin. She was squirming as the taxi pulled up to Esme's building.

"Good afternoon, Mrs. Hollender," said the doorman, holding open the taxi door.

"Hello, Eddie."

Rosemary watched her toddle into the lobby, slipping back into her skin.

Lily lay in her sofa bed, unable to fall asleep. The chemical glow from the curtainless living-room windows seemed to electrify the room. This must be what living in Lapland is like, she thought; perpetual, insomnia-inducing daylight. Though she imagined the Lapps had curtains, not to mention comfortable mattresses. An hour earlier she'd returned late from Larry's, as she did most nights. The lilies, and every bit of charm she could muster, had eased the tension between them.

A shadow moved across the small, dark hallway that led to the front door. Everyone was asleep, or so she'd thought. The shadow was headed toward the door—was one of the children sneaking out? She sprang from the bed.

"Who's there?" she said as she lunged into the hallway.

The shadow jumped, then froze.

"*Damn,* you almost gave me a fuckin' heart attack, Mrs. Grantham."

"Oh, Paco . . . I thought you were William or Sophie." So intense was her relief that it wasn't one of her children sneaking out at one in the morning on a school night that it took her a few moments to comprehend the implications, none of them positive, of Paco's leaving the apartment at that hour.

"What are you doing here this late?"

"Me?"

Lily looked behind her, then past him.

"There doesn't appear to be anyone else with us."

"No, there . . ." He turned around, then back to her, and gave an embarrassed smile. "I was with Sophie," he said.

"Really? I assumed you were playing mah-jongg with my mother."

"No, seriously, I was with Sophie," he insisted. "You can ask—"

"And where was William?"

"In his room, I guess." His *side* of the room. Poor William, having to . . . to hear his sister and Paco on the other side of the dresser they'd positioned to bifurcate the bedroom. "Don't worry, we didn't make noise or nothing to disturb him."

"How considerate. I'm going to get Sophie. We need to have a talk."

"Don't wake her up."

"She can't be in a deep sleep, considering you just left her."

"She's been sleeping for like an hour. Seriously."

"Two hours?"

"Yeah, I like . . . I like being with her, you know, when she's sleeping. It's, you know, it's nice."

Nice. In the darkness of the hallway Paco's eyebrow ring was a glistening pinpoint of light. She could barely make out his features, just the dim shadow of his lips when he spoke, and she noted that his shoulders were almost cartoonishly broad for someone of such short stature. With only that eyebrow ring and his lips and those wide shoulders visible, he seemed entirely sexual, a nocturnal creature built exclusively to attract and repeatedly impregnate the opposite sex, which wasn't exactly how she wanted to think of the boy who had just left her daughter's bed, even if he'd allegedly been doing nothing more than watch her sleep.

"You must be a light sleeper, 'cause, see, I took my shoes off and my mother always says I walk like an Indian, on account of my never making any noise when I moved."

"I was awake, yes." Lily was suddenly conscious of the fact that her T-shirt, which barely covered her hips, was all that she had on. She yanked it down and crossed her arms in front of her.

"Paco, have you ever . . . have you ever had to . . . can you get into someone's apartment when it's, you know . . ."

"Locked? You think I'm like that, breaking into people's apartments and shit?"

"No, of course not."

"I may not live in a place like this, you know? But that don't mean I steal shit."

"I wasn't suggesting you steal . . . anything. Forget I even mentioned it."

"But if you want a pick set, okay, I can get you that."

"Pick set?"

"Don't be thinking just because I can get you one, that means I use it, right?"

"No, of course not."

"Seriously, you know how to use a pick set, Mrs. Grantham?" The eyebrow ring sparkled.

"Is it . . . difficult?"

"Not if you know what you're doing."

"Could you . . ."

"Teach you? No problem. Seriously, you just choose the right pick and—"

"Can you bring the picks tomorrow?"

"Not a problem. Whose apartment you trying to bust into?"

"Whose—Oh, our old place. The government has it locked up, you see, but I need some . . . papers."

"That sucks, breaking into your own place."

It sucked more, breaking into your own nanny's place, but she spared him that observation.

He brought the picks the next day after school. They were basically metal files no thicker than emery boards. He demonstrated their use on the front door of the apartment, which he opened with unsettling ease. He handed her a pick, and as she felt the cylinder on the front door of her parents' apartment give way with a hugely satisfying though nearly imperceptible sigh of a click, like the moment when a piece of intractable gristle finally succumbs to the probing of a toothpick, she had a brief surge of self-confidence in which she felt certain that nothing was beyond her grasp.

Still high from her newfound competence in a second dark art, she waited for Nanny to report for work, then left the apartment and boarded the A train.

She'd become a counterfeiter first and then a thief, she thought with some contentment as the train hurtled northward. She glanced around the half-empty subway car and wondered what the other passengers would make of her, if they bothered to notice her at all. She'd put on ten pounds since moving out of 913 Park Avenue, as if her body sensed that it would need a thicker layer of protection from the cold wind of impoverishment. Well, relative impoverishment. Her fellow A-trainers might note her shoulder-length brown hair, which she now got cut at a Jean Louis David outlet on Broadway, where the stylists, nearly all of them newly arrived Russians (was that the dream of former Communists, to move to America and cut hair?), handed her a glossy catalog of coifs and asked her to "choose, please, how you want." Today she wore a felony-appropriate black T-shirt and black jeans and a pair of flats she'd had made for her in London, relics from Park Avenue that had set her back something like eight hundred dollars a few years ago and had held up well despite near-daily use since moving to the West Side, which at least proved that sometimes it really was worth paying more.

She walked quickly from the subway stop to Nanny's building and began pressing buttons on the intercom panel until someone buzzed open the door without asking her to identify herself. Before entering, she pressed the button for Apartment 4A, identified on the panel as belonging to a C. Griffen, and was relieved not to receive a response. She climbed to the fourth floor of the nondescript but well-maintained building, where she noted with relief that Nanny's door was secured by a basic Medeco and knob lock, with no safety strip to deal with. Like a golfer selecting her club, she carefully considered the entire pouch of picks before opting for a midsize number and got to work. After only a few moments of reaming, the Medeco cylinder gave way and it was all she could do to keep from blowing on the extracted pick like a victorious duelist. The knob lock succumbed even faster.

The apartment was dark, and her first impression was of the sickly sweet smell of potpourri. She flicked on a light switch in the living room to reveal wicker chairs with chintz cushions, framed botanical prints, floral chain-stitch carpet. The room could have illustrated a "Cozy Country Living on a Budget" article in *Good Housekeeping*, she thought—uncharitably, really, given that Nanny's budget had been set by her. Lily tried to picture her in the room—on the sofa, standing before the Bombay Company bar table pouring drinks from one of the several bottles of premium-brand spirits, lowering the moiré silk Austrian shade, replenishing the ubiquitous bowls of potpourri—and failed. It was like discovering that Nanny had a heart-shaped ass and sexy legs. It didn't fit, somehow. And there was, of course, no sign of a second woman, the "sister" Nanny had claimed to be living with.

Business called. Lily doubted that Nanny would stow evidence of embezzlement in the bucolic living room or tiny kitchen, so she headed for the bedroom, which was even more oppressively potpourried than the rest of the apartment. A canopy bed dominated the small room, which also held a pine dresser, a makeup-laden vanity, two night tables, and a desk. She started with the desk, and in the third drawer she opened she found what she wanted.

To roasting potatoes, printing money, and breaking and entering she could now safely add criminal investigation, she thought as she raised the small stack of documents to her lips and kissed them. Statements from banks in the Cayman Islands, Belize, and Switzerland, arranged chronologically, showing three balances that she'd bet every phony buck she had amounted to three million dollars, plus interest. There was no name on the account, only a long series of numbers, and they'd been sent to a post office box in Manhattan.

She secured the statements in her purse and left. She'd take a cab back to the apartment and confront Nanny directly, calling Jay DiGregorio at the Federal Prosecutor's Office on the way to arrange for him to meet her at the apartment. Unfortunately, taxis weren't as plentiful in Washington Heights as they were downtown. She spent several minutes waiting for one to appear and had just resigned herself to taking the A train when she felt a tap on her shoulder.

"Mrs. Grantham?"

Her insides went into free-fall. The man she'd seen Nanny suck face with the other day—had he caught her leave the building? She turned and saw that it wasn't Nanny's lover.

"Mrs. Grantham. I'm Howard Breslin from the Bureau of Alcohol, Tobacco, and Firearms. And this is my colleague, Rick Conklin."

Alcohol. Tobacco. Firearms. Three things she never went near, save the occasional glass of Chardonnay.

"What do you—"

"You're under arrest, Mrs. Grantham."

"Under— What for?" Suddenly the pick set in her purse felt impossibly heavy. What was the punishment for breaking and entering? Not that she'd actually broken anything. And what did any of that have to do with liquor, cigarettes, and guns?

"Knowingly passing counterfeit currency," said Howard Breslin. "If you'll come with us, I'll read you your rights in the car on the way downtown."

Arrested for passing counterfeit currency with a pick set in her pocket, having only moments earlier uncovered a diabolical plot by a trusted household employee to defraud her husband and have him take the blame—life didn't get more ironic that that. Or did it. A yellow cab, its "For Hire" sign turned on, drove slowly past.

Thirty-two

"One pair of khaki pants and one pair of white socks, seventy-four dollars at the Gap, Sixty-eighth Street. Six coffee mugs at Crate & Barrel, Sixty-ninth Street, fifty-two dollars. One haircut and blow-dry, Jean Louis David"—*Gene Lewis Dayvid*—"on Broadway and Seventy-sixth Street, twenty-five dollars . . ."

As Howard Breslin enumerated her recent purchases with allegedly counterfeit twenties, it occurred to Lily that the list was a perfect symbol for what had become of her life. Clothes from the Gap, household accessories from Crate & Barrel, hair styled by refugees from the former Iron Curtain. True, she'd have had to have printed hundred-dollar bills by the truckload to finance her old life, but it seemed a bit pathetic to risk—to risk what, ten years in prison? Twenty?—for shopping sprees at what amounted to a suburban mall of chain stores. Wouldn't she, perhaps, have felt the teeniest bit better about going to jail for "one cashmere sweater from Barneys, twelve hundred dollars"?

Well, perhaps not.

"I have no idea where the cash came from," she said with all the confidence she could muster, interrupting the shopping list. "I didn't check its authenticity. Who does?"

"We find that highly improbable, Mrs. Grantham." Like the men who had arrested Barnett a lifetime ago, Breslin was lean and pale, as if interrogating suspected counterfeiters left little time for either food or sunlight. He looked at her from across a beat-up wooden table in a small, windowless federal building downtown, not far from the site where Barnett had been arraigned, his expression a squirm-inducing blend of pity and scorn.

"*You* find it improbable?" she said. "How about me? Think about what it must feel like to learn that your every move . . ."

She thought of her nightly shuttle between Larry's apartment and her parents'. She'd managed to keep that aspect of her affair with Larry from her parents and children but not, she feared, from the federal government.

"Tell us about this man, Mrs. Grantham." Breslin slid a photo across the table. Mohammed stood in front of a height chart. He looked terrified and very sad and, at five-six, much shorter than she'd realized.

"How can I tell you about him when I don't—"

"Cut the crap," said the other man, Rick Conklin. He was as thin as his colleague and almost as pale, wearing an identically formless dark suit and plain tie. He slid another photo across the table, this one a picture of her leaving Mohammed's garage-cum-printing-plant. She looked gray and furtive and defeated, even with a handbag stuffed with several thousand dollars of self-created currency.

The game was up. She thought of all the people who would have to learn about her recent history: parents, children, Larry, all her former "friends." And, despite everything, she felt her lips slowly pulling back to a smile. If only she could be there when they found out that Lily Gimmel Grantham wasn't exactly what they'd been led to expect. She'd defied expectations once again.

"I'd like to call my lawyer," she said, though she doubted Morton Samuels would take her call, and couldn't imagine who else she'd want. It sounded like the right thing to say.

"That's fine with us," Breslin said. "You can call an army of lawyers. But you're in very deep trouble, Mrs. Grantham. First the business with your husband—"

"Different department," Conklin chimed in, as if it mattered. "But it doesn't look good, a second offense."

"I had nothing to do with that. In fact, I just learned—"

A plan took shape, not gradually but in a single moment, revealing itself to her not like a movie over time but like a Torah scroll unfurling in one smooth movement—from what memory pit had she excavated that image? She would save herself, and Mohammed.

They left her alone to call a lawyer. She removed her address book from her purse and found the number she wanted.

"Federal Prosecutor's Office," said the woman who answered.

"I'd like to speak to Jay DiGregorio," she said. "Immediately."

Guy entered his office to find the tank empty.

"Where are the fish?" he asked Dinitia, his assistant, out in the hallway.

"Oh, Guy, it was awful," she said, and indeed she looked on the verge of tears. Given her distress, he couldn't help imagining a terrible fate for his beloved fish, perhaps removal, one by one, from the tank, then a heartless thrust into the gaping maw of Sumner Freedman's open mouth. "I tried calling . . ."

Rosemary had insisted on a family outing to a park in Westchester County, without cell phones, during which the twins, deciding for their precocious selves that they were ready for solid food, had spent most of the day ripping fistfuls of dead grass from the near-frozen ground and stuffing them into their tiny mouths. The company, on the verge of being sold out from under him, had run without him for a day. But who could have anticipated ichthyic genocide?

"The fish are okay, Guy," Dinitia said. "That's the important thing."

Nod, he told himself. Just nod. The company was slipping away from him, more layoffs were a virtual certainty, and his own finances were looking precarious. But the fish were okay. He nodded.

"They came with plastic bags, which they filled with water from the tank, and then they—"

"I need to see Freedman," he said.

"—put one fish in each bag."

He turned and charged down the hall, but not before registering her look of bottomless disappointment at his disregard for his former charges.

"I insisted on one fish in each bag, not two," she called after him.

Sumner Freedman was in his office. When he noticed Guy he sat back and placed his hands on the edge of the desk, as if bracing for an impact.

"What the fuck is going on?" Guy inquired.

"You weren't reachable yesterday."

"Where are my—" He couldn't quite bring himself to finish the question: Much more was at stake than tropical fish, though symbolically they carried much weight.

"The fish will be okay, Guy. Mount Sinai has a children's ward with a big tropical tank. The move went very smoothly."

"Why wasn't I consulted?"

"We called, but you were unreachable."

"I'm sure the sick children could have lived another day without the fish."

"I don't know, Guy. Some of these kids are very ill."

How had they tumbled down this conversational hole?

"What's going on?"

"Aquinas assumed control yesterday, officially. They've called for an immediate thirty percent reduction in overall expenses. We haven't drawn up the plan for achieving that amount yet, but the fish seemed like a good place to start. We're on a very aggressive schedule. In fact, Mel Armitrage wants to meet with you this afternoon."

"He's here?"

"At the company suite at the Carlyle. He'd like you to be there at two o'clock."

"Am I being fired?"

"I don't know."

"Of course you know."

"It's complicated, Guy."

"No, it's not. There's a children's hospital somewhere with a big tank full of technology company founders. The sick kids get a real lift seeing these once-powerful creatures swimming about with big fishy frowns on their faces."

"I'm sorry, Guy."

"Or maybe they'll just sell us to the fish market—fillet of founder."

"I'm glad you still have your sense of humor."

"It's all that's left. You stole my company and my balls."

Sumner held his hands up in protest, revealing dark sweat stains under his arms, an unexpectedly mammalian response. Though bloodless, he had sweat glands.

. . .

Rosemary was inside the elevator of 218 West End Avenue when she saw Peggy and a man who was most likely her husband Monroe, crossing the lobby. She jabbed at the close-door button but to no avail.

"Hello!" Peggy called across the marble lobby. Reluctantly, Rosemary pressed the open-door button as the couple approached. The old man was walking with difficulty.

"We're visiting the Weinsteins on eleven. How are you enjoying the apartment?"

"We're scheduled to move in next month."

"Next month? But it's been . . ." She glanced at the twins in their double stroller, half expecting teenagers. "It's been forever."

"Tell me about it."

The Gimmels squeezed around the stroller and Rosemary released the door.

"Oh, look, Monroe, I've pressed six by accident," Peggy said. She made no move, however, to press eleven.

After a brief silence Rosemary gave in. "Would you like to see the apartment?"

Walking through the empty but nearly finished apartment, Monroe and Peggy Gimmel were like emigrants revisiting the old country, marveling with a mixture of awe and sadness at how much had changed.

"What the hell did you do to the foyer?" Monroe asked. "Where did it go?"

"It's part of the great room now."

"What's a great room?" He didn't wait for an answer, tottering into the forty-by-forty-foot ocean of gleaming white plaster and molding. He looked so small and tentative, Rosemary expected him to vanish into another space-time dimension.

"Come on, Monroe, I hear they made a powder room."

"It's this way," Rosemary said, wondering if that was what people gossiped about on the Upper West Side, the appearance of new rooms in old buildings.

"Imagine, having to get directions in our own apartment," Peggy said. "Well, technically it's not ours anymore."

Technically. Rosemary had to smile.

"Where did this come from?" Monroe demanded when all three had squeezed into the tiny half-bath.

"We took the guest-room closet and combined it with . . ." What *had* they combined it with? Already the original contours of 6D were a fading memory.

"I always wanted a powder room," Peggy said, caressing the edge of the pedestal sink.

Rosemary caught a glimpse of herself in the small mirror over the sink. She looked haggard and drained, but the light was more forgiving of the Gimmels, who looked pink and healthy as medium-rare lamb.

"Your daughter is Lily, right?"

"Last I checked." Peggy said. "Why?"

"I found her name inscribed in the floorboards in one of the bedrooms."

"Well, don't forget you had a full inspection before the closing," Peggy said quickly, squaring her shoulders. "I'm sorry if you—"

"No, no, it's not a problem. It's just that . . . well, it said, 'Lily plus Larry forever.' I wondered what happened to them."

Peggy seemed unable to reply at first. "She became Lily Grantham," she finally said.

"She came to all our benefits at the auction house. I think she chaired one or two."

"But not lately," Peggy said.

Rosemary decided not to bring up the scandal.

"Would you like to see the inscription? I didn't let the floor men remove it."

Both Gimmels nodded.

For a while the three of the them stood silently over the etched words, as if meditating over the tomb of an ancient prophet. Finally Peggy broke the silence.

"I would have killed her if I'd known she was ruining my floors."

"I wonder how she pulled up the carpet," Monroe said. "Wasn't it tacked down?"

"I recall reading about your daughter, but I don't remember reading that she married her high-school sweetheart. Isn't her husband a banker or something?"

"*Was* a banker or something. Now he's a fugitive."

"Oh."

"She changed after she wrote this. She wanted nothing about her life to last forever, not Larry or this room or this apartment or this neighborhood. And she did it, she changed it all."

"You should have seen her place on Park Avenue," Monroe said. "Like a museum, only she let you sit on the chairs."

"She thought you could change everything just by moving across town and buying a big place, one apartment to a floor, the elevator opens and there you are, inside. But you can move across the country and you're still who you were in the beginning. She was wiser when she wrote this"—Peggy pointed a Nike-d toe at the inscription—"than she's ever been since then. The room you were raised in, that's forever. You can tear down the walls, put new ones up, but you can't run from it."

"I get so tired of real estate," Rosemary said. "Half the city is either buying or selling their apartments, and the other half are real-estate agents helping them do it." People changing their skins, as Esme Hollender put it. "Maybe everyone should put an inscription in the rooms they live in, and there should be a law that you can't remove it."

Peggy bent down and traced a finger across the inscription.

"She left so early this morning, Monroe," Peggy said after a while. "I wonder where she is?"

Lily finished her story, after speaking for thirty uninterrupted minutes, and glanced around the room. Jay DiGregorio from the Federal Prosecutor's Office, along with Special Agent Sammet, who'd come to her apartment (her former apartment) on Park Avenue that night a lifetime ago to inform her that her husband had skipped town. Howard Breslin and Rick Conklin from the Bureau of Alcohol, Tobacco, and Firearms—she still couldn't get over the name. No one said anything, and for a moment she feared she'd just dug herself a deeper hole than her work with Mohammed had already excavated. She'd told them about Nanny, and the proof she now had. How she'd guessed it was Nanny when she'd realized that all the checks had been written—and, presumably, deposited—on Thursday, Nanny's day off. About a year earlier Nanny had insisted on Thursdays off (not the traditional Saturday or Sunday—something about physical therapy for lower-back pain) just as she'd insisted on following them to the West Side to keep tabs on the family. That's how she discovered that Lily was going to break into Manny Zelma's office, looking for evidence, and she'd almost succeeded in having her boyfriend steal the envelope with the canceled checks on William Street that night.

She threatened to use all of her old media contacts to go public with a story sure to garner front-page coverage: innocent, high-profile family attacked by a trusted employee (treacherous child-minders always made headlines), unfairly persecuted by the federal government, forcing the head of said family to flee the country or face unfair imprisonment, and condemning the wife and mother to a life of crime that she would never, under any other circumstances, have pursued. "You'll look cold and unfeeling," she'd said to DiGregorio, and when this didn't get a reaction, she'd added "and completely incompetent," which turned his pale face a sickly purple.

She hadn't expected them to break down in sobs of remorse, though that wouldn't have been an unwelcome reaction. The ability or inclination to apologize had probably been drilled out of them during basic training. Still, *some* reaction would have been nice.

"So, are you going to pursue these . . . charges against me? Because if you are, I'd like to call my . . ." She almost said *lawyer*. "My publicist." In her old life, few of her friends had had paying jobs, but many of them had had publicists whose responsibility it was to get their client's name and, ideally, photo in the right newspapers and magazines. Counterfeiting twenty-dollar bills seemed a far saner way to make a living, she now thought, than securing ink for indolent socialites. She'd never actually had a publicist, but she knew a few names, and any one of them would be more than happy to take her on, under the circumstances.

"That's it," she said after a long pause, standing up. "I'm calling my publicist."

The word cast a shadow of anxiety across the four horsemen of the federal government.

"We need to talk," said Conklin of Alcohol, Tobacco, and Firearms. They left her.

Several hours later she was allowed to go home (well, to her parents' apartment), after stern warnings not to leave Manhattan without consulting the Bureau, as they called it. As soon as she got home she called Morton Samuels, who consented to help her out once he realized that she stood a good chance of being rich again. She repeated to him the deal she'd concocted while detained downtown: She'd agree not to pursue harassment charges against the government—which had all but thrown her and the children onto the street—if the Feds dropped all counterfeiting charges against her and Mohammed. Samuels, it turned out, was the perfect emissary to offer the deal. Only a month earlier, one of his patently guilty clients had been found not guilty of insider trading, and that client was not only making the rounds of talk shows, he was suing the federal government for fifty million dollars in damages, and he wasn't nearly as telegenic as Lily. Moreover, he hadn't been evicted from his home, nor had he been forced—*forced*—by the U.S. government to print money to feed children. "If you had turned tricks, that might have been worth more," was Samuels's unironic lament. "But we'll work with what we have."

Thirty-three

Lily stood among a swarm of livery drivers in the waiting area of Terminal 4 at JFK. Each time the swinging doors flew open, the drivers waved cardboard or plastic signs containing the handwritten name of their charges. She briefly considered making a sign of her own: MR. GRANTHAM. Would Barnett recognize her otherwise? She'd put on ten pounds since he'd fled the country—poverty pounds, she thought of them—and her low-maintenance, gray-flecked hair now fell casually to her shoulders. The Banana Republic cashmere sweater and Gap jeans, purchased with homemade money, would look equally unfamiliar to him.

The unraveling of their lives had been swift, and so had the . . . reraveling? Nanny had been arrested in the living room at 124 West Sixty-seventh Street the day after Lily had been detained and released. The Feds had apparently spent the night plotting strategy and obtaining a search warrant for Nanny's apartment. As the federal agents led Nanny out in handcuffs, Lily had leapt at her. But one of the Feds stepped between them, preventing a physical confrontation.

"It was 'im what made me stay in this . . . this dump," Nanny snarled at Lily as she was led away, stress coarsening her accent from Poppins to Doolittle. "Me boyfriend—didn't I tell him we should get the hell away from this place? 'You can't bolt right after they arrest 'im, it'll look suspicious like,' is what 'e said. Then when the mister flew the coop, it was the same story. 'Stick around to see what the bitch knows.' Fat lot of good it did me."

Lily could only gape at the seething tower of rage that had lovingly diapered and bathed and fed shepherd's pie to her children. But Peggy exhibited no such paralysis.

"Dump? Who do you think you are, calling my home a dump?"

"She called me a bitch, Mother."

"Yes, well . . ." Peggy shrugged and ran into the hallway, where Nanny was being led toward the elevators.

"I'll have you know this *dump*, as you call it, cost us almost one million dollars. And since we've lived in this *dump*, it's gone up twenty-eight percent—it was in the paper this week. That's two hundred and twenty-three thousand dollars, just for living here! Just for living! It's like they're paying us, every day"—Lily watched her mother do the math in her head, lips moving quickly as she totted up what *they* were paying her—"two thousand dollars every day, we get paid two thousand dollars every single day we live in this *dump*, and we don't have to do anything! Think about *that* while you're rotting in prison."

And now the final loop in the rewinding of their lives: Barnett's return.

Each time the swinging doors flew open, Lily was reminded of a funhouse attraction; would the doors reveal a clown or a monster? Why so nervous? After all, Barnett had asked her to be there. Morton Samuels had contacted him the day Nanny was arrested—funny, how he suddenly remembered his client's address—and Barnett had left a voice message a few hours later with flight information. "Can't wait to see you at the airport, sweetie," he'd said a bit tentatively.

And he looked a bit tentative when he finally strode through the swinging doors, hesitating a few long seconds after spotting her in the crowd. He'd lost weight in Switzerland; his navy blazer and khaki pants, which she recognized from Before, hung limply on him. He appeared older and tired, but in fact it was his familiarity that startled, even angered her. So much had changed—he'd become a different person to her—it struck her as unfair that he hadn't morphed in appearance to reflect that. Instead, it was the same Barnett she'd last seen at 913 Park Avenue: a bit less doughy but with his pampered, hygenic WASPiness intact. It seemed wrong. At the very least he should have gone gray, or bald, or be covered in oozing boils.

After his initial hesitation he smiled at her, a broad, confident smile for the future, for *their* future, for the Grantham Restoration.

It was a smile aimed at her. *You're a very lucky girl.*

She'd come to JFK not knowing what she was going to say or do, half-hoping that he'd make the important decisions for her. And he had, in a way, with that proprietary, presumptuous, it's-all-been-a-bad-dream smile. That smile let her know just what she had to do.

"Darling," he said.

She deflected his kiss, which landed behind her right ear.

"Looks like we're out of practice," he said, and tried again. This time she stepped aside, causing him to lose balance and stagger forward.

"I shouldn't have come," she said to his back as he righted himself. "What was I thinking?" She turned and headed for the exit.

"Darling . . ."

She turned back to him. "Don't call me that."

"Dar—Lily, if this is about my leaving, you need to understand . . ."

"Leaving?"

"And I understand from Morton that you know about Francine, but what you don't know is that it's over, it was never—"

"It's not that," she said. "In fact, it's not about you at all."

"It's not . . ." He looked crushed, his expression darkening as his eyes glanced up and down her new form, evidence that life had, amazingly, gone on without him.

She had to say it again, slowly and out loud, just to remind herself that it was true.

"It's not about you."

His shoulders sagged and he seemed about to say something but didn't. Lily shook her head and walked away.

She was almost out the door when she heard her name. But it wasn't Barnett.

"Oh my, good grief, who would have imagined meeting you here, on this of all days."

The collision of worlds made her briefly dizzy. Instinctively she spread her arms, and after a momentary hesitation Mohammed stepped into the embrace, their first physical contact. He wore a tie and jacket and his hair had recently been cut.

"Are you meeting someone?" she asked him.

"Yes, but you notice, no sign?" He held up both patently empty hands. "I have sold my medallion and cashed in my inwestments. Very successfully, I might add. I am here to meet Kassie and the boys. Their plane landed fifteen minutes ago."

"How wonderful!"

"Yes, yes," he said a bit too quickly.

"It will be fine," she said. "I'm sure they can't wait to see you."

"I still haven't bought a new home for us, you see. But I couldn't wait any longer. After that business with the American government, I decided I must see them, never mind that I am living in a shack."

"It's not a shack, Mohammed."

"We will shop for a suitable home right away. I want to inwest my cash in real estate."

"People are saying that housing prices are already too high."

"Nonsense. Everybody will always want a home, the bigger, the better. The American dream is not a bubble."

"Here we are, discussing real estate on the most important day of your life."

"What is more important than the place you live? Anyway, what brings *you* here, Lily?"

She loved how her name floated from his lips like a lover's sigh.

"I came to meet my husband's flight." She glanced back and saw Barnett standing where she'd left him, staring at her with a look of affronted incredulity.

"Ah, so the candy man is out of the picture."

"Not necessarily."

He frowned. "You have not progressed wery far since we last spoke. Remember we talked of the need for a plan."

"Yes, but my new plan is to see what happens."

"Not much of a plan." He shook his head slowly, then his face lit up. "Good grief, here they come. Oh . . ."

She turned and saw four boys walking toward them, their bodies rigid with uncertainty. Behind them, as if hiding, was a small, pretty woman with long, straight black hair. All five wore jeans, T-shirts, and sneakers.

Mohammed began walking toward them, then broke into a run. Lily waited until he'd reached the first son, the smallest, and scooped him up, before turning to leave.

Thirty-four

"All the principal rooms face Park Avenue," Lucinda Wells said as she crossed the grand sitting room of Apartment 9A at 913 Park Avenue. She tapped a fingernail on the double-insulated windows. "Major sunlight," she said, *for Park Avenue.*

The paunchy investment banker and his pretty wife joined her at the window. Clients always followed her like young children on a class trip to the zoo, huddling close lest they get left behind.

"Wasn't this the Grantham apartment?" the wife asked.

"A million years ago." Ten months. Barnett Grantham had regained control of the place from the Feds and decided not to move back in. Since she already had the listing, he agreed to let her sell it for him. During his exile in Switzerland, the apartment had increased by a fourth, or something like one-point-nine million, which came to about six thousand dollars for every day he was out of the city. Try making that kind of money on Wall Street!

The wife turned and studied the empty sitting room with newfound reverence. For a certain species of aspiring socialite, Lily Grantham had once sat atop the evolutionary chain.

"The sitting room is twenty by twenty. Square is very rare, you know, and quite desirable. This apartment nailed ten pages in *Architectural Digest,* and three were devoted to this room."

"Do they ever cover the same apartment twice?" the wife asked anxiously. "I mean, after it's been done over, of course."

Damn, she shouldn't have brought up the *Ark Digest* feature. She never made mistakes like that, but the karma on the Grantham apartment was for shit.

"If you do it right," she said lightly, and ushered them back into the gallery. "The coat closet is nicely tucked away, don't you think?" She opened it to reveal a mirror on the back of the door. The three of them froze in contemplation of their reflections, startled by the sudden evidence of life amid so much arid real estate. She was several inches taller than the wife, who was herself a good head taller than her husband, who stood between them like a fat child squeezed into a new suit for an outing with two stylish aunts. Still, he had pulled in twenty-six million dollars last year running a hedge fund, the new cliché. She always checked these things, since there was no point in showing an apartment to people who couldn't afford it. You wouldn't believe the number of people who liked to tour apartments just to see how the other half lived.

The hedge hog was the first to step away from the mirror. Well, who could blame him?

"Where to?" he huffed.

"Whatever happened to Lily Grantham?" the wife asked. "Didn't I hear that the husband came back?"

"He was exonerated," the husband said. "Turns out it was the baby-sitter or something who stole the money. She's locked away for twenty years."

"You can comfortably entertain twenty-six in here," Lucinda said in the dining room, pulling the number from a mental hat.

The wife ran a finger along the glazed walls.

"The color's called Caravaggio Red," Lucinda said. "It was all the rage a million years ago. It took like twelve coats to achieve this luster." She saw the banker's jowls start to quiver and quickly added, "But it comes off like *that*. Not a big job, trust me."

"Where are they living now?" the wife asked.

"Separately," Lucinda replied. "Notice the light. Very bright." *For Park Avenue.*

"They're not together?"

Lucinda sighed. She hadn't brought up the Granthams, but she hadn't nipped the story in the bud, either. Now she'd have to rehash the whole sordid tale, which would do zero for the apartment.

"He came back to New York all set to pick up where he'd left off. Lily Grantham said no dice."

"Didn't he have a girlfriend?"

"Didn't want to marry her, apparently."

"Lily Grantham was a major rainmaker for Grantham, Wiley & Zelma," said the husband. "She brought the firm more business than the three principals combined. Why ditch her?"

"The kitchen," Lucinda said, unfurling one arm like a car-show model. "Custom millwork, honed granite countertops, Sub-Zero, Viking, Miele." The husband made a beeline for the Sub-Zero.

"Where is she living?" the wife asked.

"That's a long story," Lucinda said. It was *always* a long story—where you lived told the story of your life. "She took up with an old flame. High-school sweetheart. Neighborhood boy."

"What neighborhood?"

"Upper West Side. She moved into his rent-controlled classic six." The real-estate broker's nightmare.

"Who is it?" Meaning, *Do we know him? Does anyone?*

"Nobody. Owns a candy store on Broadway. I was showing an apartment in the neighborhood and happened to walk by. Lily was behind the counter, dishing out nuts."

The husband was methodically opening and closing drawers in the vast Sub-Zero. A twelve-million-dollar apartment, and fatso was inspecting the fridge for freebies. Visibly frustrated, the wife turned back to Lucinda.

"Lily Grantham is working in a candy store?"

"She looked radiant. And her boyfriend . . ."

"What about him?"

"A major improvement in the looks department." Lucinda couldn't help glancing at the porcine husband, now rooting through the empty cabinets. "To die for, really. He was just returning from a run when I walked by. Tight shorts, T-shirt all clingy with sweat. You should have seen the kiss he gave her."

"A lot of women are going for physical attraction these days," the wife said somewhat wistfully. "I read somewhere it's a trend."

The husband opened the microwave. Perhaps the Granthams had left a bag of popcorn behind on their flight from the East Side.

"Two maids' rooms, generously sized."

They crowded into one of the narrow maids'. It wasn't completely sunless, but the light felt sullen and gray, as if the journey around the back of the building and down the narrow courtyard had exhausted it. The husband looked even shorter and heavier in the small space and seemed to know it.

"Seen one, seen 'em all," he pronounced as he squeezed by them.

"Where was she before she moved in with the . . . candy man?"

"Where was she living? With her parents in a postwar across from Lincoln Center. I sold it to them. I also sold their old place. Twice, actually."

"How do you sell the same apartment twice?" asked the husband. Finally something he could get excited about.

"They had a big classic seven on West End. Total wreck, but good bones. First I sold it to an Internet executive and his wife. Gut renovation with Victor Ozeri, who would be perfect for this place, BTW, if you could get him. I don't have to tell you what happened to software companies. Practically the day the renovation was done, they put the place back on the market."

"Which software company?" the husband wanted to know.

"Positano."

He grunted and once again Lucinda wished she hadn't stumbled onto this path. The market was on the way back, but no one wanted to hear about dead dot-coms when they were considering forking over twelve million for an apartment with shitty light and walls lacquered in fuchsia nail polish that would require several weeks and half the population of Guatemala to sand off.

"They managed to scratch together enough cash to buy their old place back, at a twenty percent premium, of course. My exclusive. Way too small for them—they have twin girls. Or boys. Two of the same, at any rate. But at least it's a roof over their heads. I sold the renovated West End Avenue place to a Guyanese man and his family."

"Chinese?"

"*Guyanese.* From Guyana." People were *so* ignorant, not to mention insensitive. "He was referred to me by Lily Grantham, of all people. He was a taxi driver, if you can believe it. Notice the sweep from the sitting room right to the dining room as you pass through the gallery. Seventy-two feet. You could play football if you wanted." Silence. She'd remember to say lacrosse next time. All the East Side kids played lacrosse at their private schools—it didn't even help them get into The Ivy League anymore, that's how ordinary it was. Lacrosse! Thank God she'd never had children. "Let's have a look at the library."

"How did a taxi driver get past a co-op board?"

"Ex–taxi driver. And he's paying all cash. Plus, he's . . . well, he's not exactly black, but dark enough to bring a discrimination suit if he's rejected. His name is Mohammed, which can't hurt, either. People are soooo worried about offending Arabs. He *sailed* through the approval process."

"But how did he make all that money? Even on West End a classic seven—"

"Two-point-seven, triple mint. Notice the bookshelves, burled walnut. I wouldn't change a thing in here. He invested every cent he had in the market."

"And *made* money?" the husband asked. He'd become comparatively animated in the library, visions of surround-sound stereo, flat-panel HDTV, and gilt-framed equestrian prints no doubt dancing in his mind.

"Sold short. Every cent he had. Put options, covered calls, the whole nine yards. Then, when the market turned around, he invested all the proceeds long. Still, I think he must have had a side income—a lot of these cabdrivers do, you know."

"That's rich," the husband said. "We're standing in the apartment of the grandson of Ben 'Sell 'Em' Grantham, the most famous short-seller of all time. And you just sold an apartment to . . . what exactly was the connection?"

"The apartment on West End used to belong to the parents of Lily Grantham."

"Exactly. You sold it to a taxi driver who made millions short-selling."

"I'll tell you what's perfect," Lucinda said as she led them down the hallway to the bedrooms. "This taxi driver, Mohammed? Has four kids, just brought them over from Guyana. He wouldn't dream of making them share a room, though you can only imagine how they must have lived back in Africa. So he's hired Victor Ozeri to redo the entire apartment. They're putting back the wall between the living room and one of the bedrooms that the previous owners, Guy and Rosemary Pierce, had taken down. I mean, in my next life I want to come back as a contractor!"

As if. She'd netted more selling and then reselling Apartment 6D than Ozeri would clear gutting it twice. And without all that plaster dust and plumbing talk and having to supervise an army of little men from Central America who worked hard, God knows, but always seemed to be sharing a secret joke at your expense. And if Mohammed's luck in the market turned—and luck always turned, in Lucinda's experience—she'd be perfectly positioned to sell it a third time.

"This was a girl's room, obviously." She led the couple into a large bedroom with pink wall-to-wall carpeting and white curtains with pastel appliqués of bonnets and ribbons. It was the only room with any personality left, and it was extremely depressing. For some crazy reason, Lucinda thought of Anne Frank, though the Grantham girl had hardly been shipped off to a concentration camp. Still, leaving behind a nicely decorated room, curtains and carpet and fresh paint, for an unrenovated rental was a kind of, well, maybe not a death sentence, but a . . . what did that phony psychic with the TV show call it? *A passing.* She made a mental note to have the curtains taken down before showing the apartment again.

"What an amazing story," the wife said. "From Lily Grantham to a short-selling taxi driver."

Lucinda worried that she wasn't focusing the couple's attention on the charms of the apartment, but she couldn't help trumping her own story.

"There's more," she said coyly.

"More?"

"Let's look at the second bedroom."

This one, thankfully, had no remnants of its former occupant, other than a variety of scuff marks on the hunter-green walls.

"Four bedrooms in all, with three bathrooms. A lot of people divide this bathroom." She pointed to the bathroom that connected the room they were in to Anne Frank's.

"You said there was more."

"Rosemary Pierce, the wife of the Positano Software founder? She works at Atherton's."

The husband and wife shuffled toward her, the better to catch her next utterance. Atherton's would be seeing a lot of them if they ended up buying the apartment, which would need a palace's worth of French antiques and acres of old Oriental rugs to render it comfy.

"Her boss, I forget his name, a flamer who specializes in glass, he was investigated for buying Positano shares with inside information."

"I think I read about that," the husband said. "Half of Atherton's was implicated."

"Never indicted, though, since in the end they lost money, and who goes to jail for losing money—your own money, at least. Anyway, this Rosemary, who worked for him, one of her clients is an ancient woman named Esme Hollender. Her father was Frederick Packard, who was very big in something."

"*The Importance of Unimportance*," the husband said reverently. "Frederick Packard was a genius."

"Yeah, well, he wasn't genius enough to teach his daughter how to pick a husband. She married a flamer, a different one, who bilked her out of most of her money. All she had left was the apartment. Thank God it was at 700 Fifth. Views to die for. I got her eleven-point-five, cash."

"Amazing."

"That's not the amazing part. Notice that the third bedroom has its own bathroom, as you can see. A lot of people"—*a lot of people—there were exactly eleven apartments in the entire building!*—"use this as a guest room, though some turn it into a dressing room with en suite bath."

"What was the amazing part?" the wife asked.

"I sold Esme Hollender's apartment"—she stepped closer to the already looming couple—"to a pornographer."

The wife, gratifyingly, gasped.

"Richer than God, apparently. Who knew online porno was so lucrative? Truckloads of money coming in every month, and all he has to do is point a Webcam at a drug-addicted slut willing to . . . to open wide, as my dentist says, LOL. In my next life I want to come back as a pornographer!"

"At least someone's making money off the Internet," the husband grumbled. Lucinda worried that he might have lost a bit too much in the bubble and never fully recovered since then. The board at 913 Park Avenue liked to see liquid assets totaling ten times the purchase price, which in this case would mean cash and securities worth at least ninety million bucks, assuming they negotiated down the asking price by a few mil. That was an ocean of liquid, even in the recent, relatively strong market.

"Of course, I had no idea he was into porno," Lucinda said as she led the charge into the master bedroom. "Rosemary Pierce referred him to me. Seems he and her husband had some sort of business connection—trust me, I had no interest in going *there*!" She Vanna Whited an arm toward the master bedroom's windows. "You won't find a larger master on Park."

"How did this pornographer ever get through the co-op board?" the wife asked.

"Amazonian mahogany or something, very rare," she said upon opening the closet. "They needed a special dispensation from the World Wildlife Foundation to import it. How did he get by the co-op board? All cash, natch. And he didn't exactly announce that he was into porn. His company's called Ventnor Place, which sounds legitimate enough."

"Ventnor . . ." The husband flushed and turned away. No wonder Ventnor could afford an apartment at 700 Fifth, if the likes of Porky the Hedge Hog was jerking off to his pay-for-pussy sites. Lucinda had, of course, undertaken her usual due diligence on Ventnor, which entailed visiting a few of his more successful URLs. She'd never seen such tits in her life—how did those women brush their hair? She looked at the wife, fashionably flat-chested, and wondered if she knew or even cared that her husband downloaded videos of women with jugs the size of her Dolce and Gabbana satchel.

"Esme Hollender hadn't paid her maintenance in over a year, so the board was desperate to get her out of there. But the apartment was in such bad shape, a lot of buyers were put off. Not this Ventnor fellow. In fact, he came to the second showing with Victor Ozeri. Very shrewd to get Ozeri on board pre-sale. You're gonna love the master bath, right over there. The tiles were brought over from a monastery outside Assisi. Trust me, those nuns will never have to worry where their next bowl of porridge is coming from."

The wife hadn't made it past the small dressing area, which she was studying as if she were a pilgrim at a saint's shrine. "I read somewhere that Lily Grantham used to get her dresses sewed onto her before big parties. I mean, the designer himself would come here to work on her. And she'd also have someone sent up from Alexendre's to blow out her hair at the same time."

Imagine aspiring to such a life, being trussed like a Thanksgiving turkey before dinner.

"Yeah, well, I doubt anyone's sewing on her clothes at the Broadway Nut Shoppe. She did look radiant, though, in a Banana Republicly way. And she hasn't given up all remnants of her old life." Lucinda led them on the long trek back to the gallery. "She got basically nothing from her husband. A few million, if that. I mean, he wanted her back—*she* was the one who wanted out of the marriage, so what did she expect? There are rumors that she'd somehow managed to stash away some cash, but who knows. Anyway, the kids insisted on staying in this public school she had them in, even though their father, of course, offered to put them back in private. Kids."

"You said she still kept part of her old life."

"Right. Not her old life exactly, but she's having some work done in the candy man's rent-controlled six. Nothing major, just the bathrooms and the kitchen and the floors and the walls. New wiring. Windows. It's a crime to invest in a rental, but when you're paying that little for a classic six, you know you're never going to move. And here's the kicker. Guess who she's hired as a contractor?"

"Not Victor Ozeri?"

"Like he'd take on a rental! Guy Pierce! The founder of Positano I told you about? He's in the contracting business! He's still got a few million shares of stock, Aquinas stock, the company that bought him out and fired him the same day, but they're selling for, like, twenty cents, even today, with the market semi back up, so he's changing careers. I put him in touch with Lily and her candy man, and from what I hear, both sides are delirious. He loves this stuff, apparently."

"You wouldn't recommend him for . . ."

"For this place? Noooooo. There are only two or three names the board will even consider. Are you thinking of making an offer?"

"We'll want to think it over," the wife said. "It certainly has good bones."

Lucinda nodded—someone had been reading the shelter magazines. But the wife was right, if unoriginal. The apartment's bones were impeccable: good light (for Park Avenue), large, well-proportioned rooms—and plenty of them—a logical, no-nonsense floor plan. But a pall of defeat hung over the place; everyone sensed it even before they realized that this was where Lily Grantham had made her last stand, even after they remembered that Barnett Grantham had been exonerated (though of embezzlement, not desertion or adultery) and was back to making money down on Wall Street. Walls *always* talked, in Lucinda's experience.

"Something about the Granthams living here . . ." the husband said. "I don't know, it just doesn't feel right."

"But there's a happy ending."

"Happy ending? I don't see them moving back in here," the husband said, causing Lucinda to marvel, not for the first time, at the remarkably low minimum intelligence required to make a fortune on Wall Street.

"You should see her," she said, prepared to launch into a sales pitch about the rare opportunity to own a world-class apartment in a top building, and how the board was eager to get someone into the apartment, which had been empty for almost a year. But her mind drifted irresistibly to Central Park, where she jogged twice a week with Marque, her trainer, a toffee-skinned Apollo with big biceps that glistened like fresh challah loaves when he flexed them at her frequent request, and pecs as swollen and sturdy as the tits on the girls of Ventnor Place. Usually they circled the reservoir twice, for a total of three miles, before he handed her the small weights he jogged with and they power-walked back to her building, where he obligingly fucked her if she had the energy for it. But every so often he led her into other areas of the park, particularly the Rambles, where the hills added a deeper, more humbling level of torture to the workout. It was during one such excursion, earlier that week, on a glorious spring day, that she'd seen Lily Grantham.

She had on a navy polo shirt tucked into jeans and had pulled her hair back into a simple ponytail. Lucinda hadn't recognized her at first because her face was obscured by a pair of binoculars, through which she was looking up at a tree. But when she lowered them, she was instantly familiar, though quite changed. She looked heavier and plainer but also younger— her face benefited from the extra flesh, that much was evident even on a quick jog-by. On the return trip she saw her on a bench, binoculars on her lap, her head on the shoulder of the man from the candy store. She was pointing up at the sky, and like the candy man, Lucinda followed her outstretched arm to a lone hawk, the celebrity one who lived for free at 927 Fifth Avenue, its outstretched wings unmoving as it lazily circled the Rambles on a current of air. She envied the hawk at that moment, and she envied Lily Grantham and the candy man, too. They seemed to belong to a secret society, a guild of blessed creatures without worries and responsibilities and board rejections, who floated above non-members on warm, invisible currents. She was sorely tempted to stop and stare, if only for the chance to understand how one entered such a society, but Marque must have sensed her momentary lack of resolve and exhorted her to sprint the last half-mile to Fifth Avenue, and what choice did she have? Just before turning a corner, she looked back and saw them kissing, not a chummy, comfortable kiss but the connecting of two people who felt they had to snatch every available moment from a hostile world.

"I have a few other places to show you," she told the couple as she led them to the elevator landing. "None of them quite as perfect as this place, I might as well tell you right now." She locked the front door with the key she'd been sent a million years ago from some bureaucrat in the federal building downtown. "If you're interested, I'd make an offer soon. Trust me, you won't see another place like this one."